The Discworld series is a continuous history of a world not totally unlike our own, except that it is a flat disc carried on the backs of four elephants astride a giant turtle floating through space, and that it is peopled by, among others, wizards, dwarfs, policemen, thieves, beggars, vampires and witches. Within the history of Discworld there are many individual stories, which can be read in any order, but reading them in sequence can in_____ _our enjoyment through the accumulation of all th_ _____ __es to the teeming imaginative comp_____.

BOOKS BY TE_____

DISCARDED

DISCARDED

Other books about Discworld

TURTLE RECALL: THE DISCWORLD COMPANION ... SO FAR
(with Stephen Briggs)

NANNY OGG'S COOKBOOK
(with Stephen Briggs, Tina Hannan and Paul Kidby)

THE PRATCHETT PORTFOLIO
(with Paul Kidby)

THE DISCWORLD ALMANAK
(with Bernard Pearson)

THE UNSEEN UNIVERSITY CUT-OUT BOOK
(with Alan Batley and Bernard Pearson)

WHERE'S MY COW?
(illustrated by Melvyn Grant)

THE ART OF DISCWORLD
(with Paul Kidby)

THE WIT AND WISDOM OF DISCWORLD
(compiled by Stephen Briggs)

THE FOLKLORE OF DISCWORLD
(with Jacqueline Simpson)

THE WORLD OF POO
(with the Discworld Emporium)

MRS BRADSHAW'S HANDBOOK
(with the Discworld Emporium)

THE COMPLEAT ANKH-MORPORK
(with the Discworld Emporium)

THE STREETS OF ANKH-MORPORK
(with Stephen Briggs, painted by Stephen Player)

THE DISCWORLD MAPP
(with Stephen Briggs, painted by Stephen Player)

A TOURIST GUIDE TO LANCRE – A DISCWORLD MAPP
(with Stephen Briggs, illustrated by Paul Kidby)

DEATH'S DOMAIN (with Paul Kidby)

THE DISCWORLD ATLAS
(with the Discworld Emporium)

A complete list of Terry Pratchett ebooks and audio books as well as other books based on the
Discworld series – illustrated screenplays, graphic novels, comics and plays – can be found on
www.terrypratchett.co.uk

THE TRUTH

A Discworld® Novel

Terry Pratchett

CORGI BOOKS

TRANSWORLD PUBLISHERS
61-63 Uxbridge Road, London W5 5SA
A Random House Group Company
www.transworldbooks.co.uk

THE TRUTH
A CORGI BOOK : 9780552167635

First published in Great Britain
in 2000 by Doubleday
an imprint of Transworld Publishers
Corgi edition published 2001
Corgi edition reissued 2008
Corgi edition reissued 2013

A CIP catalogue record for this book
is available from the British Library

Addresses for Random House Group Ltd companies outside the UK
can be found at: www.randomhouse.co.uk
The Random House Group Ltd Reg. No. 954009.

Typeset in Minion by Falcon Oast Graphic Art Ltd.

011

Penguin Random House is committed to a sustainable future for
our business, our readers and our planet. This book is made from
Forest Stewardship Council® certified paper.

Printed and bound in Great Britain by Clays Ltd, Elcograf S.p.A.

AUTHOR'S NOTE

Sometimes a fantasy author has to point out the strangeness of reality. The way Ankh-Morpork dealt with its flood problems (see p. 319 and onwards) is curiously similar to that adopted by the city of Seattle, Washington, towards the end of the nineteenth century. Really. Go and see. Try the clam chowder while you're there.

THE TRUTH

The rumour spread through the city like wildfire (which had quite often spread through Ankh-Morpork since its citizens had learned the words 'fire insurance').

The dwarfs can turn lead into gold . . .

It buzzed through the fetid air of the Alchemists' quarter, where they had been trying to do the same thing for centuries without success but were certain that they'd manage it by tomorrow, or next Tuesday at least, or the end of the month for definite.

It caused speculation among the wizards at Unseen University, where they knew you *could* turn one element into another element, provided you didn't mind it turning back again next day, and where was the good in that? Besides, most elements were happy where they were.

It seared into the scarred, puffy and sometimes totally missing ears of the Thieves' Guild, where people put an edge on their crowbars. Who cared where the gold *came* from?

The dwarfs can turn lead into gold . . .

It reached the cold but incredibly acute ears of the Patrician, and it did that fairly quickly, because you did not stay ruler of Ankh-Morpork for long if you were second with the news. He sighed and made a note of it, and added it to a lot of other notes.

The dwarfs can turn lead into gold . . .

It reached the pointy ears of the dwarfs.

'Can we?'

'Damned if I know. *I* can't.'

'Yeah, but if you could, you wouldn't say. *I* wouldn't say, if *I* could.'

'Can you?'

'No!'

'Ah-*ha*!'

It came to the ears of the Night Watch of the city guard, as they did gate duty at ten o'clock on an icy night. Gate duty in Ankh-Morpork was not taxing. It consisted mainly of waving through anything that wanted to go through, although traffic was minimal in the dark and freezing fog.

They hunched in the shelter of the gate arch, sharing one damp cigarette.

'You can't turn something into something else,' said Corporal Nobbs. 'The Alchemists have been trying it for years.'

'They can gen'rally turn a house into a hole in the ground,' said Sergeant Colon.

'That's what I'm talking about,' said Corporal Nobbs. 'Can't be done. It's all to do with . . . elements. An alchemist told me. Everything's made up of elements, right? Earth, Water, Air, Fire and . . . sunnink. Well-known fact. Everything's got 'em all mixed up just right.'

He stamped his feet in an effort to get some warmth into them.

'If it was possible to turn lead into gold, everyone'd be doing it,' he said.

'Wizards could do it,' said Sergeant Colon.

'Oh, well, *magic*,' said Nobby dismissively.

A large cart rumbled out of the yellow clouds and entered the arch, splashing Colon as it wobbled through one of the puddles that were such a feature of Ankh-Morpork's highways.

'Bloody dwarfs,' he said, as it continued on into the city. But he didn't say it too loudly.

'There were a lot of them pushing that cart,' said Corporal Nobbs reflectively. It lurched slowly round a corner and was lost to view.

'Prob'ly all that gold,' said Colon.

'Hah. Yeah. That'd be it, then.'

And the rumour came to the ears of William de Worde, and in a sense it stopped there, because he dutifully wrote it down.

It was his job. Lady Margolotta of Uberwald sent him five dollars a month to do it. The Dowager Duchess of Quirm also sent him five dollars. So did King Verence of Lancre, and a few other Ramtop notables. So did the Seriph of Al Khali, although in his case the payment was half a cartload of figs, twice a year.

All in all, he considered, he was on to a good thing. All he had to do was write one letter very carefully, trace it backwards on to a piece of boxwood provided for him by Mr Cripslock the engraver in the Street of Cunning Artificers, and then pay Mr Cripslock twenty dollars to carefully remove the wood that wasn't letters and make five impressions on sheets of paper.

Of course, it had to be done thoughtfully, with spaces left after 'To my Noble Client the', and so on, which he had to fill in later, but even deducting expenses it still left him the best part of thirty dollars for little more than one day's work a month.

A young man without too many responsibilities could live modestly in Ankh-Morpork on thirty or forty dollars a month; he always sold the figs, because although it was possible to live on figs you soon wished you didn't.

And there were always additional sums to be picked up here and there. The world of letters was a closed boo— mysterious papery object to many of Ankh-Morpork's citizens, but if they ever *did* need to commit things to paper quite a few of them walked up the creaky stairs past the sign 'William de Worde: Things Written Down'.

Dwarfs, for example. Dwarfs were always coming to seek work in the city, and the first thing they did was send a letter home saying how well they were doing. This was such a predictable occurrence, even if the dwarf in question was so far down on his luck that he'd been forced to eat his helmet, that William had Mr Cripslock produce several dozen stock letters which needed only a few spaces filled in to be perfectly acceptable.

Fond dwarf parents all over the mountains treasured letters which looked something like this:

Dear [Mume & Dad],
    Well, I arrived here all right and I am staying,

at [109 Cockbill Street The Shades Ankh-Morpk].
Everythyng is fine. I have got a goode job working for [Mr C.M.O.T. Dibbler, Merchant Venturer]
and will be makinge lots of money really soon
now. I am rememberinge alle your gode advyce
and am not drinkynge, in bars or mixsing with
Trolls. Well thas about itte mu*ſ*t goe now, looking forwade to seing you and [Emelia] agane,
your loving son,
   [Tomas Brokenbrow]

. . . who was usually swaying while he dictated it. It
was twenty pence easily made, and as an additional
service William carefully tailored the spelling to the
client and allowed them to choose their own
punctuation.

On this particular evening, with the sleet gurgling in
the downspouts outside his lodgings, William sat in the
tiny office over the Guild of Conjurors and wrote carefully, half listening to the hopeless but painstaking
catechism of the trainee conjurors at their evening class
in the room below.

'. . . pay attention. Are you ready? Right. Egg.
Glass . . .'

'*Egg. Glass,*' the class droned listlessly.

'. . . Glass. Egg . . .'

'*Glass. Egg . . .*'

'. . . Magic word . . .'

'*Magic word . . .*'

'Fazammm. Just like that. Ahahahahaha . . .'

'*Faz-ammm. Just like that. Aha-ha-ha-ha-ha . . .*'

William pulled another sheet of paper towards him,

sharpened a fresh quill, stared at the wall for a moment and then wrote as follows:

And finally, on the lighter Side, it is being said that the Dwarfs can Turn Lead into Gold, though no one knows whence the rumour comes, and Dwarfs going about their lawful occafions in the City are hailed with cries such as, e.g., 'Hollah, short stuff, let's see you make some Gold then!' although only Newcomers do this because all here know what happens if you call a Dwarf 'short stuff', viz., you are Dead.

Yr. obdt. servant, William de Worde

He always liked to finish his letters on a happy note.

He fetched a sheet of boxwood, lit another candle and laid the letter face down on the wood. A quick rub with the back of a spoon transferred the ink, and thirty dollars and enough figs to make you really ill were as good as in the bank.

He'd drop it in to Mr Cripslock tonight, pick up the copies after a leisurely lunch tomorrow, and with any luck should have them all away by the middle of the week.

William put on his coat, wrapped the wood block carefully in some waxed paper and stepped out into the freezing night.

The world is made up of four elements: Earth, Air, Fire and Water. This is a fact well known even to Corporal Nobbs. It's also wrong. There's a fifth element, and generally it's called Surprise.

For example, the dwarfs found out how to turn lead into gold by doing it the hard way. The difference between that and the easy way is that the hard way works.

The dwarfs dwarfhandled their overloaded, creaking cart along the street, peering ahead in fog. Ice formed on the cart and hung from their beards.

All it needed was one frozen puddle.

Good old Dame Fortune. You can *depend* on her.

The fog closed in, making every light a dim glow and muffling all sounds. It was clear to Sergeant Colon and Corporal Nobbs that no barbarian horde would be including the invasion of Ankh-Morpork in their travel plans for this evening. The watchmen didn't blame them.

They closed the gates. This was not the ominous activity that it might appear, since the keys had been lost long ago and latecomers usually threw gravel at the windows of the houses built on top of the wall until they found a friend to lift the bar. It was assumed that foreign invaders wouldn't know which windows to throw gravel at.

Then the two watchmen trailed through the slush and muck to the Water Gate, by which the river Ankh had the good fortune to enter the city. The water was invisible in the dark, but the occasional ghostly shape of an ice floe drifted past below the parapet.

'Hang on,' said Nobby, as they laid hands on the windlass of the portcullis. 'There's someone down there.'

'In the river?' said Colon.

He listened. There was the creak of an oar, far below.

Sergeant Colon cupped his hands around his mouth and issued the traditional policeman's cry of challenge.

'Oi! You!'

For a moment there was no sound but the wind and the gurgling of the water. Then a voice said: 'Yes?'

'Are you invading the city or what?'

There was another pause. Then:

'What?'

'What what?' said Colon, raising the stakes.

'What were the other options?'

'Don't mess me about . . . Are *you*, down there in the boat, *invading* this *city*?'

'No.'

'Fair enough,' said Colon, who on a night like this would happily take someone's word for it. 'Get a move on, then, 'cos we're going to drop the gate.'

After a while the splash of the oars resumed and disappeared downriver.

'You reckon that was enough, just *askin*' 'em?' said Nobby.

'Well, they ought to know,' said Colon.

'Yeah, but—'

'It was a tiny little rowin' boat, Nobby. Of course, if you want to go all the way down to them nice icy steps on the jetty—'

'No, Sarge.'

'Then let's get back to the Watch House, all right?'

* * *

William turned up his collar as he hurried towards Cripslock the engraver. The usually busy streets were deserted. Only those people with the most pressing business were out of doors. It was turning out to be a very nasty winter indeed, a gazpacho of freezing fog, snow and Ankh-Morpork's ever-present, ever-rolling smog.

His eye was caught by a little pool of light by the Watchmakers' Guild. A small hunched figure was outlined in the glow.

He wandered over.

A hopeless sort of voice said, 'Hot sausages? Inna bun?'

'Mr Dibbler?' said William.

Cut-Me-Own-Throat Dibbler, Ankh-Morpork's most enterprisingly unsuccessful businessman, peered at William over the top of his portable sausage-cooking tray. Snowflakes hissed in the congealing fat.

William sighed. 'You're out late, Mr Dibbler,' he said politely.

'Ah, Mr Word. Times is hard in the hot sausage trade,' said Dibbler.

'Can't make both ends meat, eh?' said William. He couldn't have stopped himself for a hundred dollars and a shipload of figs.

'Definitely in a period of slump in the comestibles market,' said Dibbler, too sunk in gloom to notice. 'Don't seem to find anyone ready to buy a sausage in a bun these days.'

William looked down at the tray. If Cut-Me-Own-Throat Dibbler was selling hot sausages, it was a sure sign that one of his more ambitious enterprises had gone wahoonie-shaped yet again. Selling hot sausages from a tray was by way of being the ground state of Dibbler's existence, from which he constantly sought to extricate himself and back to which he constantly returned when his latest venture went all runny. Which was a shame, because Dibbler was an extremely good hot sausage salesman. He had to be, given the nature of his sausages.

'I should have got a proper education like you,' said Dibbler despondently. 'A nice job indoors with no heavy lifting. I could have found my nitch, if'n I'd have got a good education.'

'Nitch?'

'One of the wizards told me about 'em,' said Dibbler. 'Everything's got a nitch. You know. Like: where they ought to be. What they was cut out for?'

William nodded. He was good with words. 'Niche?' he said.

'One of them things, yes.' Dibbler sighed. 'I missed out on the semaphore. Just didn't see it coming. Next thing you know, everyone's got a clacks company. Big money. Too rich for my blood. I could've done all right with the Fung Shooey, though. Sheer bloody bad luck there.'

'I've certainly felt better with my chair in a different position,' said William. That advice had cost him two dollars, along with an injunction to keep the lid down on the privy so that the Dragon of Unhappiness wouldn't fly up his bottom.

'You were my first customer and I thank you,' said Dibbler. 'I was all set up, I'd got the Dibbler wind-chimes and the Dibbler mirrors, it was gravy all the way – I mean, everything was positioned for maximum harmony, and then . . . smack. Bad karma plops on me once more.'

'It was a week before Mr Passmore was able to walk again, though,' said William. The case of Dibbler's *second* customer had been very useful for his news letter, which rather made up for the two dollars.

'I wasn't to know there really *is* a Dragon of Unhappiness,' said Dibbler.

'I don't think there was until you convinced him that one exists,' said William.

Dibbler brightened a little. 'Ah, well, say what you like, I've always been good at selling ideas. Can I convince you of the idea that a sausage in a bun is what you desire at this time?'

'Actually, I've really got to get this along to—' William began, and then said, 'Did you just hear someone shout?'

'I've got some cold pork pies, too, somewhere,' said Dibbler, ferreting in his tray. 'I can give you a convincingly bargain price on—'

'I'm sure I heard something,' said William.

Dibbler cocked an ear. 'Sort of like a rumbling?' he said.

'Yes.'

They stared into the slowly rolling clouds that filled Broad Way.

Which became, quite suddenly, a huge tarpaulin-covered cart, moving unstoppably and very fast . . .

And the last thing William remembered, before something flew out of the night and smacked him between the eyes, was someone shouting, 'Stop the press!'

The rumour, having been pinned to the page by William's pen like a butterfly to a cork, didn't come to the ears of some people, because they had other, darker things on their mind.

Their rowboat slid through the hissing waters of the river Ankh, which closed behind it slowly.

Two men were bent over the oars. The third sat in the pointy end. Occasionally he spoke.

He said things like 'My nose itches.'

'You'll just have to wait till we get there,' said one of the rowers.

'You could let me out again. It really itches.'

'We let you out when we stopped for supper.'

'It didn't itch then.'

The other rower said, 'Shall I hit him up alongside the —ing head with the —ing oar again, Mr Pin?'

'Good idea, Mr Tulip.'

There was a dull thump in the darkness.

'Ow.'

'Now no more fuss, friend, otherwise Mr Tulip will lose his temper.'

'Too —ing right.' Then there was a sound like an industrial pump.

'Hey, go easy on that stuff, why don't you?'

'Ain't —ing killed me yet, Mr Pin.'

The boat oozed to a halt alongside a tiny, little-used landing stage. The tall figure who had so recently been the focus of Mr Pin's attention was bundled ashore and hustled down an alley.

A moment later there was the sound of a carriage rolling away into the night.

It would seem quite impossible, on such a mucky night, that there could have been anyone to witness this scene.

But there was. The universe requires everything to be observed, lest it cease to exist.

A figure shuffled out from the shadows of the alley, close by. There was a smaller shape wobbling uncertainly by its side.

Both of them watched the departing coach as it disappeared into the snow.

The smaller of the two figures said, 'Well, well, well. There's a fing. Man all bundled up and hooded. An interesting fing, eh?'

The taller figure nodded. It wore a huge old greatcoat several sizes too big, and a felt hat that had been reshaped by time and weather into a soft cone that overhung the wearer's head.

'Scraplit,' it said. 'Thatch and trouser, a blewit the grawney man. I told 'im. I told 'im. Millennium hand and shrimp. Bugrit.'

After a pause it reached into its pocket and produced a sausage, which it broke into two pieces. One bit disappeared under the hat, and the other was tossed to the smaller figure, who was doing most of the talking or, at least, most of the coherent talking.

'Looks like a dirty deed to me,' said the smaller figure, which had four legs.

The sausage was consumed in silence. Then the pair set off into the night again.

In the same way that a pigeon can't walk without

bobbing its head, the taller figure appeared unable to move without a sort of low-key, random mumbling:

'I *told* 'em, I *told* 'em. Millennium hand and shrimp. I said, I said, I said. Oh, no. But they only run out, I *told* 'em. Sod 'em. Doorsteps. I said, I said, I said. Teeth. Wassa name of age, I said I *told* 'em, not my fault, matterofact, matterofact, stands to reason . . .'

The rumour did come to his ears later on, but by then he was part of it.

As for Mr Pin and Mr Tulip, all that need be known about them at this point is that they are the kind of people who call you 'friend'. People like that aren't friendly.

William opened his eyes. I've gone blind, he thought.

Then he moved the blanket.

And then the pain hit him.

It was a sharp and insistent sort of pain, centred right over the eyes. He reached up gingerly. There seemed to be some bruising and what felt like a dent in the flesh, if not the bone.

He sat up. He was in a sloping-ceilinged room. A bit of grubby snow crusted the bottom of a small window. Apart from the bed, which was just a mattress and blanket, the room was unfurnished.

A thump shook the building. Dust drifted down from the ceiling. He got up, clutching at his forehead, and staggered to the door. It opened into a much larger room or, more accurately, a workshop.

Another thump rattled his teeth.

William tried to focus.

The room was full of dwarfs, toiling over a couple of long benches. But at the far end several of them were clustered around something like a complex piece of weaving machinery.

It went thump again.

William rubbed his head. 'What's happening?' he said.

The nearest dwarf looked up at him and nudged a colleague urgently. The nudge passed itself along the rows, and the room was suddenly filled wall to wall with a cautious silence. A dozen solemn dwarf faces looked hard at William.

No one can look harder than a dwarf. Perhaps it's because there is only quite a small amount of face between the statutory round iron helmet and the beard. Dwarf expressions are more *concentrated*.

'Um,' he said. 'Hello?'

One of the dwarfs in front of the big machine was the first to unfreeze.

'Back to work, lads,' he said, and came and looked William sternly in the groin.

'You all right, your lordship?' he said.

William winced. 'Um . . . what happened?' he said. 'I, uh, remember seeing a cart, and then something hit . . .'

'It ran away from us,' said the dwarf. 'Load slipped, too. Sorry about that.'

'What happened to Mr Dibbler?'

The dwarf put his head on one side. 'The skinny man with the sausages?' he said.

'That's right. Was he hurt?'

'I don't think so,' said the dwarf carefully. 'He sold

25

young Thunderaxe a sausage in a bun, I do know that.'

William thought about this. Ankh-Morpork had many traps for the unwary newcomer.

'Well, then, is Mr *Thunderaxe* all right?' he said.

'Probably. He shouted under the door just now that he was feeling a lot better but would stay where he was for the time being,' said the dwarf. He reached under a bench and solemnly handed William a rectangle wrapped in grubby paper.

'Yours, I think.'

William unwrapped his wooden block. It was split right across where a wheel of the cart had run over it, and the writing had been smudged. He sighed.

''scuse me,' said the dwarf, 'but what was it meant to be?'

'It's a block prepared for a woodcut,' said William. He wondered how he could possibly explain the idea to a dwarf from outside the city. 'You know? Engraving? A . . . a sort of very nearly magical way of getting *lots* of copies of writing? I'm afraid I shall have to go and make another one now.'

The dwarf gave him an odd look, and then took the block from him and turned it over and over in his hands.

'You see,' said William, 'the engraver cuts away bits of—'

'Have you still got the original?' said the dwarf.

'Pardon?'

'The original,' said the dwarf patiently.

'Oh, yes.' William reached inside his jacket and produced it.

'Can I borrow it for a moment?'

'Well, all right, but I shall need it again to—'

The dwarf scanned the letter a while, and then turned and hit the nearest dwarf a resounding *boing* on the helmet.

'Ten point across three,' he said, handing him the paper. The struck dwarf nodded, and then its right hand moved quickly across the rack of little boxes, selecting things.

'I ought to be getting back so I can—' William began.

'This won't take long,' said the head dwarf. 'Just you step along this way, will you? This might be of interest to a man of letters such as yourself.'

William followed him along the avenue of busy dwarfs to the machine, which had been thumping away steadily.

'Oh. It's an engraving press,' said William vaguely.

'This one's a bit different,' said the dwarf. 'We've ... modified it.' He took a large sheet of paper off a pile by the press and gave it to William, who read:

GUNILLA GOODMOUNTAIN & CO.
Respectfully Solicit
Work for their New
WORD SMITHY
A method of taking multiple impressions
the like of which
Hath not hiterto been seen.

Reasonable rates.
At the Sign of The Bucket, Gleam Street,
off Treacle Mine Road, Ankh-Morpork.

'What do you think?' said the dwarf shyly.

'Are you Gunilla Goodmountain?'

'Yes. What do you think?'

'We-ell . . . you've got the letters nice and regular, I must say,' said William. 'But I can't see what's so new about it. And you've spelled "hitherto" wrong. There should be another h after the first t. You'll have to cut it all out again unless you want people to laugh at you.'

'Really?' said Goodmountain. He nudged one of his colleagues.

'Just give me a ninety-six-point lower-case h, will you, Caslong? Thank you.'

Goodmountain bent over the press, picked up a spanner and busied himself somewhere in the mechanical gloom.

'You must have a really steady hand to get the letters so neat,' said William. He felt a bit sorry that he'd pointed out the mistake. Probably no one would have noticed in any case. Ankh-Morpork people considered that spelling was a sort of optional extra. They believed in it in the same way they believed in punctuation; it didn't matter where you put it so long as it was there.

The dwarf finished whatever arcane activity he had been engaged in, dabbed with an inked pad at something inside the press, and got down.

'I'm sure it won't' – *thump* – 'matter about the spelling,' said William.

Goodmountain opened the press again and wordlessly handed William a damp sheet of paper.

William read it.

The extra h was in place.

'How—?' he began.

'This is a very nearly magical way of getting lots of copies quickly,' said Goodmountain. Another dwarf appeared at his elbow, holding a big metal rectangle. It was full of little metal letters, back to front. Goodmountain took it and gave William a big grin.

'Want to make any changes before we go to press?' he said. 'Just say the word. A couple of dozen prints be enough?'

'Oh dear,' said William. 'This is *printing*, isn't it . . . ?'

The Bucket was a tavern, of sorts. There was no passing trade. The street was if not a dead end then seriously wounded by the area's change in fortunes. Few businesses fronted on to it. It consisted mainly of the back ends of yards and warehouses. No one even remembered why it was called Gleam Street. There was nothing very sparkling about it.

Besides, calling a tavern the Bucket was not a decision destined to feature in Great Marketing Decisions of History. Its owner was Mr Cheese, who was thin, dry and only smiled when he heard news of some serious murder. Traditionally he had sold short measure but, to make up for it, had short-changed as well. However, the pub had been taken over by the City Watch as the unofficial policemen's pub, because policemen like to drink in places where no one else goes and they don't have to be reminded that they are policemen.

This had been a benefit in some ways. Not even

licensed thieves tried to rob the Bucket now. Policemen didn't like their drinking disturbed. On the other hand, Mr Cheese had never found a bigger bunch of petty criminals than those wearing the Watch uniform. He saw more dud dollars and strange pieces of foreign currency cross his bar in the first month than he'd found in ten years in the business. It made you depressed, it really did. But some of the murder descriptions were quite funny.

He made part of his living by renting out the rat's nest of old sheds and cellars that backed on to the pub. They tended to be occupied very temporarily by the kind of enthusiastic manufacturer who believed that what the world really, really needed today was an inflatable dartboard.

But there *was* a crowd outside the Bucket now, reading one of the slightly misprinted posters that Goodmountain had nailed up on the door. Goodmountain followed William out and nailed up the corrected version.

'Sorry about your head,' he said. 'Looks like we made a bit of an impression on you. Have this one on the house.'

William skulked home, keeping in the shadows in case he met Mr Cripslock. But he folded his printed sheets into their envelopes and took them down to the Hubward Gate and gave them to the messengers, reflecting as he did so that he was doing this several days before he had expected to.

The messengers gave him some very odd looks.

He went back to his lodgings and had a look at himself in the mirror over the washbasin. A large R, printed in bruise colours, occupied a lot of his forehead.

He stuck a bandage over it.

And he still had eighteen more copies. As an after-thought, and feeling rather daring, he looked through his notes for the addresses of eighteen prominent citizens who could probably afford it, wrote a short covering letter to each one offering this service for . . . he thought for a while and then carefully wrote '$5' . . . and folded the free sheets into eighteen envelopes. Of course, he could always have asked Mr Cripslock to do more copies as well, but it had never seemed *right*. After the old boy had spent all day chipping out the words, asking him to sully his craftsmanship by making dozens of duplicates seemed disrespectful. But you didn't have to respect lumps of metal and machines. Machines weren't alive.

That, really, was where the trouble was going to start. And there *was* going to be trouble. The dwarfs had seemed quite unconcerned when he'd told them how much of it there was going to be.

The coach arrived at a large house in the city. A door was opened. A door was shut. Another door was knocked on. It was opened. It shut. The carriage pulled away.

One ground-floor room was heavily curtained, and only the barest gleam of light filtered out. Only the faintest of noises filtered out, too, but any listener would have heard a murmur of conversation die down. Then a chair was knocked over and several people shouted, all at once.

'That *is* him!'

'It's a trick . . . isn't it?'

'I'll be damned!'

'If it *is* him, so are we all!'

The hubbub died away. And then, very calmly, someone began to talk.

'Good. Good. Take him away, gentlemen. Make him comfortable in the cellar.'

There were footsteps. A door opened and closed.

A more querulous voice said, 'We could simply replace—'

'*No*, we could not. I understand that our guest is, fortunately, a man of rather low intelligence.' There was this about the first speaker's voice. It spoke as if disagreeing was not simply unthinkable but impossible. It was used to being in the company of listeners.

'But he looks the spit and image—'

'Yes. Astonishing, isn't it? Let us not overcomplicate matters, though. We are a bodyguard of lies, gentlemen. We are all that stands between the city and oblivion, so let us make this one chance work. Vetinari may be quite willing to see humans become a minority in their greatest city, but frankly his death by assassination would be . . . unfortunate. It would cause turmoil, and turmoil is hard to steer. And we all know that there are people who take too much of an interest. No. There is a third way. A gentle slide from one condition to another.'

'And what will happen to our new friend?'

'Oh, our employees are known to be men of resource, gentlemen. I'm sure they know how to deal with a man whose face no longer fits, eh?'

There was laughter.

* * *

Things were a little fraught in Unseen University. The wizards were scuttling from building to building, glancing at the sky.

The problem, of course, was the frogs. Not rains of frogs, which were uncommon now in Ankh-Morpork, but specifically foreign treefrogs from the humid jungles of Klatch. They were small, brightly coloured, happy little creatures who secreted some of the nastiest toxins in the world, which is why the job of looking after the large vivarium where they happily passed their days was given to first-year students, on the basis that if they got things wrong there wouldn't be too much education wasted.

Very occasionally a frog was removed from the vivarium and put into a rather smaller jar where it briefly became a very happy frog indeed, and then went to sleep and woke up in that great big jungle in the sky.

And thus the University got the active ingredient which it made up into pills and fed to the Bursar, to keep him sane. At least, *apparently* sane, because nothing was that simple at good old UU. In fact he was incurably insane and hallucinated more or less continuously, but by a remarkable stroke of lateral thinking his fellow wizards had reasoned that, in that case, the whole business could be sorted out if only they could find a formula that caused him to *hallucinate that he was completely sane.**

This had worked well. There had been a few false

---

* This is a very common hallucination, shared by most people.

starts. For several hours, at one point, he had hallucinated that he was a bookcase. But now he was permanently hallucinating that he was a bursar, and that almost made up for the small side-effect that also led him to hallucinate that he could fly.

Of course, many people in the universe have also had the misplaced belief that they can safely ignore gravity, mostly after taking some local equivalent of dried frog pills, and this has led to much extra work for elementary physics and caused brief traffic jams in the street below. When a wizard hallucinates that he can fly, things are different.

'Bursaar! You come down here right this minute!' Archchancellor Mustrum Ridcully barked through his megaphone. 'You know what I said about goin' higher than the walls!'

The Bursar floated gently down towards the lawn. 'You wanted me, Archchancellor?'

Ridcully waved a piece of paper at him. 'You were tellin' me the other day we were spendin' a ton of money with the engravers, weren't you?' he barked.

The Bursar got his mind up to something approaching the correct speed. 'I was?' he said.

'Breakin' the budget, you said. Remember it distinctly.'

A few cogs meshed in the jittery gearbox of the Bursar's brain. 'Oh. Yes. Yes. Very true,' he said. Another gear clonked into place. 'A fortune every year, I'm afraid. The Guild of Engravers—'

'Chap here says,' the Archchancellor glanced at the sheet, 'he can do us ten copies of a thousand words each for a dollar. Is that cheap?'

'I think, uh, there must be a mis-carving there, Archchancellor,' said the Bursar, finally managing to get his voice into the smooth and soothing tones he found best in dealing with Ridcully. 'That sum would not keep him in boxwood.'

'Says here' – rustle – 'down to ten-point size,' said Ridcully.

The Bursar lost control for a moment. 'Ridiculous!'

'What?'

'Sorry, Archchancellor. I mean, that can't be right. Even if anyone could consistently carve that fine, the wood would crumble after a couple of impressions.'

'Know about this sort of thing, do you?'

'Well, my great-uncle was an engraver, Archchancellor. And the print bill is a major drain, as you know. I think I can say with some justification that I have been able to keep the Guild down to a very—'

'Don't they invite you to their annual blow-out?'

'Well, as a major customer of course the University is invited to their official dinner and as the designated officer I naturally see it as part of my duties to—'

'Fifteen courses, I heard.'

'—and of course there is our policy of maintaining a friendly relationship with the other Gui—'

'*Not* including the nuts and coffee.'

The Bursar hesitated. The Archchancellor tended to combine wooden-headed stupidity with distressing insight.

'The problem, Archchancellor,' he tried, 'is that we have always been *very much* against using movable type printing for magic purposes because—'

'Yes, yes, I know all about *that*,' said the Archchancellor. 'But there's all the other stuff, more of it every day . . . forms and charts and gods know what. You know I've always wanted a paperless office—'

'Yes, Archchancellor, that's why you hide it all in cupboards and throw it out of the window at night.'

'Clean desk, clean mind,' said the Archchancellor. He thrust the leaflet into the Bursar's hand.

'Just you trot down there, why don't you, and see if it's just a lot of hot air. But walk, please.'

William felt drawn back to the sheds behind the Bucket the next day. Apart from anything else, he had nothing to do and he didn't like being useless.

There are, it has been said, two types of people in the world. There are those who, when presented with a glass that is exactly half full, say: this glass is half full. And then there are those who say: this glass is half empty.

The world *belongs*, however, to those who can look at the glass and say: What's up with this glass? Excuse me? Excuse *me*? *This* is my glass? I don't *think* so. *My* glass was full! *And* it was a bigger glass!

And at the other end of the bar the world is full of the other type of person, who has a broken glass, or a glass that has been carelessly knocked over (usually by one of the people calling for a larger glass), or who had no glass at all, because they were at the back of the crowd and had failed to catch the barman's eye.

William was one of the glassless. And this was odd, because he'd been born into a family that not only had a very large glass indeed but could afford to have people discreetly standing around with bottles to keep it filled up.

It was self-imposed glasslessness, and it had started at a fairly early age when he'd been sent away to school.

William's brother Rupert, being the elder, had gone to the Assassins' School in Ankh-Morpork, widely regarded as being the best school in the world for the full-glass class. William, as a less-important son, had been sent to Hugglestones, a boarding school so bleak and spartan that only the upper glasses would dream of sending their sons there.

Hugglestones was a granite building on a rain-soaked moor, and its stated purpose was to make men from boys. The policy employed involved a certain amount of wastage, and consisted in William's recollection at least of very simple and violent games in the healthy outdoor sleet. The small, slow, fat or merely unpopular were mown down, as nature intended, but natural selection operates in many ways and William found that he had a certain capacity for survival. A good way to survive on the playing fields of Hugglestones was to run very fast and shout a lot while inexplicably always being a long way from the ball. This had earned him, oddly enough, a reputation for being keen, and keenness was highly prized at Hugglestones, if only because actual achievement was so rare. The staff at Hugglestones believed that in sufficient quantities 'being keen' could take the place of lesser attributes like intelligence, foresight and training.

He *had* been truly keen on anything involving words. At Hugglestones this had not counted for a great deal, since most of its graduates never expected to have to do much more with a pen than sign their names (a feat which most of them could manage after three or four years), but it had meant long mornings peacefully reading anything that took his fancy while around him the hulking front-row forwards who would one day be at least the deputy-leaders of the land learned how to hold a pen without crushing it.

William left with a good report, which tended to be the case with pupils that most of the teachers could only vaguely remember. Afterwards, his father had faced the problem of what to do with him.

He was the younger son, and family tradition sent youngest sons into some church or other, where they couldn't do much harm on a physical level. But too much reading had taken its toll. William found that he now thought of prayer as a sophisticated way of pleading with thunderstorms.

Going into land management was just about acceptable, but it seemed to William that land managed itself pretty well, on the whole. He was all in favour of the countryside, provided that it was on the other side of a window.

A military career somewhere was unlikely. William had a rooted objection to killing people he didn't know.

He enjoyed reading and writing. He *liked* words. Words didn't shout or make loud noises, which pretty much defined the rest of his family. They didn't involve getting muddy in the freezing cold. They didn't hunt inoffensive animals, either. They did what he told them to. So, he'd said, he wanted to write.

His father had erupted. In his personal world a scribe was only one step higher than a teacher. Good gods, man, they didn't even ride a horse! So there had been Words.

As a result, William had gone off to Ankh-Morpork, the usual destination for the lost and the aimless. There he'd made words his living, in a quiet sort of way, and considered that he'd got off easily compared to brother Rupert, who was big and good natured and a Hugglestones natural apart from the accident of birth.

And then there had been the war against Klatch . . .

It was an insignificant war, which was over before it started, the kind of war that both sides pretended hadn't really happened, but one of the things that did happen in the few confused days of wretched turmoil was the death of Rupert de Worde. He had died for his beliefs; chief among them was the very Hugglestonian one that bravery could replace armour, and that Klatchians would turn and run if you shouted loud enough.

William's father, during their last meeting, had gone on at some length about the proud and noble traditions of the de Wordes. These had mostly involved unpleasant deaths, preferably of foreigners, but somehow, William gathered, the de Wordes had always considered that it was a decent second prize to die themselves. A de Worde was always to the fore when the city called. That was why they *existed*. Wasn't the family motto *Le Mot Juste*? The Right Word

In The Right Place, said Lord de Worde. He simply could not understand why William did not want to embrace this fine tradition and he dealt with it, in the manner of his kind, by not dealing with it.

And now a great frigid silence had descended between the de Wordes that made the winter chill seem like a sauna.

In this gloomy frame of mind it was positively cheering to wander into the print room to find the Bursar arguing the theory of words with Goodmountain.

'Hold on, hold on,' said the Bursar. 'Yes, indeed, *figuratively* a word is made up of individual letters but they have only a,' he waved his long fingers gracefully, '*theoretical* existence, if I may put it that way. They are, as it were, words *partis in potentia*, and it is, I am afraid, unsophisticated in the extreme to imagine that they have any *real* existence *unis et separato*. Indeed, the very concept of letters having their own physical existence is, philosophically, extremely worrying. Indeed, it would be like noses and fingers running around the world all by themselves—'

That's three 'indeeds', thought William, who noticed things like that. Three indeeds used by a person in one brief speech generally meant an internal spring was about to break.

'We got whole boxes of letters,' said Goodmountain flatly. 'We can make any words you want.'

'That's the trouble, you see,' said the Bursar. 'Supposing the metal remembers the words it has printed? At least engravers melt down their plates, and the cleansing effect of fire will—'

''scuse me, your reverence,' said Goodmountain. One of the dwarfs had tapped him gently on the shoulder and handed him a square of paper. He passed it up to the Bursar.

'Young Caslong here thought you might like this as a souvenir,' he said. 'He took it down directly from the case and pulled it off on the stone. He's very quick like that.'

The Bursar tried to look the young dwarf sternly up and down, although this was a pretty pointless intimidatory tactic to use on dwarfs since they had very little up to look down from.

'Really?' he said. 'How very . . .' His eyes scanned the paper.

And then bulged.

'But these are . . . when I said . . . I only just said . . . How did you know I was going to say . . . I mean, my actual words . . .' he stuttered.

'Of course they're not properly justified,' said Goodmountain.

'Now just a *moment*—' the Bursar began.

William left them to it. The stone he could work out – even the engravers used a big flat stone as a workbench. And he'd seen dwarfs pulling paper sheets off the metal letters, so that made sense, too. And what the Bursar said *had* been unjustified. It wasn't as if metal had a soul.

He looked over the head of a dwarf who was busily assembling letters in a little metal hod, the stubby fingers darting from box to box in the big tray of type in front of him. Capital letters all in the top, small letters all in the bottom. It was even possible to get an idea of what the dwarf was assembling, just by watching the movements of his hands across the tray.

'M-a-k-e-$-$-$-I-n-n-Y-o-u-r-e-S-p-a-r-e-T-y-m—' he murmured.

A certainty formed. He glanced down at the sheets of grubby paper beside the tray.

They were covered with the dense spiky handwriting that identified its owner as an anal-retentive with a poor grip.

There were no flies on C.M.O.T. Dibbler. He would have charged them rent.

With barely a conscious thought, William pulled out his notebook, licked his pencil and wrote, very carefully, in his private shorthand:

'Amzg scenes hv ocrd in the Ct with the Openg o t Prntg Engn at the Sgn o t Bucket by G. Goodmountain, Dwf, which hs causd mch intereſt amng all prts inc. chfs of commerſe.'

He paused. The conversation at the other end of the room was definitely taking a more conciliatory turn.

'*How* much a thousand?' said the Bursar.

'Even cheaper for bulk rates,' said Goodmountain. 'Small runs no problem.'

The Bursar's face had that warm glaze of someone who deals in numbers and can see one huge and inconvenient number getting smaller in the very near future, and in those circumstances philosophy doesn't stand much of a chance. And what was visible of Goodmountain's face had the cheerful scowl of some-one who's worked out how to turn lead into still more gold.

'Well, of course, a contract of this size would have to be ratified by the Archchancellor himself,' said the Bursar, 'but I can assure you that he *listens very carefully* to everything I say.'

'I'm sure he does, your lordship,' said Goodmountain cheerfully.

'Uh, by the way,' said the Bursar, 'do you people have an Annual Dinner?'

'Oh, yes. Definitely,' said the dwarf.

'When is it?'

'When would you like it?'

William scribbled: 'Mch businfs sms likly wth a Certain Educational Body in t Ct,' and then, because he had a truly honest nature, he added, 'we hear.'

Well, that was pretty good going. He'd got one letter away only this morning and already he had an important note for the next—

—except, of course, the customers weren't expecting another one for almost a month. He had a certain feeling that by then no one would be very interested. On the *other* hand, if he *didn't* tell them about it, someone would be bound to complain. There had been all that trouble with the rain of dogs in Treacle Mine Road last year, and it wasn't as if that had even happened.

But even if he got the dwarfs to make the type really big, one item of gossip wasn't going to go very far.

Blast.

He'd have to scuttle around a bit and find some more.

On an impulse he wandered over to the departing Bursar.

'Excuse me, sir,' he said.

The Bursar, who was feeling in a very cheerful mood, raised an eyebrow in a good-humoured way.

'Hmm?' he said. 'It's Mr de Worde, isn't it?'

'Yes, sir. I—'

'I'm afraid we do all our own writing down at the University,' said the Bursar.

'I wonder if I could just ask you what you think of Mr Goodmountain's new printing engine, sir?' said William.

'Why?'

'Er . . . Because I'd quite like to know? And I'd like to write it down for my news letter. You know? Views of a leading member of Ankh-Morpork's thaumaturgical establishment?'

'Oh?' The Bursar hesitated. 'This is the little thing you send out to the Duchess of Quirm and the Duke of Sto Helit and people like that, isn't it?'

'Yes, sir,' said William. Wizards were terrible snobs.

'Er. Well, then . . . you can say that I said it is a step in the right direction that will . . . er . . . be welcomed by all forward-thinking people and will drag the city kicking and screaming into the Century of the Fruitbat.' He watched eagle-eyed as William wrote this down. 'And my name is Dr A.A. Dinwiddie, D.M.(7th), D.Thau., B.Occ., M.Coll., B.F. That's Dinwiddie with an o.'

'Yes, Dr Dinwiddie. Er . . . the Century of the Fruitbat is nearly over, sir. Would you like the city to be dragged kicking and screaming *out* of the Century of the Fruitbat?'

'Indeed.'

William wrote this down. It was a puzzle why things were always dragged kicking and screaming. No one ever seemed to want to, for example, lead them gently by the hand.

'And I'm sure you will send me a copy when it comes out, of course,' said the Bursar.

'Yes, Dr Dinwiddie.'

'And if you want anything from me at any other time, don't hesitate to ask.'

'Thank you, sir. But I'd always understood, sir, that Unseen University was against the use of movable type?'

'Oh, I think it's time to embrace the exciting challenges presented to us by the Century of the Fruitbat,' said the Bursar.

'We . . . That's the one we're just about to leave, sir.'

'Then it's high time we embraced them, don't you think?'

'Good point, sir.'

'And now I must fly,' said the Bursar. 'Except that I mustn't.'

Lord Vetinari, the Patrician of Ankh-Morpork, poked at the ink in his inkwell. There was ice in it.

'Don't you even have a proper fire?' said Hughnon Ridcully, Chief Priest of Blind Io and unofficial spokesman for the city's religious establishment. 'I mean, I'm not one for stuffy rooms, but it's freezing in here!'

'Brisk, certainly,' said Lord Vetinari. 'It's odd, but the ice isn't as dark as the rest of the ink. What causes that, do you think?'

'Science, probably,' said Hughnon vaguely. Like his wizardly brother, Archchancellor Mustrum, he didn't like to bother himself with patently silly questions. Both gods and magic required solid, sensible men, and the brothers Ridcully were solid as rocks. And, in some respects, as sensible.

'Ah. Anyway . . . you were saying?'

'You must put a stop to this, Havelock. You know the . . . understanding.'

Vetinari seemed engrossed in the ink. 'Must, your reverence?' he said calmly, without looking up.

'You *know* why we're all against this movable type nonsense!'

'Remind me again . . . Look, it bobs up and down . . .'

Hughnon sighed. 'Words are too important to be left to machinery. We've got nothing against engraving, you know that. We've nothing against words being nailed down properly. But words that can be taken apart and used to make other words . . . well, that's downright dangerous. And I thought you weren't in favour, either?'

'Broadly, yes,' said the Patrician. 'But many years of ruling this city, your reverence, have taught me that you cannot apply brakes to a volcano. Sometimes it is best to let these things run their course. They generally die down again after a while.'

'You have not always taken such a relaxed approach, Havelock,' said Hughnon.

The Patrician gave him a cool stare that went on for a couple of seconds beyond the comfort barrier.

'Flexibility and understanding have always been my watchwords,' he said.

'My god, have they?'

'Indeed. And what I would like you and your brother to understand now, your reverence, in a flexible way, is that this enterprise is being undertaken by dwarfs. And do you know where the largest dwarf city is, your reverence?'

'What? Oh . . . let's see . . . there's that place in—'

'Yes, everyone starts by saying that. But it's Ankh-Morpork, in fact. There are more than fifty thousand dwarfs here now.'

'Surely not?'

'I assure you. We have currently very good relationships with the dwarf communities in Copperhead and Uberwald. In dealings with the dwarfs I have seen to it that the city's hand of friendship is permanently outstretched in a slightly downward direction. And in this current cold snap I am sure we are all very glad that bargeloads of coal and lamp oil are coming down from the dwarf mines every day. Do you catch my meaning?'

Hughnon glanced at the fireplace. Against all probability, one lump of coal was smouldering all by itself.

'And of course,' the Patrician went on, 'it is increasingly hard to ignore this new type, aha, of printing when vast printeries now exist in the Agatean Empire and, as I am sure you are aware, in Omnia. And from Omnia, as you no doubt know, the Omnians export huge amounts of their holy Book of Om and these pamphlets they're so keen on.'

'Evangelical nonsense,' said Hughnon. 'You should have banned them long ago.'

Once again the stare went on a good deal too long.

'*Ban* a *religion*, your reverence?'

'Well, when I say *ban*, I mean—'

'I'm *sure* no one could call me a despot, your reverence,' said Lord Vetinari severely.

Hughnon Ridcully made a misjudged attempt to lighten the mood. 'Not twice at any rate, ahaha.'

'I'm sorry?'

'I said . . . not twice at any rate . . . ahaha.'

'I do apologize, but you seem to have lost me there.'

'It was, uh, a minor witticism, Hav— my lord.'

'Oh. Yes. Ahah,' said Vetinari, and the words withered in the air. 'No, I'm afraid you will find that the Omnians are quite free to distribute their good news about Om. But take heart! Surely you have some good news about Io?'

'What? Oh. Yes, of course. He had a bit of a cold last month, but he's up and about again.'

'Capital. That *is* good news. No doubt these printers will happily spread the word on your behalf. I'm sure they will work to your exacting requirements.'

'And these are your reasons, my lord?'

'Do you think I have others?' said Lord Vetinari. 'My motives, as ever, are entirely transparent.'

Hughnon reflected that 'entirely transparent' meant either that you could see right through them or that you couldn't see them at all.

Lord Vetinari shuffled through a file of paper. '*However*, the Guild of Engravers has put its rates up three times in the past year.'

'Ah. I see,' said Hughnon.

'A civilization runs on words, your reverence. Civilization *is* words. Which, on the whole, should not be too expensive. The world turns, your reverence, and we must spin with it.' He smiled. 'Once upon a time nations fought like great grunting beasts in a swamp. Ankh-Morpork ruled a large part of that swamp because it had the best claws. But today gold has taken the place of steel and, my goodness, the Ankh-Morpork dollar seems to be the currency of choice. Tomorrow . . . perhaps the weaponry will be just words. The most words, the quickest words, the last words. Look out of the window. Tell me what you see.'

'Fog,' said the Chief Priest.

Vetinari sighed. Sometimes the weather had no sense of narrative convenience.

'*If it was a fine day,*' he said sharply, 'you would see the big semaphore tower on the other side of the river. Words flying back and forth from every corner of the continent. Not long ago it would take me the better part of a month to exchange letters with our ambassador in Genua. Now I can have a reply tomorrow. Certain things become easier, but this makes them harder in other ways. We have to change the way we think. We have to move with the times. Have you heard of c-commerce?'

'Certainly. The merchant ships are always—'

'I mean that you may now send a clacks all the way to Genua to order a . . . a pint of prawns, if you like. Is that not a notable thing?'

'They would be pretty high when they got here, my lord!'

'Certainly. That was just an example. But now think of a prawn as merely an assemblage of information!' said Lord Vetinari, his eyes sparkling.

'Are you suggesting that prawns could travel by semaphore?' said the Chief Priest. 'I suppose that you might be able to flick them from—'

'I was endeavouring to point out the fact that information is *also* bought and sold,' said Lord Vetinari. 'And also that what was once considered impossible is now quite easily achieved. Kings and lords come and go and leave nothing but statues in a desert, while a couple of young men tinkering in a workshop change the way the world works.'

He walked over to a table on which was spread out a map of the world. It was a workman's map; this is to say, it was a map used by someone who needed to refer to it a lot. It was covered with notes and markers.

'We've always looked beyond the walls for the invaders,' he said. 'We always thought change came from outside, usually on the point of a sword. And then we look around and find that it comes from the inside of the head of someone you wouldn't notice in the street. In certain circumstances it may be convenient to remove the head, but there seem to be such a lot of them these days.'

He gestured towards the busy map.

'A thousand years ago we thought the world was a bowl,' he said. 'Five hundred years ago we knew it was a globe. Today we know it is flat and round and carried through space on the back of a turtle.' He turned and gave the High Priest another smile. 'Don't you wonder what shape it will turn out to be tomorrow?'

But a family trait of all the Ridcullys was not to let go of a thread until you've unravelled the whole garment.

'Besides, they have these little pincer things, you know, and would probably hang on like—'

'What do?'

'Prawns. They'd hang on to—'

'You are taking me rather too literally, your reverence,' said Vetinari sharply.

'Oh.'

'I was merely endeavouring to indicate that if we do not grab events by the collar they will have us by the throat.'

'It'll end in trouble, my lord,' said Ridcully. He'd found it a good general comment in practically any debate. Besides, it was so often true.

Lord Vetinari sighed. 'In my experience, practically everything does,' he said. 'That is the nature of things. All we can do is sing as we go.'

He stood up. 'However, I will pay a personal visit to the dwarfs in question.' He reached out to ring a bell on his desk, stopped, and with a smile at the priest moved his hand instead to a brass and leather tube that hung from two brass hooks. The mouthpiece was in the shape of a dragon.

He whistled into it, and then said, 'Mr Drumknott? My coach, please.'

'Is it me,' said Ridcully, giving the new-fangled speaking tube a nervous glance, 'or is there a terrible smell in here?'

Lord Vetinari gave him a quizzical look and glanced down.

There was a basket just underneath his desk. In it was what appeared to be, at first glance and certainly at first smell, a dead dog. It lay with all four legs in the air. Only the occasional gentle expulsion of wind suggested that some living process was going on.

'It's his teeth,' he said coldly. The dog Wuffles turned over and regarded the priest with one baleful black eye.

'He's doing very well for a dog of his age,' said Hughnon, in a desperate attempt to climb a suddenly tilting slope. 'How old would he be now?'

'Sixteen,' said the Patrician. 'That's over a hundred in dog years.'

Wuffles dragged himself into a sitting position and growled, releasing a gust of stale odours from the depths of his basket.

'He's very healthy,' said Hughnon while trying not to breathe. 'For his age, I mean. I expect you get used to the smell.'

'What smell?' said Lord Vetinari.

'Ah. Yes. Indeed,' said Hughnon.

As Lord Vetinari's coach rattled off through the slush towards Gleam Street it may have surprised its occupant to know that, in a cellar quite near by, someone looking very much like him was chained to the wall.

It was quite a long chain, giving him access to a table and chair, a bed, and a hole in the floor.

Currently he was at the table. On the other side of

it was Mr Pin. Mr Tulip was leaning menacingly against the wall. It would be clear to any experienced person that what was going on here was 'good cop, bad cop' with the peculiar drawback that there were no cops. There was just an apparently endless supply of Mr Tulip.

'So . . . Charlie,' said Mr Pin, 'how about it?'

'It's not illegal, is it?' said the man addressed as Charlie.

Mr Pin spread his hands. 'What's legality, Charlie? Just words on paper. But you won't be doing anything *wrong*.'

Charlie nodded uncertainly. 'But ten thousand dollars doesn't sound like the kind of money you get for doing something *right*,' he said. 'Not for just saying a few words.'

'Mr Tulip here once got even more money than that for saying just a few words, Charlie,' said Mr Pin soothingly.

'Yeah, I said, "Give me all the —ing cash or the girl gets it," ' said Mr Tulip.

'Was that *right*?' said Charlie, who seemed to Mr Pin to have a highly developed death wish.

'Absolutely right for that occasion, yes,' he said.

'Yes, but it's not often people make money like that,' said the suicidal Charlie. His eyes kept straying to the monstrous bulk of Mr Tulip, who was holding a paper bag in one hand and, in the other hand, a spoon. He was using the spoon to ferry a fine white powder to his nose, his mouth and once, Charlie would have sworn, his ear.

'Well, you are a special man, Charlie,' said Mr Pin.

'And afterwards you will have to stay out of sight for a long time.'

'Yeah,' said Mr Tulip, in a spray of powder. There was a sudden strong smell of mothballs.

'All right, but why did you have to kidnap me, then? One minute I was locking up for the night, next minute – bang! *And* you've got me chained up.'

Mr Pin decided to change tack. Charlie was arguing too much for a man in the same room as Mr Tulip, especially a Mr Tulip who was halfway through a bag of powdered mothballs. He gave him a big friendly smile.

'There's no point in dwelling on the past, my friend,' he said. 'This is business. All we want is a few days of your time, and then you end up with a fortune and – and I believe this is *important*, Charlie – a *lifetime* in which to spend it.'

Charlie was turning out to be very stupid indeed.

'But how do you know I won't tell someone?' he insisted.

Mr Pin sighed. 'We trust you, Charlie.'

The man had run a clothes shop in Pseudopolis. Small shopkeepers had to be smart, didn't they? They were usually sharp as knives when it came to making just the right amount of wrong change. So much for physiognomy, thought Mr Pin. This man could pass for the Patrician even in a good light, but while by all accounts Lord Vetinari would have already worked out all the nasty ways the future could go, Charlie was actually entertaining the idea that he was going to come out of this alive and might even outsmart Mr Pin. He was actually trying to be *cunning*! He was sitting a few feet away from Mr Tulip, a man trying to snort crushed moth repellant, and he was trying *guile*. You almost had to admire the man.

'I'll need to be back by Friday,' said Charlie. 'It'll all be over by Friday, will it?'

The shed that was now leased by the dwarfs had in the course of its rickety life been a forge and a laundry and a dozen other enterprises, and had last been used as a rocking-horse factory by someone who had thought something was the Next Big Thing when it was by then one day away from becoming the Last Big Flop. Stacks of half-finished rocking horses that Mr Cheese had been unable to sell for the back rent still filled one wall all the way to the tin roof. There was a shelf of corroding paint tins. Brushes had fossilized in their jars.

The press occupied the centre of the floor, with several dwarfs at work. William had seen presses. The engravers used them. This one had an organic quality, though. The dwarfs spent as much time changing the press as they did using it. Extra rollers appeared, endless belts were threaded into the works. The press grew by the hour.

Goodmountain was working in front of several of the large sloped boxes, each one of which was divided into several dozen compartments.

William watched the dwarf's hand fly over the little boxes of leaden letters.

'Why's there a bigger box for the Es?'

''cos that's the letter we use most of.'

'Is that why it's in the middle of the box?'

'Right. Es then Ts then As . . .'

'I mean, people would expect to see A in the middle.'

'We put E.'

'But you've got more Ns than Us. And U is a vowel.'

'People use more Ns than you think.'

On the other side of the room Caslong's stubby dwarf fingers danced across his own boxes of letters.

'You can almost read what he's working on—' William began.

Goodmountain glanced up. His eyes narrowed for a moment.

'"... Make ... more ... money ... inn ... youre ... Spare ... Time ..."' he said. 'Sounds like Mr Dibbler has been back.'

William stared down at the box of letters again. Of course, a quill pen *potentially* contained anything you wrote with it. He could understand that. But it did so in a clearly theoretical way, a *safe* way. Whereas these dull grey blocks looked threatening. He could understand why they worried people. Put us together in the right way, they seemed to say, and we can be anything you want. We could even be something you don't want. We can spell anything. We can certainly spell trouble.

The ban on movable type wasn't *exactly* a law. But he knew the engravers didn't like it, because they had the world operating just as they wanted it, thank you very much. And Lord Vetinari was said not to like it, because too many words only upset people. And the wizards and the priests didn't like it because words were important.

An engraved page was an engraved page, complete

and unique. But if you took the leaden letters that had previously been used to set the words of a god, and then used them to set a cookery book, what did that do to the holy wisdom? For that matter, what would it do to the pie? As for printing a book of spells, and then using the same type for a book of navigation – well, the voyage might go *anywhere*.

On cue, because history likes neatness, he heard the sound of a carriage drawing up in the street outside. A few moments later Lord Vetinari stepped inside and stood leaning heavily on his stick and surveying the room with mild interest.

'Why . . . Lord de Worde,' he said, looking surprised. 'I had no idea that you were involved in this enterprise . . .'

William coloured as he hurried over to the city's supreme ruler. 'It's *Mister* de Worde, my lord.'

'Ah, yes. Of course. Indeed.' Lord Vetinari's gaze traversed the inky room, paused a moment on the pile of madly smiling rocking horses, and then took in the toiling dwarfs. 'Yes. Of course. And are you in charge?'

'No one is, my lord,' said William. 'But Mr Goodmountain over there seems to do most of the talking.'

'So what exactly is *your* purpose here?'

'Er . . .' William paused, which he knew was never a good tactic with the Patrician. 'Frankly, sir, it's warm, my office is freezing, and . . . well, it's fascinating. Look, I know it's not really—'

Lord Vetinari nodded and raised a hand. 'Be so good as to ask Mr Goodmountain to come over here, will you?'

William tried to whisper a few instructions into Gunilla's ear as he hustled him over to the tall figure of the Patrician.

'Ah, good,' said the Patrician. 'Now, I would just like to ask one or two questions, if I may?'

Goodmountain nodded.

'Firstly, is Mr Cut-My-Own-Throat Dibbler involved in this enterprise in any significant managerial capacity?'

'What?' said William. He hadn't been expecting *this*.

'Shifty fellow, sells sausages—'

'Oh, him. No. Just the dwarfs.'

'I *see*. And is this building built on a crack in space-time?'

'What?' said Gunilla.

The Patrician sighed. 'When one has been ruler of this city as long as I have,' he said, 'one gets to know with a sad certainty that whenever some well-meaning soul begins a novel enterprise they always, with some kind of uncanny foresight, site it at the point where it will do maximum harm to the fabric of reality. There was that Holy Wood moving picture fiasco a few years ago, yes? And that Music with Rocks In business not long after, we never got to the bottom of that. And of course the wizards seem to break into the Dungeon Dimensions so often they might as well install a revolving door. And I'm sure I don't have to remind you what happened when the late Mr Hong chose to open his Three Jolly Luck Take-Away Fish Bar in Dagon Street during the lunar eclipse. Yes? You see, gentlemen, it would be nice to think that *someone*, somewhere in this city, is engaged in some simple enterprise that is *not* going to end up causing tentacled monsters and dread apparitions to stalk the streets eating people. So . . . ?'

'What?' said Goodmountain.

'We haven't noticed any cracks,' said William.

'Ah, but possibly *on this very site* a strange cult once engaged in eldritch rites, the very essence of which permeated the neighbourhood, and which seeks only the rite, ahah, circumstances to once again arise and walk around eating people?'

'What?' said Gunilla. He looked helplessly at William, who could only add:

'They made rocking horses here.'

'Really? I've always thought there was something slightly sinister about rocking horses,' said Lord Vetinari, but he looked subtly disappointed. Then he brightened up. He pointed to the big stone on which the type was arranged.

'Aha,' he said. 'Innocently taken from the overgrown ruins of a megalithic stone circle, this stone is redolent with the blood of thousands, I have no doubt, who will emerge to seek revenge, you may depend upon it.'

'It was cut specially for me by my brother,' said Gunilla. 'And I don't have to take that kind of talk, mister. Who do you think you are, coming in here and talking daft like that?'

William stepped forward at a healthy fraction of the speed of terror.

'I wonder if I might just take Mr Goodmountain aside and explain one or two things to him?' he said quickly.

The Patrician's bright, enquiring smile did not so much as flicker.

'What a good idea,' he said, as William frogmarched the dwarf to a corner. 'He will be sure to thank you for it later.'

Lord Vetinari stood leaning on his stick and looking at the press with an air of benevolent interest, while behind him William de Worde explained the political realities of Ankh-Morpork, especially those relating to sudden death. With gestures.

After thirty seconds of this, Goodmountain came back and stood foursquare in front of the Patrician, with his thumbs in his belt.

'I speak as I find, me,' he said. 'Always have done, always will—'

'And what is it that you call a spade?' said Lord Vetinari.

'What? Never use spades,' said the glowering dwarf. '*Farmers* use spades. But I call a shovel a shovel.'

'Yes, I thought you would,' said Lord Vetinari.

'Young William here says you're a ruthless despot who doesn't like printing. But I say you're a fair-minded man who won't stand in the way of an honest dwarf making a bit of a living, am I right?'

Once again Lord Vetinari's smile remained in place.

'Mr de Worde, a moment, please . . .'

The Patrician put his arm companionably around William's shoulders and walked him gently away from the watching dwarfs.

'I only said that *some* people call you—' William began.

'Now, sir,' said the Patrician, waving this away. 'I

think I might just be persuaded, against all experience, that we have here a little endeavour that might just be pursued without filling my streets with inconvenient occult rubbish. It is hard to imagine such a thing in Ankh-Morpork, but I could just about accept it as a possibility. And it so happens that I feel the question of "printing" is one that might, with care, be re-opened.'

'You *do*?'

'Yes. So I am minded to allow your friends to proceed with their folly.'

'Er, they're not exactly—' William began.

'*Of course*, I should add that, in the event of there being any problems of a tentacular nature, you would be held personally responsible.'

'Me? But I—'

'Ah. You feel that I am being unfair? Ruthlessly despotic, perhaps?'

'Well, I, er—'

'Apart from anything else, the dwarfs are a very hard-working and valuable ethnic grouping in the city,' said the Patrician. 'On the whole, I wish to avoid any low-level difficulties at this time, what with the unsettled situation in Uberwald and the whole Muntab question.'

'Where's Muntab?' said William.

'Exactly. How is Lord de Worde, by the way? You should write to him more often, you know.'

William said nothing.

'I always think it is a very sad thing when families fall out,' said Lord Vetinari. 'There is far too much mutton-headed ill-feeling in the world.' He gave

William a companionable pat. 'I'm sure you will see to it that the printing enterprise stays firmly in the realms of the cult, the canny and the scrutable. Do I make myself clear?'

'But I don't have any control ov—'

'Hmm?'

'Yes, Lord Vetinari,' said William.

'Good. Good!' The Patrician straightened up, turned, and beamed at the dwarfs.

'Jolly good,' he said. 'My word. Lots of little letters, all screwed together. Possibly an idea whose time has come. I may even have an occasional job for you myself.'

William waved frantically at Gunilla from behind the Patrician's back.

'Special rate for government jobs,' the dwarf muttered.

'Oh, but I wouldn't dream of paying any less than other customers,' said the Patrician.

'I wasn't going to charge you less than—'

'Well, I'm sure we've all been very pleased to see you here, your lordship,' said William brightly, swivelling the Patrician in the direction of the door. 'We look forward to the pleasure of your custom.'

'Are you quite *sure* Mr Dibbler isn't involved in this concern?'

'I think he's having some things printed, but that's all,' said William.

'Astonishing. Astonishing,' said Lord Vetinari, getting into his coach. 'I do hope he isn't ill.'

Two figures watched his departure from the rooftop opposite.

One of them said, very, *very* quietly, '—!'

The other said, 'You have a point of view, Mr Tulip?'

'And *he*'s the man who runs the city?'

'Yeah.'

'So where's his —ing bodyguards?'

'If we wanted to scrag him, here and now, how useful would, say, four bodyguards be?'

'As a —ing chocolate kettle, Mr Pin.'

'There you are, then.'

'But I could knock him over from here with a —ing brick!'

'I gather there are many organizations who hold Views on that, Mr Tulip. People tell me this dump is thriving. The man at the top has a lot of friends when everything is going well. You would soon run out of bricks.'

Mr Tulip looked down at the departing coach. 'From what I hear he mostly doesn't do a —ing thing!' he complained.

'Yeah,' said Mr Pin smoothly. 'One of the hardest things to do properly, in politics.'

Mr Tulip and Mr Pin brought different things to their partnership, and in this instance what Mr Pin brought was political savvy. Mr Tulip respected this, even if he didn't understand it. He contented himself with muttering, 'It'd be simpler to —ing kill him.'

'Oh, for a —ing simple world,' said Mr Pin. 'Look, lay off the Honk, eh? That stuff's for *trolls*. It's worse than Slab. And they cut it with ground glass.'

''s chemical,' said Mr Tulip sullenly.

Mr Pin sighed. 'Shall I try again?' he said. 'Listen

carefully. Drugs equals chemicals, *but*, and please do *listen* to this part, sheesh, chemicals do not equal drugs. Remember all that trouble with the calcium carbonate? When you paid the man five dollars?'

'Made me feel good,' muttered Mr Tulip.

'Calcium carbonate?' said Mr Pin. 'Even for you, I mean . . . Look, you put up your actual nose enough chalk that someone could probably cut your head off and write on a blackboard with your neck?'

That was the major problem with Mr Tulip, he thought, as they made their way to the ground. It wasn't that he had a drugs habit. He *wanted* to have a drugs habit. What he *had* was a stupidity habit, which cut in whenever he found anything being sold in little bags, and this had resulted in Mr Tulip seeking heaven in flour, salt, baking powder and pickled beef sandwiches. In a street where furtive people were selling Clang, Slip, Chop, Rhino, Skunk, Triplin, Floats, Honk, Double Honk, Gongers and Slack, Mr Tulip had an unerring way of finding the man who was retailing curry powder at what worked out as six hundred dollars a pound. It was so —ing *embarrassing*.

Currently he was experimenting with the whole range of recreational chemicals available to Ankh-Morpork's troll population, because at least when dealing with trolls Mr Tulip had a moderate chance of outsmarting somebody. In theory Slab and Honk shouldn't have any effect on the human brain, apart from maybe dissolving it. Mr Tulip was hanging in there. He'd tried normality once and hadn't liked it.

Mr Pin sighed again. 'Come on,' he said. 'Let's feed the geek.'

In Ankh-Morpork it is very hard to watch without being watched in turn, and the two furtive watchers were indeed under careful observation.

They were being watched by a small dog, variously coloured but mainly a rusty grey. Occasionally it scratched itself, with a noise like someone trying to shave a wire brush.

There was a piece of string around its neck. This was attached to another piece of string or, rather, to a length made up of pieces of string inexpertly knotted together.

The string was being held in the hand of a man. At least, such might be deduced from the fact that it disappeared into the same pocket of the grubby coat as one sleeve, which presumably had an arm in it, and theoretically therefore a hand on the end.

It was a strange coat. It stretched from the pavement almost to the brim of the hat above it, which was shaped rather like a sugar loaf. There was a suggestion of grey hair around the join. One arm burrowed in the suspicious depths of a pocket and produced a cold sausage.

'Two men spyin' on the Patrician,' said the dog. 'An interestin' fing.'

'Bugrem,' said the man, and broke the sausage into two democratic halves.

William wrote a short paragraph about Patrician Visits The Bucket, and examined his notebook.

Amazing, really. He'd found no less than a dozen

items for his news letter in only a day. It was astonishing what people would tell you if you asked them.

Someone had stolen one of the golden fangs of the statue of Offler the Crocodile God; he'd promised Sergeant Colon a drink for telling him that, but in any case had got some way towards payment by appending to his paragraph the sentence: 'The Watch are Mightily in Pursuit of the Wrongdoer, and are Confident of Apprehenſion at an Early Juncture.'

He was not entirely sure about this, although Sergeant Colon had looked very sincere when he said it.

The nature of truth always bothered William. He had been brought up to tell it or, more correctly, to 'own up' and some habits are hard to break if they've been beaten in hard enough. And Lord de Worde had inclined to the old proverb that, as you bend the twig, so grows the tree. William had not been a particularly flexible twig. Lord de Worde had not, himself, been a violent man. He'd merely employed them. Lord de Worde, as far as William could recall, had no great enthusiasm for anything that involved touching people.

Anyway, William always told himself, he was no good at making things up; anything that wasn't the truth simply unravelled for him. Even little white lies, like 'I shall definitely have the money by the end of the week', always ended in trouble. That was 'telling stories', a sin in the de Worde compendium that was worse than lying; it was trying to make lies *interesting*.

So William de Worde told the truth, out of cosmic self-defence. He'd found a hard truth less hard than an easy lie.

There had been rather a good fight in the Mended Drum. William was very pleased with that one: 'Whereupon Brezock the Barbarian picked up a table and delivered a blow to Moltin the Snatcher, who in his turn seized hold of the Chandeliers and swung thereon, the while crying, "Take that, thou B*st*rd that you are!!!", at which juncture, a ruckus commenced and 5 or 6 people were hurt.'

He took it all down to the Bucket.

Gunilla read it with interest; it seemed to take very little time for the dwarfs to set it up in type.

And it was odd, but . . .

. . . once it *was* in type, all the letters so neat and regular . . .

. . . it looked more *real*.

Boddony, who seemed to be second in command of the print room, squinted at the columns of type over Goodmountain's shoulders.

'Hmm,' he said.

'What do you think?' said William.

'Looks a bit . . . grey,' said the dwarf. 'All the type bunched up. Looks like a book.'

'Well, that's all right, isn't it?' said William. Looking like a book sounded like a good thing.

'Maybe you want it more sort of spaced out?' said Gunilla.

William stared at the printed page. An idea crept over him. It seemed to evolve from the page itself.

'How about,' he said, 'if we put a little title on each piece?'

He picked up a scrap of paper and doodled: 5/6 Hurt in Tavern Brawl.

Boddony read it solemnly. 'Yes,' he said eventually. 'That looks . . . suitable.' He passed the paper across the table.

'What do you call this news sheet?' he said.

'I don't,' said William.

'You've got to call it something,' said Boddony. 'What do you put at the top?'

'Generally something like "To my Lord the . . ."' William began. Boddony shook his head.

'You can't put that,' he said. 'You want something a bit more general. More *snappy*.'

'How about "Ankh-Morpork Items"?' said William. 'Sorry, but I'm not much good at names.'

Gunilla pulled his little hod out of his apron and selected some letters from one of the cases on the table. He screwed them together, inked them, and rolled a sheet of paper over them.

William read: Ankh-Morpork tImes.

'Messed that up a bit. Wasn't paying attention,' muttered Gunilla, reaching for the type. William stopped him.

'I don't know,' he said. 'Er. Leave it as it is . . . just make it a bigger T and a smaller i.'

'That's it, then,' said Gunilla. 'All done. All right, lad? How many copies do you want?'

'Er . . . twenty? Thirty?'

'How about a couple of hundred?' Gunilla nodded at the dwarfs, who set to work. 'It's hardly worth going to press for less.'

'Good grief! I can't imagine there's enough people in the city that'd pay five dollars!'

'All right, charge 'em half a dollar. Then it'll be

fifty dollars for us and the same for you.'

'My word! Really?' William stared at the beaming dwarf. 'But I've still got to sell them,' he said. 'It's not as though they're cakes in a shop. It's not like—'

He sniffed. His eyes began to water.

'Oh dear,' he said. 'We're going to have another visitor. I know that smell.'

'What smell?' said the dwarf.

The door creaked open.

There was this to be said about the Smell of Foul Ole Ron, an odour so intense that it took on a personality of its own and fully justified the capital letter: after the initial shock the organs of smell just gave up and shut down, as if no more able to comprehend the thing than an oyster can comprehend the ocean. After some minutes in its presence, wax would trickle out of people's ears and their hair would begin to bleach.

It had developed to such a degree that it now led a semi-independent life of its own, and often went to the theatre by itself, or read small volumes of poetry. Ron was *outclassed* by his Smell.

Foul Ole Ron's hands were thrust deeply into his pockets, but from one pocket issued a length of string, or rather a great many lengths of string tied into one length. The other end was attached to a small dog of the greyish persuasion. It was possibly a terrier. It walked with a limp and also in a kind of oblique fashion, as though it was trying to insinuate its way through the world. It walked like a dog who has long ago learned that the world contains more thrown boots than meaty bones. It walked like a dog that was prepared, at any moment, to run.

It looked up at William with crusted eyes and said: 'Woof.'

William felt that he ought to stand up for mankind.

'Sorry about the smell,' he said. Then he stared at the dog.

'What's this smell you keep on about?' said Gunilla. The rivets on his helmet were beginning to tarnish.

'It, er, belongs to Mr ... er ... Ron,' said William, still giving the dog a suspicious look. 'People say it's glandular.'

He was sure he'd seen the dog before. It was always in the corner of the picture, as it were – ambling through the streets, or just sitting on a corner, watching the world go by.

'What does he want?' said Gunilla. 'D'you think he wants us to print something?'

'Shouldn't think so,' said William. 'He's a sort of beggar. Only they won't let him in the Beggars' Guild any more.'

'He isn't saying anything.'

'Well, usually he just stands there until people give him something to go away. Er . . . you've heard of things like the Welcome Wagon, where various neighbours and traders greet newcomers to an area?'

'Yes.'

'Well, this is the dark side.'

Foul Ole Ron nodded and held out a hand. ''s right, Mister Push. Don't try the blarney gobble on me, juggins, I *told* 'em, I ain't slanging the gentry, bugrit. Millennium hand and shrimp. Dang.'

'Woof.'

William glared at the dog again.

'Growl,' it said.

Gunilla scratched somewhere in the recesses of his beard.

'One thing I already noticed about this here town,' he said, 'is that people'll buy practically *anything* off a man in the street.'

He picked up a handful of the news sheets, still damp from the press.

'Can you understand me, mister?' he said.

'Bugrit.'

Gunilla nudged William in the ribs. 'Does that mean yes or no, d'you think?'

'Probably yes.'

'Okay. Well, see here now, if you sell these things at, oh, twenty pence each, you can keep—'

'Hey, you can't sell it *that* cheap,' said William.

'Why not?'

'Why? Because ... because ... because, well, anyone will be able to read it, that's why!'

'Good, 'cos that means anyone'll be able to pay twenty pence,' said Gunilla calmly. 'There's lots more poor folk than rich folk and it's easier to get money out of 'em.' He grimaced at Foul Ole Ron. 'This may seem a strange question,' he said, 'but have you got any friends?'

'I told 'em! I *told* 'em! Bugrem!'

'Probably yes,' said William. 'He hangs out with a bunch of ... er ... unfortunates who live under one of the bridges. Well, not exactly "hangs out". More "droops".'

'Well now,' said Gunilla, waving the copy of the *Times* at Ron, 'you can tell them that if they can sell these to people for twenty pence each, I'll let you keep one nice shiny penny.'

'Yeah? And you can put yer nice shiny penny where the sun don't shine,' said Ron.

'Oh, so you—' Gunilla began.

William laid a hand on his arm. 'Sorry, just a minute— What was that you said, Ron?' he said.

'Bugrit,' said Foul Ole Ron.

It had *sounded* like Ron's voice and it had seemed to come from the general area of Ron's face, it was just that it had demonstrated a coherence you didn't often get.

'You want more than a penny?' said William carefully.

'Got to be worth five pence a time,' said Ron. More or less.

For some reason William's gaze was dragged down to the small grey dog. It returned it amiably and said, 'Woof?'

He looked back up again. 'Are you all right, Foul Ole Ron?' he said.

'Gottle o' geer, gottle o' geer,' said Ron mysteriously.

'All right . . . two pence,' said Gunilla.

'Four,' Ron seemed to say. 'But let's not mess about, okay? One dollar per thirty?'

'It's a deal,' said Goodmountain, who spat on his hand and would have held it out to seal the contract if William hadn't gripped it urgently.

'Don't.'

'What's wrong?'

William sighed. 'Have you got any horribly disfiguring diseases?'

'No!'

'Do you *want* some?'

'Oh.' Gunilla lowered his hand. 'You tell your friends to get round here right now, okay?' he said. He turned to William.

'Trustworthy, are they?'

'Well . . . *sort* of,' said William. 'It's probably not a good idea to leave paint thinners around.'

Outside, Foul Ole Ron and his dog ambled down the street. And the strange thing was that a conversation was going on, even though there was technically only one person there.

'See? I *told* you. You just let me do the talkin', all right?'

'Bugrit.'

'Right. You stick with me and you won't go far wrong.'

'Bugrit.'

'Really? Well, I s'pose that'll have to do. Bark, bark.'

Twelve people lived under the Misbegot Bridge and in a life of luxury, although luxury is not hard to achieve when you define it as something to eat at least once a day and *especially* when you have such a broad definition of 'something to eat'. Technically they were beggars, although they seldom had to beg. Possibly they were thieves, although they only took what had been thrown away, usually by people hurrying to be out of their presence.

Outsiders considered that the leader of the group was Coffin Henry, who would have been the city's champion expectorator if anyone else had wanted the title. But the group had the true democracy of the voteless. There was Arnold Sideways, whose lack of legs only served to give him an extra advantage in any pub fight, where a man with good teeth at groin height had it all his own way. And if it wasn't for the duck whose presence on his head he consistently denied, the Duck Man would have been viewed as well-spoken and educated and as sane as the next man. Unfortunately, the next man was Foul Ole Ron.

The other eight people were Altogether Andrews.

Altogether Andrews was one man with considerably more than one mind. In a rest state, when he had no particular problem to confront, there was no sign of this except a sort of background twitch and flicker as his features passed randomly under the control of, variously, Jossi, Lady Hermione, Little Sidney, Mr Viddle, Curly, the Judge and Tinker; there was also Burke, but the crew had only ever seen Burke once and never wanted to again, so the other seven personalities kept him buried. Nobody in the body answered to the name of Andrews. In the opinion of the Duck Man, who was probably the best in the crew at thinking in a straight line, Andrews had probably been some innocent and hospitable person of a psychic disposition who had simply been overwhelmed by the colonizing souls.

Only among the gentle crew under the bridge could a consensus person like Andrews find an accommodating niche. They'd welcomed him, or them, to the fraternity around the smoky fire. Someone who wasn't the same person for more than five minutes at a time could fit right in.

One other thing that united the crew – although probably nothing could unite Altogether Andrews – was a readiness to believe that a dog could talk. The group around the smouldering fire believed they had heard a lot of things talk, such as walls. A dog was easy by comparison. Besides, they respected the fact that Gaspode had the sharpest mind of the lot and never drank anything that corroded the container.

'Let's try this again, shall we?' he said. 'If you sell thirty of the things, you'll get a dollar. A whole dollar. Got that?'

'Bugrit.'

'Quack.'

'Haaargghhh . . . gak!'

'How much is that in old boots?'

Gaspode sighed. 'No, Arnold. You can use the money to buy as many old—'

There was a rumble from Altogether Andrews, and the rest of the crew went very still. When Altogether Andrews was quiet for a while you never knew who he was going to be.

There was always the possibility that it would be Burke.

'Can I ask a question?' said Altogether Andrews, in a rather hoarse treble.

The crew relaxed. That sounded like Lady Hermione. She wasn't a problem.

'Yes . . . your ladyship?' said Gaspode.

'This wouldn't be . . . *work*, would it?'

The mention of the word sent the rest of the crew into a fugue of stress and bewildered panic.

'Haaaruk . . . gak!'

'Bugrit!'

'Quack!'

'No, no, no,' said Gaspode hurriedly. 'It's hardly work, is it? Just handing out stuff and takin' money? Doesn't sound like *work* to me.'

'I ain't working!' shouted Coffin Henry. 'I am socially inadequate in the whole area of doin' anything!'

'We do *not* work,' said Arnold Sideways. 'We is gentlemen of les-u-are.'

'Ahem,' said Lady Hermione.

'Gentlemen and *ladies* of les-u-are,' said Arnold gallantly.

'This is a very nasty winter. Extra money would certainly come in handy,' said the Duck Man.

'What for?' said Arnold.

'We could live like kings on a dollar a day, Arnold.'

'What, you mean someone'd chop our heads off?'

'No, I—'

'Someone'd climb up inside the privy with a red-hot poker and—'

'No! I meant—'

'Someone'd drown us in a butt of wine?'

'No, that's *dying* like kings, Arnold.'

'I shouldn't reckon there's a butt of wine big enough that you couldn't drink your way out of it,' muttered Gaspode. 'So, what about it, masters? Oh, and mistress, o' course. Shall I— shall *Ron* tell that lad we're up for it?'

'Indeed.'

'Okay.'

'Gawwwark . . . pt!'

'Bugrit!'

They looked at Altogether Andrews. His lips moved, his face flickered. Then he held up five democratic fingers.

'The ayes have it,' said Gaspode.

Mr Pin lit a cigar. Smoking was his one vice. At least, it was his only vice that he thought of as a vice. All the others were just job skills.

Mr Tulip's vices were also limitless, but he owned up to cheap aftershave because a man has to drink *something*. The drugs didn't count, if only because the only time he'd ever got real ones was when they'd robbed a horse doctor and he'd taken a couple of big pills that had made every vein in his body stand out like a purple hosepipe.

The pair were not thugs. At least they did not see themselves as thugs. Nor were they thieves. At least they never thought of themselves as thieves. They did not think of themselves as assasins. Assassins were posh and had rules. Pin and Tulip – the New Firm, as Mr Pin liked to refer to themselves – did not have rules.

They thought of themselves as *facilitators*. They were men who made things happen, men who were going places.

It has to be added that when one says 'they thought' it means 'Mr Pin thought'. Mr Tulip used his *head* all the time, from a distance of about eight inches, but he was not, except in one or two unexpected areas, a man given much to using his brain. On the whole, he left Mr Pin to do the polysyllabic cogitation.

Mr Pin, on the other hand, was not very good at sustained, mindless violence, and admired the fact that Mr Tulip had an apparently bottomless supply. When they had first met, and had recognized in each other the qualities that would make their partnership greater than the sum of its parts, he'd seen that Mr Tulip was not, as he appeared to the rest of the world, just another nutjob. Some negative qualities can reach a pitch of perfection that changes their very nature, and Mr Tulip had turned anger into an art.

It was not anger *at* anything. It was just pure, platonic anger from somewhere in the reptilian depths of the soul, a fountain of never-ending red-hot grudge; Mr Tulip lived his life on that thin line most people occupy just before they haul off and hit some-one repeatedly with a spanner. For Mr Tulip, anger was the ground state of being. Pin had occasionally wondered what had happened to the man to make him as angry as that, but to Tulip the past was another country with very, very well-guarded borders. Sometimes Mr Pin heard him screaming at night.

It was quite hard to hire Mr Tulip and Mr Pin. You had to know the right people. To be more accurate, you had to know the *wrong* people, and you got to know them by hanging around a certain kind of bar and surviving, which was kind of a first test. The wrong people, of course, would not know Mr Tulip and Mr Pin. But they would know a man. And that man would, in a general sense, express the guarded opinion that he might know how to get in touch with men of a Pin-like or Tulipolitic disposition. He could not exactly recall much more than that at the moment, due to memory loss brought on by lack of money. Once cured, he might indicate in a general kind of way another address where you would meet, in a dark corner, a man who would tell you emphatically that he had never heard of anyone called Tulip *or* Pin. He would also ask where you would be at, say, nine o'clock tonight.

And then you would meet Mr Tulip and Mr Pin. They would know you had money, they would know you had something on your mind and, if you had been really stupid, they now knew your address.

And it had therefore come as a surprise to the New Firm that their latest client had come straight to them. This was worrying. It was also worrying that he was dead. Generally the New Firm had no problem with corpses, but they didn't like them to speak.

Mr Slant coughed. Mr Pin noticed that this created a small cloud of dust. For Mr Slant was a zombie.

'I must reiterate,' said Mr Slant, 'that I am a mere facilitator in this matter—'

'Just like us,' said Mr Tulip.

Mr Slant indicated with a look that he would never in a thousand years be just like Mr Tulip, but he *said*: 'Quite so. My clients wished me to find some ... experts. I found you. I gave you some sealed instructions. You have accepted the contract. And I understand that as a result of this you have made certain ... arrangements. I do not know what those arrangements are. I will *continue* not to know what those arrangements are. My relationship with you is, as they say, on the long finger. Do you understand me?'

'What —ing finger is that?' said Mr Tulip. He

was getting jittery in the presence of the dead lawyer.

'We see each other only when necessary, we say as little as possible.'

'I hate —ing zombies,' said Mr Tulip. That morning he'd tried something he'd found in a box under the sink. If it cleaned drains, he'd reasoned, that meant it was *chemical*. Now he was getting strange messages from his large intestine.

'I am sure the feeling is mutual,' said Mr Slant.

'I understand what you're saying,' said Mr Pin. 'You're saying that if this goes bad you've never seen us in your life—'

'Ahem . . .' Mr Slant coughed.

'Your afterlife,' Mr Pin corrected himself. 'Okay. What about the money?'

'As requested, thirty thousand dollars for special expenses will be included in the sum already agreed.'

'In gems. Not cash.'

'Of course. And my clients would hardly write you a cheque. It will be delivered tonight. And perhaps I should mention one other matter.' His dry fingers shuffled through the dry papers in his dry briefcase, and he handed Mr Pin a folder.

Mr Pin read it. He turned a few pages quickly.

'You may show it to your monkey,' said Mr Slant.

Mr Pin managed to grab Mr Tulip's arm before it reached the zombie's head. Mr Slant did not even flinch.

'He's got the story of our lives, Mr Tulip!'

'So? I can still rip his —ing stitched-on head right off!'

'No, you cannot,' said Mr Slant. 'Your colleague will tell you why.'

'Because our legal friend here will have made a lot of copies, won't you, Mr Slant? And probably lodged them in all kinds of places in case he di— in case—'

'. . . of accidents,' said Mr Slant smoothly. 'Well done. You have had an interesting career so far, gentlemen. You are quite young. Your talents have taken you a long way in a short time and given you quite a reputation in your chosen profession. While of course I have no idea about the task you are under-taking – no idea whatsoever, I must stress – I have no doubt that you will impress us all.'

'Does he know about the contract in Quirm?' said Mr Tulip.

'Yes,' said Mr Pin.

'That stuff with the wire netting and the crabs and that —ing banker?'

'Yes.'

'And the thing with the puppies and that kid?'

'He does now,' said Mr Pin. 'He knows nearly every-thing. Very clever. You believe you know where the bodies are buried, Mr Slant?'

'I've talked to one or two of them,' said Mr Slant. 'But it would appear that you have never committed a crime within Ankh-Morpork, otherwise *of course* I could not talk to *you*.'

'Who says we've never committed a —ing crime in Ankh-Morpork?' Mr Tulip demanded in an offended tone.

'As I understand it, you have never been to this city before.'

'Well? We've had all —ing day!'

'Have you been caught?' said Mr Slant.

'No!'

'Then you have committed no crime. May I express the hope that your business here does not involve any kind of criminal activity?'

'Perish the thought,' said Mr Pin.

'The City Watch here are quite dogged in some respects. And the various Guilds jealously guard their professional territories.'

'We hold the police in high regard,' said Mr Pin. 'We have a great respect for the work they do.'

'We —ing *love* policemen,' said Mr Tulip.

'If there was a policemen's ball, we would be among the first to buy a ticket,' said Mr Pin.

''specially if it was mounted on a plinth, or a little display stand of some sort,' said Mr Tulip. ''cos we like beautiful things.'

'I just wanted to be sure that we understood one another,' said Mr Slant, snapping his case closed. He stood up, nodding to them, and walked stiffly out of the room.

'What a—' Mr Tulip began, but Mr Pin raised a finger to his lips. He crossed silently to the door and opened it. The lawyer had gone.

'He *knows* what we're —ing here for,' Mr Tulip whispered hotly. 'What's he —ing pretending for?'

'Because he's a lawyer,' said Mr Pin. 'Nice place, this,' he added, in a slightly over-loud voice.

Mr Tulip looked around. 'Nah,' he said dismissively. 'I fort that at the start, but it's just a late eighteenth-century copy of the —ing Baroque Style. They got the dimensions all wrong. Didja see them pillars in the hall? Didja? —ing sixth-century Ephebian with Second-Empire Djelibeybian —ing finials! It was all I could do not to laugh.'

'Yes,' said Mr Pin. 'As I have remarked before, Mr Tulip, in many ways you are a very unexpected man.'

Mr Tulip walked over to a shrouded picture and tweaked the cloth aside.

'Well, — me, it's a —ing da Quirm,' he said. 'I seen a print of it. *Woman Holding Ferret*. He did it just after he moved from Genua and was influenced by —ing Caravati. Look at that —ing brushwork, will ya? See the way the line of the hand draws the —ing eye into the picture? Look at the quality of the light on the landscape you can see through the —ing window there. See the way the ferret's nose follows you around the room? That's —ing genius, that is. I don't mind telling you that if I was here by myself I'd be in —ing *tears*.'

'It's very pretty.'

'*Pretty*?' said Mr Tulip, despairing of his colleague's taste. He walked over to a statue by the door and stared hard at it, then ran his fingers lightly across the marble.

'I *fort* so! This is a —ing Scolpini! I'd bet anything. But I've never seen it in a catalogue. And it's been left in an empty house, where anyone could just —ing walk in and nick it!'

'This place is under powerful protection. You saw the seals on the door.'

'Guilds? Bunch of —ing *amateurs*. We could go through this place like a hot knife through —ing thin ice and you know it. Amateurs and rocks and lawn ornaments and dead men walking about . . . We could knock this —ing city *over*.'

Mr Pin said nothing. A similar idea had occurred to him, but unlike with his colleague deed did not automatically follow upon what passed for thought.

The Firm had, indeed, not operated in Ankh-Morpork before. Mr Pin had kept away because, well, there were plenty of other cities, and an instinct for survival had told him that the Big Wahoonie* should wait a while. He'd had a Plan, ever since he'd met Mr Tulip and found that his own inventiveness combined with Tulip's incessant anger promised a successful career. He'd developed their business in Genua, Pseudopolis, Quirm – cities smaller and easier to navigate than Ankh-Morpork although, these days, it seemed they increasingly resembled it.

The reason that they had done well, he'd realized, was that sooner or later people went soft. Take the trollish Breccia, f'rinstance. Once the Honk and Slab route had been established all the way to Uberwald, and the rival clans had been eliminated, the trolls had got soft. The *tons* acted like society lords. It was the same everywhere – the big old gangs and families reached some kind of equilibrium with society and settled down to be a specialist kind of businessman. They cut down on henchmen and employed butlers instead. And then, when there was a bit of difficulty,

* The world's rarest and most evil-smelling vegetable, and consequently much prized by connoisseurs (who seldom prize anything cheap and common). Also a slang name for Ankh-Morpork, although it does not smell as bad as that.

they needed muscle that could think . . . and there was the New Firm, ready and willing.

And waiting.

One day there'd be time for a new generation, Mr Pin thought. One with a new way of doing things, one without the shackles of tradition holding them back. Happening people. Mr Tulip, for example, happened all the time.

'Hey, will you —ing look at this?' said the happening Tulip, who had uncovered another painting. 'Signed by Gogli, but it's a —ing fake. Look at the way the light falls here, willya? And the leaves on this tree? If —ing Gogli painted that, it was with his —ing *foot*. Probably by some —ing pupil . . .'

While they had been marking time in the city Mr Pin had followed Mr Tulip, trailing scouring powder and canine worming tablets, through one after another of the city's art galleries. The man had insisted. It had been an education, mostly for the curators.

Mr Tulip had the *instinct* for art which he did not have for chemistry. Sneezing icing sugar and dribbling foot powder, he was ushered into private galleries, where he ran his bloodshot eye over nervously proffered trays of ivory miniatures.

Mr Pin had watched in silent admiration while his colleague spoke colourfully and at length on the differences between ivory faked the old way, with bones, and the —ing new way the —ing dwarfs had come up with, using —ing refined oil, chalk and —ing Spirits of Nacle.

He'd lurched over to the tapestries, declaimed at length about high and low weaving, burst into tears in front of a verdant scene, and then demonstrated that the gallery's prized thirteenth-century Sto Lat tapestry couldn't be more than a hundred years old because, see that —ing bit of purple there? No way was that —ing dye around then. 'And ... what's this? An Agatean embalming pot from the P'gi Su Dynasty? Someone took you to the —ing *cleaners*, mister. The glaze is *rubbish*.'

It was astounding, and Mr Pin had been so enthralled that he had all but forgotten to slip a few small valuable items into his pocket. But in truth he was familiar with Tulip on art. When they had occasionally to torch a premises Mr Tulip always made sure that any truly irreplaceable pieces were removed first, even though that meant taking extra time to tie the inhabitants to their beds. Somewhere under that self-inflicted scar tissue and at the heart of that shuddering anger was the soul of a true connoisseur with an unerring instinct for beauty. It was a strange thing to find in the body of a man who would mainline bath salts.

The big doors at the other end of the room swung open, revealing the dark space beyond.

'Mr Tulip?' said Mr Pin.

Tulip drew himself away from a painstaking examination of a possible Tapasi table, with its magnificent inlay work involving dozens of —ing rare veneers.

'Huh?'

'Time to meet the bosses again,' said Mr Pin.

William was just getting ready to leave his office for good when someone knocked at his door.

He opened it cautiously, but it was pushed the rest of the way.

'You utterly, utterly – ungrateful person!'

It wasn't a nice thing to be called, especially by a young lady. She used a simple word like 'ungrateful' in a way that would require a dash and an 'ing' in the mouth of Mr Tulip.

William had seen Sacharissa Cripslock before, generally helping her grandfather in his tiny work-shop. He'd never paid her much attention. She wasn't particularly attractive, but she wasn't particularly bad-looking, either. She was just a girl in an apron, doing slightly dainty things in the background, such as light dusting and arranging flowers. Insofar as he'd formed any opinion of her, it was that she suffered from misplaced gentility and the mistaken belief that etiquette meant good breeding. She mistook mannerisms for manners.

Now he could see her a lot plainer, mostly because she was advancing towards him across the room, and in the light-headed way of people who think they're just about to die he realized that she was quite good-looking if considered *over several centuries*. Concepts of beauty change over the years, and two hundred years ago Sacharissa's eyes would have made the great painter Caravati bite his brush in half; three hundred years ago the sculptor Mauvaise would have taken one look at her chin and dropped his chisel on his foot; a thousand years ago the Ephebian poets would have agreed that her nose alone was capable of launching at least forty ships. And she had good medieval ears.

Her hand was quite modern, though, and it

caught William a stinging blow on the cheek.

'That twenty dollars a month was nearly all we had!'

'Sorry? What?'

'All right, he isn't very fast, but in his day he was one of the best engravers in the business!'

'Oh . . . yes. Er . . .' William had a sudden flash of guilt about Mr Cripslock.

'And you took it away, just like that!'

'I didn't *mean* to! The dwarfs just . . . things just happened!'

'You're working for them?'

'Sort of . . . with them . . .' said William.

'While *we* starve, I suppose?'

Sacharissa stood there panting. She had a well-crafted supply of other features that never go out of fashion at all and are perfectly at home in any century. She clearly believed that severe, old-fashioned dresses toned these down. They did not.

'Look, I'm stuck with them,' said William, trying not to stare. 'I mean, stuck with the *dwarfs*. Lord Vetinari was very . . . *definite* about it. And it's suddenly all become very complicated—'

'The Guild of Engravers is going to be livid about this, you do know that?' she demanded.

'Er . . . yes.' A desperate idea struck William rather harder than her hand. 'That's a point. You wouldn't like to, er, be official about that, would you? You know: "We are livid," says spokesm— spokeswoman for the Guild of Engravers?'

'Why?' she said suspiciously.

'I'm desperate for things to put in my next edition,'

said William desperately. 'Look, can you help me? I can give you – oh, twenty pence an item, and I could use at least five a day.'

She opened her mouth to snap a reply, but calculation cut in. 'A dollar a day?' she said.

'More, if they're nice and long,' said William wildly.

'For that letter thing you do?'

'Yes.'

'A dollar?'

'Yes.'

She eyed him with mistrust. 'You can't afford that, can you? I thought you only got thirty dollars yourself. You told grandfather.'

'Things have moved on a bit. I haven't caught up with it myself, to tell you the truth.'

She was still looking at him doubtfully, but natural Ankh-Morpork interest in the distant prospect of a dollar was gaining the upper hand.

'Well, I hear things,' she began. 'And ... well, writing things down? I suppose that's a suitable job for a lady, isn't it? It's practically *cultural*.'

'Er ... close, I suppose.'

'I wouldn't like to do anything that wasn't ... proper.'

'Oh, I'm sure it's proper.'

'And the Guild can't object to *that*, can they? You've been doing it for years, after all ...'

'Look, I'm just me,' said William. 'If the Guild object, they'll have to sort it out with the Patrician.'

'Well ... all right ... if you're *sure* it's an acceptable job for a young lady ...'

'Come down to the printing works tomorrow,

then,' said William. 'I think we ought to be able to produce another paper of news in a few days.'

This was a ballroom, still plush in red and gold, but musty in the semi-darkness and ghostly with its shrouded chandeliers. The candlelight in the centre was dimly reflected from the mirrors around the walls; they had probably once brightened the place up considerably but over the years some sort of curious tarnish had blotched its way across them, so that the reflections of the candles looked like dim sub-aqueous glows through a forest of seaweed.

Mr Pin was halfway across the floor when he realized that the only footsteps he could hear were his own. Mr Tulip had veered off in the gloom and was dragging the shroud off something that had been pushed against one wall.

'Well. I'll be a . . .' the man began. 'This is a —ing *treasure*! I *fort* so! A genuine —ing Intaglio Ernesto, too. See that mother-of-pearl work there?'

'This isn't the time, Mr Tulip—'

'He only made six of them. Oh, no, they haven't even kept it —ing *tuned*!'

'Godsdammit, we're supposed to be *pro-fessionals . . .*'

'Perhaps your – colleague would like it as a present?' said a voice from the centre of the room.

There were half a dozen chairs around the circle of candlelight. They were an old-fashioned kind, and the backs curved out and up to form a deep leathery arch that had, presumably, been designed to keep out the draughts but now gave the occupants their own deep pools of shadow.

Mr Pin had been here before. He'd admired the set-up. Anyone inside the ring of candles couldn't see who was in the depths of the chairs, while at the same time being fully visible themselves.

It occurred to him now that the arrangement also meant that the people in the chairs couldn't see who was in the other chairs.

Mr Pin was a rat. He was quite happy with the description. Rats had a lot to recommend them. And this layout had been dreamed up by someone who thought like him.

One of the chairs said, 'Your friend Daffodil—'

'Tulip,' said Mr Pin.

'Your friend Mr Tulip would perhaps like part of your payment to be the harpsichord?' said the chair.

'It's not a —ing harpsichord, it's a —ing virginal,' growled Mr Tulip. 'One —ing string to a note instead of two! So called because it was an instrument for —ing young ladies!'

'My word, was it?' said one of the chairs. 'I thought it was just a sort of early piano!'

'Intended to be *played* by young ladies,' said Mr Pin smoothly. 'And Mr Tulip does not collect art, he merely ... *appreciates* it. Our payment will be in gems, as agreed.'

'As you wish. Please step into the circle . . .'

'—ing harpsichord,' muttered Mr Tulip.

The New Firm came under the hidden gaze of the chairs as they took up their positions.

What the chairs saw was this:

Mr Pin was small and slim and, like his namesake, slightly larger in the head than ought to be the case. If there was a word for him apart from 'rat' it was 'dapper'; he drank little, he watched what he ate and considered that his body, slightly malformed though it was, was a temple. He also used too much oil on his hair and parted it in the middle in a way that was twenty years out of style, and his black suit was on the greasy side, and his little eyes were constantly moving, taking in everything.

It was hard to see Mr Tulip's eyes, because of a certain puffiness probably caused by too much enthusiasm for things in bags.* The bags had also possibly caused the general blotchiness and the thick veins that stood out on his forehead, but Mr Tulip was in any case the kind of heavy-set man who is on the verge of bursting out of his clothes and, despite his artistic inclinations, projected the image of a would-be wrestler who had failed the intelligence test. If his body was a temple, it was one of those strange ones where people did odd things to animals in the basement, and if he watched what he ate it was only to see it wriggle.

Several of the chairs wondered, not if they were doing the right thing, since that was indisputable, but whether they were doing it with the right people. Mr Tulip, after all, wasn't a man you'd want to see standing too close to a naked flame.

---

* Your Brain On Drugs is a terrible sight, but Mr Tulip was living proof of the fact that so was Your Brain on a cocktail of horse liniment, sherbet and powdered water-retention pills.

'When will you be ready?' said a chair. 'How is your . . . protégé today?'

'We think Tuesday morning would be a good time,' said Mr Pin. 'By then he'll be as good as he's going to get.'

'And there will be no deaths involved,' said a chair. 'This is important.'

'Mr Tulip will be as gentle as a lamb,' said Mr Pin.

Unseen gazes avoided the sight of Mr Tulip, who had chosen this moment to suck up his nose a large quantity of Slab.

'Er, yes,' said a chair. 'His lordship is not to be harmed any more than is strictly necessary. Vetinari dead would be more dangerous than Vetinari alive.'

'And at all costs there must be no trouble with the Watch.'

'Yeah, we know about the Watch,' said Mr Pin. 'Mr Slant told us.'

'Commander Vimes is running a very . . . efficient Watch.'

'No problem,' said Mr Pin.

'And it employs a werewolf.'

White powder fountained into the air. Mr Pin had to slap his colleague on the back.

'A —ing *werewolf*? Are you —ing *crazy*?'

'Uh . . . why does your partner keep saying "ing", Mr Pin?' said a chair.

'You must be out of your —ing *minds*!' Tulip growled.

'Speech impediment,' said Pin. 'A werewolf? Thank you for telling us. Thank you very much. They're worse than vampires when they're on the trail! You do know that, do you?'

'You were recommended to us as men of resource.'

'*Expensive* men of resource,' said Mr Pin.

A chair sighed. 'There are seldom any other kind. Very well, very well. Mr Slant will discuss this with you.'

'Yeah, but they've got a sense a' smell that you wouldn't believe,' Mr Tulip went on. 'Money's no use to a —ing dead man.'

'Are there any other surprises?' said Mr Pin. 'You've got bright watchmen and one of 'em's a werewolf. Anything *else*? They've got trolls too?'

'Oh, yes. Several. And dwarfs. And zombies.'

'In a *Watch*? What kind of a city are you running here?'

'*We* are not running the city,' said a chair.

'But we care about the way it is going,' said another.

'Ah,' said Mr Pin. 'Right. I remember. You are concerned citizens.' He knew about *concerned citizens*. Wherever they were, they all spoke the same private language, where 'traditional values' meant 'hang someone'. He did not have a problem with this, broadly speaking, but it never hurt to understand your employer.

'You could have got someone else,' he said. 'You've got a guild of Assassins here.'

A chair made a sucking sound between its teeth.

'The trouble with the city at present,' it said, 'is that a number of otherwise intelligent people find the status quo ... convenient, even though it will undoubtedly ruin the city.'

'Ah,' said Mr Pin. 'They are *un*concerned citizens.'

'Precisely, gentlemen.'

'There's a lot of them?'

The chair ignored this.

'We look forward to seeing you again, gentlemen. Tomorrow night. When, I trust, you will announce your readiness. Good evening.'

The circle of chairs was silent for a while after the New Firm had left. Then a black-clad figure entered soundlessly through the big doors, approached the light, nodded and hurried away.

'They're well outside the building,' said a chair.

'What *ghastly* people.'

'We should have used the Assassins' Guild, though.'

'Hah! They've done *rather well* out of Vetinari. In any case, we do *not* want him dead. However, it occurs to me that we may eventually have a job for the Guild, later on.'

'Quite so. When our friends have safely left the city . . . the roads can be so dangerous at this time of year.'

'*No*, gentlemen. We will stick to our plan. The one called Charlie will be kept around until everything is *entirely* settled, in case he can be of further use, and then our gentlemen will take him a long, long way away to, hah, pay him off. Perhaps later we will call the Assassins in, just in case Mr Pin has any clever ideas.'

'Good point. Although it does seem such a waste. The things one could do with Charlie . . .'

'I told you, it would not work. The man is a clown.'

'I suppose you are right. Better something once-and-for-all, then.'

'I'm sure we understand one another. And now . . .
this meeting of the Committee to Unelect the
Patrician is declared closed. And hasn't happened.'

Lord Vetinari by habit rose so early that bedtime was
merely an excuse to change his clothes.

He liked the time just before a winter's dawn. It was
generally foggy, which made it hard to see the city, and
for a few hours there was no sound but the occasional
brief scream.

But the tranquillity was broken this morning by a
cry just outside the palace gates.

'Hoinarylup!'

He went to the window.

'Squidaped-*oyt*!'

The Patrician walked back to his desk and rang the
bell for his clerk Drumknott, who was despatched to
the walls to investigate.

'It is the beggar known as Foul Ole Ron, sir,'
Drumknott reported five minutes later. 'Selling this
. . . paper full of things.' He held it between two
fingers as though expecting it to explode.

Lord Vetinari took it and read through it. Then he
read through it again.

'Well, well,' he said. ' "The *Ankh-Morpork Times*".
Was anyone else buying this?'

'A number of people, my lord. People coming off
the night shifts, market people and so on.'

'I see no mention of Hoinarylup or Squidaped-*oyt*.'

'No, my lord.'

'How very strange.' Lord Vetinari read for a
moment and said, 'Hm-*hm*. Clear my appointments

this morning, will you? I will see the Guild of Towncriers at nine o'clock and the Guild of Engravers at ten past.'

'I wasn't aware they had appointments, sir.'

'They will have,' said Lord Vetinari. 'When they see this, they will have. Well, well . . . I see fifty-six people were hurt in a tavern brawl.'

'That seems rather a lot, my lord.'

'It must be true, Drumknott,' said the Patrician. 'It's in the paper. Oh, and send a message to that nice Mr de Worde, too. I will see him at nine thirty.'

He ran his eye down the grey type again. 'And please also put out the word that I wish to see no harm coming to Mr de Worde, will you?'

Drumknott, usually so adept in his understanding of his master's requirements, hesitated a moment.

'My lord, do you mean that you want no *harm* to come to Mr de Worde, or that *you* want *no* harm to *come* to *Mr de Worde*?'

'Did you wink at me, Drumknott?'

'No, sir!'

'Drumknott, I believe it is the right of every citizen of Ankh-Morpork to walk the streets unmolested.'

'Good gods, sir! Is it?'

'Indeed.'

'But I thought you were very much against movable type, sir. You said that it would make printing too cheap, and people would—'

'Sheearna-plp!' shouted the newspaper seller, down by the gates.

'Are you poised for the exciting new millennium that

lies before us, Drumknott? Are you ready to grasp the future with a willing hand?'

'I don't know, my lord. Is special clothing required?'

The other lodgers were already at the breakfast table when William hurried down. He was hurrying because Mrs Arcanum had Views about people who were late for meals.

Mrs Arcanum, proprietress of Mrs Eucrasia Arcanum's Lodging House for Respectable Working Men, was what Sacharissa was unconsciously training to be. She wasn't just respectable, she was Respectable; it was a lifestyle, religion and hobby combined. She liked respectable people who were Clean and Decent; she used the phrase as if it was impossible to be one without being the other. She kept respectable beds and cooked cheap but respectable meals for her respectable lodgers, who apart from William were mostly middle-aged, unmarried and extremely sober. They were mainly craftsmen in small trades, and were almost all heavily built, well-scrubbed, owned serious boots and were clumsily polite at the dining table.

Oddly enough – or, at least, oddly enough to William's expectations of people like Mrs Arcanum – she wasn't averse to dwarfs and trolls. At least, the clean and decent ones. Mrs Arcanum rated Decency above species.

'It says here fifty-six people were hurt in a brawl,' said Mr Mackleduff, who by dint of being the longest-surviving lodger acted as a kind of president at mealtimes. He had bought a copy of the *Times* on his way home from the bakery, where he was night-shift foreman.

'Fancy,' said Mrs Arcanum.

'I think it must have been five or six,' said William.

'Says fifty-six here,' said Mr Mackleduff sternly. 'In black and white.'

'It must be right,' said Mrs Arcanum, to general agreement, 'otherwise they wouldn't let them put it in.'

'I wonder who's doing it?' said Mr Prone, who travelled in wholesale boots and shoes.

'Oh, they'd be special people for doing this,' said Mr Mackleduff.

'Really?' said William.

'Oh, yes,' said Mr Mackleduff, who was one of those large men who were instantly expert on anything. 'They wouldn't allow just anyone to write what they like. That stands to reason.'

So it was in a thoughtful mood that William made his way to the shed behind the Bucket.

Goodmountain looked up from the stone where he was carefully setting the type for a playbill.

'There's a spot of cash for you over there,' he said, nodding to a bench.

It was mostly in coppers. It was almost thirty dollars.

William stared at it. 'This can't be right,' he whispered.

'Mr Ron and his friends kept coming back for more,' said Goodmountain.

'But . . . but it was only usual stuff,' said William. 'It wasn't even anything very important. Just . . . stuff that happened.'

'Ah, well, people like to know about stuff that happened,' said the dwarf. 'And I reckon we can sell three times as many tomorrow if we halve the price.'

'*Halve* the price?'

'People like to be in the know. Just a thought.' The dwarf grinned again. 'There's a young lady in the back room.'

In the days when this place had been a laundry, back in the pre-rocking-horse age, one area had been partitioned off with some cheap panelling to waist height, to segregate the clerks and the person whose job it was to explain to customers where their socks had gone. Sacharissa was sitting primly on a stool, clutching her handbag to her with her elbows close to her sides in order to expose herself to as little of the grime as possible.

She gave him a nod.

Now, why had he asked her to come along? Oh, yes . . . she was sensible, more or less, and did her grandfather's books and, frankly, William didn't meet many literate people. He met the sort to whom a pen was a piece of difficult machinery. If she knew what an apostrophe was, he could put up with the fact that she acted as if she was living in a previous century.

'Is this your office now?' she whispered.

'I suppose so.'

'You didn't tell me about the dwarfs!'

'Do you mind?'

'Oh, no. Dwarfs are very law-abiding and respectable, in my experience.'

William now realized that he was talking to a girl

who had *never* been in certain streets when the bars were closing.

'I've already got two good items for you,' Sacharissa went on, as if imparting state secrets.

'Er . . . yes?'

'My grandfather says this is the longest, coldest winter he can remember.'

'Yes?'

'Well, he's eighty. That's a long time.'

'Oh.'

'And the meeting of the Dolly Sisters' Baking and Flower Circle Annual Competition had to be abandoned last night because the cake table got knocked over. I found out all about it from the secretary, and I've written it all down neatly.'

'Oh? Um. Is that really *interesting*, do you think?'

She handed him a page torn from a cheap exercise book.

He read: '"The Dolly Sisters' Baking and Flower Circle Annual Competition was held in the Reading Room in Lobbin Clout Street, Dolly Sisters. Mrs H. Rivers was the President. She welcomed all members and commented on the Sumptuous Offerings. Prizes were awarded as follows . . ."'

William ran his eye down the meticulous list of names and awards.

'"Specimen in Jar"?' he queried.

'That was the competition for dahlias,' said Sacharissa.

William carefully inserted the word 'dahlia' after the word 'specimen', and read on.

' "A fine display of Loose Stool Covers"?'

'Well?'

'Oh . . . nothing.' William carefully changed this to 'Loose Covers for stools', which was barely an improvement, and continued to read with the air of a jungle explorer who might expect any kind of exotic beast to spring out of the peaceful undergrowth. The story concluded:

'However, everyone's Spirits were Dampened when a naked man, hotly pursued by Members of the Watch, burst through the Window and ran around the Room, causing much Disarray of the Tarts before being Apprehended by the Trifles. The meeting closed at 9 p.m. Mrs Rivers thanked all Members.'

'What do you think?' said Sacharissa, with just a hint of nervousness.

'You know,' said William, in a sort of *distant* voice, 'I think it is quite likely that it would be impossible to improve this piece in any way. Um . . . what would you say was the most *important* thing that happened at the meeting?'

Her hand flew to her mouth in dismay. 'Oh, yes! I forgot to put that in! Mrs Flatter won first prize for her sponge! She's been runner-up for six years, too.'

William stared at the wall. 'Well done,' he said. 'I should put that in, if I was you. But you could drop in at the Watch House in Dolly Sisters and ask about the naked man—'

'I shall do no such thing! Respectable women don't have anything to do with the Watch!'

'I meant, ask why he was being chased, of course.'

'But why should I do that?'

William tried to put words around a vague idea. 'People will want to know,' he said.

'But won't the Watch *mind* me asking?'

'Well, they're *our* Watch. I don't see why they should. And perhaps you could find some more really old people to ask about the weather? Who is the oldest inhabitant in the city?'

'I don't know. One of the wizards, I expect.'

'Could you go to the University and ask him if he remembers it ever being colder than this?'

'Is this where you put things in the paper?' said a voice at the doorway.

It belonged to a small man with a beaming red face, one of those people blessed with the permanent expression of someone who has just heard a rather saucy joke.

'Only I grew this carrot,' he went on, 'and I reckon it's grown into a very interesting shape. Eh? What d'you think, eh? Talk about a giggle, eh? I took it down the pub and everyone was killin' 'emselves! They said I should put it in your paper!'

He held it aloft. It was a very interesting shape. And William went a very interesting shade.

'That's a *very* strange carrot,' said Sacharissa, eyeing it critically. 'What do you think, Mr de Worde?'

'Er ... er ... you go along to the University, why don't you? And I'll see to this ... gentleman,' said William, when he felt he could speak again.

'My wife couldn't stop laughin'!'

'What a lucky man you are, sir,' said William solemnly.

'It's a shame you can't put pictures in your paper, eh?'

'Yes, but I think I may be in enough trouble already,' said William, opening his notebook.

When the man and his hilarious vegetable had been dealt with, William wandered out into the printing shop. The dwarfs were talking in a group, around a trapdoor in the floor.

'Pump's frozen again,' said Goodmountain. 'Can't mix up any more ink. Old man Cheese says there used to be a well somewhere round here . . .'

There was a shout from below. A couple of dwarfs descended the ladder.

'Mr Goodmountain, can you think of any reason I should put *this* in the paper?' said William, handing him Sacharissa's report of the Flowers and Cookery meeting. 'It's a bit . . . dull . . .'

The dwarf read the copy. 'There's seventy-three reasons,' he said. 'That's 'cos there's seventy-three names. I expect people like to see their names in the paper.'

'But what about the naked man?'

'Yeah . . . shame she didn't get his name.'

There was another shout from below.

'Shall we have a look?' said Goodmountain.

To William's complete lack of surprise, the little cellar under the shed was much better built than the shed itself. But then, practically everywhere in Ankh-Morpork had cellars that were once the first or even second or third floors of ancient buildings, built at the time of one of the city's empires when men thought that the future was going to last for ever. And then the river had flooded and brought mud with it, and walls had gone higher and, now, what Ankh-Morpork was built on was mostly Ankh-Morpork. People said that anyone with a good sense of direction and a pickaxe could cross the city underground by simply knocking holes in walls.

Rusted tins and piles of timber rotted to tissue strength were piled up against one wall. And in the middle of the wall was a bricked-up doorway, the more recent bricks already looking worn and tatty compared to the ancient stone surrounding them.

'What's through there?' said Boddony.

'The old street, probably,' said William.

'The *street* has a cellar? What does it keep there?'

'Oh, when parts of the city get badly flooded people just keep building on up,' said William. 'This was probably a ground-floor room once, you see. People just bricked up the doors and windows and built on another storey. In some parts of the city, they say, there's six or seven levels underground. Mostly full of mud. And that's choosing my words with care—'

'I am looking for Mister William der Worde,' rumbled a voice above them.

An enormous troll was blocking out the light from the cellar trapdoor.

'That's me,' said William.

'Der Patrician will see you now,' said the troll.

'I don't have an appointment with Lord Vetinari!'

'Ah, well,' said the troll, 'you'd be amazed at how many people has appointments wid der Patrician an' dey don't know it. So you'd better hurry. I would hurry, if I was you.'

* * *

There was no sound but the ticking of the clock. William watched in apprehension as, apparently forgetting his presence, Lord Vetinari read his way through the *Times* again.

'What a very . . . interesting document,' said the Patrician, suddenly laying it aside. 'But I'm forced to ask . . . *Why?*'

'It's just my news sheet,' said William, 'but bigger. Er . . . people like to know things.'

'Which people?'

'Well . . . everyone, really.'

'Do they? Did they tell you this?'

William swallowed. 'Well . . . no. But you know I've been writing my news letter for some time now—'

'For various foreign notables and similar people.' Lord Vetinari nodded. 'People who *need* to know. Knowing things is part of their profession. But you are selling this to anyone in the street, is that correct?'

'I suppose so, sir.'

'Interesting. Then you wouldn't entertain the idea, would you, that a state is, say, rather like one of those old rowing galleys? The ones which had banks of oarsmen down below, and a helmsman and so on above? It is certainly in everyone's interest that the ship does not founder but, I put it to you, it is perhaps not in the interest of the rowers that they know of every shoal avoided, every collision fended off. It would only serve to worry them and put them off their stroke. What the rowers need to know is how to row, hmm?'

'And that the helmsman is a good one,' said William. He couldn't stop the sentence. It said itself. It was out there, hanging in the air.

Lord Vetinari gave him a stare that went on for several seconds beyond the necessary time. Then his face *instantly* broke into a broad smile.

'To be sure. And so they should, so they should. This is the age of words, after all. Fifty-six hurt in tavern brawl, eh? Astounding. What further news do you have for us, sir?'

'Well, er . . . it's been very cold . . .'

'Has it? Has it, indeed? My word!' On his desk the tiny iceberg bumped against the side of Lord Vetinari's inkwell.

'Yes, and there was a bit of a . . . fracas . . . at some cookery meeting last night . . .'

'A fracas, eh?'

'Well, probably more of a rumpus, really.* And someone has grown a funny-shaped vegetable.'

'That's the stuff. What shape?'

'A . . . an amusing shape, sir.'

'Could I give you a little bit of advice, Mr de Worde?'

'Please do, sir.'

'Be careful. People like to be told what they already know. Remember that. They get uncomfortable when you tell them *new* things. New things . . . well, new things aren't what they expect. They like to know

---

* Words resemble fish in that some specialist ones can survive only in a kind of reef, where their curious shapes and usages are protected from the hurly-burly of the open sea. 'Rumpus' and 'fracas' are found only in certain newspapers (in much the same way that 'beverages' are found only in certain menus). They are never used in normal conversation.

that, say, a dog will bite a man. That is what dogs do. They don't want to know that a man bites a dog, because the world is not supposed to happen like that. In short, what people *think* they want is news, but what they really crave is *olds*. I can see you've got the hang of it already.'

'Yes, sir,' said William, not at all sure he fully understood this but certain that he didn't like the bit he did understand.

'I believe the Guild of Engravers has some things it wishes to discuss with Mr Goodmountain, William, but I have always thought that we should go forward to the future.'

'Yes, sir. Quite hard to go any other way.'

Once again, there was the too-long stare and then the sudden unfreezing of the face.

'Indeed. Good day, Mr de Worde. Oh . . . and do tread carefully. I'm sure you wouldn't want to become news . . . would you?'

William turned over the Patrician's words as he walked back to Gleam Street, and it is not wise to be thinking too deeply when walking the streets of Ankh-Morpork.

He walked past Cut-Me-Own-Throat Dibbler with barely a nod, but in any case Mr Dibbler was otherwise engaged. He had two customers. Two at once, unless one was daring another, was a great rarity. But these two were worrying him. They were *inspecting* the merchandise.

C.M.O.T. Dibbler sold his buns and pies all around the city, even outside the Assassins' Guild. He was a good judge of people, especially when it involved judging when to step innocently round a corner and then run like hell, and he had just decided that he was really unlucky to be standing here and also that it was too late.

He didn't often meet killers. Murderers, yes, but murderers usually had some strange reason and in any case generally murdered friends and relations. And he'd met plenty of assassins, but assassination had a certain style and even certain rules.

These men were killers. The big one with the powdery streaks down his jacket and the smell of mothballs was just a vicious thug, no problem there, but the small one with the lank hair had the smell of violent and spiteful death about him. You didn't often look into the eyes of someone who'd kill because it seemed like a good idea at the time.

Moving his hands carefully, Dibbler opened the *special* section of his tray, the high-class one that contained sausages whose contents were 1) meat, 2) from a known four-footed creature, 3) probably land-dwelling.

'Or may I recommend these, gentlemen,' he said, and because old habits died hard he couldn't stop himself from adding, 'Finest pork.'

'Good, are they?'

'You'll never want to eat another, sir.'

The other man said, 'How about the other sort?'

'Pardon?'

'Hooves and pig snot and rats what fell in the —ing mincer.'

'What Mr Tulip here means,' said Mr Pin, 'is a more *organic* sausage.'

'Yeah,' said Mr Tulip. 'I'm very —ing environmental like that.'

'Are you sure? No, no, fine!' Dibbler raised a hand. The manner of the two men had changed. They were clearly very sure of everything. 'We-ell, you want a bad— a less good sausage, then . . . er?'

'With —ing fingernails in it,' said Mr Tulip.

'Well, er . . . I do . . . I could . . .' Dibbler gave up. He was a salesman. You sold what you sold. 'Let me tell you about *these* sausages,' he went on, smoothly shifting an internal motor into reverse. 'When someone chopped off his thumb in the abattoir, they didn't even stop the grinder. You prob'ly won't find any rat in them 'cos rats don't go near the place. There's animals in there that . . . well, you know how they say life began in some kind of big soup? Same with these sausages. If you want a bad sausage, you won't get better than these.'

'You keep 'em for your special customers, do you?' said Mr Pin.

'To me, sir, every customer is special.'

'And you got mustard?'

'People *call* it mustard,' Dibbler began, getting carried away, 'but I call it—'

'I *like* —ing mustard,' said Mr Tulip.

'—really *great* mustard,' said Dibbler, not missing a beat.

'We'll take two,' said Mr Pin. He did not reach for his wallet.

'On the house!' said Dibbler. He stunned two

sausages, enbunned them and thrust them forward. Mr Tulip took both of them, and the mustard pot.

'Do you know what they called a sausage-in-a-bun in Quirm?' said Mr Pin, as the two walked away.

'No?' said Mr Tulip.

'They called it le sausage-in-le-bun.'

'What, in a —ing foreign language? You're —ing kidding!'

'I'm not a —ing kidder, Mr Tulip.'

'I mean, they ought to call it a . . . a . . . sausage dans lar derrière,' said Mr Tulip. He took a bite of his Dibbler delight. 'Hey, that's what this —ing thing tastes of,' he added, with his mouth full.

'In a *bun*, Mr Tulip.'

'I know what I meant. This is a —ing awful sausage.'

Dibbler watched them go. It wasn't often you heard language like that in Ankh-Morpork. Most people talked without leaving gaps in their sentences, and he wondered what the word 'ing' meant.

A crowd was gathered outside a large building in Welcome Soap, and the cart traffic was already backed up all the way to Broad Way. And, thought William, wherever a large crowd is gathered, someone ought to write down why.

The reason in this case was clear. A man was standing on the flat parapet just outside the fourth-storey window, back against the wall, staring downwards with a frozen expression.

Far below, the crowd were trying to be helpful. It was not in the robust Ankh-Morpork nature to *dissuade* anyone in this position. It was a free city, after all. So was the advice.

'Much better to try the Thieves' Guild!' a man yelled. 'Six floors, and then you're on good solid cobbles! Crack your skull first go!'

'There's proper flagstones around the palace,' advised the man next to him.

'Well, certainly,' said his immediate neighbour. 'But the Patrician'll kill him if he tries to jump from up there, am I right?'

'Well?'

'Well, it's a question of *style*, isn't it?'

'Tower of Art's good,' said a woman confidently. 'Nine hundred feet, almost. And you get a good view.'

'Granted, granted. But you also get a long time to think about things. On the way down, I mean. Not a good time for introspection, in my view.'

'Look, I've got a load of prawns on my wagon and if I'm held up any longer they're gonna be *walking* home,' moaned a carter. 'Why doesn't he just *jump*?'

'He's thinking about it. It's a big step, after all.'

The man on the edge turned his head when he heard a shuffling noise. William was sidling along the ledge, trying hard not to look down.

''Morning. Come to try and talk me out of it, 'ave yer?'

'I . . . I . . .' William *really* tried not to look down. The ledge had looked a lot wider from below. He was regretting the whole thing. 'I wouldn't dream of it . . .'

'I'm always open to being talked out of it.'

'Yes, yes . . . er . . . would you care to give me your name and address?' said William. There was a hitherto unsuspected nasty breeze up here, gusting treacherously around the rooftops. It fluttered the pages of his notebook.

'Why?'

'Er . . . because from this height on to solid ground it's often hard to find out that sort of thing afterwards,' said William, trying not to breathe out too much. 'And if I'm going to put this in the paper, it'd look much better if I say who you were.'

'What paper?'

William pulled a copy of the *Times* out of his pocket. It rattled in the wind as he wordlessly handed it over.

The man sat down and read it, his lips moving, his legs dangling over the drop.

'So this is, like, things that happen?' he said. 'Like a towncrier, but written down?'

'That's right. So, what was your name?'

'What do you mean, *was*?'

'Well, you know . . . obviously . . .' said William wretchedly. He waved his hand towards the void, and almost lost his balance. 'If you . . .'

'Arthur Crank.'

'And where did you live, Arthur?'

'Prattle Alley.'

'And what was your job?'

'There you go with the *was* again. The Watch usually give me a cup of tea, you know.'

A warning bell went off in William's head. 'You . . . jump a lot, do you?'

'Only the difficult bits.'

'And they are?'

113

'The climbing-up bits. I don't do the actual *jump-ing*, obviously. That's not a skilled job. I'm more into the "cry for help" aspect.'

William tried to grip sheer wall. 'And the help you want is . . . ?'

'Could you make it twenty dollars?'

'Or you jump?'

'Ah, well, not exactly *jump*, obviously. Not the *whole* jump. Not as per such. But I shall continue to threaten to jump, if you get my drift.'

The building seemed a lot higher to William than it had done when he climbed the stairs. The people below were a lot smaller. He could make out faces looking up. Foul Ole Ron was there, with his scabby dog and the rest of the crew, because they had an uncanny gravitational attraction to impromptu street theatre. He could even make out Coffin Henry's 'Will Threaten For Food' sign. And he could see the queues of wagons, by now paralysing half the city. He could feel his knees buckling . . .

Arthur grabbed him. 'Oi, this is *my* patch,' he said. 'Find your own spot.'

'You said the jumping-off wasn't a skilled job,' said William, trying to concentrate on his notes as the world spun gently around him. 'What *was* your job, Mr Crank?'

'Steeplejack.'

'*Arthur Crank, you come down here right this minute!*'

Arthur looked down.

'Oh gawds, they've gone and fetched the wife,' he said.

'*Constable Fiddyment here says you're . . .*' the distant pink face of Mrs Crank paused to listen again to the watchman standing next to her, '*interferin' with the merc-ant-ile well-bein' of the city, you ole fool!*'

'Can't argue with the wife,' said Arthur, giving William a sheepish look.

'*I'll hide your trousers another time, you silly ole man! You come down here or I'll give you what for!*'

'Three happy married years,' said Arthur cheerfully, waving at the distant figure. 'The other thirty-two haven't been too bad, either. But she can't cook cabbage worth a damn.'

'Really?' said William, and dreamily fell forward.

He woke up lying on the ground, which was what he'd expected, but still in a three-dimensional shape, which he hadn't. He realized that he was not dead. One reason for this was the face of Corporal Nobbs of the Watch looking down at him. William considered that he had lived a relatively blameless life and, if he died, did not expect to encounter anything with a face like Corporal Nobbs, the worst thing ever to hit a uniform if you didn't count seagulls.

'Ah, you're all right,' said Nobbs, looking slightly disappointed.

'Feel . . . faint,' William murmured.

'I could give you the kiss of life if you like,' said Nobbs.

Unbidden by William, various muscles spasmed and jerked him vertical so fast that his feet momentarily left the ground.

'Much better now!' he shouted.

'Only we learned it down the Watch House and I haven't had a chance to try it yet . . .'

'Fit as a fiddle!' William wailed.

'. . . I've been practising on my hand and everything . . .'

'Never felt better!'

'Old Arthur Crank's always doing that,' said the watchman. 'He's just after tobacco money. Still, everyone clapped when he carried you down. It's amazing how he can still climb drainpipes like that.'

'Is it really . . . ?' William felt oddly empty.

'It was great when you were sick. I mean, from four storeys up it looked quite pretty. Someone ought to have taken a picture—'

'Got to be going!' William screamed.

I must be going mad, he thought, as he hurried towards Gleam Street. Why the hell did I do it? It wasn't as if it was my *business*.

Except, come to think of it, it is now.

Mr Tulip burped. 'What're we going to do now?' he said.

Mr Pin had acquired a map of the city and was examining it closely.

'We are not your old-style bother boys, Mr Tulip. We are thinking men. We *learn*. We learn *fast*.'

'What're we going to do now?' Mr Tulip repeated. Sooner or later he'd be able to catch up.

'We're going to buy ourselves a little insurance, that's what we're going to do. I don't like no lawyer having all that muck on us. Ah . . . here we are. It's the other side of the University.'

'We're going to buy some magic?' said Mr Tulip.

'Not *exactly* magic.'

'I fort you said this city was a —ing pushover?'

'It has its good points, Mr Tulip.'

Mr Tulip grinned. '—ing *right*,' he said. 'I want to go back to the Museum of Antiquities!'

'Now, now, Mr Tulip. Business first, pleasure later,' said Mr Pin.

'I want to —ing see *all* of 'em!'

'Later on. Later on. Can you wait twenty minutes without exploding?'

The map led them to the Thaumatological Park, just hubwards of Unseen University. It was still so new that the modern flat-roofed buildings, winners of several awards from the Guild of Architects, hadn't even *begun* to let in water and shed window panes in a breeze.

An attempt had been made to pretty up the immediate area with grass and trees, but since the site had been built partly on the old ground known as the 'unreal estate' this had not worked as planned. The area had been a dump for Unseen University for thousands of years. There was a lot more below that turf than old mutton bones, and magic *leaks*. On any map of thaumic pollution the unreal estate would be the centre of some extremely concentric circles.

Already the grass was multicoloured and some of the trees had walked away.

Nevertheless, several businesses were thriving there, products of what the Archchancellor, or at least his speech writer, had called 'a marriage between magic and modern business; after all, the modern world doesn't need very many magic rings and magic

117

swords, but it does need some way to keep its appointments in order. Lot of garbage, really, but I suppose it makes everyone happy. Is it time for that lunch yet?'

One of the results of this joyful union was now on the counter in front of Mr Pin.

'It's the Mk II,' said the wizard, who was *glad* there was a counter between him and Mr Tulip. 'Er . . . cutting edge.'

'That's good,' said Mr Tulip. 'We —ing *love* cutting edges.'

'How does it work?' said Mr Pin.

'It's got contextual help,' said the wizard. 'All you have to do is, er, open the lid.'

To the wizard's horror a very thin knife appeared magically in his customer's hand and was used to release the catch.

The lid sprang back. A small green imp sprang up.

'Bingely-bingely-bee—'

It froze. Even a creation of biothaumic particles will hesitate when a knife is pressed to its throat.

'What the hell's this?' said Mr Pin. 'I said I want something that *listens*!'

'It does listen, it does listen!' said the wizard hurriedly. 'But it can say things too!'

'Like what? Bingely-bingely?'

The imp gave a nervous cough. 'Good for you!' it said. 'You have wisely purchased the Dis-organizer Mk II, the latest in biothaumaturgic design, with a host of useful features and no resemblance whatsoever to the Mk I which you may have inadvertently destroyed by stamping on it heavily!' it said, adding,

'This device is provided without warranty of any kind as to reliability, accuracy, existence or otherwise or fitness for any particular purpose and Bioalchemic Products specifically does not warrant, guarantee, imply or make any representations as to its merchantability for any particular purpose and furthermore shall have no liability for or responsibility to you or any other person, entity or deity with respect of any loss or damage whatsoever caused by this device or object or by any attempts to destroy it by hammering it against a wall or dropping it into a deep well or any other means whatsoever and moreover asserts that you indicate your acceptance of this agreement or any other agreement that may be substituted at any time by coming within five miles of the product or observing it through large telescopes or by any other means because you are such an easily cowed moron who will happily accept arrogant and unilateral conditions on a piece of highly priced garbage that you would not dream of accepting on a bag of dog biscuits and is used solely at your own risk.'

The imp took a deep breath. 'May I introduce to you the rest of my wide range of interesting and amusing sounds, Insert Name Here?'

Mr Pin glanced at Mr Tulip. 'All right.'

'For example, I can go "tra-la!"'

'No.'

'An amusing bugle call?'

'No.'

' "Ding!"?'

'No.'

'Or I can be instructed to make droll and diverting comments when performing various actions.'

'Why?'

'Er . . . some people like us to say things like "I'll be back when you open the box again", or something like that . . .'

'Why do you do noises?' said Mr Pin.

'People like noises.'

'We don't,' said Mr Pin.

'We —ing *hate* noises,' said Mr Tulip.

'Good for you! I can do *lots* of silence,' the imp volunteered. But suicidal programming forced it to continue: 'And would you like a different colour scheme?'

'What?'

'What colour would you like me to be?' As it spoke, one of the imp's long ears slowly turned purple and its nose became a vaguely disquieting shade of blue.

'We don't want any colours,' said Mr Pin. 'We don't want noises. We don't want cheerfulness. We just want you to do what you're told.'

'Perhaps you would like to take a moment to fill in your registration card?' said the imp desperately, holding it up.

A knife thrown at snake speed snapped the card out of its hand and nailed it to the desk.

'Or perhaps you would like to leave it until later . . .'

'Your man here—' Mr Pin began. 'Where did he go?'

Mr Tulip reached behind the counter and hauled up the wizard.

'Your man here says you're one of those imps that can repeat everything you hear,' said Pin.

'Yes, Insert Name Here, sir,' said the imp.

'And you don't make stuff up?'

'They can't,' the wizard panted. 'They have no imagination at all.'

'So if someone heard it, they'd know it was real?'

'Yes, indeed.'

'Sounds just the thing we're looking for,' said Mr Pin.

'And how will you be paying?' said the wizard.

Mr Pin snapped his fingers. Mr Tulip drew himself

up and out, squared his shoulders and cracked knuckles that were like two bags of pink walnuts.

'Before we —ing talk about *paying*,' said Mr Tulip, 'we want to talk to the bloke that wrote that —ing warranty.'

What William now had to think of as his office had changed quite a lot. The old laundry fixings, dismembered rocking horses and other rubbish had been spirited away and two desks stood back to back in the middle of the floor.

They were ancient and battered and to stop them wobbling they needed, against all common sense, bits of folded cardboard under *all four* legs.

'I got them from the secondhand shop along the road,' said Sacharissa nervously. 'They weren't very expensive.'

'Yes, I can see that. Er ... Miss Cripslock ... I've been thinking ... your grandfather can engrave a picture, can he?'

'Yes, of course. Why have you got mud all over you?'

'And if we got an iconograph and learned how to use it to take pictures,' William went on, ignoring this, 'could he engrave the picture that the imp paints?'

'I suppose so.'

'And do you know any good iconographers in the city?'

'I could ask around. What happened to you?'

'Oh, there was a threatened suicide in Welcome Soap.'

'Any good?' Sacharissa looked startled at the sound of her own voice. 'I mean, *obviously* I wouldn't wish anyone to die, but, er, we've got quite a lot of space . . .'

'I might be able to make something of it. He, er, saved the life of the man who climbed up to talk him down.'

'How brave. Did you get the name of the man who climbed up after him?'

'Um, no. Er, he was a Mystery Man,' said William.

'Oh, well, that's something. There's some people waiting to see you outside,' said Sacharissa. She glanced at her notes. 'There's a man who's lost his watch, a zombie who . . . well, I can't make out what he wants. There's a troll who wants a job, and there's someone who's got a complaint about the story of the fight at the Mended Drum and wants to behead you.'

'Oh, dear. All right, one at a time . . .'

The watch-loser was easy.

'It was one of the new clockwork ones my father gave to me,' said the man. 'I've been looking for it all week!'

'It's not exactly—'

'If you can put in the paper that I've lost it, maybe someone who has found it will turn it in?' said the man, with unwarranted hopefulness. 'And I'll give you sixpence for your trouble.'

Sixpence was sixpence. William made a few notes.

The zombie was more difficult. For a start he was grey, shading to green in places, and smelled very strongly of artificial hyacinth aftershave, some of the more recent zombies having realized that their chance of making friends in their new life would be greatly improved if they smelled of flowers rather than just smelled.

'People like to know about people who are dead,' he said. His name was Mr Bendy, and he pronounced it in a way that made it clear that the 'Mr' was very much a part of the name.

'They do?'

'Yes,' said Mr Bendy emphatically. 'Dead people can be very interesting. I expect people would be very interested in reading about dead people.'

'Do you mean obituaries?'

'Well, yes, I suppose they would be. I could write them in an interesting way.'

'All right. Twenty pence each, then.'

Mr Bendy nodded. It was clear that he would have done it for nothing. He handed William a wad of yellow, crackling paper.

'Here's an interesting one to start you off,' he said.

'Oh? Whose is it?'

'Mine. It's very interesting. Especially the bit where I died.'

The next man to come in was in fact a troll. Unusually for trolls, who usually wore just enough to satisfy humanity's mysterious demands for decency, this one actually wore a suit. At least, it was largely tubes of cloth that covered his body, and 'suit' was about the only word.

''m Rocky,' he mumbled, looking down. 'I'll take any job, guv.'

'What was your last job?' said William.

'Boxer, guv. But I wasn't happy wiv it. Kept getting knocked down.'

'Can you write or take pictures?' said William, wincing.

'No, guv. I can do heavy liftin'. 'n' I can whistle tunes, guv.'

'That's . . . a *good* talent, but I don't think we—'

The door flew open and a thick-shouldered, leather-clad man burst in, flourishing an axe.

'You got no right putting that about me in the paper!' he said, waving the blade under William's nose.

'Who are you?'

'I'm Brezock the Barbarian, and I—'

The brain works fast when it thinks it is about to be cut in half.

'Oh, if it's a *complaint* you have, you have to take it up with the Complaints, Beheadings and Horsewhippings Editor,' said William. 'Mr Rocky here.'

'Dat's me,' boomed Rocky cheerfully, laying a hand on the man's shoulder. There was only room for three of his fingers. Brezock sagged.

'I . . . just . . . want to say,' said Brezock, slowly, 'that you put in I hit someone with a table. I never done that. What'd people think of me if they heard I go around hitting people with tables? What'd that do to my reputation?'

'I see.'

'I knifed him. A table's a cissy weapon.'

'We shall certainly print a correction,' said William, picking up his pencil.

'You couldn't add that I tore Slicer Gadley's ear off with my teeth, could you? That'd make people sit up. Ears aren't easy to do.'

When they had all gone, Rocky to sit on a chair

outside the door, William and Sacharissa stared at one another.

'It's been a *very* strange morning,' he said.

'I've found out about the winter,' said Sacharissa. 'And there was an unlicensed theft from a jewellery shop in the Artificers Street. They got quite a lot of silver.'

'How did you find that out?'

'One of the journeyman jewellers told me.' Sacharissa gave a little cough. 'He, um, always comes to have a little chat with me when he sees me walking past.'

'Really? Well done!'

'And while I was waiting for you I had an idea. I got Gunilla to set this in type.' She shyly pushed a piece of paper across the desk.

'THE TRUTH SHALL MAKE YE FREE' • EXTRA!

'It looks more impressive at the top of the page,' she said nervously. 'What do you think?'

'What are all the fruit salads and leaves and things?' said William.

Sacharissa blushed. 'I did that. A bit of unofficial engraving. I thought it might make it look . . . you know, high class and impressive. Er . . . do you like it?'

'It's very good,' said William hurriedly. 'Very nice
. . . er, cherries—'

'—grapes—'

'Yes, of course, I meant grapes. What's the quote
from? It's very meaningful without, er, meaning anything very much.'

'I think it's just a quote,' said Sacharissa.

Mr Pin lit a cigarette and blew a stream of smoke into
the still damp air of the wine cellar.

'Now, it seems to me what we got here is a failure
to communicate,' he said. 'I mean, it's not like we're
asking you to memorize a book or anything. You
just got to *look* at Mr Tulip here. Is this hard? Lots
of people do it without any kinda special
training.'

'I sort of . . . l-lose my bottle,' said Charlie. His feet
clanked against several empty ones.

'Mr Tulip is not a scary man,' said Mr Pin. This was
flying in the face of the current evidence, he had to
admit. His partner had bought a twist of what the
dealer had sworn was Devil Dust but which looked to
Mr Pin very much like powdered copper sulphate,
and this had apparently reacted with the chemicals
from the Slab which had been Mr Tulip's afternoon
snack and turned one of his sinuses into a small
bag of electricity. His right eye was spinning slowly, and
sparks twinkled on his nasal hairs.

'I mean, does he *look* scary?' Mr Pin went on.
'Remember, you are Lord Vetinari. Understand?
You're not going to take *anything* from some guard. If
he talks back to you, just *look* at him.'

'Like *this*,' said Mr Tulip, half of his face flashing on and off.

Charlie leapt back.

'Not quite like that, perhaps,' said Mr Pin. 'But close.'

'I don't want to *do* this any more!' Charlie wailed.

'Ten thousand dollars, Charlie,' said Mr Pin. 'That's a lot of money.'

'I've heard of this Vetinari,' said Charlie. 'If this goes wrong he'll have me thrown into the scorpion pit!'

Mr Pin spread his hands expansively. 'Well, the scorpion pit isn't as bad as it's cracked up to be, you know?'

'It's a —ing picnic compared to me,' rumbled Mr Tulip, his nose lighting up.

Charlie's eyes sought a way out. Unfortunately, one of them was cleverness. Mr Pin hated the sight of Charlie trying to be clever. It was like watching a dog try to play the trombone.

'I'm not doing it for ten thousand dollars,' he said. 'I mean . . . you *need* me . . .'

He let it hang in the air, which was very much what Mr Pin was considering doing with Charlie.

'We had a deal, Charlie,' he said mildly.

'Yeah, well, I reckon there's more money in this now,' said Charlie.

'What do you think, Mr Tulip?'

Tulip opened his mouth to reply but sneezed instead. A thin bolt of lightning earthed itself on Charlie's chain.

'Maybe we could go to fifteen thousand,' said Mr Pin. 'And that's coming out of *our* share, Charlie.'

'Yeah, well . . .' said Charlie. He was as far away from Mr Tulip as possible now, because the man's dry hair was standing out from his head.

'But we want to see some extra effort, right?' said Mr Pin. 'Starting right now. All you have to do is say . . . What do you have to say?'

' "You are relieved of your post, my man. Go away," ' said Charlie.

'Except we don't say it like that, do we, Charlie?' said Mr Pin. 'It's an *order*. You are his *boss*. And you have to give him a haughty stare . . . Look, how can I put it? You're a shopkeeper. Imagine that he's asked for credit.'

It was six in the morning. Freezing fog held the city in its breathless grip.

Through the mists they came, and into the press room behind the Bucket they lurched, and out into the mists they went again, on a variety of legs, crutches and wheels.

'Mrpikeerah-tis!'

Lord Vetinari heard the cry and sent the overnight clerk down to the gate again.

He noted the title. He smiled at the motto.

He read the words:

IT IS THE COLDEST WINTER IN LIVING MEMORY, AND THAT IS OFFICIAL.

Dr Fettle Dodgast (132) of Unfeen University, told the *Times*: 'It if as cold as I can remember. Mind you, we don't get the winter thefe days that we had when I was ½young.'

Isicles as long as a man's arm have been seen on gutters about the city and many pumps have frozen.

Dr Dodgast (132) says the winter is worse than the one in 1902 when wolves invaded te acity. He added 'and we were glad of that, because we hadn't seen fresh meat for a fortnight'

. . .

Mr Josia Wintler (45) of 12b Martlebury Street has %a Humerous Vegetable that he will exhibit to all comers upon payment of a small sum. It is most droll.

. . .

Mr Clarence Harry (39) begs to inform the public that he has lost a valuable watch, probably in the area of Dolly Sisters. Reward to finder. Please report to *Times* office.

. . .

A icongrapher with thier own equipptment vanted by this publication. Apply at the *Times* office, The sign of the Bucket.

. . .

> A miscreatn stole $200 worth of silver
> from H. Hogland and Son, Jewllrs., of
> Nonsuch Street yesterday p.m. Mr
> Hogland, (32) who was threatened at
> knifepoint, told the *Times*: 'I shall
> recognise the man if I should see him
> again because not many people have a
> ftocking on their head.'

And Lord Vetinari smiled.

And someone knocked softly at the door.

And he glanced at the clock.

'Come,' he said.

Nothing happened. After a few seconds, the soft knock came again.

'Come *in*.'

And there was the pregnant silence again.

And Lord Vetinari touched an apparently ordinary part of his desktop.

And a long drawer appeared out of what had seemed to be the solid walnut of the desk, sliding forward as though on oil. It contained a number of slim devices on a bed of black velvet, and a description of any one of them would certainly involve the word 'sharp'.

And he chose one, held it casually by his side, crossed soundlessly towards the door and turned the handle, stepping back quickly in case of a sudden rush.

No one pushed.

And the door, yielding to an unevenness in the hinges, swung inwards.

* * *

Mr Mackleduff smoothed out the paper. It was already accepted by all around the breakfast table that, as the man who bought the paper, he was not simply its owner but, as it were, its priest, relaying its contents to the appreciative masses.

'It says here a man in Martlebury Street has grown a vegetable that's a funny shape,' he said.

'I should very much like to see that,' said Mrs Arcanum. There was a choking noise from further down the table. 'Are you all right, Mr de Worde?' she added, as Mr Prone thumped him on the back.

'Yes, yes, really,' gasped William. 'S-sorry. Some tea went down the wrong way.'

'There's good soil in that part of the city,' opined Mr Cartwright, travelling seed salesman.

William concentrated desperately on his toast, while over his head every news item was presented with the care and veneration of a blessed relic.

'Someone held up a shopkeeper at knifepoint,' Mr Mackleduff went on.

'Soon we will not be safe in our beds,' said Mrs Arcanum.

'I don't think this is the coldest winter for more than a hundred years, though,' said Mr Cartwright. 'I'm sure that one we had ten years ago was worse. Hit my sales something cruel.'

'It's in the paper,' said Mr Mackleduff, in the quiet voice of someone laying down an ace.

'It was a very strange obituary that you read out, too,' said Mrs Arcanum. William nodded silently over his boiled egg. 'I'm sure it's not usual to talk about the things someone's done *since* they died.'

Mr Longshaft, who was a dwarf and something in the jewellery business, helped himself to another slice of toast.

'I suppose it takes all sorts,' he said calmly.

'The city *is* getting rather crowded, though,' said Mr Windling, who had some unspecified clerical job. 'Still, at least zombies are human. No offence meant, of course.'

Mr Longshaft smiled faintly as he buttered the toast, and William wondered why he always disliked people who said 'no offence meant'. Maybe it was because they found it easier to say 'no offence meant' than actually refrain from giving offence.

'Well, I suppose we have to move with the times,' said Mrs Arcanum. 'And I hope that other poor man finds his watch.'

In fact Mr Harry was waiting outside the office when William arrived. He grabbed William's hand and shook it.

'Amazing, sir, amazing!' he said. 'How *did* you do it? It must be magic! You put that notice in your paper and when I got home, blow me down if the watch wasn't in my other jacket! Gods bless your paper, say I!'

Inside, Goodmountain gave William the news. The *Times* had sold eight hundred copies so far today. At five pence each, William's share came to sixteen dollars. In pennies, it came to quite a large heap on the desk.

'This is insane,' said William. 'All we did was write things down!'

'There is a bit of a problem, lad,' said

132

Goodmountain. 'Are you going to want to do another one for tomorrow?'

'Good gods, I hope not!'

'Well, I've got a story for you,' said the dwarf glumly. 'I hear the Guild of Engravers are already setting up their own press. They've got a lot of money behind 'em, too. They could put us right out of business when it comes to general printing.'

'Can they do that?'

'Of course. They use presses anyway. Type isn't hard to make, especially when you've got a lot of engravers. They can do really good work. To be honest, we didn't reckon they'd cotton on this soon.'

'I'm amazed!'

'Well, younger members of the Guild have seen the work coming out of Omnia and the Agatean Empire. Turns out they've been looking for a chance like this. I hear there was a special meeting last night. A few changes of officers.'

'That must have been worth seeing.'

'So if you could keep your paper going . . .' said the dwarf.

'I don't *want* all this money!' William wailed. 'Money causes problems!'

'We could sell the *Times* cheaper,' said Sacharissa, giving him an odd look.

'We'd only make *more* money,' said William gloomily.

'We could . . . we could pay the street vendors more,' said Sacharissa.

'Tricky,' said Goodmountain. 'A body can only take so much turpentine.'

'Then we could at least make sure they get a good breakfast,' said Sacharissa. 'A big stew with named meat, perhaps.'

'But I'm not even sure there *is* enough news to fill a—' William began, and stopped. That wasn't the way it worked, was it? If it was in the paper, it *was* news. If it was news it went in the paper, and if it was in the paper it *was* news. And it was the truth.

He remembered the breakfast table. 'They' wouldn't let 'them' put it in the paper if it wasn't true, would they?

William wasn't a very political person. But he found himself using unfamiliar mental muscles when he thought about 'they'. Some of them had to do with memory.

'We could employ more people to help us get the news,' said Sacharissa. 'And what about news from other places? Pseudopolis and Quirm? We just have to talk to passengers getting off the coaches—'

'Dwarfs would like to hear what's been happening in Uberwald and Copperhead,' said Goodmountain, stroking his beard.

'It takes nearly a week for a coach to get there from here!' said William.

'So? It's still *news*.'

'I suppose we couldn't use the clacks, could we?' said Sacharissa.

'The semaphore towers? Are you mad?' said William. 'That's really expensive!'

'Well? You were the one who was worried we had too much money!'

There was a flash of light. William spun around.

A . . . thing occupied the doorway. There was a tripod. There was a pair of skinny, black-clad legs behind it and a large black box on top of it. One black-clad arm extended out from behind the box and was holding a sort of small hod, which was smoking.

'Nice vun,' said a voice from behind the box. 'The light vas shinink so good off the dvarf's helmet, I could not resist it. You vanted an iconographer? My name is Otto Chriek.'

'Oh. Yes?' said Sacharissa. 'Are you any good?'

'I am a vizard in zer darkroom. I am experimenting all the time,' said Otto Chriek. 'And I have all my own eqvipment and also a keen and positive attitude!'

'Sacharissa!' hissed William urgently.

'We could probably start you at a dollar a day—'

'*Sacharissa!*'

'Yes? What?'

'He's a *vampire!*'

'I object most stronkly,' said the hidden Otto. 'It iss such an easy assumption to believe that everyvun with an Uberwald accent is a vampire, is it not? There are many thousands of people from Uberwald who are *not* vampires!'

William waved his hand aimlessly, trying to shrug off the embarrassment. 'All right, I'm sorry, but—'

'I *am* a vampire, as it happens,' Otto went on. 'But if I had said "Hello my cheeky cock sparrow mate old boy by crikey" vot vould you have said *zen*, eh?'

'We'd have been completely taken in,' said William.

'Anyway, your notice did say "vanted", so I thought it vas, you know, affirmative action,' said Otto. 'Alzo, I have *zis* . . .' A thin, blue-veined hand was held up, gripping a small twist of shiny black ribbon.

'Oh? You've signed the pledge?' said Sacharissa.

'At the Meeting Rooms in Abattoirs Lane,' said Otto triumphantly, 'vhere I attend every veek for our big singsong and tea and a bun and wholesome conversation on themes of positive reinforcement keeping off the whole subject of bodily fluids by strict instruction. I am not any longer any stupid sucker!'

'What do you think, Mr Goodmountain?' said William.

Goodmountain scratched his nose. 'It's up to you,' he said. 'If he tries anything with my lads he'll be looking for his legs. What's this pledge?'

'It's the Uberwald Temperance Movement,' said Sacharissa. 'A vampire signs up and forswears any human blood—'

Otto shuddered. 'Ve prefer "zer b-vord",' he said.

'The b-word,' Sacharissa corrected herself. 'The movement is becoming very popular. They know it's the only chance they've got.'

'Well . . . okay,' said William. He was uneasy about vampires himself, but turning the newcomer down after all this would be like kicking a puppy. 'Do you mind setting up your stuff in the cellar?'

'A cellar?' said Otto. 'Top hole!'

First the dwarfs had come, William thought as he went back to his desk. They'd been insulted because of their diligence and because of their height, but they had kept their heads down* and prospered. Then the trolls had come, and they got on a little better, because people don't throw as many stones at creatures seven feet tall who could throw rocks back. Then the zombies had come out of the casket. One or two were-wolves had crept in under the door. The gnomes had integrated quickly, despite a bad start, because they were tough and even more dangerous to cross than a troll; at least a troll couldn't run up your trouser leg. There weren't that many species *left*.

The vampires had never made it. They weren't sociable, even amongst themselves, they didn't think as a species, they were unpleasantly weird and they sure as hell didn't have their own food shops.

So now it was dawning on some of the brighter ones that the only way people would accept vampires was if they stopped *being* vampires. That was a large price to pay for social acceptability, but perhaps not so large as the one that involved having your head cut off and your ashes scattered on the river. A life of steak *tartare* wasn't too bad if you compared it with a death of stake *au naturelle*.†

'Er, I think we'd like to see who we're employing, though,' William said aloud.

Otto emerged, very slowly and nervously, from behind the lens. He was thin, pale and wore little oval dark glasses. He still clutched the twist of black ribbon as if it was a talisman, which it more or less was.

---

* Which was not hard, as unkind people pointed out.
† In any case, anyone eating raw steak from an Ankh-Morpork slaughterhouse was embarking on a life of danger and excitement that should satisfy anyone.

'It's all right, we won't bite you,' said Sacharissa.

'And one good turn deserves another, eh?' said Goodmountain.

'That was a bit tasteless, Mr Goodmountain,' said Sacharissa.

'So am I,' said the dwarf, turning back to the stone. 'Just so long as people know where I stand, that's all.'

'You vill not be sorry,' said Otto. 'I am completely reformed, I assure you. Vot is it you vant me to take pictures of, please?'

'News,' said William.

'Vot is news, please?'

'News is . . .'. William began. 'News . . . is what we put in the paper—'

'What d'you think of *this*, eh?' said a cheerful voice.

William turned. There was a horribly familiar face looking at him over the top of a cardboard box.

'Hello, Mr Wintler,' he said. 'Er, Sacharissa, I wonder if you could go and—'

He wasn't quick enough. Mr Wintler, a man of the variety that thinks a whoopee cushion is the last word in repartee, was not the kind to let a mere freezing reception stand in his way. 'I was digging my garden this morning and up came this parsnip, and I thought: that young man at the paper will laugh himself silly when he sees it, 'cos my lady wife couldn't keep a straight face, and—'

To William's horror he was already reaching into the box. 'Mr Wintler, I really don't think—'

But the hand was already rising, and there was the

sound of something scraping on the side of the box. 'I bet the young lady here would like a good chuckle too, eh?'

William shut his eyes.

He heard Sacharissa gasp. Then she said, 'Golly, it's amazingly lifelike!'

William opened his eyes. 'Oh, it's a *nose*,' he said. 'A parsnip with a sort of knobbly face and a huge *nose*!'

'You vant I should take a picture?' said Otto.

'Yes!' said William, drunk with relief. 'Take a big picture of Mr Wintler and his wonderfully nasal parsnip, Otto! Your first job! Yes, indeed!'

Mr Wintler beamed. 'And shall I run back home and fetch my carrot?' he said.

'No!' said William and Goodmountain in whiplash unison.

'You vant the picture right now?' said Otto.

'We certainly do!' said William. 'The sooner we can let him go home, the sooner our Mr Wintler can find *another* wonderfully humorous vegetable, eh, Mr Wintler? What will it be next time? A bean with ears? A beetroot shaped like a potato? A sprout with an enormous hairy tongue?'

'Right here and now is ven you vant the picture?' said Otto, anxiety hanging off every syllable.

'Right now, yes!'

'As a matter of fact, there *is* a swede coming along that I've got great hopes of—' Mr Wintler began.

'Oh, vell . . . if you vill look zis vay, Mr Vintler,' said Otto. He got behind the iconograph and uncovered the lens. William got a glimpse of the imp peering out, brush poised. In his spare hand Otto slowly held up, on a stick, a cage containing a fat and drowsing salamander, finger poised on the trigger that would bring a small hammer down on its head just hard enough to annoy it.

'Be smiling, please!'

'Hold on,' said Sacharissa. 'Should a vampire really—?'

Click.

The salamander flared, etching the room with searing white light and dark shadows.

Otto screamed. He fell to the floor, clutching at his throat. He sprang to his feet, goggle-eyed and gasping, and staggered, knock-kneed and wobbly-legged, the length of the room and back again. He sank down behind a desk, scattering paperwork with a wildly flailing hand.

'Aarghaarghaaargh . . .'

And then there was a shocked silence.

Otto stood up, adjusted his cravat and dusted himself off. Only then did he look up at the row of shocked faces.

'Vell?' he said sternly. 'Vot are you all looking at? It is just a normal reaction, zat is all. I am vorking on it. Light in all its forms is mine passion. Light is my canvas, shadows are my brush.'

'But strong light hurts you!' said Sacharissa. 'It hurts vampires!'

'Yes. It iss a bit of a bugger, but zere you go.'

'And, er, that happens every time you take a picture, does it?' said William.

'No, sometimes it iss a lot vorse.'

'*Worse?*'

'I sometimes crumble to dust. But zat vich does not kill us makes us stronk.'

'Stronk?'

'Indeed!'

William caught Sacharissa's gaze. Her look said it all: we've hired him. Have we got the heart to fire him now? And don't make fun of his accent unless your Uberwaldean is *really good*, okay?

Otto adjusted the iconograph and inserted a fresh sheet.

'And now, shall ve try vun more?' he said brightly. 'And zis time – everybody smile!'

Mail was arriving. William was used to a certain amount, usually from clients of his news letter complaining that he hadn't told them about the double-headed giants, plagues and rains of domestic animals that they had heard had been happening in Ankh-Morpork; his father had been right about one thing, at least, when he'd asserted that lies could run round the world before the truth could get its boots on. And it was amazing how people wanted to believe them.

These were . . . well, it was as if he'd shaken a tree and all the nuts had fallen out. Several letters were complaining that there had been much colder winters than this, although no two of them could agree when it was. One said vegetables were not as funny as they used to be, especially leeks. Another asked what the Guild of Thieves was doing about unlicensed crime in the city. There was one saying that all these robberies were down to dwarfs who shouldn't be allowed into the city to steal the work out of honest humans' mouths.

'Put a title like "Letters" on the top and put them in,' said William. 'Except the one about the dwarfs. That sounds like Mr Windling. It sounds like my father, too, except that at least he can *spell* "undesirable" and wouldn't use crayon.'

'Why *not* that letter?'

'Because it's offensive.'

'Some people think it's true, though,' said Sacharissa. 'There's been a lot of trouble.'

'Yes, but we shouldn't print it.'

William called Goodmountain over and showed him the letter. The dwarf read it.

'Put it in,' he suggested. 'It'll fill a few inches.'

'But people will object,' said William.

'Good. Put their letters in, too.'

Sacharissa sighed. 'We'll probably need them,' she said. 'William, grandfather says no one in the Guild will engrave the iconographs for us.'

'Why not? We can afford the rates.'

'We're not Guild members. It's all getting unpleasant. Will you tell Otto?'

William sighed and walked over to the ladder.

The dwarfs used the cellar as a bedroom, being naturally happier with a floor over their heads. Otto had been allowed to use a dank corner, which he'd made his own by hanging an old sheet across on a rope.

'Oh, hello, Mr Villiam,' he said, pouring something noxious from one bottle into another.

'I'm afraid it looks as if we won't get anyone to engrave your pictures,' said William.

The vampire seemed unmoved by this. 'Yes, I vundered about zat.'

'So I'm sorry to say that—'

'No problem, Mr Villiam. Zere is alvays a vay.'

'How? You can't engrave, can you?'

'No, but . . . all ve are printing is black and vite, yes? And zer paper is vite zo all ve are really *printink* is black, okay? I looked at how zer dvarfs do zer letters, and zey haf all zese bits of metal lying around and . . . you know how zer engravers can engrave metal viz acid?'

'Yes?'

'Zo, all I haf to do is teach zer imps to *paint* viz acid. End of problem. Getting grey took a bit of thought, but I zink I haf—'

'You mean you can get the imps to etch the picture straight on to a plate?'

'Yes. It is vun of those ideas that are obvious ven you zink about it.' Otto looked wistful. 'And I zink about light all zer time. All zer . . . time.'

William vaguely remembered something someone had once said: the only thing more dangerous than a vampire crazed with blood lust was a vampire crazed with anything else. All the meticulous single-mindedness that went into finding young women who slept with their bedroom window open was channelled into some other interest, with merciless and painstaking efficiency.

'Er, why do you need to work in a dark room, though?' he said. 'The imps don't need it, do they?'

'Ah, zis is for my experiment,' said Otto proudly.

'You know zat another term for an iconographer would be "photographer"? From the old word *photus* in Latation, vhich means—'

'"To prance around like a pillock ordering everyone about as if you owned the place",' said William.

'Ah, you know it!'

William nodded. He'd always wondered about that word.

'Vell, I am vorking on an obscurograph.'

William's forehead wrinkled. It was turning into a long day. 'Taking pictures with darkness?' he ventured.

'Viz *true* darkness, to be precise,' said Otto, excitement entering his voice. 'Not just absence of light. Zer light on zer *ozzer* side of darkness. You could call it . . . living darkness. Ve can't see it, but imps can. Did you know zer Uberwaldean Deep Cave land eel emits a burst of dark light ven startled?'

William glanced at a large glass jar on the bench. A couple of ugly things were coiled up in the bottom.

'And that will work, will it?'

'I zink so. Hold it vun minute.'

'I really ought to be getting back—'

'Zis vill not take a second . . .'

Otto gently lifted one of the eels out of its jar and put it into the hod usually occupied by a salamander. He carefully aimed one of his iconographs at William and nodded.

'Vun . . . two . . . three . . . BOO!'

There was—

—there was a soft noiseless implosion, a very brief sensation of the world being screwed up small, frozen, smashed into tiny little sharp pins and hammered through every cell of William's body.* Then the gloom of the cellar flowed back.

'That was . . . very strange,' said William, blinking. 'It was like something very cold walking through me.'

'Much may be learnt about dark light now ve have left our disgusting past behind us and haf emerged into zer bright new future vhere ve do not zink about zer b-vord all day in any vay at all,' said Otto, fiddling with the iconograph. He looked hard at the picture the imp had painted and then glanced up at William. 'Oh vell, back to zer drawink board,' he said.

'Can I see?'

'It vould embarrass me,' said Otto, putting the square of cardboard down on his makeshift bench. 'All zer time I am doing things wronk.'

'Oh, but I'd—'

'Mister de Worde, dere's something happening!'

The bellow came from Rocky, whose head eclipsed the hole.

'What is it?'

'Something at der palace. Someone's been killed!'

William sprang up the ladder. Sacharissa was sitting at her desk, looking pale.

'Someone's assassinated Vetinari?' said William.

'Er, no,' said Sacharissa. 'Not . . . exactly.'

Down in the cellar Otto Chriek picked up the dark light iconograph and looked at it again. Then he scratched it with a long pale finger, as if trying to remove something.

'Strange . . .' he said.

* In many ways William de Worde had quite a graphic imagination.

The imp hadn't imagined it, he knew. Imps had no imagination whatsoever. They didn't know how to lie.

He looked around the bare cellar suspiciously.

'Is zere anyvun zere?' he said. 'Is anyvun playink zer silly buggers?'

Thankfully there was no answer.

Dark light. Oh dear. There were lots of theories about dark light . . .

'Otto!'

He glanced up, shoving the picture into his pocket.

'Yes, Mr Villiam?'

'Get your stuff together and come with me! Lord Vetinari's murdered someone! Er, it is alleged,' William added. 'And it can't possibly be true.'

It sometimes seemed to William that the whole population of Ankh-Morpork was simply a mob waiting to happen. It was mostly spread thin, like some kind of great amoeba, all across the city. But when something happened somewhere it contracted around that point, like a cell around a piece of food, filling the streets with people.

It was growing around the main gates to the palace. It came together apparently at random. A knot of people would attract other people, and become a bigger, more complicated knot. Carts and sedan chairs would stop to find out what was going on. The invisible beast grew bigger.

There were watchmen on the gate instead of the palace guard. This was a problem. 'Let me in, I'm nosy,' was not a request likely to achieve success. It lacked a certain authority.

'Vy are ve stoppink?' said Otto.

'That's Sergeant Detritus on the gate,' said William.

'Ah. A troll. Very stupid,' opined Otto.

'But hard to fool. I'm afraid I shall have to try the truth.'

'Vy vill zat vork?'

'He's a policeman. The truth usually confuses them. They don't often hear it.'

The big troll sergeant watched William impassively as he approached. It was a proper policeman's stare. It gave nothing away. It said: I can see you, now I'm waiting to see what you're going to do that's wrong.

'Good morning, Sergeant,' said William.

A nod from the troll indicated that he was prepared to accept, on available evidence, that it was morning and, in certain circumstances, by some people, it might be considered good.

'I urgently need to see Commander Vimes.'

'Oh, yes?'

'Yes. Indeed.'

'And does he urgently need to see you?' The troll leaned closer. 'You're Mr de Worde, right?'

'Yes. I work for the *Times*.'

'I don't read dat,' said the troll.

'Really? We'll bring out a large-print edition,' said William.

'Dat was a very funny joke,' said Detritus. 'Fing is, fick though I am, I am der one that's sayin' you can stay outside, so— What's dat vampire doing?'

'Hold it just vun second!' said Otto.

WHOOMPH.

'—damndamndamn!'

Detritus watched Otto roll around on the cobbles screaming.

'What was dat about?' he said, eventually.

'He's taken a picture of you not letting me into the palace,' said William.

Detritus, although born above the snowline on some distant mountain, a troll who had never seen a human until he was five years old, nevertheless was a policeman to his craggy, dragging fingertips and reacted accordingly.

'He can't do dat,' he said.

William pulled out his notebook and poised his pencil. 'Could you explain to my readers exactly why not?' he said.

Detritus looked around, a little worried. 'Where are dey?'

'No, I mean I'm going to write down what you say.'

Basic policing rushed to Detritus's aid once again. 'You can't do dat,' he said.

'Then can I write down why I can't write anything down?' William said, smiling brightly.

Detritus reached up and moved a little lever on the side of his helmet. A barely audible whirring noise became fractionally louder. The troll had a helmet with a clockwork fan, to blow air across his silicon brain when overheating threatened to reduce its operating efficiency. Right now he obviously needed a cooler head.

'Ah. Dis is some kind of politics, right?' he said.

'Um, maybe. Sorry.'

Otto had staggered to his feet and was fiddling with the iconograph again.

Detritus reached a decision. He nodded to a constable.

'Fiddyment, you take dese . . . two to Mister Vimes. Dey are not to fall down any steps on der way or any stuff like dat.'

Mister Vimes, thought William, as they hurried after the constable. All the watchmen called him that. The man had been a knight and was now a duke and a commander, but they called him *Mister*. And it was *Mister*, too, the full two syllables, not the everyday unheeded 'Mr'; it was the 'mister' you used when you wanted to say things like 'Put down that crossbow and turn around real slow, mister.' He wondered why.

William had not been brought up to respect the Watch. They weren't our kind of people. It was conceded that they were useful, like sheepdogs, because clearly someone had to keep people in order, heavens knew, but only a fool would let a sheepdog sleep in the parlour. The Watch, in other words, was a regrettably necessary sub-set of the criminal classes, a section of the population informally defined by Lord de Worde as anyone with less than a thousand dollars a year.

William's family and everyone they knew also had a mental map of the city that was divided into parts where you found upstanding citizens and other parts where you found criminals. It had come as a shock to them . . . no, he corrected himself, it had come as an *affront* to learn that Vimes operated on a different map. Apparently he'd *instructed* his men to use the front door when calling at any building, even in broad daylight, when sheer common sense said that they should use the back, just like any other servant.* The man simply had no *idea*.

That Vetinari had made him a duke was just another example of the Patrician's lack of grip.

William therefore felt predisposed to like Vimes, if only because of the type of enemies he made, but as far as he could see everything about the man could be prefaced by the word 'badly', as in -spoken, -educated and -in need of a drink.

Fiddyment stopped in the big hall of the palace.

'Don't you go anywhere and don't you do anything,' he said. 'I'll go and—'

But Vimes was already coming down the wide stairs, trailed by a giant of a man William recognized as Captain Carrot.

You could add '-dressed' to Vimes's list. It wasn't that he wore bad clothes. He just seemed to generate an internal scruffiness field. The man could rumple a helmet.

Fiddyment met them halfway. There was a muttered conversation, out of which the unmistakable words 'He's *what*?' arose, in Vimes's voice. He glared darkly at William. The expression was clear. It said: it's been a bad day and now there's *you*.

Vimes walked the rest of the way down the stairs and looked William up and down.

'What is it you're wanting?' he demanded.

'I want to know what's happened here, please,' said William.

---

* William's class understood that justice was like coal or potatoes. You ordered it when you needed it.

'Why?'

'Because people will want to know.'

'Hah! They'll find out soon enough!'

'But who from, sir?'

Vimes walked round William as if he was examining some strange new thing.

'You're Lord de Worde's boy, aren't you?'

'Yes, your grace.'

'Commander will do,' said Vimes sharply. 'And you write that little gossipy thing, right?'

'Broadly, sir.'

'What was it you did to Sergeant Detritus?'

'I only wrote down what he said, sir.'

'Aha, pulled a pen on him, eh?'

'Sir?'

'Writing things down at people? Tch, tch . . . that sort of thing only causes trouble.'

Vimes stopped walking round William, but having him glare from a few inches away was no improvement.

'This has not been a nice day,' he said. 'And it's going to get a lot worse. Why should I waste my time talking to you?'

'I can tell you one good reason,' said William.

'Well, go on, then.'

'You should talk to me so that I can write it down, sir. All neat and correct. The actual words you say, right down there on the paper. And you know who I am, and if I get them wrong you know where to find me.'

'So? You're telling me that if I do what you want you'll do what you want?'

'I'm saying, sir, that a lie can run round the world before the truth has got its boots on.'

'Ha! Did you just make that up?'

'No, sir. But you know it's true.'

Vimes sucked on his cigar. 'And you'll let me see what you've written?'

'Of course. I'll make sure you get one of the first papers off the press, sir.'

'I meant *before* it gets published, and you know it.'

'To tell you the truth, no, I don't think I should do that, sir.'

'I *am* the Commander of the Watch, lad.'

'Yes, sir. And I'm not. I think that's my point, really, although I'll work on it some more.'

Vimes stared at him a little too long. Then, in a slightly different tone of voice, he said:

'Lord Vetinari was seen by three cleaning maids of the household staff, all respectable ladies, after they were alerted by the barking of his lordship's dog at about seven o'clock this morning. He said' – here Vimes consulted his own notebook – ' "I've killed him, I've killed him, I'm sorry." They saw what looked very much like a body on the floor. Lord Vetinari was holding a knife. They ran downstairs to fetch someone. On their return they found his lordship missing. The body was that of Rufus Drumknott, the Patrician's personal secretary. He had been stabbed and is seriously ill. A search of the buildings located Lord Vetinari in the stables. He was unconscious on the floor. A horse was saddled. The saddlebags contained ... seventy thousand dollars ... Captain, this is damn *stupid*.'

'I know, sir,' said Carrot. 'They are the facts, sir.'

'But they're not the right facts! They're *stupid* facts!'

'I know, sir. I can't imagine his lordship trying to kill anyone.'

'Are you mad?' said Vimes. 'I can't imagine him saying sorry!'

Vimes turned and glared at William, as if surprised to find him still there. 'Yes?' he demanded.

'Why was his lordship unconscious, sir?'

Vimes shrugged. 'It looks as though he was trying to get on the horse. He's got a game leg. Maybe he slipped— I can't believe I'm saying this. Anyway, that's your lot, understand?'

'I'd like to get an iconograph of you, please,' William persisted.

'Why?'

William thought fast. 'It will reassure the citizens that you are on the case and handling this personally, Commander. My iconographer is just downstairs. Otto!'

'Good gods, a damn vamp—' Vimes began.

'He's a Black Ribboner, sir,' Carrot whispered. Vimes rolled his eyes.

'Good mornink,' said Otto. 'Do not be movink, please, you are making a good pattern of light and shade.' He kicked out the legs of the tripod, peered into the iconograph and raised a salamander in its cage.

'Looking this vay, please—'

Click.

WHOOMPH.

'—oh, shee-yut!'

Dust floated to the floor. In the midst of it a twist of black ribbon spiralled down.

There was a moment of shocked silence. Then Vimes said, 'What the hell happened just then?'

'Too much flash, I think,' said William. He reached down with a trembling hand and retrieved a small square of card that was sticking out of the little grey cone of the late Otto Chriek.

'"DO NOT BE ALARMED,"' he read. '"The former bearer of this card has suffered a minor accident. You vill need a drop of blood from any species, and a dust-pan and brush."'

'Well, the kitchens are over that way,' said Vimes. 'Sort him out. I don't want my men treading him in all over the damn place.'

'One last thing, sir. Would you like me to say that if anyone saw anything suspicious they should tell you, sir?' said William.

'In this town? We'd need every man on the Watch just to control the queue. Just you be careful what you write, that's all.'

The two watchmen strode away, Carrot giving William a wan smile as he passed.

William busied himself in carefully scraping up Otto with two pages from his notebook and depositing the dust in the bag the vampire used to carry his equipment.

Then it dawned on him that he was alone – Otto probably didn't count at the moment – in the palace with Commander Vimes's *permission* to be there, if 'the kitchens are over that way' could be parlayed into 'permission'. And William was good with words. Truth was what he told. Honesty was sometimes not the same thing.

He picked up the bag and found his way to the back stairs and the kitchen, whence came a hubbub.

Staff were wandering around with the bewildered air of people with nothing to do who were nevertheless still being paid to do it. William sidled over to a maid who was sobbing into a grubby handkerchief.

'Excuse me, miss, but could you let me have a drop of blood— Yes, perhaps this isn't the right moment,' he added nervously, as she fled shrieking.

''ere, what did you say to our Rene?' said a thickset man, putting down a tray of hot loaves.

'Are you the baker?' said William.

The man gave him a look. 'What does it look like?'

'I can see what it *looks* like,' said William. There was another look, but this one had just a measure of respect in it. 'I'm still asking the question,' he went on.

'I'm the butcher, as it happens,' said the man. 'Well done. The baker's off sick. And who are you, askin' me questions?'

'Commander Vimes sent me down here,' said William. He was appalled at the ease with which the truth turned into a something that was almost a lie, just by being positioned correctly. He opened his notebook. 'I'm from the *Times*. Did you—'

'What, the paper?' said the butcher.

'That's right. Did you—'

'Hah! You got it completely up your bum about the winter, y'know. You should've said it was the Year of the Ant, that was the worst. You should've arsked me. I could've put you right.'

'And you are—?'

'Sidney Clancy and Son, aged thirty-nine, Eleven Long Hogmeat, Purveyors of Finest Cat and Dog Meats to The Gentry ... Why aren't you writing it down?'

'Lord Vetinari eats pet food?'

'He doesn't eat much of anything from what I hear. No, I delivers for his dog. Finest stuff. Prime. We sell only the best at Eleven Long Hogmeat, open every day from six a.m. to mid—'

'Oh, his dog. Right,' said William. 'Er.' He looked around at the throng. Some of those people could *tell* him things, and he was talking to a dogmeat man. Still ...

'Could you let me have a tiny piece of meat?' he said.

'Are you going to put it in the paper?'

'Yes. Sort of. In a way.'

William found a quiet alcove hidden from the general excitement and gingerly let the piece of meat dribble one drop of blood on to the little grey pile.

The dust mushroomed up into the air, became a mass of coloured flecks, became Otto Chriek.

'How vas that vun?' he said. 'Oh ...'

'I think you got the picture,' said William. 'Er, your jacket ...'

Part of the sleeve of the vampire's jacket was now the colour and texture of the stair carpet in the big hall, a rather dull pattern of red and blue.

'Carpet dust got mixed in, I expect,' said Otto. 'Do not be alarmed. Happens all zer time.' He sniffed the sleeve. 'Finest steak? Thank you!'

'It was dog food,' said William the Truthful.

'Dog food?'

'Yes. Grab your stuff and follow me.'

'*Dog* food?'

'You did say it was finest steak. Lord Vetinari is kind to his dog. Look, don't complain to *me*. If this sort of thing happens a lot then you ought to carry a little bottle of emergency blood! Otherwise people will do the best they can!'

'Vell, yes, fine, zank you anyvay,' the vampire mumbled, trailing behind him. 'Dog food, dog food, oh dear me . . . vhere are ve goink now?'

'To the Oblong Office to see where the attack was made,' said William. 'I just hope it isn't being guarded by someone clever.'

'Ve will get into a lot off trouble.'

'Why?' said William. He'd been thinking the same thing, but: why? The palace belonged to the city, more or less. The Watch probably wouldn't *like* him going in there, but William felt in his bones that you couldn't run a city on the basis of what the Watch liked. The Watch would probably *like* it if everyone spent their time indoors, with their hands on the table where people could see them.

The door to the Oblong Office was open. Guarding it, if you could truly be said to be on guard whilst leaning against the wall staring at the opposite wall, was Corporal Nobbs. He was smoking a surreptitious cigarette.

'Ah, just the man I was looking for!' said William. That was true. Nobby was more than he'd hoped for.

The cigarette disappeared by magic.

'Am I?' wheezed Nobbs, smoke curling out of his ears.

'Yes, I've been talking to Commander Vimes, and now I would like to see the room where the crime was committed.' William had great hopes of that sentence. It *seemed* to contain the words 'and he gave me permission to' without actually doing so.

Corporal Nobbs looked uncertain, but then he noticed the notebook. And Otto. The cigarette appeared between his lips again.

''ere, are you from that news paper?'

'That's right,' said William. 'I thought people would be interested in seeing how our brave Watch swings into action at a time like this.'

Corporal Nobbs's skinny chest visibly swelled.

'Corporal Nobby Nobbs, sir, probably thirty-four, bin in uniform since prob'ly ten years old, man and boy.'

William felt he ought to make a show of writing this down. '*Probably* thirty-four?'

'Our mam has never been one for numbers, sir. Always a bit vague on fine detail, our mam.'

'And . . .' William took a closer look at the corporal. You had to assume he was a human being because he was broadly the right shape, could talk and wasn't covered in hair. 'Man and boy and . . .?' he heard himself say.

'Just man and boy, sir,' said Corporal Nobbs reproachfully. 'Just man and boy.'

'And were you first on the scene, Corporal?'

'Last on the scene, sir.'

'And your important job is to . . .?'

'Stop anyone going through this door, sir,' said Corporal Nobbs, trying to read William's notes upside down. 'That's "Nobbs" without a "K", sir. It's amazing how people get that wrong. What's he doing with that box?'

'Got to take a picture of Ankh-Morpork's finest,' said William, easing himself towards the door. Of course, that *was* a lie, but since it was such an obvious lie he considered that it didn't count. It was like saying the sky was green.

By now Corporal Nobbs was almost leaving the floor under the lifting power of pride.

'Could I have a copy for my mam?' he said.

'Smile, please . . .' said Otto.

'I *am* smilin'.'

'Stop smiling, please.'

Click. WHOOMPH.

'Aaarghaarghaargh . . .'

A screaming vampire is always the centre of attention. William slipped into the Oblong Office.

Just inside the door was a chalk outline. In *coloured* chalk. It must have been done by Corporal Nobbs, because he was the only person who would add a pipe and draw in some flowers and clouds.

There was also a stink of peppermint.

There was a chair, knocked over.

There was a basket, kicked upside down in the corner of the room.

There was a short, evil-looking metal arrow sticking into the floor at an angle; it had a City Watch label tied to it now.

There was a dwarf. He— no, William corrected

himself, on seeing the heavy leather skirt and the slight raised heels to the iron boots – *she* was lying down on her stomach, picking at something on the floor with a pair of tweezers. It looked like a smashed jar.

She glanced up. 'Are you new? Where's your uniform?' she said.

'Well, er, I, er . . .'

She narrowed her eyes. 'You're not a watchman, are you? Does Mister Vimes know you're here?'

The way of the truthful-by-nature is as a bicycle race in a pair of sandpaper underpants, but William clung to an indisputable fact.

'I spoke to him just now,' he said.

But the dwarf wasn't Sergeant Detritus, and certainly not Corporal Nobbs.

'And he *said* you could come in here?' she demanded.

'Not exactly *said*—'

The dwarf walked across and swiftly opened the door. 'Then get—'

'Ah, a vonderful framing effect!' said Otto, who'd been on the other side of the door.

Click!

William shut his eyes.

WHOOMPH.

'. . . oohhbuggerrrrr . . .'

This time William caught the little piece of paper before it hit the ground.

The dwarf stood open-mouthed. Then she closed her mouth. Then she opened it again to say: 'What the *hell* just happened?'

'I suppose you could call it a sort of industrial injury,' said William. 'Hang on, I think I've still got a piece of dog food somewhere. Honestly, there's *got* to be a better way than this . . .'

He unwrapped the meat from a grubby piece of newspaper and gingerly dropped it on to the heap.

The ash fountained and Otto arose, blinking.

'How vas that? Vun more? This time viz the obscurograph?' he said. He was already reaching for his bag.

'Get out of here right now!' said the dwarf.

'Oh, please' – William glanced at the dwarf's shoulder – 'Corporal, let him do his job. Give him a chance, eh? He's a Black Ribboner, after all . . .' Behind the watchman Otto took an ugly, newt-like creature out of its jar.

'Do you want me to arrest the pair of you? You're interfering with the scene of a crime!'

'What crime, would you say?' said William, flipping open his notebook.

'Out, the pair of—'

'Boo,' said Otto softly.

The land eel must have been quite tense already. In response to thousands of years of evolution in a high magical environment it discharged a night-time's worth of darkness all at once. It filled the room for a moment, sheer solid black laced with traceries of blue and violet. Again for a moment William thought he could feel it wash through him in a flood. Then light flowed back, like chilly water after a pebble has been dropped in the lake.

The corporal glared at Otto. 'That was dark light, wasn't it?'

'Ah, you too are from Uberwald—' Otto began happily.

'Yes, and I did *not* expect to see that here! Get *out*!'

They hurried past the startled Corporal Nobbs, down the wide stairs and out into the frosty air of the courtyard.

'Is there something you ought to be telling me, Otto?' said William. 'She seemed *extremely* angry when you took that second picture.'

'Vell, it's a little hard to explain,' said the vampire awkwardly.

'It's not *harmful*, is it?'

'Oh, no, zere are no physical effects vhatsoever—'

'Or *mental* effects?' said William, who had spun words too often to miss such a carefully misleading statement.

'Perhaps zis is not zer time . . .'

'That's true. Tell me about it later. *Before* you try it again, okay?'

William's head buzzed as he ran along Filigree Street. Barely an hour ago he'd been agonizing over what stupid letters to put in the newspaper and the world had seemed more or less normal. Now it had been turned upside down. Lord Vetinari was supposed to have tried to kill someone, and *that* didn't make sense, if only because the person he had tried to kill was apparently still alive. He'd been trying to get away with a load of money, too, and *that* didn't make sense either. Oh, it wasn't hard to imagine a person embezzling money and attacking someone, but if you mentally inserted someone like the Patrician into the picture it all fell apart. And what about the peppermint? The room had *reeked* of it.

There were a lot more questions. The look in the corporal's eye as she'd chased him out of the office suggested firmly to William that he was unlikely to get any more answers from the Watch.

And looming up in his mind was the gaunt shape of the press. Somehow he was going to have to make a coherent story about all this, and he'd have to do it *now* . . .

The happy figure of Mr Wintler greeted him as he strode into the press room.

'What do you think of this funny marrow, eh, Mr de Worde?'

'I suggest you stuff it, Mr Wintler,' said William, pushing past.

'Just as you say, sir, that's just what my lady wife said too.'

'I'm sorry, but he insisted on waiting for you,' Sacharissa whispered as William sat down. 'What's going on?'

'I'm not sure . . .' said William, staring hard at his notes.

'Who's been killed?'

'Er, no one . . . I think . . .'

'That's a mercy, then.' Sacharissa looked down at the papers covering her desk.

'I'm afraid we've had five other people in here with humorous vegetables,' she said.

'Oh.'

'Yes. They weren't all that funny, to tell the truth.'

'Oh.'

'No, they mainly looked like . . . um, you know.'

'Oh . . . what?'

'*You* know,' she said, beginning to go red. 'A man's . . . um, you know.'

'*Oh.*'

'Not even very much like, um, you know, too. I mean, you had to *want* to see a . . . um, you know . . . there, if you understand me.'

William hoped that no one was making notes about this conversation. 'Oh,' he said.

'But I took their names and addresses, just in case,' said Sacharissa. 'I thought it might be worth it if we're short of stuff.'

'We're never going to be that short,' said William quickly.

'You don't think so?'

'I'm positive.'

'You may be right,' she said, looking at the mess of paper on her desk. 'It's been very busy in here while you were out. People have been queueing up with all sorts of news. Things that are going to happen, lost dogs, things they want to sell—'

'That's advertising,' said William, trying to concentrate on his notes. 'If they want it in the paper they have to pay.'

'I don't see that it's up to us to decide—'

William thumped the desk, to his own amazement and Sacharissa's shock.

'Something is *happening*, do you understand? Something really real is *happening*! And it's not an amusing shape! It's really serious! And I've got to write it down as soon as possible! Can you just let me do that?'

He realized Sacharissa was staring not at him but at his fist. He followed her gaze.

'Oh, no . . . what the *hell* is *this*?'

A long sharp nail projected straight upwards from the desk, an inch from his hand. It must have been at least six inches long. Pieces of paper had been impaled on it. When he picked it up he saw that it remained upright because it had been hammered through a wooden block.

'It's a spike,' said Sacharissa quietly. 'I, I, er, brought it in to keep our papers tidy. M-my grandfather always uses one. All . . . all the engravers do. It's . . . it's sort of a cross between a filing cabinet and a waste-paper basket. I thought it would be useful. Er, it'll save you using the floor.'

'Er, right, yes, good idea,' said William, looking at her reddening face. 'Er . . .'

He couldn't think straight. 'Mr Goodmountain?' he yelled.

The dwarf looked up from a playbill he was setting.

'Can you put stuff in type if I dictate to you?'

'Yes.'

'Sacharissa, *please* go and find Ron and his . . . friends. I want to get a small paper out as soon as possible. Not tomorrow morning. Right now. Please?'

She was about to protest, and then she saw the look in his eye. 'Are you sure you're allowed to do this?' she said.

'No! I'm not! I won't know until after I've done it! That's why I've got to do it! Then I'll know! And I'm sorry I'm shouting!'

He pushed his chair aside and went over to Goodmountain, who was standing patiently by a case of type.

'All right . . . we need a line at the top . . .' William shut his eyes and pinched the bridge of his nose while he thought. 'Er . . . "Amazing Scenes In Ankh-Morpork" . . . got that? In very big type. Then in smaller type, underneath . . . "Patrician Attacks Clerk With Knife" . . . er . . .' That didn't sound right, he knew. It was grammatically inexact. It was the Patrician who had the knife, not the clerk. 'We can sort that out later . . . er . . . in smaller type again . . . "Mysterious Events In Stables" . . . go down another size of type . . . "Watch Baffled". Okay? And now we'll start the story . . .'

'Start it?' said Goodmountain, his hand dancing across the boxes of type. 'Aren't we nearly finished?'

William flicked back and forth through his notes. How to begin, how to begin . . . Something interesting . . . No, something amazing . . . Some amazing things . . . no . . . no . . . The story was surely the *strangeness* of it all . . .

'"Suspicious circumstances surround the attack" . . . make that "alleged attack" . . .'

'I thought you said he *admitted* it,' said Sacharissa, dabbing at her eyes with a handkerchief.

'I know, I know, it's just that I think that if Lord Vetinari wanted to kill someone they'd be dead . . . look him up in *Twurp's Peerage*, will you,

I'm sure he was educated in the Assassins' Guild—'

'Alleged or not?' said Goodmountain, his hand hovering over the As. 'Just say the word.'

'Make it "the *apparent* attack"', said William, ' "by Lord Vetinari on Rufus Drumknott, his clerk, in the palace today. Er . . . er . . . Palace staff heard—" '

'Do you want me to work on this or do you want me to find the beggars?' Sacharissa demanded. 'I can't do both.'

William gave her a blank stare. Then he nodded.

'Rocky?'

The troll by the door awoke with a snort. 'Yessir?'

'Go and find Foul Ole Ron and the others and get them up here as soon as possible. Tell them there'll be a bonus. Now, where was I?'

' "Palace staff heard," ' Goodmountain prompted.

' "—heard his lordship—" '

' "—who graduated with full honours from the Guild of Assassins in 1968," ' Sacharissa called out.

'Put that in,' said William urgently. 'And then go on with . . . "say 'I killed him, I killed him, I'm sorry' " . . . Good grief, Vimes is right, this is insane, he'd have to be mad to talk like this.'

'Mr de Worde, is it?' said a voice.

'Oh, what the hell is it *this* time?'

William turned. He saw the trolls first, because even when they're standing at the back a group of four big trolls are metaphorically to the fore of any picture. The two humans in front of them were a mere detail, and in any case one of them was only human by tradition. He had the grey pallor of a zombie and wore the expression of one who, while not seeking to be unpleasant in himself, was the cause of much unpleasantness in other people.

'Mr de Worde? I believe you know me. I am Mr Slant of the Guild of Lawyers,' said Mr Slant, bowing stiffly. 'This,' he indicated the slight young man next to him, 'is Mr Ronald Carney, the new chairman of the Guild of Engravers and Printers. The four gentlemen behind me do not belong to any guild, as far as I am aware—'

'Engravers *and* Printers?' said Goodmountain.

'Yes,' said Carney. 'We have expanded our charter. Guild membership is two hundred dollars a year—'

'I'm not—' William began, but Goodmountain laid a hand on his arm.

'This is the shakedown, but it isn't as bad as I thought it might be,' he whispered. 'We haven't got time to argue and at this rate we'll make it back in a few days. End of problem!'

'*However*,' said Mr Slant, in his special lawyer's voice that sucked in money at every pore, 'in this instance, in view of the special circumstances, there will also be a one-off payment of, say, two thousand dollars.'

The dwarfs went quiet. Then there was a metallic chorus. Each dwarf had laid down his type, reached under the stone and pulled out a battle axe.

'That's agreed, then, is it?' said Mr Slant, stepping aside. The trolls were straightening up. It didn't take a major excuse for trolls and dwarfs to fight; sometimes, being on the same world was enough.

This time it was William who restrained Goodmountain. 'Hold on, hold on, there must be a law against killing lawyers.'

'Are you *sure*?'

'There're still some around, aren't there? Besides, he's a zombie. If you cut him in half both bits will sue you.' William raised his voice. 'We can't pay, Mr Slant.'

'In that case, accepted law and practice allows me—'

'I want to see your charter!' Sacharissa snapped. 'I've known you since we were kids, Ronnie Carney, and you're always up to something.'

'Good afternoon, Miss Cripslock,' said Mr Slant. 'As a matter of fact we thought someone might ask, so I brought the new charter with me. I hope we are *all* law-abiding here.'

Sacharissa snatched the impressive-looking scroll, with its large dangling seal, and glared at it as if trying to burn the words off the parchment by the mere friction of reading.

'Oh,' she said. 'It . . . seems to be in order.'

'Quite so.'

'Except for the Patrician's signature,' Sacharissa added, handing back the scroll.

'That is a mere formality, my dear.'

'I'm not your dear and it's not on there, formal or not. So this isn't legal, is it?'

Mr Slant twitched. '*Clearly* we cannot get a signature from a man in prison on a *very* serious charge,' he said.

Aha, that's a wallpaper word, thought William. When people say *clearly* something, that means there's a huge crack in their argument and they know things aren't clear at all.

'Then who is running the city?' he said.

'I don't know,' said Mr Slant. 'That is not my concern. I—'

'Mr Goodmountain?' said William. 'Large type, please.'

'Got you,' said the dwarf. His hand hovered over a fresh case.

'In caps, size to fit, "WHO RUNS ANKH-MORPORK?"' said William. 'Now into body type, upper and lower case, across two columns: "Who is governing the city while Lord Vetinari is imprisoned? Asked for an opinion today, a leading legal figure said he did not know and it was no concern of his. Mr Slant of the Lawyers' Guild went on to say—"'

'You can't put that in your newspaper!' barked Slant.

'Set that directly, please, Mr Goodmountain.'

'Setting it already,' said the dwarf, the leaden slugs clicking into place. Out of the corner of his eye William saw Otto emerging from the cellar and looking puzzled at the noise.

'"Mr Slant went on to say . . ."?' said William, glaring at the lawyer.

'You will find it very hard to print that,' said Mr Carney, ignoring the lawyer's frantic hand signals, 'with no damn press!'

'". . . was the view of Mr Carney of the Guild of Engravers," spelled with an e before the y,' said William, '"who earlier today tried to put the *Times* out of business by means of an illegal document."' William realized that although his mouth felt full of acid he was enjoying this immensely. '"Asked for his opinion of this flagrant abuse of the city laws, Mr Slant said . . ."?'

'STOP TAKING DOWN EVERYTHING WE SAY!' yelled Slant.

'Full caps for the whole sentence, please, Mr Goodmountain.'

The trolls and the dwarfs were staring at William and the lawyer. They understood that a fight was going on, but they couldn't see any blood.

'And when you're ready, Otto?' said William, turning round.

'If the dvarfs vould just close up a bit more,' said Otto, squinting into the iconograph. 'Oh, zat's *good*, let's see the light *gleam* on zose big choppers . . . trolls, please vave your fists, zat's right . . . big smile, everyvun . . .'

It is *amazing* how people will obey a man pointing a lens at them. They'll come to their senses in a fraction of a second, but that's all he needs.

Click.

WHOOMPH.

'. . . aaarghaaarghaaarghaaaaaagh . . .'

William reached the falling iconograph just ahead of Mr Slant, who could move very fast for a man with no apparent knees.

'It's ours,' he said, holding it firmly, while the dust of Otto Chriek settled around them.

'What are you intending to do with this picture?'

'I don't have to tell you. This is our workshop. We didn't ask you to come here.'

'But I am here on legal business!'

'Then it can't be wrong to take a picture of you, can

it?' said William. 'But if you think differently, then I will of course be happy to quote you!'

Slant glared at him and then marched back to the group by the door. William heard him say, 'It is my considered legal opinion that we leave at this juncture.'

'But you said you could—' Carney began, glaring at William.

'My very *considered* opinion,' said Mr Slant again, 'is that we go right now, in *silence*.'

'But you said—'

'In *silence*, I suggest!'

They left.

There was a group sigh of relief from the dwarfs, and a replacement of axes.

'You want me to set this properly?' said Goodmountain.

'There'll be trouble over it,' said Sacharissa.

'Yes, but how much trouble are we in already?' said William. 'On a scale of one to ten?'

'At the moment ... about eight,' said Sacharissa. 'But when the next edition is on the streets...' she shut her eyes a moment and her lips moved in calculation '... about two thousand, three hundred and seventeen?'

'Then we'll put it in,' said William.

Goodmountain turned to his workers. 'Leave the axes where you can see 'em, boys,' he said.

'Look, I don't want anyone else to get into trouble,' said William. 'I'll even set the rest of the type myself, and I can run some copies off on the press.'

'Needs three to operate and you won't get much

speed,' said Goodmountain. He saw William's expression, grinned and slapped him as high up the back as a dwarf could manage. 'Don't worry, lad. We want to protect our investment.'

'And I'm not leaving,' said Sacharissa. 'I need that dollar!'

'Two dollars,' said William absently. 'It's time for a rise. What about you, Ott— Oh, can someone sweep up Otto, please?'

A few minutes later the restored vampire pulled himself upright against his tripod and lifted out a copper plate with trembling fingers.

'Vot is happenink next, please?'

'Are you staying with us? It could be dangerous,' said William, realizing that he was saying this to a vampire iconographer who undied every time he took a picture.

'Vot kind of danger?' said Otto, tilting the plate this way and that in order to examine it better.

'Well, legal, to start with.'

'Has anyvun mentioned garlic zo far?'

'No.'

'Can I have vun hundred and eighty dollars for the Akina TR-10 dual-imp iconograph viz the telescopic seat and big shiny lever?'

'Er . . . not yet.'

'Okay,' said Otto philosophically. 'Zen I shall require five dollars for repairs and improvements. I can see zis is a different kind of job.'

'All right. All right, then.' William looked around the press room. Everyone was silent, and everyone was watching him.

A few days ago he'd have expected today to be . . . well, dull. It usually was, just after he'd sent out his news letter. He generally spent the time wandering around the city or reading in his tiny office while waiting for the next client with a letter to be written or, sometimes, read out.

Often both kinds were difficult. People prepared to trust a postal system that largely depended on handing an envelope to some trustworthy-looking person who was heading in the right direction generally had something important to say. But the point was that they weren't *his* difficulties. It wasn't *him* making a last-minute plea to the Patrician, or hearing the terrible news about the collapse of shaft #3, although of course he did his best to make things easier for the customer. It had worked very well. If stress were food, he'd succeeded in turning his life into porridge.

The press waited. It looked, now, like a great big beast. Soon he'd throw a lot of words into it. And in a few hours it would be hungry again, as if those words had never happened. You could feed it, but you could never fill it up.

He shuddered. What had he got them all into?

But he felt on fire. There was a truth somewhere, and he hadn't found it yet. He was going to, because he knew, he *knew* that once this edition hit the streets—

'Bugrit!'

'Hawrrak . . . pwit!'

'Quack!'

He glanced at the crowd coming in. Of course, the

truth hid in some unlikely places and had some strange handmaidens.

'Let's go to press,' he said.

It was an hour later. The sellers were already coming back for more. The rumbling of the press made the tin roof shake. The piles of copper mounting up in front of Goodmountain leapt into the air at every thump.

William examined his reflection in a piece of polished brass. Somehow he'd got ink all over himself. He did the best he could with his handkerchief.

He'd sent Altogether Andrews to sell the papers near Pseudopolis Yard, reckoning him to be the most consistently sane of the fraternity. At least five of his personalities could hold a coherent conversation.

By now, surely, the Watch would have had time to read the story, even if they'd had to send out for help with the longer words.

He was aware of someone staring at him. He turned and saw Sacharissa's head bend down over her work again.

Someone sniggered, behind him.

There was no one there who was paying him any attention. There *was* a three-way argument over a matter of sixpence going on between Goodmountain, Foul Ole Ron and Foul Ole Ron, Ron being capable of keeping a pretty good row going all by himself. The dwarfs were hard at work around the press. Otto had retired to his darkroom, where he was once again mysteriously also hard at work.

Only Ron's dog was watching William. He

considered that it had, for a dog, a very offensive and knowing look.

A couple of months ago someone had tried to hand William the old story about there being a dog in the city that could talk. It was the third time this year. William had explained that it was an urban myth. It was always a friend of a friend who had heard it talk, and it was never anyone who had seen the dog. The dog in front of William didn't look as if it could talk, but it *did* look as if it could swear.

There seemed to be no stopping that kind of story. People swore that there was some long-lost heir to the throne of Ankh living incognito in the town. William certainly recognized wishful thinking when he heard it. There was the other old chestnut about a werewolf being employed in the Watch, too. Until recently he'd dismissed that one, but he was having some doubts lately. After all, the *Times* employed a vampire . . .

He stared at the wall, tapping his teeth with his pencil.

'I'm going to see Commander Vimes,' he said at last. 'It's better than hiding.'

'We're being invited to all sorts of things,' said Sacharissa, looking up from her paperwork. 'Well, I *say* invited . . . Lady Selachii has *ordered* us to attend her ball on Thursday next week and write *at least* five hundred words which we will *of course* let her see before publication.'

'Good idea,' Goodmountain called over his shoulder. 'Lots of names at balls, and—'

'—names sell newspapers,' said William. 'Yes. I know. Do you want to go?'

'Me? I haven't got anything to wear!' said Sacharissa. 'It'd cost forty dollars for the kind of dress you wear to that sort of thing. And we can't afford that kind of money.'

William hesitated. Then he said: 'Stand up and twirl around, could you?'

She actually blushed. 'Whatever for?'

'I want to see what size you are . . . you know, all over.'

She stood up and turned around nervously. There was a chorus of whistles from the crew and a number of untranslatable comments in dwarfish.

'You're pretty close,' said William. 'If I could get you a really good dress, could you find someone to make any adjustments you need? It might have to be let out a bit in the, in the, you know . . . in the top.'

'What kind of dress?' she said suspiciously.

'My sister's got *hundreds* of evening dresses and she spends all her time at our place in the country,' said William. 'The family never comes back to the city these days. I'll give you the key to the town house this evening and you can go and help yourself.'

'Won't she mind?'

'She'll probably never notice. Anyway, I think she'd be shocked to find that anyone could spend as little as forty dollars on a dress. Don't worry about it.'

'Town house? Place in the country?' said Sacharissa, displaying an inconveniently journalistic trait of picking on the words you hoped wouldn't be noticed.

'My family's rich,' said William. 'I'm not.'

He glanced at the rooftop opposite when he stepped outside, because something in its outline was different, and saw a spiky head outlined against the afternoon sky.

It was a gargoyle. William had got used to seeing them everywhere in the city. Sometimes one would stay in the same place for months at a time. You seldom saw them actually moving from one roof to another. But you also seldom saw them at all in districts like this. Gargoyles liked high stone buildings with lots of gutters and fiddly architecture, which attracted pigeons. Even gargoyles have to eat.

There was also something going on further down the street. Several large carts were outside one of the old warehouses, and crates were being carried inside.

He spotted several more gargoyles on the way across the bridge to Pseudopolis Yard. Every single one of them turned its head to watch him.

Sergeant Detritus was on duty at the desk. He looked at William in surprise.

'By damn, dat was quick. You run all der way?' he said.

'What are you talking about?'

'Mister Vimes only sent for you a coupla minutes ago,' said Detritus. 'Go on up, I should. Don't worry, he's stopped shoutin'.' He gave William a rather-you-than-me look. 'But he are not glad about being in a tent, as dey say.'

'Has he *ever* been a happy camper?'

'Not much,' said Detritus, grinning evilly.

William climbed the stairs and knocked at the door, which swung open.

Commander Vimes looked up from his desk. His eyes narrowed.

'Well, well, that was quick,' he said. 'Ran all the way, did you?'

'No, sir, I was coming here hoping to ask you some questions.'

'That was kind of you,' said Vimes.

There was a definite feeling that although the little village was quiet at the moment – women hanging out washing, cats sleeping in the sun – soon the volcano was going to explode and hundreds were going to be buried in the ash.

'So—' William began.

'*Why* did you do this?' said Vimes. William could see the *Times* on the desk in front of the commander. He could read the headlines from here:

The Ankh-Morpork Times

'THE TRUTH SHALL MAKE YE FRET' • EXTRA!

Patrician Attacks Clerk With Knife
(He had the knife, not the clerk)

MYSTERIOUS EVENTS IN STABLES
Strange Smell of Peppermint
WATCH BAFFLED

'Baffled, am I?' said Vimes.

'If you are telling me that you are not, Commander,

179

I will be happy to make a note of the fa—'

'Leave that notebook alone!'

William looked surprised. The notebook was the cheapest kind, made of paper recycled so many times you could use it as a towel, but once again someone was glaring at it as if it was a weapon.

'I won't have you doing to me what you did to Slant,' said Vimes.

'Every word of that story is true, sir.'

'I'd bet on it. It sounds like his style.'

'Look, Commander, if there's something wrong with my story, tell me what it is.'

Vimes sat back and waved his hands.

'Are you going to print *everything* you hear?' he said. 'Do you intend to run around my city like some loose . . . loose siege weapon? You sit there clutching your precious integrity like a teddy bear and you haven't the faintest idea, have you, not the *faintest idea* how hard you can make my job?'

'It's not against the law to—'

'Isn't it? Isn't it, though? In Ankh-Morpork? Stuff like this? It reads like Behaviour Likely to Cause a Breach of the Peace to *me*!'

'It might upset people, but this is *important*—'

'And what will you write next, I wonder?'

'I haven't printed that you have a werewolf employed in the Watch,' said William. He regretted it instantly, but Vimes was getting on his nerves.

'Where did you hear that?' said a quiet voice behind him. He turned in his chair. A fair-haired young woman in Watch uniform was leaning against the wall. She must have been there all the time.

'This is Sergeant Angua,' said Vimes. 'You can speak freely in front of her.'

'I've ... heard rumours,' said William. He'd seen the sergeant in the streets. She had a habit of staring a bit too sharply at people, he'd considered.

'And?'

'Look, I can see this is worrying you,' said William. 'Please let me assure you that Corporal Nobbs's secret is safe with me.'

No one spoke. William congratulated himself. It had been a shot in the dark, but he could tell by Sergeant Angua's face that he'd won this one. It seemed to have shut down, locking away all expression.

'We don't often talk about Corporal Nobbs's species,' said Vimes, after a while. 'I would deem it a small favour if you would take the same approach.'

'Yes, sir. So could I ask you why you're having me watched?'

'I am?'

'The gargoyles. Everyone knows a lot of them work for the Watch these days.'

'We're not watching you. We're watching to see what *happens* to you,' said Sergeant Angua.

'Because of *this*,' said Vimes, slapping the newspaper.

'But I'm not doing anything *wrong*,' said William.

'No, it may just be you're not doing anything *illegal*,' said Vimes. 'Although you're coming damn close. Other people do not have my kind and understanding disposition, though. All I ask is that you try not to bleed all over the street.'

'I'll try.'

'And don't write that down.'

'Fine.'

'And don't write down that I said don't write that down.'

'Okay. Can I write down that you said that I shouldn't write down that you said—' William stopped. The mountain was rumbling. 'Only joking.'

'Haha. And no tapping my officers for information.'

'And no giving dog biscuits to Corporal Nobbs,' said Sergeant Angua. She walked around behind Vimes and peered over his shoulder. '"The Truth Shall Make Ye Fret"?'

'Printer's error,' said William shortly. 'Anything else I shouldn't do, Commander?'

'Just don't get in the way.'

'I'll make a— I'll remember,' said William. 'But, if you don't mind my asking, what's in it for me?'

'I'm Commander of the Watch and I'm asking you politely.'

'And that's it?'

'I could ask you impolitely, Mr de Worde.' Vimes sighed. 'Look, can you see things my way? A crime has been committed. The Guilds are in an uproar. You've heard of too many chiefs? Well, right now there's a hundred many chiefs. I've Captain Carrot and a lot of men I really can't spare guarding the Oblong Office and the rest of the clerks, which means I'm short-handed everywhere else. I've got to deal with all this and ... actively pursue a state of non-bafflement. I've got Vetinari in the cells. And Drumknott, too—'

'But wasn't he the victim, sir?'

'One of my men is tending him.'

'Not one of the city doctors?'

Vimes stared fixedly at the notebook. 'The doctors of this city are a fine body of men,' he said in a level tone, 'and I would not see a word written against them. One of my staff just happens to have . . . special skills.'

'You mean he can tell someone else's arse from their elbow?'

Vimes was a fast learner. He sat with his hands folded and a completely impassive expression.

'Can I ask another question?' said William.

'Nothing will stop you, will it?'

'Have you found Lord Vetinari's dog?'

Again, total blankness. But this time William had the impression that behind it several dozen wheels had begun to spin.

'Dog?' said Vimes.

'Wuffles, I believe he's called,' said William.

Vimes sat watching him impassively.

'A terrier, I think,' said William.

Vimes failed to move a muscle.

'Why was there a crossbow bolt sticking in the floor?' said William. 'That doesn't make sense to me, unless there was someone else in the room. And it had gone in a long way. That's not a rebound. Someone was firing at something on the floor. Dog-sized, perhaps?'

Not a feature twitched on the commander's face.

'And then there's the peppermint,' William went on. 'There's a puzzle. I mean, why peppermint? And then I thought, maybe someone didn't want to be traced by their smell? Perhaps *they*'d heard about your werewolf too? A few jars of peppermint oil thrown down would confuse things a bit?'

There it was, a faint flicker as Vimes glanced momentarily at some paperwork in front of him. Lotto! thought William.*

At last, like some oracle that speaks once a year, Vimes said, 'I don't trust you, Mr de Worde. And I've just realized why. It's not just that you're going to cause trouble. Dealing with trouble is my job, it's what I'm paid for, that's why they give me an armour allowance. But who are you responsible to? I have to answer for what I do, although right now I'm damned if I know who to. But you? It seems to me you can do what the hell you like.'

'I suppose I'm answerable to the truth, sir.'

'Oh, really? How, exactly?'

'Sorry?'

'If you tell lies, does the truth come and smack you in the face? I'm impressed. Ordinary everyday people like me are responsible to other people. Even Vetinari always had— has one eye on the Guilds. But you . . . *you* are answerable to the truth. Amazing. What's its address? Does it read the paper?'

'She, sir,' said Sergeant Angua. 'There's a goddess of truth, I believe.'

'Can't have many followers, then,' said Vimes. 'Except our friend here.' He stared at William again over the top of his fingers, and once again the wheels turned.

'Supposing . . . just supposing . . . you came into

---

* At this point Bingo had not been introduced to Ankh-Morpork.

possession of a little drawing of a dog,' he said. 'Could you print it in your paper?'

'We *are* talking about Wuffles, are we?' said William.

'Could you?'

'I'm sure I could.'

'We would be interested in knowing why he barked just before the . . . event,' said Vimes.

'And if you could find him Corporal Nobbs could speak to him in dog language, yes?' said William.

Once again Vimes did his impression of a statue. 'We could get a drawing of the dog to you in an hour,' he said.

'Thank you. Who *is* running the city at the moment, Commander?'

'I'm just a copper,' said Vimes. 'They don't tell me these things. But I imagine a new Patrician will be elected. It's all laid down in the city statutes.'

'Who can tell me more about them?' said William, mentally adding, *'Just a copper' my bum!*

'Mr Slant is your man there,' said Vimes, and this time he smiled. 'Very helpful, I believe. Good afternoon, Mr de Worde. Sergeant, show Mr de Worde out, will you?'

'I want to see Lord Vetinari,' said William.

'You *what*?'

'It's a reasonable request, sir.'

'No. Firstly, he is still unconscious. Secondly, he is my prisoner.'

'Aren't you even letting a lawyer see him?'

'I think his lordship is in enough trouble already, lad.'

'What about Drumknott? *He* isn't a prisoner, is he?'

Vimes glanced up at Sergeant Angua, who shrugged.

'All right. There's no law against that, and we can't have people saying he's dead,' he said. He unhooked a speaking tube from a brass and leather construction on his desk and hesitated.

'Have they got that problem sorted out, Sergeant?' he said, ignoring William.

'Yes, sir. The pneumatic message system and the speaking tubes are *definitely* separated now.'

'Are you sure? You do know Constable Keenside had all his teeth knocked out yesterday?'

'They say it can't happen again, sir.'

'Well, obviously it can't. He hasn't got any more teeth. Oh, well . . .' Vimes picked up the tube, held it away from him for a moment and then spoke into it.

'Put me through to the cells, will you?'

'Wizzip? Wipwipwip?'

'Say again?'

'Sneedle flipsock?'

'This is Vimes!'

'Scitscrit?'

Vimes put the tube back on its cradle and stared at Sergeant Angua.

'They're still working on it, sir,' she said. 'They say rats have been nibbling at the tubes.'

'Rats?'

'I'm afraid so, sir.'

Vimes groaned and turned to William. 'Sergeant Angua will take you to the cells,' he said.

And then William was on the other side of the door.

'Come on,' said the sergeant.

'How did I do?' said William.

'I've seen worse.'

'Sorry to mention Corporal Nobbs, but—'

'Oh, don't worry about it,' said Sergeant Angua. 'Your powers of observation will be the talk of the station. Look, he's being kind to you because he hasn't worked out what you are yet, okay? Just be careful, that's all.'

'And you *have* worked out what I am, have you?' said William.

'Let's just say I don't rely on first impressions. Mind the step.'

She led the way down into the cells. William noted, without being so crass as to write it down, that there were two watchmen on duty at the bottom.

'Are there usually guards down here? I mean, the cells have locks, don't they?'

'I hear you've got a vampire working for you,' said Sergeant Angua.

'Otto? Oh, yes. Well, we're not prejudiced about that sort of thing . . .'

The sergeant did not answer. Instead she opened a door off the main cell corridor and called out: 'Visitor for the patients, Igor.'

'Right with you, Thargent.'

The room within was brightly lit by an uncanny, flickering blue light. Jars lined shelves on one wall. Some had strange things moving in them – very strange things. Other things just floated. Blue sparks sizzled on some complex machine, all copper balls and glass rods, in the corner. But what mainly drew William's attention was the great big eye.

Before he could actually scream a hand reached up and what he'd thought was a huge eyeball was revealed as the largest magnifying glass he'd ever seen, swivelling up on a metal bracket attached to the forehead of its owner. But the face it revealed was barely an improvement, when it came to mouth-desiccating horror.

The eyes were on different levels. One ear was larger than the other. The face was a network of scars. But that was nothing compared to the deformed hairstyle; Igor's greasy black hair had been brushed forward into an overhanging quiff in the manner of some of the city's noisier young musicians, but to a length that could take out the eye of any innocent pedestrian. By the looks of the ... *organic* nature of Igor's work area, he would then be able to help put it back.

There was a fish tank bubbling on one bench. Inside it some potatoes were idly swimming backwards and forwards.

'Young Igor here is part of our forensic department,' said Sergeant Angua. 'Igor, this is Mr de Worde. He wants to see the patients.'

William saw the quick glance Igor gave the sergeant, who added, 'Mister Vimes says it's okay.'

'Right this way, then,' said Igor, lurching past William into the corridor. 'Always nice to get visitors down here, Mr de Worde. You will find we keep a very relaxed thell down here. I'll just go and get the keys.'

'Why does he only lisp the occasional s?' said William, as Igor limped towards a cupboard.

'He's trying to be modern. You never met an Igor before?'

'Not one like that, no! He's got two thumbs on his right hand!'

'He's from Uberwald,' said the sergeant. 'Igors are very much into self-improvement. Fine surgeons, though. Just don't shake hands with one in a thunderstorm—'

'Here we are, then,' said Igor, lurching back. 'Who first?'

'Lord Vetinari?' said William.

'He's still athleep,' said Igor.

'What, after all this time?'

'Not surprithing. It was a nasty blow he had—'

Sergeant Angua coughed loudly.

'I thought he fell off a horse,' said William.

'Well, yes . . . and caught himthelf a blow when he hit the floor, I've no doubt,' said Igor, glancing at Angua.

He turned the key.

Lord Vetinari lay on a narrow bed. His face looked pale but he seemed to be sleeping peacefully.

'He's not woken up *at all*?' said William.

'No. I look in on him every fifteen minutes or tho. It can be like that. Sometimeth the body just says: thleep.'

'I heard he hardly *ever* sleeps,' said William.

'Maybe he's taking the opportunity,' said Igor, gently closing the door.

He unlocked the next cell.

Drumknott was sitting up in bed, his head bandaged. He was drinking some soup. He looked startled when he saw them, and nearly spilled it.

'And how are we?' said Igor, as cheerfully as a face full of stitches can allow.

'Er, *I'm* feeling much better . . .' The young man looked from one face to another, uncertain.

'Mr de Worde here would like to talk to you,' said Sergeant Angua. 'I'll go and help Igor sort out his eyeballs. Or something.'

William was left in an awkward silence. Drumknott was one of those people with no discernible character.

'You're Lord de Worde's son, aren't you?' said Drumknott. 'You write that news sheet.'

'Yes,' said William. It seemed he'd always be his father's son. 'Um. They say Lord Vetinari stabbed you.'

'So they say,' said the clerk.

'You were there, though.'

'I knocked on the door to take him his copy of the paper as he'd requested, his lordship opened it, I walked into the room . . . and the next thing I know I was waking up here with Mr Igor looking at me.'

'That must have come as a shock,' said William, with a momentary flash of pride that the *Times* had figured in this in some small way.

'They say I'd have lost the use of my arm if Igor hadn't been so good with a needle,' said Drumknott earnestly.

'But your head's bandaged, too,' said William.

'I think I must have fallen over when . . . when whatever it was happened,' said Drumknott.

My gods, thought William, he's *embarrassed*.

'I have every confidence that there has been a mistake,' Drumknott went on.

'Has his lordship been preoccupied lately?'

'His lordship is always preoccupied. It's his job,' said the clerk.

'Do you know that three people heard him say that he'd killed you?'

'I cannot explain that. They must have been mistaken.'

The words were clipped sharp. Any moment now, William told himself . . . 'Why do you think—' he began, and was proved right.

'I *think* I don't have to talk to you,' said Drumknott. 'Do I?'

'No, but—'

'*Sergeant!*' Drumknott shouted.

There were swift footsteps and the cell door opened.

'Yes?' said Sergeant Angua.

'I have finished talking to this gentleman,' said Drumknott. 'And I am tired.'

William sighed and put his notebook away. 'Thank you,' he said. 'You've been very . . . helpful.'

As he walked along the corridor he said, 'He doesn't want to believe his lordship might have attacked him.'

'Really,' said the sergeant.

'Looks like quite a bang he had on his head,' William went on.

'Does it?'

'Look, even I can see this smells funny.'

'Can you?'

'I *see*,' said William. 'You went to the Mister Vimes School of Communication, yes?'

'Did I?' said Sergeant Angua.

'Loyalty is a wonderful thing.'

'Is it? The way out is *this* way—'

After she had carefully ushered William into the street Sergeant Angua went back upstairs into Vimes's office and quietly shut the door behind her.

'So he only spotted the gargoyles?' said Vimes, who was watching William walk down the street.

'Apparently. But I wouldn't underestimate him, sir. He notices things. He was dead right about the peppermint bomb. And how many officers would have noticed how deeply that arrow went into the floor?'

'That's unfortunately true.'

'And he spotted Igor's second thumb, and hardly anyone else has noticed the swimming potatoes.'

'Igor hasn't got rid of them yet?'

'No, sir. He believes that instant fish and chips are only a generation away.'

Vimes sighed. 'All right, Sergeant. Forget the potatoes. What are the odds?'

'Sir?'

'I know what goes on in the duty room. They wouldn't be watchmen if someone wasn't running a book.'

'On Mr de Worde?'

'Yes.'

'Well . . . six'll get you ten that he'll be dead by next Monday, sir.'

'You might just spread the word that I don't like that sort of thing, will you?'

'Yes, sir.'

'Find out who's running the book, and when you have found out that it is Nobby, take it off him.'

'Right, sir. And Mr de Worde?'

Vimes stared at the ceiling. 'How many officers are watching him?' he said.

'Two.'

'Nobby's usually good at judging odds. Think that'll be enough?'

'No.'

'Me neither. But we're stretched. He's going to have to learn the hard way. And the trouble with the hard way is you only get one lesson.'

Mr Tulip emerged from the alleyway where he had just negotiated the purchase of a very small packet of what would shortly prove to be rat poison cut with powdered washing crystals.

He found Mr Pin reading a large piece of paper. 'What's that?' he said.

'Trouble, I expect,' said Mr Pin, folding it up and putting it in his pocket. 'Yes, indeed.'

'This city is getting on my —ing nerves,' said Mr Tulip, as they continued down the street. 'I got a —ing *headache*. And my leg hurts.'

'So? It bit me, too. You made a big mistake with that dog.'

'Are you saying I shouldn't've shot at it?'

'No, I'm saying you shouldn't've missed. It got away.'

'It's only a dog,' Mr Tulip grumbled. 'What's such a problem about a dog? It's not like it's a reliable —ing witness. They never told us about no —ing dog.' His ankle was beginning to get that hot, dark sensation that suggested that someone hadn't been brushing their teeth lately. 'You just try carrying a guy with a —ing dog snapping at your legs! *And* how come the —ing zombie never told us the guy was so —ing *fast*? If he hadn't been staring at the geek he'd have —ing *got* me!'

Mr Pin shrugged. But he'd made a note of that. Mr Slant had failed to tell the New Firm quite a lot of things, and one of them was that Vetinari moved like a snake.

This was going to cost the lawyer a lot of money. Mr Pin had nearly got *cut*.

But he was proud of stabbing the clerk and shoving Charlie out on the landing to babble to the stupid servants. That hadn't been in the script. That was the kind of service you got from the New Firm. He snapped his fingers as he walked. Yeah! They could react, they could extemporize, they could get *creative* . . .

'Excuse me, gentlemen?'

A figure had stepped out of the alleyway ahead of them, a knife in each hand.

'Thieves' Guild,' it said. 'Excuse me? This is an official robbery.'

To the surprise of the thief, Mr Pin and Mr Tulip seemed neither shocked nor frightened, despite the size of the knives. Instead they looked like a pair of lepidopterists who'd stumbled across an entirely new kind of butterfly and found it trying to wave a tiny little net.

'Official robbery?' said Mr Tulip slowly.

'Ah, you're visitors to our fair city?' said the thief.

'Then this is your lucky day, sir and . . . sir. A theft of twenty-five dollars entitles you to immunity from further street theft for a period of a full six months plus, for this week only, the choice of this handsome box of crystal wine glasses or a useful set of barbecue tools which will be the envy of your friends.'

'You mean . . . you're legal?' said Mr Pin.

'What —ing friends?' said Mr Tulip.

'Yes, sir. Lord Vetinari feels that since there'll always be *some* crime in the city, it might as well be organized.'

Mr Tulip and Mr Pin looked at one another.

'Well, "Legal" is my middle name,' said Mr Pin, shrugging. 'Over to you, Mr Tulip.'

'And since you are newcomers I can offer you an introductory hundred-dollar theft, which will give you subsequent immunity for a full twenty-six months plus this booklet of restaurant, livery hire, clothing and entertainment vouchers worth a full twenty-five dollars at today's prices. Your neighbours will admire—'

Mr Tulip's arm moved in a blur. One banana-bunch hand caught the thief around the neck and slammed his head against the wall.

'Unfortunately, Mr Tulip's middle name is "Bastard",' said Mr Pin, lighting a cigarette. The meaty sounds of his colleague's permanent anger continued behind him as he picked up the wine glasses and examined them critically.

'Tch . . . cheap paste, not crystal at all,' he said. 'Who can you trust these days? It makes you despair.'

The body of the thief slumped to the ground.

'I think I'll go for the —ing barbecue set,' said Mr Tulip, stepping over it. 'I see here where it contains a number of oh-so-useful skewers and spatulas that will add a —ing new dimension of enjoyment to those al fresco patio meals.'

He ripped open the box and dragged out a blue and white apron, which he examined critically.

' "Kill the Cook!!!" ' he said, slipping it over his head. 'Hey, this is classy stuff. I'll have to get some —ing friends so's they can envy me when I'm having a meal with —ing Al Fresco. How about them —ing vouchers?'

'There's never any good stuff in these things,' said Mr Pin. 'It's just a way of shifting stuff no one can sell. See here . . . "Twenty-five per cent off Happy Hour Prices at Furby's Castle of Cabbage". He tossed the booklet aside.

'Not bad, though,' said Mr Tulip. 'And he only had twenty dollars on him, so it's a —ing bargain.'

'I'll be glad when we leave this place,' said Mr Pin. 'It's too strange. Let's just frighten the dead man and get out of here.'

'Eyinnngg . . . GUT!'

The cry of the wild newspaper seller rang out across the twilit square as William set off back to Gleam Street. They were still selling well, he could see.

It was only by accident, as a citizen hurried past him, that he saw the headline:

WOMAN GIVES BIRTH TO COBRA

Surely Sacharissa hadn't got out another edition by

herself, had she? He ran back to the seller.

It wasn't the *Times*. The title, in big bold type that was rather better than the stuff the dwarfs made, was:

THE NEWS YOU ONLY HEAR ABOUT   2p

'What's all this?' he said to the seller, who was socially above Ron's group by several layers of grime.

'All this what?'

'All this *this*!' The stupid interview with Drumknott had left William very annoyed.

'Don't ask me, guv. I get a penny for every one I sell, that's all I know.'

'"Rain of Soup in Genua"? "Hen Lays Egg Three Times In Hurricane"? Where'd all this *come* from?'

'Look, guv, if I was a readin' man I wouldn't be flogging papers, right?'

'Someone else has started a paper!' said William. He cast his eyes down to the small print at the bottom of the single page and, in this paper, even the small print wasn't very small. 'In *Gleam* Street?'

He recalled the workmen bustling around outside the old warehouse. How could— But the Engravers' Guild could, couldn't they? They already had presses, and they certainly had the money. Tuppence was ridiculous, though, even for this single sheet of . . . of *rubbish*. If the seller got a penny, then how in the world could the printer make any money?

Then he realized: that wouldn't be the point, would it . . . the point was to put the *Times* out of business.

A big red and white sign for the *Inquirer* was already in place across the street from the Bucket. More carts were queueing outside.

One of Goodmountain's dwarfs was peering around from behind the wall.

'There's three presses in there already,' he said. 'You saw what they've done? They got it out in half an hour!'

'Yes, but it's only one sheet. And it's made-up stuff.'

'Is it? Even the one about the snake?'

'I'd bet a thousand dollars.' William remembered that the smaller print had said this had happened in Lancre. He revised his estimate. 'I'd bet at least a hundred dollars.'

'That's not the worst of it,' said the dwarf. 'You'd better come in.'

Inside the press was creaking away, but most of the dwarfs were idle.

'Shall I give you the headlines?' said Sacharissa, as he entered.

'You'd better,' said William, sitting down at his crowded desk.

'Engravers Offer Dwarfs One Thousand Dollars For Press.'

'Oh, no . . .'

'Vampire Iconographer and Hard-Working Writer Tempted with Five-Hundred Dollar Salaries,' Sacharissa went on.

'Oh, really . . .'

'Dwarfs Buggered For Paper.'

'*What?*'

'That's a direct quote from Mr Goodmountain,' said Sacharissa. 'I don't pretend to know *exactly* what it means, but I understand they've got enough for only one more edition.'

'And if we want any more it's five times the old price,' said Goodmountain, coming up. 'The Engravers are buying it up. Supply and demand, King says.'

'King?' William's brow wrinkled. 'You mean Mr King?'

'Yeah, King of the Golden River,' said the dwarf. 'And, yeah, we could just about pay that but if them across the road are going to sell their sheet for 2p we'll be working for practically nothing.'

'Otto told the man from the Guild that he'd break his pledge if he saw him here again,' said Sacharissa. 'He was very angry because the man was angling to find out how he was taking printable iconographs.'

'What about you?'

'I'm staying. I don't trust them, especially when they're so sneaky. They seemed very ... *low-class* people,' said Sacharissa. 'But what are we going to *do*?'

William bit his thumbnail and stared at his desk. When he moved his feet a boot fetched up against the money chest with a reassuring thud.

'We could cut down a bit, I daresay,' said Goodmountain.

'Yes, but then people won't buy the paper,' said Sacharissa. 'And they *ought* to buy our paper, because it's got real news in it.'

'The news in the *Inquirer* looks more interesting, I have to admit,' said Goodmountain.

'That's because it doesn't actually have to have any facts in it!' she snapped. 'Now, I don't mind going back to a dollar a day and Otto says he'd work for half a dollar if he can go on living in the cellar.'

William was still staring at nothing. 'Apart from the truth,' he said in a distant voice, 'what have we got that the Guild hasn't got? Can we print faster?'

'One press against three? No,' said Goodmountain. 'But I bet we can set type faster.'

'And that means . . . ?'

'We can probably beat them in getting the first paper on to the street.'

'Okay. That might help. Sacharissa, do you know anyone who wants a job?'

'Know? Haven't you been looking at the letters?'

'Not as such . . .'

'Lots of people want a job! This is Ankh-Morpork!'

'All right, find the three letters with the fewest spelling mistakes and send Rocky round to hire the writers.'

'One of them was Mr Bendy,' Sacharissa warned. 'He wants more work. Not many interesting people are dying. Did you know he attends meetings for fun and very carefully writes down everything that's said?'

'Does he do it accurately?'

'I'm sure he does. He's exactly that sort of person. But I don't think we've got the space—'

'Tomorrow morning we'll go to four pages. Don't look like that. I've got more stuff about Vetinari, and we've got, oh, twelve hours to get some paper.'

'I told you, King won't sell us any more paper at a decent price,' said Goodmountain.

'There's a story right there, then,' said William.

'I mean—'

'Yes, I know. I've got some stuff to write, and then you and I will go to see him. Oh, and send someone to the semaphore tower, will you? I want to send a clacks to the King of Lancre. I think I met him once.'

'Clacks cost money. Lots of money.'

'Do it anyway. We'll find the money somehow.' William leaned over towards the cellar ladder. 'Otto?'

The vampire emerged to waist height. He was holding a half-dismantled iconograph in his hand.

'Vot can I do for you?'

'Can you think of anything extra we can do to sell more papers?'

'Vot do you vant *now*? Pictures that jump out of zer page? Pictures zat talk? Pictures vhere zer eyes follow you around zer room?'

'There's no need to take offence,' said William. 'It wasn't as if I asked for colour or anything—'

'Colour?' said the vampire. 'Is that all? Colour iss easy-peasy. How soon do you vant it?'

'Can't be done,' said Goodmountain firmly.

'Oh, zo you say? Is there somevhere here that makes coloured glass?'

'Yeah, I know the dwarf who runs the stained-glass works in Phedre Road,' said Goodmountain. 'They do hundreds of shades, but—'

'I vish to see samples right now. And of inks, too. You can get coloured inks alzo?'

'That's easy,' said the dwarf, 'but you'd need hundreds of different ones . . . wouldn't you?'

'No, ziss is not so. I vill make you a list of vot I reqvire. I cannot promise a Burleigh & Ztronginzerarm job first cat out of zer bag, off course. I mean you should not ask me for zer subtle play of light on autumn leafs or anyzing like zat. But zomething with stronk shades should be fine. Zis vill be okay?'

'It'd be amazing.'

'Zank you.'

William stood up. 'And now,' he said, 'let's go and see the King of the Golden River.'

'I've always been puzzled why people call him that,' said Sacharissa. 'I mean, there's no river of gold around here, is there?'

'Gentlemen.'

Mr Slant was waiting in the hall of the empty house. He stood up when the New Firm entered and clutched his briefcase. He looked as if he was in an unusually bad temper.

'Where have you been?'

'Getting a bite, Mr Slant. You didn't turn up this morning, and Mr Tulip gets hungry.'

'I *told* you to maintain a very low profile.'

'Mr Tulip isn't good at low profiles. Anyway, it all went off well. You must have heard. Oh, we nearly got killed because you didn't tell us a lot of stuff, and that's going to cost you but, hey, who cares about us? What's the problem?'

Mr Slant glared at them. 'My time is valuable, Mr Pin. So I will not spin this out. What did you do with the dog?'

'No one said anything to us about that dog,' said Mr Tulip, and Mr Pin knew he'd got the tone wrong.

'Ah, so you encountered the dog,' said Mr Slant. 'Where is it?'

'Gone. Ran off. Bit our —ing legs and ran off.'

Mr Slant sighed. It was like the wind from an ancient tomb.

'I *did* tell you that the Watch has a werewolf on the staff,' he said.

'Well? So what?' said Mr Pin.

'A werewolf would have no difficulty in talking to a dog.'

'What? You're telling us people will listen to a *dog*?' said Mr Pin.

'Unfortunately, yes,' said Mr Slant. 'A dog has got personality. Personality counts for a lot. And the legal precedents are clear. In the history of this city, gentlemen, we have put on trial at various times seven pigs, a tribe of rats, four horses, one flea and a swarm of bees. Last year a parrot was allowed as a prosecution witness in a serious murder case, and I had to arrange a witness protection scheme for it. I believe it is now pretending to be a very large budgerigar a long way away.' Mr Slant shook his head. 'Animals, alas, have their place in a court of law. There are all kinds of objections that could be made but the point *is*, Mr Pin, that Commander Vimes *will* build a case on it. He will start questioning . . . people. He already *knows* things are not right, but he has to work within the bounds of proof and evidence, and he has neither. If he finds the dog, I think things will unravel.'

'Slip him a few thousand dollars,' said Mr Pin. 'That always works with watchmen.'

'I believe that the last person who tried to bribe Vimes still doesn't have full use of one of his fingers,' said Mr Slant.

'We did everything you —ing told us!' shouted Mr Tulip, pointing a sausage-thick finger.

Mr Slant looked him up and down, as if seeing him for the first time.

'"Kill the Cook!!!"' he said. 'How amusing. However, I understood that we were employing *professionals*.'

Mr Pin had seen this one coming and once again caught Mr Tulip's fist in mid-air, being momentarily lifted off his feet.

'The *envelopes*, Mr Tulip,' he sang. 'This man *knows* things . . .'

'Hard to know any —ing thing when you're *dead*,' snarled Mr Tulip.

'Actually the mind becomes crystal clear,' said Mr Slant. He stood up and Mr Pin noticed how a zombie rises, using pairs of muscles in turn, not so much standing as unfolding upwards.

'Your . . . *other* assistant is still safe?' Slant said.

'Back down in the cellar, drunk as a skunk,' said Mr Pin. 'I don't see why we don't just scrag him right now. He nearly turned and ran when he saw Vetinari. If the man hadn't been so surprised we'd have been in big trouble. Who'd notice one more corpse in a city like this?'

'The Watch, Mr Pin. How many times must I tell you this? They are uncannily good at noticing things.'

'Mr Tulip here won't leave 'em much to notice—'
Mr Pin stopped. 'The Watch frighten you *that* much,
do they?'

'This is Ankh-Morpork,' snapped the lawyer. 'We are
a very cosmopolitan city. Being dead in Ankh-Morpork
is sometimes only an inconvenience, do you understand? We have wizards, we have mediums of all sizes.
And bodies do have a habit of turning up. We want
nothing that is going to give the Watch a clue, do you
understand?'

'They'd listen to a —ing dead man?' said Mr Tulip.

'I don't see why not. *You* are,' said the zombie. He
relaxed a little. 'Anyway, it is always possible that there
may be further use for your ... colleague. Some
further little outing to convince the unconvinced. He
is too valuable an asset to ... *retire* just yet.'

'Yeah, okay. We'll keep him in a bottle. But we want
extra for the dog,' said Mr Pin.

'It's only a *dog*, Mr Pin,' said Slant, raising his eyebrows. 'Even Mr Tulip could out-think a dog, I
expect.'

'Got to *find* the dog first,' said Mr Pin, stepping
smartly in front of his colleague. 'Lots of dogs in this
town.'

The zombie sighed again. 'I can add another five
thousand dollars in jewels to your fee,' he said. He
held up a hand. 'And please don't insult both of us by
saying "ten" automatically. The task is not hard.
Lost dogs in this town either end up running with one
of the feral packs or begin a new life as a pair of
gloves.'

'I want to know who's giving me these orders,' said

Mr Pin. He could feel the weight of the Dis-organizer inside his jacket.

Mr Slant looked surprised. 'Me, Mr Pin.'

'Your clients, I meant.'

'Oh, really!'

'This is going to get political,' Mr Pin persisted. 'You can't fight politics. I'm going to need to know how far we've got to run when people find out what happened. And who's going to protect us if we're caught.'

'In this city, gentlemen,' said Mr Slant, 'the facts are never what they seem. Take care of the dog, and . . . others will look after you. There are plans afoot. Who can say what really happened? People are easily confused, and here I speak as one who has spent centuries in court rooms. Apparently, they say, a lie can run round the world before the truth has got its boots on. What an obnoxious little phrase, don't you think? So . . . do not panic, and all will be well. And do not be stupid, either. My . . . clients have long memories and deep pockets. Other killers can be hired. Do you understand me?' He snapped the catches on his case. 'Good day to you.'

The door swung to behind him.

There was a rattling behind Mr Pin as Mr Tulip pulled out his set of stylish executive barbecue tools.

'What are you doing?'

'That —ing zombie is going to end up on the end of a couple of —ing handy and versatile kebab skewers,' said Mr Tulip. 'An' then I'm gonna put an edge on this —ing spatula. An' then . . . then I'm gonna get *medieval* on his arse.'

There were more pressing problems, but this one intrigued Mr Pin.

'How, exactly?' he said.

'I thought maybe a maypole,' said Mr Tulip reflectively. 'An' then a display of country dancing, land tillage under the three-field system, several plagues and, if my —ing hand ain't too tired, the invention of the —ing horse collar.'

'Sounds good,' said Mr Pin. 'Now let's find that damn dog.'

'How we gonna do that?'

'Intelligently,' said Mr Pin.

'I hate that —ing way.'

He was called King of the Golden River. This was a recognition of his wealth and achievements and the source of his success, which was not quite the *classical* river of gold. It was a considerable advance on his former nickname, which was Piss Harry.

Harry King had made his fortune by the careful application of the old adage: where there's muck there's brass. There was *money* to be made out of things that people threw away. Especially the very *human* things that people threw away.

The real foundations of his fortune came when he started leaving empty buckets at various hostelries around the city centre, especially those that were more than a gutter's length from the river. He charged a very modest fee to take them away when they were full. It became part of the life of every pub landlord; they'd hear a *clank* in the middle of the night and turn over in their sleep content in the knowledge that one of Piss Harry's men was, in a small way, making the world a better-smelling place.

They didn't wonder what happened to the full buckets, but Harry King had learned something that can be the key to great riches: there is very little, however disgusting, that isn't used somewhere in some industry. There are people out there who *want* large quantities of ammonia and saltpetre. If you can't sell it to the alchemists then the farmers probably want it. If even the farmers don't want it then there is nothing, *nothing*, however gross, that you can't sell to the tanners.

Harry felt like the only man in a mining camp who knows what gold looks like.

He started taking on whole streets at a time, and branched out. In the well-to-do areas the householders paid him, *paid him*, to take away night soil, the by now established buckets, the horse manure, the dustbins and even the dog muck. Dog muck? Did they have any *idea* how much the tanners paid for the finest white dog muck? It was like being paid to take away squishy diamonds.

Harry couldn't help it. The world fell over itself to give him money. Someone, somewhere, would *pay* him for a dead horse or two tons of prawns so far beyond their best-before date it couldn't be seen with a telescope, and the most wonderful part of all was that *someone had already paid him to take them away*. If anything absolutely failed to find a buyer, not even from the catmeat men, not even from the tanners, not even from Mr Dibbler himself, there were his mighty compost heaps downstream of the city, where the volcanic heat of decomposition made fertile soil ('10p a bag, bring your own bag . . .') out of everything that was left including, according to rumour, various shadowy businessmen who had come second in a takeover battle ('. . . brings up your dahlias a treat').

He'd kept the woodpulp-and-rags business closer to home, though, along with the huge vats that contained the golden foundations of his fortune, because it was the only part of his business that his wife Effie would talk about. Rumour had it that she had also been behind the removal of the much-admired sign over the entrance to his yard, which said: H. King – Taking the Piss Since 1961. Now it read: H. King – Recycling Nature's Bounty.

A small door within the large gates was opened by a troll. Harry was very forward-looking when it came to employing the non-human races, and had been among the first employers in the city to give a job to a troll. As far as organic substances were concerned, they had no sense of smell.

'Yus?'

'I'd like to speak to Mr King, please.'

'What abaht?'

'I want to buy a considerable amount of paper from him. Tell him it's Mr de Worde.'

'Right.'

The door slammed shut. They waited. After a few minutes the door opened again.

'Der King will see you now,' the troll announced.

And so William and Goodmountain were led into the yard of a man who, rumour said, was stockpiling used paper hankies against the day somebody found a way of extracting silver from bogeys.

On either side of the door huge black Rottweilers flung themselves against the bars of their day cages. Everyone knew Harry let them have the run of the yard at night. He made *sure* that everyone knew. And any nocturnal miscreant would have to be really *good* with dogs unless they wanted to end up as a few pounds of Tanners' Grade 1 (White).

The King of the Golden River had his office in a two-storey shed overlooking the yard, from where he could survey the steaming mounds and cisterns of his empire.

Even half hidden by his big desk Harry King was an enormous man, pink and shiny faced, with a few strands of hair teased across his head; it was hard to imagine him not in shirtsleeves and braces, even when he wasn't, or not smoking a huge cigar, which he'd never been seen without. Perhaps it was some kind of defence against the odours which were, in a way, his stock in trade.

''evenin', lads,' he said amiably. 'What can I do for you? As if I didn't know.'

'Do you remember me, Mr King?' said William.

Harry nodded. 'You're Lord de Worde's son, right? You put a piece in that letter of yourn last year when our Daphne got wed, right? My Effie was that impressed, all those nobs reading about our Daphne.'

'It's a rather bigger letter now, Mr King.'

'Yes, I did hear about that,' said the fat man. 'Some of 'em's already turnin' up in our collections. Useful stuff, I'm getting the lads to store it sep'rate.'

His cigar shifted from one side of his mouth to the other. Harry could not read or write, a fact which had never stopped him besting those who could. He employed hundreds of workers to sort through the garbage; it was cheap enough to employ a few more who could sort through words.

'Mr King—' William began.

'I ain't daft, lads,' said Harry. 'I know why you're here. But business is business. You know how it is.'

'We won't *have* a business without paper!' Goodmountain burst out.

The cigar shifted again. 'And you'd be . . .?'

'This is Mr Goodmountain,' said William. 'My printer.'

'Dwarf, eh?' said Harry, looking Goodmountain up and down. 'Nothing against dwarfs, me, but you ain't good sorters. Gnolls don't cost much but the grubby little buggers eat half the rubbish. Trolls are okay. They stop with me 'cos I pays 'em well. Golems is best – they'll sort stuff all day and all night. Worth their weight in gold, which is bloody near what they want payin' these days.' The cigar began another journey back across the mouth. 'Sorry, lads. A deal's a deal. Wish I could help you. Sold right out of paper. Can't.'

'You're knocking us back, just like that?' said Goodmountain.

Harry gave him a narrow-eyed look through the haze.

'You talking to me about knocking back? Don't know what a tosheroon is, do you?' he said. The dwarf shrugged.

'Yes. I do,' said William. 'There's several meanings, but I think you're referring to a big caked ball of mud and coins, such as you might find in some crevice in an old drain where the water forms an eddy. They can be quite valuable.'

'What? You've got hands on you like a girl,' said Harry, so surprised that the cigar momentarily drooped. 'How come you know *that*?'

'I like words, Mr King.'

'I started out as a muckraker when I was three,' said Harry, pushing his chair back. 'Found me first tosheroon on day one. O' course, one of the big kids nicked it off me right there. And you tell me about being knocked back? But I had a nose for the job even then. Then I . . .'

They sat and listened, William more patiently than Goodmountain. It *was* fascinating, anyway, if you had the right kind of mind, although he knew a lot of the story; Harry King told it at every opportunity.

Young Harry King had been a mudlark with vision, combing the banks of the river and even the surface of the turbid Ankh itself for lost coins, bits of metal, useful lumps of coal, *anything* that had some value *somewhere*. By the time he was eight he was employing other kids. Whole stretches of the river belonged to him. Other gangs kept away, or were taken over. Harry wasn't a bad fighter, and he could afford to employ those who were better.

And so it had gone on, the ascent of the King through horse manure sold by the bucket (guaranteed well stamped-down) to rags and bones and scrap metal and household dust and the famous buckets, where the future really was golden. It was a kind of history of civilization, but seen from the bottom looking up.

'You're not a member of a Guild, Mr King?' said William, during a pause for breath.

The cigar travelled from one side to the other and back quite fast, a sure sign that William had hit a nerve.

'Damn Guilds,' said its owner. 'They said I should join the Beggars! Me! I never begged for nothin', not in my whole life! The *nerve*! But I've seen 'em all off. I won't deal with no Guild. I pay my lads well and they stand by me.'

'It's the Guilds that are trying to break us, Mr King. You *know* that. I know you get to hear about everything. If you can't sell us paper, we've lost.'

'What'd I be if I broke a deal?' said Harry King.

'This is my tosheroon, Mr King,' said William. 'And the kids who want to take it off me are *big*.'

Harry was silent for a while and then lumbered to his feet and crossed to the big window.

'Come and look here, lads,' he said.

At one end of the yard was a big treadmill, operated by a couple of golems. It powered a creaking endless belt which crossed most of the yard. At the other end, several trolls with broad shovels fed the belt from a heap of trash that was itself constantly refilled by the occasional cart.

Lining the belt itself were golems and trolls and even the occasional human. In the flickering torch-light they watched the moving debris carefully. Occasionally a hand would dart out and pitch something into a bin behind the worker.

'Fish heads, bones, rags, paper ... I got twenty-seven different bins so far, including one for gold and silver, 'cos you'd be amazed what gets thrown away by mistake. Tinkle, tinkle, little spoon, wedding ring will follow soon ... That's what I used to sing to my little girls. Stuff like your paper of news goes in bin six, Low Grade Paper Waste. I sells most of that to Bob Holtely up in Five and Seven Yard.'

'What does he do with it?' said William, noting the 'Low Grade'.

'Pulps it for lavatory paper,' said Harry. 'The wife swears by it. Pers'n'ly I cut out the middle man.' He sighed, apparently oblivious of the sudden sag in William's self-esteem. 'Y'know, sometimes I stand here of an evenin' when the line is rumbling and the sunset is shinin' on the settlin' tanks and, I don't mind admitting it, a tear comes to my eye.'

'To tell you the truth, it comes to mine, too, sir,' said William.

'Now then, lad ... when that kid nicked my first tosheroon, I didn't go around complaining, did I? I knew I'd got an eye for it, see? I carried on, and I found plenty more. And on my eighth birthday I paid a couple of trolls to seek out the man who'd pinched my first one and slap seven kinds of snot out of him. Did you know that?'

'No, Mr King.'

Harry King stared at William through the smoke. William felt that he was being turned over and examined, like something found in the trash.

'My youngest daughter, Hermione ... she's getting

married at the end of next week,' said Harry. 'Big show. Temple of Offler. Choirs and everything. I'm inviting all the top nobs. Effie insisted. They won't come, o' course. Not for Piss Harry.'

'The *Times* would have been there, though,' said William. 'With coloured pictures. Except we go out of business tomorrow.'

'Coloured, eh? You get someone to paint 'em in, do you?'

'No. We've ... got a special way,' said William, hoping against hope that Otto was serious. He wasn't just out on a limb here, he was dangerously out of the tree.

'That'd be something to see,' said Harry. He took out his cigar, stared reflectively at the end and put it back in his mouth. Through the smoke he watched William carefully.

William felt the distinct unease of a well-educated man who has to confront the fact that the illiterate man watching him could probably out-think him three times over.

'Mr King, we really *need* that paper,' he said, to break the thoughtful silence.

'There's something about you, Mr de Worde,' said the King. 'I buy and sell clerks when I need them, and you don't smell like a clerk to me. You've got the air about you of a man who'd scrabble through a ton o' shit to find a farthin', and I'm wonderin' why that is.'

'Look, Mr King, will you *please* sell us some paper at the old price?' said William.

'Couldn't do that. I *told* you. A deal's a deal. The Engravers've paid me,' said Harry shortly.

William opened his mouth but Goodmountain laid a hand on his arm. The King was clearly working his way to the end of a line of thought.

Harry went over to the window again and stared pensively at the yard with its steaming piles. Then . . .

'Oh, will you look at that,' he said, stepping back from the window in tremendous astonishment. 'See that cart at the other gate down there?'

They saw the cart.

'I must've told the lads a hundred times, don't leave a cart all laden up and ready to go right by an open gate like that. Someone'll nick it, I told 'em.'

William wondered who'd steal anything from the King of the Golden River, a man with all those red-hot compost heaps.

'That's the last quarter of the order for the Engravers' Guild,' said Harry, to the world in general. 'I'd have to repay 'em if it got half-inched right out of my yard. I'll have to tell the foreman. He's getting forgetful these days.'

'We should be *leaving*, William,' said Goodmountain, grabbing William's arm again.

'Why? We haven't—'

'However can we repay you, Mr King?' said the dwarf, dragging William towards the door.

'The bridesmaids'll be wearing oh-de-nill, whatever that is,' said the King of the Golden River. 'Oh, and if I don't get eighty dollars from you by the end of the month you lads will be in deep' – the cigar did a double length of the mouth – 'trouble. Head downwards.'

Two minutes later the cart was creaking out of the

yard, under the curiously uninterested eyes of the troll foreman.

'No, it's *not* stealing,' said Goodmountain emphatically, shaking the reins. 'The King pays the bastards back their money and we pay him the old price. So we're all happy except for the *Inquirer*, and who cares about them?'

'I didn't like the bit about the deep pause trouble,' said William. 'Head downwards.'

'I'm shorter'n you so I lose out either way up,' said the dwarf.

After watching the cart disappear the King yelled downstairs for one of his clerks and told him to fetch a copy of the *Times* from Bin Six. He sat impassively, except for the oscillating cigar, while the stained and crumpled paper was read to him.

After a while his smile broadened and he asked the clerk to read a few extracts again.

'Ah,' he said, when the man had finished. 'I reckoned that was it. The boy's a born muckraker. Shame for him he was born a long way from honest muck.'

'Shall I do a credit note for the Engravers, Mr King?'

'Aye.'

'You reckon you'll get your money back, Mr King?'

Harry King usually didn't take this sort of thing from clerks. They were there to do the adding-up, not discuss policy. On the other hand, Harry had made a fortune seeing the sparkle in the mire, and sometimes you had to recognize expertise when you saw it.

'What colour's oh-de-nill?' he said.

'Oh, one of those difficult colours, Mr King. A sort of light blue with a hint of green.'

'Could you get ink that colour?'

'I could find out. It'd be expensive.'

The cigar made its traverse from one side of Harry King to the other. He was known to dote on his daughters, who he felt had suffered rather from having a father who needed to take two baths just to get dirty.

'We shall just have to keep an eye on our little writing man,' he said. 'Tip off the lads, will you? I wouldn't like to see our Effie disappointed.'

The dwarfs were working on the press again, Sacharissa noticed. It seldom stayed the same shape for more than a couple of hours. The dwarfs designed as they went along.

It looked to Sacharissa that the only tools a dwarf needed were his axe and some means of making fire. That'd eventually get him a forge, and with that he could make simple tools, and with those he could make complex tools, and with *complex* tools a dwarf could more or less make anything.

A couple of them were rummaging around in the industrial junk that had been piled against the walls. A couple of metal mangles had been melted down for their iron already, and the rocking horses were being used to melt lead. One or two of the dwarfs had left the shed on mysterious errands, too, and had returned carrying small sacks and furtive expressions. A dwarf is also very good at making use of things other people have thrown away, even if they haven't actually thrown them away yet.

She was turning her attention to a report of the Nap Hill Jolly Pals annual meeting when a crash and some cursing in Uberwaldean, a good cursing language, made her run over to the cellar entrance.

'Are you all right, Mr Chriek? Do you want me to get the dustpan and brush?'

'*Bodrozvachski zhaltziet!* ... oh, sorry, Miss Sacharissa! Zere has been a minor pothole on zer road to progress.'

Sacharissa made her way down the ladder.

Otto was at his makeshift bench. Boxes of demons hung on the wall. Some salamanders dozed in their cages. In a big dark jar, land eels slithered. But a jar next to it was broken.

'I vas clumsy and knocked it over,' said Otto, looking embarrassed. 'And now zer stupid eel 'as gone behind the bench.'

'Does it bite?'

'Oh no, zey are very lazy wretches—'

'What *is* this you've been working on, Otto?' Sacharissa said, turning to look closer at something big on the bench.

He tried to dart in front of her. 'Oh, it is all very experimental—'

'The way of making coloured plates?'

'Yes, but it is just a crude lash-up—'

Sacharissa caught sight of a movement out of the corner of her eye. The escaped land eel, having got bored behind the bench, was making a very sluggish bid for new horizons where an eel could wriggle proud and horizontal.

'Please don't—' Otto began.

'Oh, it's all right, I'm not at all squeamish . . .'

Sacharissa's hand closed on the eel.

She came to with Otto's black handkerchief being flapped desperately in her face.

'Oh, my goodness . . .' she said, trying to sit up.

Otto's face was a picture of such terror that Sacharissa forgot her own splitting headache for a moment.

'What's happened to *you*?' she said. 'You look *terrible*.'

Otto jerked back, tried to stand up and half collapsed against the bench, clutching at his chest.

'Cheese!' he moaned. 'Please get me some cheese! Or a big apple! Something to *bite*! *Pleeease!*'

'There's nothing like that down here—'

'Keep avay from me! And do not breathe like zat!' Otto wailed.

'Like what?'

'Zer bosoms going in and out and up and down like zat! I am a *vampire*! A fainting young lady, please understand, zer panting, zer heaving of zer bosoms . . . it calls somezing terrible from vithin . . .' With a lurch he pushed himself upright and gripped the black twist of ribbon from his lapel. '*But I vill be stronk!*' he screamed. 'I vill not let everyvun down!'

He stood stiffly to attention, although slightly blurred because of the vibration shaking him from head to foot, and in a trembling voice sang: '*Oh vill you come to zer mission, vill you come, come, come, Zere's a nice cup of tea and a bun, and a bun—*'

The ladder was suddenly alive with tumbling dwarfs.

'Are you all right, miss?' said Boddony, running forward with his axe. 'Has he *tried* anything?'

'No, no! He's—'

'—*zer drink zat's in zer livink vein, Is not zer drink for me*—' Sweat was running down Otto's face. He stood with one hand pressed over his heart.

'That's right, Otto!' shouted Sacharissa. 'Fight it! Fight it!' She turned to the dwarfs. 'Have any of you got any raw meat?'

'—*to life anew and temperance too, And to pure cold vater ve'll come*—' Veins were throbbing on Otto's pale head.

'Got some fresh rat fillets upstairs,' muttered one of the dwarfs. 'Cost me tuppence . . .'

'You get them right now, Gowdie,' snapped Boddony. 'This looks bad!'

'—*oh ve can drink brandy and gin if it's handy, and ve can sup vhisky and rum, but zer drink ve abhor and ve drink no more, is zer*—'

'Tuppence is tuppence, that's all I'm saying!'

'Look, he's starting to *twitch*!' said Sacharissa.

'And he can't sing, either,' said Gowdie. 'All right, all right, I'm going, I'm going . . .'

Sacharissa patted Otto's clammy hand.

'You can beat it!' she said urgently. 'We're all here for you! Aren't we, everyone? *Aren't we?*' Under her baleful gaze the dwarfs responded with a chorus of half-hearted 'yesses', even though Boddony's expression suggested that he wasn't certain what Otto was here for.

Gowdie came back with a small package. Sacharissa snatched it out of his hand and held it out to Otto, who reared back.

'No, it's just rat!' said Sacharissa. 'Perfectly okay! You're allowed rat, right?'

Otto froze for a moment and then snatched up the packet.

He bit into it.

In the sudden silence Sacharissa wondered if she wasn't hearing a very faint sound, like the straw at the bottom of a milkshake.

After a few seconds Otto opened his eyes and then looked sidelong at the dwarfs. He dropped the packet.

'Oh, vot shame! Vhere can I put my face? Oh, vot must you think of me . . . ?'

Sacharissa clapped with desperate enthusiasm. 'No, no! We're all very impressed! *Aren't we*, everyone?' Out of Otto's sight, she waved one hand very deliberately at the dwarfs. There was another ragged chorus of agreement.

'I mean, I haf been going through "cold bat" now for more than three months,' muttered Otto. 'It is such a disgusting thing to break down now and—'

'Oh, raw meat's *nothing*,' said Sacharissa. 'That's allowed, isn't it?'

'Yes, but for a second there I nearly—'

'Yes, but you *didn't*,' said Sacharissa. 'That's what's important. You wanted to and didn't.' She turned to the dwarfs. 'You can all go back to what you were doing,' she said. 'Otto is *perfectly* all right now.'

'Are you sure—' Boddony began, and then nodded. He'd rather have argued with a wild vampire than Sacharissa at this moment. 'Right you are, miss.'

Otto sat down, wiping his forehead, as the dwarfs filed out.

Sacharissa patted his hand. 'Do you want a drink—'

'Oh!'

'—of *water*, Otto?' said Sacharissa.

'No, no, everythink is okay, I think. Uh. Oh dear. My goodness. I am so sorry. You think you are on top of it, and then suddenly it all comes back to you. Vot a day . . .'

'Otto?'

'Yes, miss?'

'What actually happened when I grabbed the eel, Otto?'

He winced. 'I think zis is maybe not the time—'

'Otto, I *saw* things. There were . . . flames. And people. And noise. Just for a moment. It was like watching a whole day go past in a second! What *happened*?'

'Vell,' Otto said reluctantly, 'you know how salamanders absorb light?'

'Yes, of course.'

'Vell, zer eels absorb *dark* light. Not *darkness*, exactly, but zer light vithin darkness. Dark light . . . you see, dark light . . . vell, it has not been properly studied. It is heavier than normal light, you see, so most of it is under zer sea or in zer really deep caves in Uberwald, but zer is always a little of it even in *normal* darkness. It really is very fascinating—'

'It's a kind of magical light. Right. Could we just get more towards the point a bit?'

'I have heard it said that dark light is zer *original* light from vhich all other types of light came—'

'Otto!'

He held up a pale hand. 'I haf to tell you these things! Haf you heard the theory that there is no such thing as zer present? Because if it is divisible, then it cannot *be* zer present, and if it is not divisible, then it cannot have a beginning which connects to zer past and an end that connects to zer future? The philosopher Heidehollen tells us that the universe is just a cold soup of time, all time mixed up together, and vot we call zer *passage of time* is merely qvantum fluctuations in zer fabric of space-time.'

'You have very long winter evenings in Uberwald, don't you?'

'You see, dark light is held to be zer proof of this,' Otto went on, ignoring her. 'It is a light vithout time. Vot it illuminates, you see ... is not necessarily *now*.'

He paused, as if waiting for something.

'Are you saying it takes pictures of the *past*?' said Sacharissa.

'Or zer future. Or somevhere else. Of course, in reality zere is no difference.'

'And *all this* you point at people's heads?'

Otto looked worried. 'I *am* finding strange side things. Oh, zer dvarfs say that dark light has odd ... effects, but zey are very superstitious people so I did not take that seriously. However ...'

He scrabbled among the debris on his bench and picked up an iconograph.

'Oh, dear. Zis is so complicated,' said Otto. 'Look,

zer philosopher Kling says zer mind has a dark side and a light side, you see, and dark light . . . is seen by zer dark eyes of zer mind . . .'

He paused again.

'Yes?' said Sacharissa politely.

'I vas vaiting for zer roll of thunder,' said the vampire. 'But, alas, zis is not Uberwald.'

'You've lost me there,' said Sacharissa.

'Vell, you see, if I vas to say something portentous like "zer dark eyes of zer mind" back home in Uberwald, zer would be a sudden crash of thunder,' said Otto. 'And if I vas to point at a castle on a towering crag and say "Yonder is . . . *zer castle*" a volf would be bound to howl mournfully.' He sighed. 'In zer old country, zer scenery is psychotropic and knows vot is expected of it. Here, alas, people just look at you in a funny vay.'

'All right, all right, it's a magical light that takes uncanny pictures,' said Sacharissa.

'That's a very . . . *newspaper* vay of putting it,' said Otto politely. He showed her the iconograph. 'Look at zis vun. I vanted a picture of a dvarf vorking in the Patrician's study and I *got* zis.'

The picture was a wash of blurs and swirls, and there was a *vague* outline of a dwarf, lying down on the floor and examining something. But superimposed on this was quite a clear picture of Lord Vetinari. *Two* pictures of Lord Vetinari, each figure staring at the other.

'Well, it's his office and he's always in there,' said Sacharissa. 'Does the . . . magic light pick that up?'

'Maybe,' said Otto. 'Ve know that vot is physically zere is not alvays vot is *really zere*. Look at zis vun.'

He handed her another picture.

'Oh, that's a good one of William,' she said. 'In the cellar. And ... that's Lord de Worde standing just behind him, isn't it?'

'Is it?' said the vampire. 'I don't know zer man. I do know that he vas not in zer cellar ven I took the picture. But ... you only have to talk to Mr Villiam for any length of time to see that, in a *vay*, his father is alvays looking over his shoulder—'

'That's *creepy*.'

Sacharissa looked around the cellar. The stone walls were old and stained, but they certainly weren't blackened.

'I just saw ... people. Men fighting. Flames. And ... silver rain. How can it rain underground?'

'I do not know. That's vy I study dark light.'

Noises above suggested that William and Goodmountain had returned.

'I wouldn't mention this to anyone else,' said Sacharissa, heading for the ladder. 'We've got enough to deal with. That's *creepy*.'

There was no name outside the bar, because those who knew what it was didn't need one. Those who didn't know what it was shouldn't go in. Ankh-Morpork's undead were, on the whole, a law-abiding bunch, if only because they knew the law paid them a certain amount of special attention, but if you walked into the place known as Biers on a dark night and had no business there, who would ever know?

For the vampires*, it was a place to hang up. For the werewolves, it was where you let your hair down. For the bogeymen, it was a place to come out of the closet. For the ghouls, it did a decent meat pasty and chips.

All eyes, and that was not the same thing as the number of heads multiplied by two, turned to the door when it creaked open. The newcomers were surveyed from dark corners. They wore black, but that didn't mean anything. Anyone could wear black.

They walked up to the bar and Mr Pin rapped on the stained wood.

The barman nodded. The important thing, he'd found, was to make sure ordinary people paid for their drinks as they bought them. It wasn't good business to let them run a tab. That showed an unwarranted optimism about the future.

'What can I—' he began, before Mr Tulip's hand caught him around the back of the neck and rammed his head down hard on the bar.

'I am not having a nice day,' said Mr Pin, turning to the world in general, 'and Mr Tulip here suffers from unresolved personality conflicts. Has anyone got any questions?'

An indistinct hand rose in the gloom.

'What cook?' said a voice.

Mr Pin opened his mouth to reply and then turned

---

* Those, that is, who weren't gathered around the harmonium at the Temperance Mission nervously singing songs about how much they liked cocoa.

to his colleague, who was examining the bar's array of very strange drinks. All cocktails are sticky; the ones in Biers tended to be stickier.

'Says "Kill the Cook!!!"' said the voice.

Mr Tulip rammed two long kebab skewers into the bar, where they vibrated. 'What cooks've you got?' he said.

'It's a *good* apron,' said the voice in the gloom.

'It is the —ing envy of all my friends,' Mr Tulip growled.

In the silence Mr Pin *heard* the unseen drinkers calculating the likely number of friends of Mr Tulip. It was not a calculation that would involve a simple thinker taking off their shoes.

'Ah. Right,' said someone.

'Now, we don't want any trouble with you people,' said Mr Pin. 'Not as such. We simply wish to meet a werewolf.'

Another voice in the gloom said: 'Vy?'

'Got a job for him,' said Mr Pin.

There was some muffled laughter in the darkness and a figure shuffled forward. It was about the size of Mr Pin; it had pointy ears; it had a hairstyle that clearly continued to its ankles, inside its ragged clothes. Tufts of hair stuck out of holes in its shirt and densely thatched the backs of its hands.

''m part werewolf,' it said.

'Which part?'

'That's a funny joke.'

'Can you talk to dogs?'

The self-confessed part-werewolf looked around at its unseen audience, and for the first time Mr Pin felt a twinge of disquiet. The sight of Mr Tulip's slowly spinning eye and throbbing forehead were not having their usual effect. There were rustlings in the dark. He was sure he heard a snigger.

'Yep,' said the werewolf.

The hell with this, thought Mr Pin. He pulled out his pistol bow in one practised movement and held it an inch from the werewolf's face.

'This is tipped with silver,' he said.

He was amazed at the speed of movement. Suddenly a hand was against his neck and five sharp points pressed into his skin.

'These ain't,' said the werewolf. 'Let's see who finishes squeezin' first, eh?'

'Yeah, right,' said Mr Tulip, who was also holding something.

'That's just a barbecue fork,' said the werewolf, giving it barely a glance.

'You want to see how —ing fast I can throw it?' said Mr Tulip.

Mr Pin tried to swallow, but got only halfway. Dead people, he knew, didn't squeeze that hard, but it was at least ten steps to the door and the space seemed to be getting wider by the heart beat.

'Hey,' he said. 'There's no need for this, right? Why don't we all loosen up? And, hey, it would help me talk to you if you were your normal shape . . .'

'No problem, my friend.'

The werewolf winced and shuddered, but without at any point letting go of Mr Pin's neck. The face contorted so much, features flowing together, that even Mr Pin, who in other circumstances quite enjoyed that sort of thing, had to look away.

This allowed him to see the shadow on the wall. It was, contrary to expectations, growing. So were its ears.

'Any qvestions?' said the werewolf. Now its teeth seriously interfered with its speech. Its breath smelled even worse than Mr Tulip's suit.

'Ah . . .' said Mr Pin, standing on tiptoe. 'I think we've come to the wrong place.'

'I think zat also.'

At the bar Mr Tulip bit the top off a bottle in a meaningful way.

Once again the room was filled with the ferocious silence of calculation and the personal mathematics of profit and loss.

Mr Tulip smashed a bottle against his forehead. At this point, he did not appear to be paying much attention to the room. He'd just happened to have a bottle in his hand which he did not need any more. Putting it on to the bar would have required an unnecessary expenditure of hand-eye co-ordination.

People recalculated.

'Is he *human*?' said the werewolf.

'Well, of course, "human" is just a word,' said Mr Pin.

He felt weight slowly press down on to his toes as he was lowered to the floor.

'I think perhaps we'll just be going,' he said carefully.

'Right,' said the werewolf. Mr Tulip had smashed open a big jar of pickles, or at least things that were long, chubby and green, and was trying to insert one up his nose.

'If we wanted to stay, we would,' said Mr Pin.

'Right. But you want to go. So does your . . . friend,' said the werewolf.

Mr Pin backed towards the door. 'Mr Tulip, we have business elsewhere,' he said. 'Sheesh, take the damn pickle out of your nose, will you? We're supposed to be professionals!'

'That's not a pickle,' said a voice in the dark.

Mr Pin was uncharacteristically thankful when the door slammed behind them. To his surprise, he also heard the bolts shoot home.

'Well, that could have gone better,' he said, brushing dust and hair off his coat.

'What now?' said Mr Tulip.

'Time to think of a plan B,' said Pin.

'Why don't we just —ing hit people until someone tells us where the dog is?' said Mr Tulip.

'Tempting,' said Mr Pin. 'But we'll leave that for plan C—'

'Bugrit.'

They both turned.

'Bent treacle edges, I told 'em,' said Foul Ole Ron, lurching across the street, a wad of *Times*es under one arm and the string of his nondescript mongrel in his other hand. He caught sight of the New Firm.

'Harglegarlyurp?' he said. '*Lay*arrrB*nip*! You gents want a paper?'

It seemed to Mr Pin that the last sentence, while in pretty much the same voice, had an intrusive, not-quite-right quality. Apart from anything else, it made sense.

'You got some change?' he said to Mr Tulip, patting his pockets.

'You're going to —ing *buy* one?' said his partner.

'There's a time and a place, Mr Tulip, a time and a place. Here you are, mister.'

'Millennium hand and shrimp, bugrit,' said Ron, adding, 'Much obliged, gents.'

Mr Pin opened the *Times*. 'This thing has got—' He stopped and looked closer.

' "Have You Seen This Dog?" ' he said. 'Sheesh . . .' He stared at Ron.

'You sell lots of these things?' he said.

'Qeedle the slops, I told 'em. Yeah, hundreds.'

There it was again, the slight sensation of two voices.

'Hundreds,' said Mr Pin. He looked down at the paper seller's dog. It looked pretty much like the one in the paper, but all terriers looked alike. Anyway, this one was on a string. 'Hundreds,' he said again, and read the short article again.

He stared. 'I think we have a plan B,' he said.

At ground level the newspaper seller's dog watched them carefully as they walked away.

'That was too close for comfort,' it said, when they'd turned the corner.

Foul Ole Ron put down his papers in a puddle and pulled a cold sausage from the depths of his hulking coat.

He broke it into three equal pieces.

* * *

The Ankh-Morpork Times

'THE TRUTH SHALL MAKE YE FRED' • EXTRA!

☞ HAVE YOU SEEN THIS DOG? ☜
$25 Reward for Information

William had dithered over that, but the Watch had supplied quite a good drawing and he felt right now that a little friendly gesture in that direction would be a good idea. If he found himself in deep trouble, head downwards, he'd need someone to pull him out.

He had rewritten the Patrician story, too, adding as much as he was certain of, and there wasn't much of that. He was, frankly, stuck.

Sacharissa had penned a story about the opening of the *Inquirer*. William had hesitated about this, too. But it *was* news, after all. They couldn't just ignore it, and it filled some space.

Besides, he liked the opening line, which began: 'A would-be rival to Ankh-Morpork's old-established newspaper, the *Times*, has opened in Gleam Street . . .'

'You're getting good at this,' he said, looking across the desk.

'Yes,' she said. 'I now know that if I see a naked man I should definitely get his name and address, because—'

William joined in the chorus: '—names sell newspapers.'

He sat back and drank the really horrible tea the dwarfs made. Just for a moment there was an unusual feeling of bliss. Strange word, he thought. It's one of those words that described something that does not make a noise but if it *did* make a noise would sound just like that. *Bliss*. It's like the sound of a soft meringue melting gently on a warm plate.

Here, and now, he was free. The paper was put to bed, tucked up, had its prayers listened to. It was *finished*. The crew were already filing back in for more copies, cursing and spitting; they'd commandeered a variety of old trolleys and prams to cart their papers out into the streets. Of course, in an hour or so the mouth of the press would be hungry again and he'd be back pushing the huge rock uphill, just like that character in mythology ... what was his name ...?

'Who was that hero who was condemned to push a rock up a hill and every time he got it to the top it rolled down again?' he said.

Sacharissa didn't look up. 'Someone who needed a wheelbarrow?' she said, spiking a piece of paper with some force.

William recognized the voice of someone who still has an annoying job to do.

'What are you working on?' he said.

'A report from the Ankh-Morpork Recovering Accordion Players Society,' she said, scribbling fast.

'Is there something wrong with it?'

'Yes. The punctuation. There isn't any. I think we might have to order an extra box of commas.'

'Why are you bothering with it, then?'

'Twenty-six people are mentioned by name.'

'As accordionists?'

'Yes.'

'Won't they complain?'

'They didn't *have* to play the accordion. Oh, and there was a big crash on Broad Way. A cart overturned and several tons of flour fell on to the road, causing a couple of horses to rear and upset their cartload of fresh eggs, and *that* caused another cart to shed thirty churns of milk ... So what do you think of this as a headline?'

She held up a piece of paper on which she'd written:

CITY'S BIGGEST CAKE MIX-UP!!

William looked at it. Yes. Somehow it had everything. The sad attempt at humour was exactly right. It was just the sort of thing that would cause much mirth around Mrs Arcanum's table.

'Lose the second exclamation mark,' he said. 'Otherwise I think it's perfect. How did you hear about it?'

'Oh, Constable Fiddyment dropped in and told me,' said Sacharissa. She looked down and shuffled papers unnecessarily. 'I think he's a bit sweet on me, to tell you the truth.'

A tiny, hitherto-unregarded bit of William's ego instantly froze solid. An awful lot of young men seemed happy to tell Sacharissa things. He heard himself say: 'Vimes doesn't want any of his officers to speak to us.'

'Yes, well, I don't think telling me about a lot of smashed eggs counts, does it?'

'Yes, but—'

'Anyway, I can't help it if young men want to tell me things, can I?'

'I suppose not, but—'

'Anyway, that's it for tonight.' Sacharissa yawned. 'I'm going home.'

William got up so quickly he skinned his knees on the desk. 'I'll walk you there,' he said.

'Good grief, it's nearly a quarter to eight,' said Sacharissa, putting on her coat. 'Why do we keep on working?'

'Because the press doesn't go to sleep,' said William.

As they stepped out into the silent street he wondered if Lord Vetinari had been right about the press. There was something . . . *compelling* about it. It was like a dog that stared at you until you fed it. A slightly dangerous dog. Dog bites man, he thought. But that's not news. That's *olds*.

Sacharissa let him walk her to the end of her street, where she made him stop.

'It'll embarrass Grandfather if you're seen with me,' she said. 'I know it's stupid, but . . . neighbours, you know? And all this Guild stuff . . .'

'I know. Um.'

The air hung heavy for a moment as they looked at each other.

'Er, I don't know how to put this,' said William, knowing that sooner or later it had to be said, 'but I ought to say that, though you are a very attractive girl, you're not my type.'

236

She gave him the *oldest* look he had ever seen, and then said: 'That took a lot of saying, and I would like to thank you.'

'I just thought that with me and you working together all the time—'

'No, I'm glad one of us said it,' she said. 'And with smooth talk like that I bet you have the girls just lining up, right? See you tomorrow.'

He watched her walk down the street to her house. After a few seconds a lamp went on in an upper window.

By running very fast he arrived back at his lodgings just late enough for a Look from Mrs Arcanum, but not so late as to be barred from the table for impoliteness; serious latecomers had to eat their supper at the table in the kitchen.

It was curry tonight. And one of the strange things about eating at Mrs Arcanum's was that you got more leftovers than you got original meals. That is, there were far more meals made up from what were traditionally considered the prudently usable remains of earlier meals – stews, bubble-and-squeak, curry – than there were meals at which those remains could have originated.

The curry was particularly strange, since Mrs Arcanum considered foreign parts only marginally less unspeakable than private parts and therefore added the curious yellow curry powder with a very small spoon, lest everyone should suddenly tear their clothes off and do foreign things. The main ingredients appeared to be swede and gritty rainwater-tasting sultanas and the remains of some cold mutton, although William couldn't remember when they'd had the original mutton, at any temperature.

This was not a problem for the other lodgers. Mrs Arcanum provided big helpings, and they were men who measured culinary achievement by the amount you got on your plate. It might not taste astonishing, but you went to bed full and that was what mattered.

At the moment, the news of the day was being discussed. Mr Mackleduff had bought the *Inquirer* and both editions of the *Times*, in his role as keeper of the fire of communication.

It was generally agreed that the news in the *Inquirer* was more interesting, although Mrs Arcanum ruled that the whole subject of snakes was not one for the dinner table and papers ought not to be allowed to disturb people like this. Rains of insects and so on, though, fully confirmed everyone's view of distant lands.

Olds, thought William, forensically dissecting a sultana. His lordship was right. Not news but *olds*, telling people that what they think they already know is true . . .

The Patrician, it was agreed, was a shifty one. The meeting concurred that they were all alike, the lot of them. Mr Windling said the city was in a mess and there ought to be some changes. Mr Longshaft said that he couldn't speak for the city, but from what he had heard the gemstone business had been very brisk of late. Mr Windling said that it was all right for some. Mr Prone put forth the opinion that the Watch could not find their bottom with both hands, a turn of phrase that almost earned him a place at the kitchen table to finish his meal. It was agreed that Vetinari had done it all right and should be put away. The main course adjourned at 8.45 p.m., and was followed by disintegrating plums in runny custard, Mr Prone getting slightly fewer plums as an unspoken reprimand.

William went up to his room early. He had adapted to Mrs Arcanum's cuisine, but nothing except radical surgery would make him like her coffee.

He lay down on the narrow bed in the dark (Mrs Arcanum supplied one candle weekly, and what with one thing and another he had forgotten to buy any extra) and tried to *think*.

Mr Slant walked across the floor of the empty ballroom, his feet echoing on the wood.

He took his position in the circle of candlelight with a slight twanging of nerves. As a zombie, he was always a little edgy about fire.

He coughed.

'Well?' said a chair.

'They didn't get the dog,' said Mr Slant. 'In all other respects, I have to say, they did a masterly job.'

'How bad could it be if the Watch find it?'

'As I understand it, the dog in question is quite old,' said Mr Slant, into the candlelight. 'I have instructed Mr Pin to look for it, but I don't believe he will find it easy to get access to the city's canine underground.'

'There are other werewolves here, aren't there?'

'Yes,' said Mr Slant smoothly. 'But they won't help. There are very few of them, and Sergeant Angua of the Watch is *very* important in the werewolf

239

community. They won't help strangers, because she *will* find out.'

'And bring the Watch down on them?'

'I believe she would not bother with the Watch,' said Slant.

'The dog is probably in some dwarf's stewpot by now,' said a chair. There was general laughter.

'If things go . . . wrong,' said a chair, 'who do these men know?'

'They know me,' said Mr Slant. 'I would not worry unduly. Vimes works by the rules.'

'I've always understood him to be a violent and vicious man,' said a chair.

'Quite so. And because this is what he knows himself to be, he always works by the rules. In any case, the Guilds will be meeting tomorrow.'

'Who will be the new Patrician?' said a chair.

'That will be a matter for careful discussion and the consideration of all shades of opinion,' said Mr Slant. His voice could have oiled watches.

'Mr Slant?' said a chair.

'Yes?'

'Do not try that on us. It *is* going to be Scrope, isn't it?'

'Mr Scrope is certainly well thought of by many of the leading figures in the city,' said the lawyer.

'Good.'

And the musty air was loud with unspoken conversation.

Absolutely no one needed to say: A lot of the most powerful men in the city owe their positions to Lord Vetinari.

And nobody replied: Certainly. But to the kind of men who seek power, gratitude has very poor keeping qualities. The kind of men who seek power tend to deal with *matters as they are*. They would never try to depose Vetinari, but if he was gone then they would *be practical*.

No one said: Will anyone speak up for Vetinari?

Silence replied: Oh, *everyone*. They'll say things like: 'Poor fellow . . . it was the strain of office, you know.' They'll say: 'It's the quiet ones that crack.' They'll say: 'Quite so . . . We should put him somewhere where he can do no harm to himself or others. Don't you think?' They'll say: 'Perhaps a small statue would be in order, too?' They'll say: 'The least we can do is call off the Watch, we owe him that much.' They'll say: 'We must look to the future.' And so, quietly, things change. No fuss, and very little mess.

No one said: Character assassination. What a wonderful idea. Ordinary assassination only works once, but this one works every day.

A chair *did* say: 'I wondered whether Lord Downey or even Mr Boggis—'

Another chair said: 'Oh, *come* now! Why should they? Much better this way.'

'True, true. Mr Scrope is a man of fine qualities.'

'A good family man, I understand.'

'Listens to the common people.'

'Not *just* to the common people, I trust?'

'Oh, no. He's very open to advice. From informed . . . focus groups.'

'He'll need plenty of that.'

No one said: He's a useful idiot.

'Nevertheless . . . the Watch will have to be brought to heel.'

'Vimes *will* do what he is told. He *must* do. Scrope will be at least as legitimate a choice as Vetinari was. Vimes is the kind of man who must have a boss, because that gives him legitimacy.'

Slant coughed. 'Is that all, gentlemen?' he said.

'What about the *Ankh-Morpork Times*?' said a chair. 'Bit of a problem shaping up there?'

'People find it amusing,' said Mr Slant. 'And nobody takes it seriously. The *Inquirer* outsells it two to one already, after just one day. And it is underfinanced. And it has, uh, difficulty with supplies.'

'Good tale in the *Inquirer* about that woman and the snake,' said a chair.

'Was there?' said Mr Slant.

The chair that had first mentioned the *Times* had something on its mind.

'I'd feel happier if a few likely lads smashed up the press,' it said.

'That would attract attention,' said a chair. 'The *Times wants* attention. The . . . writer craves to be noticed.'

'Oh, well, if you insist.'

'I would not dream of insisting. But the *Times* will collapse,' said the chair, and this was the chair that other chairs listened to. 'The young man is also an idealist. He has yet to find out that what's in the public interest is not what the public is interested in.'

'Say again?'

'I mean, gentlemen, that people probably think he's

doing a good job, but what they are buying is the *Inquirer*. The news is more interesting. Did I ever tell you, Mr Slant, that a lie will go round the world before the truth has got its boots on?'

'A great many times, sir,' said Slant, with slightly less than his usual keen diplomacy. He realized this, and added, 'A valuable insight, I'm sure.'

'Good.' The most important chair sniffed. 'Keep an eye on our . . . workmen, Mr Slant.'

It was midnight in the Temple of Om in the Street of Small Gods, and one light burned in the vestry. It was a candle in a very heavy ornate candlestick and it was, in a way, sending a prayer to heaven. The prayer, from the Gospel According to the Miscreants, was: don't let anyone find us pinching this stuff.

Mr Pin rummaged in a cupboard.

'I can't find anything in your size,' he said. 'It looks as though— Oh, no . . . sheesh, incense is for *burning*.'

Tulip sneezed, pebble-dashing the opposite wall with sandalwood.

'You could've —ing told me before,' he muttered. 'I've got some papers.'

'Have you been Chasing the Oven Cleaner again?' said Mr Pin accusingly. 'I want you focused, understand? Now, the only thing I can find in here that will fit you—'

The door creaked open and a small elderly priest wandered into the room. Mr Pin instinctively grasped the big candlestick.

'Hello? Are you here for the, mm, midnight service?' said the old man, blinking in the light.

243

This time it was Tulip who grabbed Mr Pin's arm as he raised the candlestick.

'Are you mad? What kind of person are you?' he growled.

'What? We can't let him—'

Mr Tulip snatched the silver stick out of his partner's hand.

'I mean, *look* at the —ing thing, will you?' he said, ignoring the bemused priest. 'That's a genuine Sellini! Five hundred years old! Look at the chasing work on that snuffer, will you? Sheesh, to you it's nothing more than five —ing pounds of silver, right?'

'Actually, mm, it's a Futtock,' said the old priest, who still hadn't yet got up to mental speed.

'What, the pupil?' said Mr Tulip, his eyes ceasing their spin out of surprise. He turned the candlestick over and looked at the base. 'Hey, that's right! There's the Sellini mark, but it's stamped with a little "f", too. First time I've ever seen his —ing early stuff. He was a better —ing silversmith, too, it's just a shame he had such a —ing stupid name. You know how much it'd sell for, Reverend?'

'We thought about seventy dollars,' said the priest, looking hopeful. 'It was in a lot of furniture that an old lady left to the church. Really, we kept it for sentimental value . . .'

'Have you still got the box it came in?' said Mr Tulip, turning the candlestick over and over in his hands. 'He did wonderful —ing presentation boxes. Cherrywood.'

'Er . . . no, I don't think so . . .'

'—ing shame.'

'Er . . . is it still worth anything? I think we've got another one somewhere.'

'To the right collector, maybe four thousand —ing dollars,' said Mr Tulip. 'But I reckon you could get twelve thousand if you've got a —ing pair. Futtock is very collectable at the moment.'

'Twelve thousand!' burbled the old man. His eyes gleamed with a deadly sin.

'Could be more,' Mr Tulip nodded. 'It's a —ing delightful piece. I feel quite privileged to have seen it.' He looked sourly at Mr Pin. 'And you were going to use it as a —ing blunt instrument.'

He put the candlestick reverentially on the vestry table and buffed it carefully with his sleeve. Then he spun round and brought his fist down hard on the head of the priest, who folded up with a sigh.

'And they were just keepin' it in a —ing cupboard,' he said. 'Honestly, I could —ing *spit*!'

'You want to take it with us?' said Mr Pin, stuffing clothes into a bag.

'Nah, all the fences round here'd probably just melt it down for the silver,' said Mr Tulip. 'I couldn't have something like that on my —ing conscience. Let's find this —ing dog and get right out of this dump, shall we? It makes me so —ing *despondent*.'

William turned over, woke up and stared wide-eyed at the ceiling.

Two minutes later Mrs Arcanum came downstairs and into the kitchen armed with a lamp, a poker and most importantly with her hair in curlers. The combination would be a winner against all but the most iron-stomached intruder.

'Mr de Worde! What *are* you doing? It's midnight!'

William glanced up and then went back to opening cupboards. 'Sorry I knocked the saucepans over, Mrs Arcanum. I'll pay for any damage. Now, *where* are the scales?'

'Scales?'

'Scales! Kitchen scales! Where are they?'

'Mr de Worde, I—'

'Where are the damn scales, Mrs Arcanum?' said William desperately.

'Mr de Worde! For shame!'

'The future of the city hangs in the balance, Mrs Arcanum!'

Perplexity slowly took the place of stern affront. 'What, in *my* scales?'

'Yes! Yes! It could very well be!'

'Well, er . . . they're in the pantry by the flour bag. The whole city, you say?'

'Quite possibly!' William felt his jacket sag as he forced the big brass weights into his pocket.

'Use the old potato sack, do,' said Mrs Arcanum, now quite flustered by events.

William grabbed the sack, rammed everything in and ran for the door.

'The University and the river and everything?' said the landlady nervously.

'Yes! Yes indeed!'

Mrs Arcanum set her jaw. 'You will wash it out *thoroughly* afterwards, won't you?' she said to his retreating back.

William's progress slowed towards the end of the

road. Big iron kitchen scales and a full set of weights aren't carried lightly.

But that was the point, wasn't it? Weight! He ran and walked and dragged them through the freezing, foggy night until he reached Gleam Street.

The lights were still on in the *Inquirer* building. How late do you need to stay up when you can make up the news as you go along? thought William. But *this* is real. Heavy, even.

He hammered on the door of the *Times* shed until a dwarf opened up. The dwarf was amazed to see a frantic William de Worde rush past and drop the scales and weights on a desk.

'Please get Mr Goodmountain up. We've got to get out another edition! And can I have ten dollars, please?'

It took Goodmountain to sort things out when, night-shirted but still firmly helmeted, he clambered out of the cellar.

'No, ten *dollars*,' William was explaining to the bewildered dwarfs. 'Ten dollar *coins*. Not ten dollars' worth of money.'

'Why?'

'To see how much seventy thousand dollars weigh!'

'We haven't got seventy thousand dollars!'

'Look, even one dollar coin would do,' said William patiently. 'Ten dollars would just be more accurate, that's all. I can work it out from there.'

Ten assorted coins were eventually procured from the dwarfs' cash box and were duly weighed. Then William turned to a fresh page in his notebook and bent his head in ferocious calculation. The dwarfs watched him solemnly, as if he was conducting an alchemical experiment. Finally he looked up from his figures, the light of revelation in his eyes.

'That's almost a third of a ton,' he said. 'That's how much seventy thousand dollar coins weigh. I suppose a really good horse could carry that *and* a rider, but . . . Vetinari walks with a stick, you *saw* him. It'd take him for ever to load the horse up, and even if he got away he could hardly travel fast. Vimes must have worked it out. He *said* the facts were stupid facts!'

Goodmountain had stationed himself before the rows of cases. 'Ready when you are, chief,' he said.

'All right . . .' William hesitated. He knew the facts, but what did the facts suggest?

'Er . . . make the heading: "Who framed Lord Vetinari?" and then the story starts . . . er . . .' William watched the hand pounce and grab among the little boxes of type, 'A . . . er . . . "Ankh-Morpork City Watch now believe that at least one other person was involved in the . . . the . . ."'

'Fracas?' suggested Goodmountain.

'No.'

'Rumpus?'

'". . . in the *attack* at the palace on Tuesday night."' William waited until the dwarf had caught up. It was getting easier and easier to read the words forming in Goodmountain's hands as the fingers jumped from box to box: m-i-g-h-t . . .

'You got an m for an n there,' he said.

'Oh, yes. Sorry. Carry on.'

'Er . . . "Evidence suggests that far from attacking

his clerk as believed, Lord Vetinari may have discovered a crime in progress."'

The hand flew across the type . . . *c-r-i-m-e-space-i-n* . . .

It stopped.

'Are you *sure* about this?' said Goodmountain.

'No, but it's as good a theory as any other,' said William. 'That horse hadn't been loaded to escape, it had been loaded to be *discovered*. Someone had some plan and it went wrong. I'm sure of *that* at least. Right . . . new paragraph. "A horse in the stables had been loaded with a third of a ton of coins, but in his current state of health the Patrician—"'

One of the dwarfs had lit the stove. Another was stripping out the formes that contained the last edition. The room was coming alive again.

'That's about eight inches plus the heading,' said Goodmountain, when William had finished. 'That should rattle people. You want to add any more stuff? Miss Sacharissa did something about Lady Selachii's ball, and there's a few small things.'

William yawned. He didn't seem to be getting enough sleep these days.

'Put them in,' he said.

'And there's this clacks from Lancre that came in when you'd gone home,' said the dwarf. 'That'll cost us another 50p for the messenger. You remember you sent a clacks this afternoon? About snakes?' he added, in the face of William's blank expression.

William read the flimsy sheet of paper. The message had been carefully transcribed in the neat handwriting of the semaphore operator. It was probably the strangest message yet sent on the new technology.

King Verence of Lancre had also mastered the idea that the clacks charged by the word.

```
WOMEN OF LANCRE NOT RPT NOT IN HABIT BEARING SNAKES
STOP CHILDREN BORN THIS MONTH WILLIAM WEAVER
CONSTANCE THATCHER CATASTROPHE CARTER ALL PLUS ARMS
LEGS MINUS SCALES FANGS
```

'Hah! We have them!' said William. 'Give me five minutes and I'll put together a story on this. We shall soon see if the sword of truth can't beat the dragon of lies.'

Boddony gave him a kind look. 'Didn't you say a lie can run round the world before the truth has got its boots on?' he said.

'But this is the *truth*.'

'So? Where's its boots?'

Goodmountain nodded to the other dwarfs, who were yawning. 'You get back to bed, lads. I'll pull it all together.'

He watched them disappear down the ladder to the cellar. Then he sat down, took out a small silver box and opened it.

'Snuff?' he said, offering the box to William. 'Best thing you humans ever invented. Watson's Red Roasted. Clears the mind a treat. No?'

William shook his head.

'What are you doing all this for, Mr de Worde?' said Goodmountain, taking a monstrous suction of snuff up each nostril.

'What do you mean?'

'I'm not saying we don't appreciate it, mark you,' said Goodmountain. 'It's keeping the money coming in. The jobbing stuff is drying up more every day. Seems like every engraving shop was poised to go over to printing. All we did was give the young rips an opening. They'll get us in the end, though. They've got money behind them. I don't mind saying some of the lads are talking about selling up and going back to the lead mines.'

'You can't do that!'

'Ah, well,' said Goodmountain. 'You *mean* you don't want us to. I understand that. But we've been putting money by. We should be all right. I daresay we can flog the press to someone. We might have a spot of cash to take back home. That's what this was all about. Money. What were you doing it for?'

'Me? Because—' William stopped. The *truth* was that he'd never decided to do *anything*. He'd never really made that kind of decision in his whole life. One thing had just gently led to another, and then the press had to be fed. It was waiting there now. You worked hard, you fed it, and it was still just as hungry an hour later and out in the world all your work was heading for Bin Six in Piss Harry's and that was only the *start* of its troubles. Suddenly he had a proper job, with working hours, and yet everything he did was only as real as a sandcastle, on a beach where the tide only ever came in.

'I don't know,' he admitted. 'I suppose it's because I'm no good at anything else. Now I can't imagine *doing* anything else.'

'But I heard your family's got pots of money.'

'Mr Goodmountain, I'm useless. I was educated to be useless. What we've always been supposed to do is hang around until there's a war and do something really stupidly brave and then get killed. What we've mainly done is hang on to things. Ideas, mostly.'

'You don't get on with them, then.'

'Look, I don't need a heart-to-heart about this, can you understand? My father is not a nice man. Do I have to draw you a picture? He doesn't much like me and I don't like him. If it comes to that, he doesn't like anyone very much. Especially dwarfs and trolls.'

'No law says you have to like dwarfs and trolls,' said Goodmountain.

'Yes, but there ought to be a law against disliking them the way he does.'

'Ah. *Now* you've drawn me a picture.'

'Maybe you've heard the term "lesser races"?'

'And now you've coloured it in.'

'He won't even live in Ankh-Morpork any more. Says it's polluted.'

'That's observant of him.'

'No, I mean—'

'Oh, I know what you mean,' said Goodmountain. 'I've met humans like him.'

'You said this was all about money?' said William. 'Is that true?'

The dwarf nodded at the ingots of lead stacked up neatly by the press. 'We wanted to turn lead into gold,' he said. 'We'd got a lot of lead. But we need gold.'

William sighed. 'My father used to say that gold is all dwarfs think about.'

'Pretty much.' The dwarf took another pinch of snuff. 'But where people go wrong is . . . see, if all a human thinks about is gold, well, he's a miser. If a dwarf thinks about gold, he's just being a dwarf. It's *diff'rent*. What do you call them black humans that live in Howondaland?'

'I know what my father calls them,' said William. 'But I call them "people who live in Howondaland".'

'Do you really? Well, I hear tell there's one tribe where, before he can get married, a man has to kill a leopard and give the skin to the woman? It's the same as that. A dwarf needs gold to get married.'

'What . . . like a dowry? But I thought dwarfs didn't differentiate between—'

'No, no, the two dwarfs getting married each buy the other dwarf off their parents.'

'*Buy?*' said William. 'How can you buy people?'

'See? Cultural misunderstanding once again, lad. It costs a lot of money to raise a young dwarf to marriageable age. Food, clothes, chain mail . . . it all adds up over the years. It needs repaying. After all, the other dwarf is getting a valuable commodity. And it has to be paid for in gold. That's *traditional*. Or gems. They're fine, too. You must've heard our saying "worth his weight in gold"? Of course, if a dwarf's been working for his parents that gets taken into account on the other side of the ledger. Why, a dwarf who's left off marrying till late in life is probably owed quite a tidy sum in wages – you're still looking at me in that funny way . . .'

'It's just that we don't do it like that . . .' mumbled William.

Goodmountain gave him a sharp look. 'Don't you, now?' he said. 'Really? What do you use instead, then?'

'Er . . . gratitude, I suppose,' said William. He wanted this conversation to stop, right now. It was heading out over thin ice.

'And how's that calculated?'

'Well . . . it isn't, as such . . .'

'Doesn't that cause problems?'

'Sometimes.'

'Ah. Well, we know about gratitude, too. But our way means the couple start their new lives in a state of . . . *g'daraka* . . . er, free, unencumbered, *new* dwarfs. *Then* their parents might well give them a huge wedding present, much bigger than the dowry. But it is between dwarf and dwarf, out of love and respect, not between debtor and creditor . . . though I have to say these human words are not really the best way of describing it. It works for us. It's worked for a thousand years.'

'I suppose to a human it sounds a bit . . . chilly,' said William.

Goodmountain gave him another studied look.

'You mean by comparison to the warm and wonderful ways humans conduct their affairs?' he said. 'You don't have to answer that one. Anyway, me and Boddony want to open up a mine together, and we're expensive dwarfs. We know how to work lead, so we thought a year or two of this would see us right.'

'You're getting married?'

'We want to,' said Goodmountain.

'Oh ... well, congratulations,' said William. He knew enough not to comment on the fact that both dwarfs looked like small barbarian warriors with long beards. All traditional dwarfs looked like that.*

Goodmountain grinned. 'Don't worry too much about your father, lad. People change. My grandmother used to think humans were sort of hairless bears. She doesn't any more.'

'What changed her mind?'

'I reckon it was the dying that did it.'

Goodmountain stood up and patted William on the shoulder. 'Come on, let's get the paper finished. We'll start the run when the lads wake up.'

Breakfast was cooking when William got back, and Mrs Arcanum was waiting. Her mouth was set in the firm line of someone hot on the trail of unrespectable behaviour.

'I shall require an explanation of last night's affair,' she said, confronting him in the hallway, 'and a week's notice, if you please.'

William was too exhausted to lie. 'I wanted to see how much seventy thousand dollars weighed,' he said.

Muscles moved in various areas of the landlady's face. She knew William's background, being the kind

---

* Most dwarfs were still referred to as 'he' as well, even when they were getting married. It was generally assumed that somewhere under all that chain mail one of them was female and that both of them knew which one this was. But the whole subject of sex was one that traditionally minded dwarfs did not discuss, perhaps out of modesty, possibly because it didn't interest them very much and certainly because they took the view that what two dwarfs decided to do together was entirely their own business.

of woman who finds out about that kind of thing very quickly, and the twitching was a sign of some internal struggle based around the definite fact that seventy thousand dollars was a *respectable* sum.

'I may perhaps have been a *little* hasty,' she ventured. 'Did you find out how much the money weighed?'

'Yes, thank you.'

'Would you like to keep the scales for a few days in case you want to weigh any more?'

'I think I've finished the weighing, Mrs Arcanum, but thank you all the same.'

'Breakfast has already begun, Mr de Worde, but . . . well, perhaps I can make allowances this time.'

He was given a second boiled egg, too. This was a rare sign of favour.

The latest news was already the subject of deep discussion.

'I am frankly amazed,' said Mr Cartwright. 'It beats me how they find this stuff out.'

'It certainly makes you wonder what's going on that we aren't told,' said Mr Windling.

William listened for a while, until he couldn't wait any longer.

'Something interesting in the paper?' he asked innocently.

'A woman in Kicklebury Street says her husband has been kidnapped by elves,' said Mr Mackleduff, holding up the *Inquirer*. The heading was very clear on the subject:

ELVES STOLE MY HUSBAND!

'That's made up!' said William.

'Can't be,' said Mackleduff. 'There's the lady's name and address, right there. They wouldn't put that in the paper if they were telling lies, would they?'

William looked at the name and address. 'I *know* this lady,' he said.

'There you are, then!'

'*She* was the one last month who said her husband had been carried off by a big silver dish that came out of the sky,' said William, who had a good memory for this sort of thing. He'd nearly put it in his news letter as an 'On a lighter note' but had thought better of it. 'And you, Mr Prone, said everyone *knew* her husband had carried himself off with a lady called Flo who used to work as a waitress in Harga's House of Ribs.'

Mrs Arcanum gave William a sharp look which said that the whole subject of nocturnal kitchenware theft could be reopened at any time, extra egg or no.

'I am not partial to that kind of talk at the table,' she said coldly.

'Well, then, it's obvious,' said Mr Cartwright. 'He must've come back.'

'From the silver dish or from Flo?' said William.

'Mr de Worde!'

'I was only asking,' said William. 'Ah, I see they're revealing the name of the man who broke into the jeweller's the other day. Shame it's Done It Duncan, poor old chap.'

'A notorious criminal, by the sound of it,' said Mr Windling. 'It's shocking that the Watch won't arrest him.'

'Especially since he calls on them every day,' said William.

'Whatever for?'

'A hot meal and a bed for the night,' said William. 'Done It Duncan confesses to *everything*, you see. Original sin, murders, minor thefts ... everything. When he's desperate he tries to turn himself in for the reward.'

'Then they ought to do something about him,' said Mrs Arcanum.

'I believe they generally give him a mug of tea,' said William. He paused and then ventured: 'Is there anything in the other paper?'

'Oh, they're still trying to say that Vetinari didn't do it,' said Mr Mackleduff. 'And the King of Lancre says women in Lancre don't give birth to snakes.'

'Well, he would say that, wouldn't he?' said Mrs Arcanum.

'Vetinari must've done *something*,' said Mr Windling. 'Otherwise why would he be helping the Watch with their inquiries? That's not the action of an innocent man, in my humble opinion.'*

'I believe there's plenty of evidence that throws doubt on his guilt,' said William.

---

* The best way to describe Mr Windling would be like this: you are at a meeting. You'd like to be away early. So would everyone else. There really isn't very much to discuss, anyway. And just as everyone can see Any Other Business coming over the horizon and is already putting their papers neatly together, a voice says, 'If I can raise a minor matter, Mr Chairman . . .' and with a horrible wooden feeling in your stomach you *know*, now, that the evening will go on for twice as long with much referring back to the minutes of earlier meetings. The man who has just said that, and is now sitting there with a smug smile of dedication to the committee process, is as near Mr Windling

'Really,' said Mr Windling, making the word suggest that William's opinion was considerably more humble than his. 'Anyway, I understand the Guild leaders are meeting today.' He sniffed. 'It's time for a change. Frankly, we could do with a ruler who is a little more responsive to the views of ordinary people.'

William glanced at Mr Longshaft, the dwarf, who was peacefully cutting some toast into soldiers. Perhaps he hadn't noticed. Perhaps there was nothing *to* notice and William was being oversensitive. But years of listening to Lord de Worde's opinions had given him a certain ear. It told him when phrases like 'the views of ordinary people', innocent and worthy in themselves, were being used to mean that someone should be whipped.

'How do you mean?' he said.

'The ... city is getting too big,' said Mr Windling. 'In the old days the gates were kept shut, not left open to all and sundry. And people could leave their doors unlocked.'

'We didn't have anything worth stealing,' said Mr Cartwright.

'That's true. There's more money around,' said Mr Prone.

'It doesn't all stay here, though,' said Mr Windling. That was true, at least. 'Sending money home' was the major export activity of the city, and dwarfs were right

---

as makes no difference. And something that distinguishes the Mr Windlings of the universe is the term 'in my humble opinion', which they think *adds* weight to their statements rather than indicating, in reality, 'these are the mean little views of someone with the social grace of duckweed'.

at the front of it. William also knew that most of it came back again, because dwarfs bought from the best dwarf craftsmen and, mostly, the best dwarf craftsmen worked in Ankh-Morpork these days. And *they* sent money back home. A tide of gold coins rolled back and forth and seldom had a chance to go cold. But it upset the Windlings of the city.

Mr Longshaft quietly picked up his boiled egg and inserted it into an eggcup.

'There's just too many people in the city,' Mr Windling repeated. 'I've nothing against . . . outsiders, heavens know, but Vetinari let it go far too far. Everyone knows we need someone who is prepared to be a little more firm.'

There was a metallic noise. Mr Longshaft, still staring fixedly at his egg, had reached down and drawn a smallish but still impressively *axe-like* axe from his bag. Watching the egg carefully, as if it was about to run away, he leaned slowly back, paused for a moment, then brought the blade round in an arc of silver.

The top of the egg flew up with hardly a noise, turned over in mid-air several feet above the plate, and landed beside the eggcup.

Mr Longshaft nodded to himself and then looked up at the frozen expressions.

'I'm sorry?' he said. 'I wasn't listening.'

At which point, as Sacharissa would have put it, the meeting broke up.

William purchased his own copy of the *Inquirer* on the way to Gleam Street and wondered, not for the first time, who was writing this stuff. They were better at it than he would be, that was certain. He'd wondered once about making up a few innocent paragraphs, when not much was happening in the city, and found that it was a lot harder than it looked. Try as he might, he kept letting common sense and intelligence get the better of him. Besides, telling lies was Wrong.

He noted glumly that they'd used the talking dog story. Oh, and one he hadn't heard before: a strange figure had been seen swooping around the rooftops of Unseen University at night, HALF MAN HALF MOTH? Half invented and half made up, more likely.

The curious thing was, if the breakfast table jury was anything to go by, that denying stories like this only proved that they were true. After all, no one would bother to deny something if it didn't exist, would they?

He took a short cut through the stables in Creek Alley. Like Gleam Street, Creek Alley was there to mark the back of places. This part of the city had no real existence other than as a place you passed through to somewhere more interesting. The dull street was made up of high-windowed warehouses and broken-down sheds and, significantly, Hobson's Livery Stable.

It was huge, especially since Hobson had realized that you could go multi-storey.

Willie Hobson was another businessman in the mould of the King of the Golden River; he'd found a niche, occupied it and forced it open so wide that lots of money dropped in. Many people in the city occasionally needed a horse, and hardly anyone had a place to park one. You needed a stable, you needed a groom, you needed a hayloft . . . but to hire a horse from Willie you just needed a few dollars.

Lots of people kept their own horses there, too. People came and went all the time. The bandy-legged, goblin-like little men who ran the place never bothered to stop anyone unless they appeared to have hidden a horse about their person.

William looked around when a voice out of the gloom of the loose-boxes said, ''scuse me, friend.'

He peered into the shadows. A few horses were watching him. In the distance, around him, other horses were being moved, people were shouting, there was the general bustle of the stables. But the voice had come out of a little pool of ominous silence.

'I've still got two months to go on my last receipt,' he said to the darkness. 'And may I say that the free canteen of cutlery seemed to be made of an alloy of lead and horse manure?'

'I'm not a thief, friend,' said the shadows.

'Who's there?'

'Do you know what's good for you?'

'Er . . . yes. Healthy exercise, regular meals, a good night's sleep.' William stared at the long lines of loose-boxes. 'I think what you *meant* to ask was: do I know what's bad for me, in the general context of blunt instruments and sharp edges. Yes?'

'Broadly, yes. No, don't move, mister. You stand where I can see you and no harm will come to you.'

William analysed this. 'Yes, but if I stand where you *can't* see me, I don't see how any harm could come to me there, either.'

Something sighed. 'Look, meet me halfway here—No! Don't move!'

'But you said to—'

'Just stand still and shut up and *listen*, will you?'

'All right.'

'I am hearing where there's a certain dog that people are lookin' for,' said the mystery voice.

'Ah. Yes. The Watch want him, yes. And . . . ?' William thought he could just make out a slightly darker shape. More importantly, he could smell a Smell, even above the general background odour of the horses.

'Ron?' he said.

'Do I *sound* like Ron?' said the voice.

'Not . . . exactly. So who am I talking to?'

'You can call me . . . Deep Bone.'

'*Deep Bone?*'

'Anything wrong with that?'

'I suppose not. What can I do for you, Mr Bone?'

'Just supposin' someone knew where the doggie was but didn't want to get involved with the Watch?' said the voice of Deep Bone.

'Why not?'

'Let's just say the Watch can be trouble to a certain kind of person, eh? That's one reason.'

'All right.'

'And let's just say there's people around who'd much prefer the little doggie didn't tell what it knew, shall we? The Watch might not take enough care. They're very uncaring about dogs, the Watch.'

'Are they?'

263

'Oh yes, the Watch fink a dog has no human rights at all. That's another reason.'

'Is there a third reason?'

'Yes. I read in the paper where there's a reward.'

'Ah. Yes?'

'Only it got printed wrong, 'cos it said twenty-five dollars instead of a hundred dollars, see?'

'Oh. I *see*. But a hundred dollars is a lot of money for a dog, Mr Bone.'

'Not for this dog, if you know what I mean,' said the shadows. 'This dog's got a *story* to tell.'

'Oh, yes? It's the famous talking dog of Ankh-Morpork, is it?'

Deep Bone growled. 'Dogs can't talk, everyone knows that. But there's them as can understand dog language, if you catch my drift.'

'Werewolves, you mean?'

'Could be people of that style of kidney, yes.'

'But the only werewolf I know is in the Watch,' said William. 'So you're just telling me to pay you a hundred dollars so that I could hand Wuffles over to the Watch?'

'That'd be a feather in your cap with old Vimes, wouldn't it?' said Deep Bone.

'But *you* said you didn't trust the Watch, Mr Bone. I do *listen* to what people say, you know.'

Deep Bone went quiet for a while. Then:

'All right, the dog *and* an interpreter, one hundred and fifty dollars.'

'And the story this dog could tell deals with events in the palace a few mornings ago?'

'Could be. Could be. Could *very well* be.

Could be exactly the kind of fing I'm referrin' to.'

'I want to see who I'm talking to,' said William.

'Can't do that.'

'Oh, *well*,' said William. 'That's reassuring. I'll just go and get a hundred and fifty dollars, shall I, and bring it back to this place and hand it over to you, just like that?'

'Good idea.'

'Not a chance.'

'Oh, so you don't trust me, eh?' said Deep Bone.

'That's right.'

'Er . . . supposin' I was to tell you a little piece of free news information for gratis and nothin'. A lick of the lolly. A little taste, style of fing.'

'Go on . . .'

'It wasn't Vetinari who stabbed the other man. It was another man.'

William wrote this down, and then looked at it. 'Exactly how helpful is this?' he said.

'That's a good bit of news, that is. Hardly anyone knows it.'

'There's not a lot to know! Isn't there a description?'

'He's got a dog bite on his ankle,' said Deep Bone.

'That'll make him easy to find in the street, won't it? What are you expecting me to do, try a little surreptitious trouser lifting?'

Deep Bone sounded hurt. 'That's kosher news, that is. It'd worry certain people if you put that in your paper.'

'Yes, they'd worry that I'd gone mad! You've got to tell me something better than that! Can you give me a description?'

Deep Bone went silent for a while, and when the voice spoke again it sounded uncertain. 'You mean, what he looked like?' it said.

'Well, yes!'

'Ah . . . well, it dunt work like that with dogs, see? What w— what your average dog does, basic'ly, is look *up*. People are mostly just a wall with a pair of nostril holes at the top, is my point.'

'Not a lot of help, then,' said William. 'Sorry we can't do busin—'

'What he *smells* like, now, that's somethin' else,' said the voice of Deep Bone, hurriedly.

'All right, tell me what he *smells* like.'

'Do I see a pile of cash in front of me? I don't think so.'

'Well, Mr Bone, I'm not even going to *think* about getting that kind of money together until I've got some *proof* that you really know something.'

'All right,' said the voice from the shadows after a while. 'You know there's a Committee to Unelect the Patrician? Now *that's* news.'

'What's new about that? People have plotted to get rid of him for *years*.'

There was another pause.

'Y'know,' said Deep Bone, 'it'd save a lot of trouble if you just gave me the money and I told you everything.'

'So far you haven't told me anything. Tell me everything, and *then* I'll pay you, if it's the truth.'

'Oh, yes, pull one of the others, it's got bells on!'

'Then it looks like we can't do business,' said William, putting his notebook away.

'Wait, wait . . . this'll do. You ask Vimes what Vetinari did just before the attack.'

'Why, what did he do?'

'See if you can find out.'

'That's not a lot to go on.'

There was no reply. William thought he heard a shuffling noise.

'Hello?'

He waited a moment and then very carefully stepped forward.

In the gloom a few horses turned to look at him. Of an invisible informant there was no sign.

A lot of thoughts jostled for space in his mind as he headed out into the daylight, but surprisingly enough it was a small and theoretically unimportant one that kept oozing into centre stage. What kind of expression was 'pull one of the others, it's got bells on'? Now, 'pull the *other* one, it's got bells on', he'd heard of – it stemmed from the days of a crueller than usual ruler in Ankh-Morpork who had had any Morris dancers ritually tortured. But 'one of the others' . . . where was the sense in that?

Then it struck him.

Deep Bone must be a foreigner. It made sense. It was like the way Otto spoke perfectly good Morporkian but hadn't got the hang of colloquialisms.

He made a note of this.

He smelled the smoke at the same time as he heard the pottery clatter of golem feet. Four of the clay people thudded past him, carrying a long ladder. Without thinking he fell in behind, automatically turning to a new page in his notebook.

Fire was always the terror in those parts of the city where wood and thatch predominated. That was why everyone had been so dead set against any form of fire brigade, reasoning – with impeccable Ankh-Morpork logic – that any bunch of men who were paid to put out fires would naturally see to it that there was a plentiful supply of fires to put out.

Golems were different. They were patient, hard-working, intensely logical, virtually indestructible and they *volunteered*. Everyone knew golems couldn't harm people.

There was some mystery about how the golem fire brigade had got formed. Some said the idea had come from the Watch, but the generally held theory was that golems simply would not allow people and property to be destroyed. With eerie discipline and no apparent communication they would converge on a fire from all sides, rescue any trapped people, secure and carefully pile up all portable property, form a bucket chain along which the buckets moved at a blur, trample every last ember . . . and then hurry back to their abandoned tasks.

These four were hurrying to a blaze in Treacle Mine Road. Tongues of fire curled out of first-floor rooms.

'Are you from the paper?' said a man in the crowd.

'Yes,' said William.

'Well, I reckon this is another case of mysterious spontaneous combustion, just like you reported yesterday,' and he craned his neck to see if William was writing this down.

William groaned. Sacharissa *had* reported a fire in

Lobbin Clout, in which one poor soul had died, and had left it at that. But the *Inquirer* had called it a Mystery Fire.

'I'm not sure that one was *very* mysterious,' he said. 'Old Mr Hardy decided to light a cigar and forgot that he was bathing his feet in turpentine.' Apparently someone had told him this was a cure for athlete's foot and, in a way, they had been right.

'That's what they *say*,' said the man, tapping his nose. 'But there's a lot we don't get told.'

'That's true,' said William. 'I heard only the other day that giant rocks hundreds of miles across crash into the country every week, but the Patrician hushes it up.'

'There you are, then,' said the man. 'It's amazing the way they treat us as if we're stupid.'

'Yes, it's a puzzle to me, too,' said William.

'Gangvay, gangvay, please!'

Otto pushed through the onlookers, struggling under the weight of a device the size and general shape of an accordion. He elbowed his way to the front of the crowd, balanced the device on its tripod and aimed it at a golem who was climbing out of a smoking window holding a small child.

'All right, boys, zis is zer big vun!' he said, and raised the flash cage. 'Vun, two, thre—aarghaarghaarghaargh . . .'

The vampire became a cloud of gently settling dust. For a moment something hovered in the air. It looked like a small jar on a necklace made of string.

Then it fell and smashed on the cobbles.

The dust mushroomed up, took on a shape . . . and

Otto stood blinking and running his hands over himself to check that he was all there. He caught sight of William and gave him the kind of big broad smile that only a vampire can give.

'Mr Villiam! It vorked, your idea!'

'Er . . . which one?' said William. A thin plume of yellow smoke was creeping out from under the lid of the big iconograph.

'You said carry a little drop of emergency b-vord,' said Otto. 'Zo I thought: if it is in a little bottle around my neck, zen if I crumble to dust, hoopla! It vill crash and smash unt here I am!'

He lifted the lid of the iconograph and waved the smoke away. There was the sound of very small coughing from within. 'And if I am not mistaken, ve have a successfully etched picture! All of vich only goes to show vot ve can achieve ven our brains are not clouded by thoughts of open vindows and bare necks, vich never cross my mind at all zese days because I am completely beetotal.'

Otto had made changes to his clothing. Away had gone the traditional black evening dress preferred by his species, to be replaced by an armless vest containing more pockets than William had ever seen on one garment. Many of them were stuffed with packets of imp food, extra paint, mysterious tools and other essentials of the iconographer's art.

In deference to tradition, though, Otto had made it black, with a red silk lining, and had added tails.

On making gentle inquiries of a family watching disconsolately as the smoke from the fire was turned to steam, William ascertained that the blaze had been mysteriously caused by mysterious spontaneous combustion in an overflowing mysterious chip pan full of boiling fat.

William left them picking through the blackened remains of their home.

'And it's just a story,' he said, putting away the note-book. 'It does makes me feel a bit of a vampire— oh . . . sorry.'

'It is okay,' said Otto. 'I understand. And I should like to thank you for givink me zis job. It means a lot to me, especially since I can see how nervous you are. Vich is understandable, of course.'

'I'm not nervous! I'm very much at home with other species!' said William hotly.

Otto's expression was amicable, but it was also as penetrative as the smile of a vampire can be.

'Yes, I notice how careful you are to be friendly with the dvarfs and you are kind to me, also. It is a big effort vich is very commendable—'

William opened his mouth to protest, and gave up. 'All right, look, it's the way I was brought up, all right? My father was definitely very . . . in favour of humanity, well, ha, not humanity in the sense of . . . I mean, it was more that he was against—'

'Yes, yes, I understand.'

'And that's all there is to it, okay? We can all decide who we're going to be!'

'Yes, yes, sure. And if you vant any advice about vimmin, you only have to ask.'

'Why should I want advice about vi— women?'

'Oh, no reason. No reason at all,' said Otto innocently.

'Anyway, you're a vampire. What advice could a vampire give me about women?'

'Oh, my vord, vake up and smell zer garlic! Oh, zer stories I could tell you.' Otto paused. 'But I von't because I don't do zat sort of thing any more, now that I have seen the daylight.' He nudged William, who was red with embarrassment. 'Let us just say, zey don't *alvays* scream.'

'That's a bit tasteless, isn't it?'

'Oh, that vas in zer bad old days,' said Otto hurriedly. 'Now I like nothing better than a nice mug of cocoa and a good sing-song around zer harmonium, I assure you. Oh, yes. My vord.'

Getting into the office to write up the story turned out to be a problem. In fact, so was getting into Gleam Street.

Otto caught William up as he stood and stared.

'Vell, I suppose ve asked for it,' he shouted. 'Twenty-five dollars is a lot of money.'

'What?' shouted William.

'I SAID TVENTY-FIVE DOLLARS IS A LOT OF MONEY, VILLIAM!'

'WHAT?'

Several people pushed past them. They were carrying dogs. *Everyone* in Gleam Street was carrying a dog, or leading a dog, or being dragged by a dog, or being savaged, despite the owner's best efforts, by a dog belonging to someone else. The barking had already gone beyond mere sounds, and was now some kind of perceptible force, hitting the eardrums like a hurricane made of scrap iron.

William pulled the vampire into a doorway,

where the din was merely unbearable.

'Can't *you* do something?' he screamed. 'Otherwise we'll never get through!'

'Like vot?'

'Well, you know . . . all that *children of the night* business?'

'Oh, zat,' said Otto. He looked glum. 'Zat's really very stereotypical, you know. Vy don't you ask me to turn into a bat vhile you're about it? I told you, I don't do zat stuff no more!'

'Have you got a better idea?'

A few feet away a Rottweiler was doing its best to eat a spaniel.

'Oh, very *vell*.' Otto waved his hands vaguely.

The barking ceased instantly. And then every dog sat on its haunches and howled.

'Not a *huge* improvement, but at least they're not fighting,' said William, hurrying forward.

'Vell, I'm sorry. Stake me as you pass,' said Otto. 'I shall have a very embarrassing five minutes explaining this at the next meeting, you understand? I know it's not zer . . . sucking item, but I mean, vun should care about zer *look* of zer thing . . .'

They climbed over a rotting fence and entered the shed via the back door.

People and dogs were squeezing in through the other door and were only held at bay by a barricade of desks and also by Sacharissa, who was looking harassed as she faced a sea of faces and muzzles. William could just make out her voice above the din.

'—no, that's a poodle. It doesn't look a bit like the dog we're after—'

'—no, that's not it. How do I know? Because it's a *cat*. All right, then why's it washing itself? No, I'm sorry, dogs *don't* do that—'

'—no, madam, that's a bulldog—'

'—no, that's not it. No, sir, I *know* that's not it. Because it's a parrot, that's why. You've taught it to bark and you've painted "DoG" on the side of it but it's still a parrot—'

Sacharissa pushed her hair out of her eyes and caught sight of William.

'Well, now, who's been a clever boy?' she said.

'*Wh's a cl'r boy?*' said the DoG.

'How many more out there?'

'Hundreds, I'm afraid,' said William.

'Well, I've just had the most unpleasant half-hour of— That's a chicken! It's a *chicken*, you stupid woman, it's just laid an *egg*! – of my life and I would like to thank you *very* much. You'll never *guess* what happened! No, that's a Shnauswitzer! And you know what, William?'

'What?' said William.

'Some complete *muffin* offered a reward! In Ankh-Morpork! Can you believe that? They were queueing three deep when I got here! I mean, what kind of idiot would do a thing like that? I mean, one man had a cow! A *cow*! I had a huge argument about animal physiology before Rocky hit him over the head! The poor troll's out there now trying to keep order! There's *ferrets* out there!'

'Look, I'm *sorry*—'

'I wonder, ah, if we can be of any assistance?'

They turned.

The speaker was a priest, dressed in the black, unadorned and unflattering habit of the Omnians. He had a flat, broad-brimmed hat, the Omnians' turtle symbol around his neck, and an expression of almost terminal benevolence.

'Mm, I am Brother Upon-Which-The-Angels-Dance Pin,' said the priest, stepping aside to reveal a mountain in black, 'and this is Sister Jennifer, who is under a vow of *silence*.'

They stared up at the apparition of Sister Jennifer, while Brother Pin went on: 'That means she does not, mm, talk. *At all*. In *any* circumstances.'

'Oh dear,' said Sacharissa weakly. One of Sister Jennifer's eyes was revolving, in a face that was like a brick wall.

'Yes, mm, and we happened to be in Ankh-Morpork as part of the Bishop Horn Ministry to Animals and heard that you were looking for a little doggie who is in trouble,' said Brother Pin. 'I can see you are, mm, a little overwhelmed, and perhaps we can help? It would be our duty.'

'The dog's a little terrier,' said Sacharissa, 'but you'd be *amazed* at what people are bringing in—'

'Dear me,' said Brother Pin. 'But Sister Jennifer is *very* good at this sort of thing . . .'

Sister Jennifer strode to the front desk. A man hopefully held up what was clearly a badger.

'He's been a bit ill—'

Sister Jennifer brought her fist down on the man's head.

William winced.

'Sister Jennifer's order believes in tough love,' said

Brother Pin. 'A little correction at the right time can prevent a lost soul taking the wrong path.'

'Vich order is this she belongs to, please?' said Otto, as the lost soul carrying his badger staggered out, his legs trying to take several paths at once.

Brother Pin gave him a damp smile. 'The Little Flowers of Perpetual Annoyance,' he said.

'Really? I had not heard of zis vun. Very . . . out-reaching. Vell, I must go and see if the imps have done zere job properly . . .'

Certainly the crowd was thinning rapidly under the stress of seeing the advancing Sister Jennifer, especially that segment of it that had brought dogs which purred or ate sunflower seeds. Many of those who *had* brought an actual living dog were looking nervous as well.

A sense of unease crept over William. He knew that some sections of the Omnian church still believed that the way to send a soul to heaven was to give the body hell. And Sister Jennifer couldn't be blamed for her looks, or even the size of her hands. And even if the backs of said hands were rather hairy, well, that was the sort of thing that happened out in the rural districts.

'What exactly is she doing?' he said. There were yelps and shouts in the queue as dogs were grabbed, glared at and thrust back with more than minimum force.

'As I said, we're trying to find the little dog,' said Brother Pin. 'It may need ministering to.'

'But . . . that wire-haired terrier there looks pretty

much like the picture,' said Sacharissa. 'And she's just ignored it.'

'Sister Jennifer is very sensitive in these matters,' said Brother Pin.

'Oh well, this is not getting the next edition filled,' said Sacharissa, heading back to her desk.

'I expect it would help if we could print in colour,' said William, when he was left alone with Brother Pin.

'Probably,' said the reverend brother. 'It was a kind of greyish brown.'

William knew then that he was dead. It was only a matter of time.

'You *know* what colour you're looking for,' he said quietly.

'You just get on with sorting out the words, writer boy,' said Brother Pin, for his ears only. He opened the jacket of his frock coat just enough for William to see the range of cutlery holstered there, and closed it again. 'This isn't anything to do with you, okay? Shout out and someone gets killed. Try to be a hero and someone gets killed. Make any kind of sudden move and some-one gets killed. In fact, we might as well kill someone *anyway* and save some time, eh? You know that stuff about the pen being mightier than the sword?'

'Yes,' said William hoarsely.

'Want to try?'

'No.'

William caught sight of Goodmountain, who was staring at him.

'What's that dwarf doing?' said Brother Pin.

'He's setting type, sir,' said William. It was always wise to be polite to edged weapons.

'Tell him to get on with it,' said Pin.

'Er ... if you could just get on with it, Mr Goodmountain,' said William, raising his voice over the growls and yelps. 'Everything is fine.'

Goodmountain nodded and turned his back. He held up one hand theatrically and then started to assemble type.

William watched. It was better than semaphore, as the hand dipped from box to box.

Hes[space]a[space]fawe?

W was in the box next to K ...

'Yes indeed,' said William.

Pin glanced at him. 'Yes indeed what?'

'I, er, it was just nerves,' said William. 'I'm always nervous in the presence of swords.'

Pin glanced at the dwarfs. They all had their backs to them.

Goodmountain's hand moved again, flicking letter after letter from its nest.

Armed?[space]coff[space]4[space]yes

'Something wrong with your throat?' said Pin, after William coughed.

'Just nerves again . . . sir.'

OK[space]will[space]get[space]Otto

'Oh no,' William muttered.

'Where's that dwarf going?' said Pin, his hand reaching into his coat.

'Just into the cellar, sir. To ... fetch some ink.'

'Why? Looks like you've got lots of ink up here already.'

'Er, the white ink, sir. For the spaces. And the

middle of the Os.' William leaned towards Mr Pin and shuddered when the hand reached inside the jacket again. 'Look, the dwarfs are all armed, too. With axes. And they get excited very easily. I'm the only person anywhere near you who hasn't got a weapon. Please? I don't want to die just yet. Just do whatever you came to do and go?'

It was a pretty good impression of an abject coward, he thought, because it was casting for type.

Pin glanced away. 'How are we doing, Sister Jennifer?' he said.

Sister Jennifer held a struggling sack. 'Got all the —ing terriers,' he said.

Brother Pin shook his head sharply.

'*Got all the —ing terriers!*' fluted Sister Jennifer, in a much higher register. '*And there's —ing watchmen at the end of the street!*'

Out of the corner of his eye William saw Sacharissa sit bolt upright. Death was certainly somewhere on the agenda now.

Otto was climbing unconcernedly up the cellar steps, one of his iconograph boxes swinging from his shoulder.

He nodded at William. Behind him Sacharissa was pushing her chair back.

Back in front of his case of type Goodmountain was feverishly setting:

Hide[space]your[space]eyes

Mr Pin turned to William. 'What do you mean, white ink for the spaces?'

Sacharissa was looking angry and determined, like Mrs Arcanum after an uncalled-for remark.

The vampire raised his box.

William saw the hod above it, crammed with Uberwaldean land eels.

Mr Pin thrust back his coat.

William leapt towards the advancing girl, rising through the air like a frog through treacle.

Dwarfs started to jump over the low barrier to the print room with axes in their hands. And . . .

'Boo,' said Otto.

Time stopped. William felt the universe fold away, the little globe of walls and ceilings peeling back like the skin of an orange, leaving a chilly, rushing darkness filled with needles of ice. There were voices, cut off, random syllables of sound, and again the feeling that he'd felt before, that his body was as thin and insubstantial as a shadow.

Then he landed on top of Sacharissa, threw his arms around her, and rolled them both behind the welcome barrier of the desks.

Dogs howled. People swore. Dwarfs yelled. Furniture smashed. William lay still until the thunder died away.

It was replaced by groans and swearing.

Swearing was a positive indication. It was dwarfish swearing, and it meant that the swearer was not only alive but angry too.

He raised his head carefully.

The far door was open. There was no queue, no dogs. There *was* the sound of running feet and furious barking out in the street.

The back door was swinging on its hinges.

William was aware of the pneumatic warmth of

Sacharissa in his arms. This was an experience of the sort which, in a life devoted to arranging words in a pleasing order, he had not dreamed would – well, obviously *dreamed*, his inner editor corrected him, better make that *expected* – would have come his way.

'I'm *dreadfully* sorry,' he said. That was technically a white lie, the editor said. Like thanking your aunt for the lovely handkerchiefs. It's okay. It's okay.

He drew away carefully and got unsteadily to his feet. The dwarfs were also staggering upright. One or two of them were being noisily sick.

The body of Otto Chriek was crumpled on the floor. The departing Brother Pin had got one expert cut in, at neck height, before leaving.

'Oh, my gods,' said William. 'What a dreadful thing to happen . . .'

'What, having your head cut off?' said Boddony, who'd never liked the vampire. 'Yes, I expect you could say that.'

'We . . . ought to do something for him . . .'

'Really?'

'Yes! I'd have been killed for sure if he hadn't used those eels!'

'Excuse me? Excuse me, please?'

The sing-song voice was coming from under the printers' bench. Goodmountain knelt down.

'Oh, no . . .' he said.

'What is it?' said William.

'It's . . . er . . . well, it's Otto.'

'Excuse me, please? Could somevun get me out of here?' Goodmountain, grimacing, pushed his hand into the darkness, while the voice continued: 'Oh, crikey, zere is a dead rat under here, somevun must've dropped zere lunch, how sordid— Not zer ear please, *not zer ear* . . . By the hair, please . . .'

The hand came out again, holding Otto's head by the hair as requested. The eyes swivelled.

'Everyvun all right?' said the vampire. 'Zat vas a close shave, yes?'

'Are you . . . all right, Otto?' said William, realizing that this was a winning entrant in the Really Stupid Things to Say contest.

'Vot? Oh, yes. Yes, I zink so. Mustn't grumble. Pretty good, really. It's just that I seem to have had my head cut off, vich you could say is a bit of a drawback—'

'That's not Otto,' said Sacharissa. She was shaking.

'Of course it is,' said William. 'I mean, who else could it—'

'Otto's taller than that,' said Sacharissa and burst out laughing. The dwarfs started to laugh, too, because at that moment they would laugh at anything. Otto didn't join in very enthusiastically.

'Oh, yes. Ho ho ho,' he said. 'Zer famous Ankh-Morpork sense of humour. Vot a funny joke. Talk about laugh. Do not mind me.'

Sacharissa was gasping for breath. William grabbed her as gently as he could, because this was the kind of laughter you died of. And now she was crying, great racking sobs that bubbled up through the laughs.

'I wish I was dead!' she sobbed.

'You should try it some time,' said Otto. 'Mr Goodmountain, take me to my body, please? It is around here somevhere.'

'Do you . . . should we . . . do you have to sew—'
Goodmountain tried.

'No. Ve heal easily,' said Otto. 'Ah, zere it is. If you
could just put me down by me, please? And turn
round? Zis is a bit, you know, embarrassing? Like the
making of zer vater?' Still wincing in the after-effects
of the dark light, the dwarfs obeyed.

After a moment they heard: 'Okay, you can look
now.'

Otto, all in one piece, was sitting up and dabbing at
his neck with a handkerchief.

'Got to be a stake in zer heart as vell,' he said, as they
stared. 'Zo . . . vot vas all *zat* about, please? Zer dvarf
said to make a distraction—'

'We didn't know you used dark light!' snapped
Goodmountain.

'Excuse me? All I had ready vas the land eels and
you said it looked urgent! Vot did you expect me to
do? I'm *reformed*!'

'That's bad luck, that stuff!' said a dwarf William
had come to know as Dozy.

'Oh yes? You zink? Vell, *I'm* zer von who is going to
have to have his collar laundered!' snapped Otto.

William did his best to comfort Sacharissa, who was
still trembling.

'Who *were* they?' she said.

'I'm . . . not sure, but they certainly wanted Lord
Vetinari's dog . . .'

'I'm *sure* that she wasn't a proper virgin, you know!'

'Sister Jennifer certainly looked very odd,' was the
most William was going to concede.

Sacharissa snorted. 'Oh, no, I was taught by worse

than her at school,' she said. 'Sister Credenza could bite through a door . . . No, it was the *language*! I'm *sure* "ing" is a bad word. She certainly used it like one. I mean, you could *tell* it was a bad word. And that priest, he had a *knife*!'

Behind them Otto was in trouble.

'You use it to take *pictures*?' said Goodmountain.

'Vy, yes.'

Several of the dwarfs slapped their thighs, half turned away and did the usual little pantomime that people do to indicate that they just can't *believe* someone else could be so damn *stupid*.

'You *know* it is dangerous!' said Goodmountain.

'Mere superstition!' said Otto. 'All zat possibly happens is that a subject's own morphic signature aligns zer resons, or thing-particles, in phase-space according to zer Temporal Relevance Theory, creating zer effect of multiple directionless vindows vich intersect vith the illusion of zer present and create metaphoric images according to zer dictates of qvasi-historical extrapolation. You see? Nothing mysterious about it at all!'

'It certainly frightened off those people,' said William.

'It was the axes that did *that*,' said Goodmountain firmly.

'No, it was the feeling that the top of your head has been opened and icicles have been pounded into your brain,' said William.

Goodmountain blinked. 'Yeah, okay, that too,' he said, mopping his forehead. 'You've got a way with words, right enough . . .'

A shadow appeared in the doorway. Goodmountain grabbed his axe.

William groaned. It was Vimes. Worse, he was smiling, in a humourless predatory way.

'Ah, Mr de Worde,' he said, stepping inside. 'There are several thousand dogs stampeding through the city at the moment. This is an interesting fact, isn't it?'

He leaned against the wall and produced a cigar. 'Well, I *say* dogs,' he said, striking a match on Goodmountain's helmet. '*Mostly* dogs, perhaps I *should* say. Some cats. More cats now, in fact, 'cos, hah, there's nothing like a, yes, a tidal wave of dogs, fighting and biting and howling, to sort of, how can I put it, give a city a certain ... busyness. Especially underfoot, because – did I mention it? – they're very *nervous* dogs too. Oh, and did I mention cattle?' he went on, conversationally. 'You know how it is, market day and so on, people are driving the cows and, my goodness, around the corner comes a wall of wailing dogs ... Oh, and I forgot about the sheep. And the chickens, although I imagine there's not much left of the chickens now ...'

He stared at William. 'Anything you feel you want to tell me?' he said.

'Uh ... we had a bit of a problem ...'

'Never! Really? Do tell!'

'The dogs took fright when Mr Chriek took a picture of them,' said William. This was absolutely true. Dark light was frightening enough even if you knew what was happening.

Vimes glared at Otto, who looked miserably at his feet.

'Well now,' said Vimes. 'Shall I tell you something? They're electing a new Patrician today—'

'Who?' said William.

'*I* don't know,' said Vimes.

Sacharissa blew her nose and said: 'It'll be Mr Scrope, of the Shoemakers and Leatherworkers.'

Vimes gave William a suspicious look. 'How do you know that?' he said.

'Everyone knows,' said Sacharissa. 'That's what the young man in the bakery said this morning.'

'Oh, where would we be without rumour?' said Vimes. 'So this is not a day, Mr de Worde, for . . . things to go wrong. My men are talking to some of the people who brought dogs along. Not many of them, I have to admit. Most of them don't want to talk to the Watch. Can't think why, we're very good listeners. *Now* is there anything you want to tell me?' Vimes looked around the room and back to William. 'Everyone's staring at you, I notice.'

'The *Times* does not need any help from the Watch,' said William.

'Helping wasn't what I had in mind.'

'We haven't done anything wrong.'

'I'll decide that.'

'Really? That's an interesting point of view.'

Vimes glanced down. William had taken his notebook out of his pocket. 'Oh,' he said. 'I see.' He reached down to his own belt and pulled out a blunt, dark length of wood.

'You know what this is?' he said.

'It's a truncheon,' said William. 'A big stick.'

'Always the last resort, eh?' said Vimes evenly.

'Rosewood and Llamedos silver, a lovely piece of work. And it says on this little plate here that I'm supposed to keep the peace, and *you*, Mr de Worde, don't look like part of that right now.'

They locked gazes.

'What was the odd thing Lord Vetinari did just before the . . . accident?' said William, so quietly that probably only Vimes heard it.

Vimes didn't even blink. But after a moment he laid the truncheon down on the desk, with a click that sounded unnaturally loud in the silence.

'Now you put your notebook down, lad,' he suggested, in a quiet voice. 'That way, it's just me and you. No . . . clash of symbols.'

This time, William could see where the path of wisdom lay. He put down the book.

'Right,' said Vimes. 'And now you and me are going to go over to the corner there, while your friends tidy up. Amazing, isn't it, how much furniture can get broken, just by taking a picture?'

He went and sat down on an upturned washtub. William made do with a rocking horse.

'All right, Mr de Worde, we'll do this your way,' said Vimes.

'I didn't know I *had* a way.'

'You're not going to tell me what you know, are you?'

'I'm not sure what I know,' said William. 'But I . . . think . . . Lord Vetinari did something remarkable not long before the crime.'

Vimes pulled out his own notebook and thumbed through it.

'He entered the palace by the stables some time before seven o'clock and dismissed the guard,' he said.

'He'd been out all night?'

Vimes shrugged. 'His lordship comes and goes. The guards don't ask him where and why. Have they been talking to you?'

William was ready for the question. He just didn't have an answer. But the palace guard, insofar as he'd met them, weren't men chosen for imagination or flair but for a kind of obstructive loyalty. They didn't sound like a potential Deep Bone.

'I don't think so,' he said.

'Oh, you don't *think* so?'

Hold on, hold on . . . Deep Bone claimed to know the dog Wuffles, and a dog ought to know if his master was acting oddly, dogs *liked* routine . . .

'I think it's very unusual for his lordship to be outside the palace at that time,' said William carefully. 'Not part of the . . . routine.'

'Nor is stabbing your clerk and trying to run off with a very heavy sack of cash,' said Vimes. 'Yes, we noticed that, too. We're not stupid. We only *look* stupid. Oh . . . and the guard said he smelled spirits on his lordship's breath.'

'Does he drink?'

'Not so's you'd notice.'

'He's got a drinks cabinet in his office.'

Vimes smiled. 'You noticed that? He likes other people to drink.'

'But all that might mean was that he was plucking up the courage to—' William began, and stopped. 'No, that's not Vetinari. He's not that sort.'

'No. He isn't,' said Vimes. He sat back. 'Perhaps you'd better . . . *think* again, Mr de Worde. Maybe . . . maybe . . . you can find someone to help you think better.'

Something in his manner suggested that the informal part of the discussion was well and truly over.

'Do you know much about Mr Scrope?' said William.

'Tuttle Scrope? Son of old Tuskin Scrope. President of the Guild of Shoemakers and Leatherworkers for the past seven years,' said Vimes. 'Family man. Old-established shop in Wixon's Alley.'

'That's all?'

'Mr de Worde, that's all the Watch knows about Mr Scrope. You understand? You wouldn't want to know about some of the people we know a *lot* about.'

'Ah.' William's brow wrinkled. 'But there's not a shoe shop in Wixon's Alley.'

'I never mentioned shoes.'

'In fact the only shop that is even, er, remotely connected with leather is—'

'That's the one,' said Vimes.

'But that sells—'

'Comes under the heading of leatherwork,' said Vimes, picking up his truncheon.

'Well, *yes* . . . and rubber work, and . . . feathers . . . and whips . . . and . . . little jiggly things,' said William, blushing. 'But—'

'Never been in there myself, although I believe Corporal Nobbs gets their catalogue,' said Vimes. 'I don't think there's a Guild of Makers of Little Jiggly Things, though it's an interesting thought. Anyway,

Mr Scrope is all nice and legal, Mr de Worde. Nice old family atmosphere, I understand. Makes buying ... this and that, and little jiggly things ... as pleasant as half a pound of humbugs, I don't doubt. And what rumour is telling *me* is that the first thing nice Mr Scrope will do is pardon Lord Vetinari.'

'What? Without a trial?'

'Won't that be nice?' said Vimes, with horrible cheerfulness. 'A good start to his term of office, eh? Clean sheet, fresh start, no sense in raking up unpleasantness. Poor chap. Overwork. Bound to crack. Didn't get enough fresh air. And so on. So he can be put away in some nice quiet place and we'll be able to stop worrying about this whole wretched affair. A bit of a relief, eh?'

'But you *know* he didn't—'

'Do I?' said Vimes. 'This is an official truncheon of office, Mr de Worde. If it was a club with a nail in it this'd be a different sort of city. I'm off now. You've been thinking, you tell me. Maybe you ought to think some more.'

William watched him go.

Sacharissa had pulled herself together, perhaps because no one was trying to comfort her any more.

'What are we going to do now?' she said.

'I don't know. Get a paper out, I suppose. That's our job.'

'But what happens if those men come back?'

'I don't think they will. This place is being watched now.'

Sacharissa started to pick papers up off the floor. 'I suppose I'll feel better if I do *something*...'

'That's the spirit.'

'If you can give me a few paragraphs about that fire . . .'

'Otto got a decent picture,' said William. 'Didn't you, Otto?'

'Oh yes. That vun is okay. But . . .'

The vampire was staring down at his iconograph. It was smashed.

'Oh, I'm so sorry,' said William.

'I have ozzers.' Otto sighed. 'You know, I thought it vould be *easy* in zer big city,' he said. 'I thought it would be *civilized.* Zey told me mobs don't come after you viz pitchforks in zer big city like zey do back in Schüschien. I mean, I *try.* Gods know I try. Three months, four days and seven hours on zer vagon. I give up zer whole thing! Even zer pale ladies viz the velvet basques vorn on zer outside and zer fetching black lace dresses and zose little tiny, you know, high-heeled boots – and zat vas a wrench, I don't mind telling you . . .' He shook his head miserably, and stared at his ruined shirt. 'And stuff all gets broken and now my best shirt is all covered viz . . . blood . . . covered viz red, red *blood* . . . rich *dark* blood . . . zer blood . . . covered with zer blood . . . zer *blood* . . . '

'Quick!' said Sacharissa, pushing past William. 'Mr Goodmountain, you hold his arms!' She waved at the dwarfs. 'I was ready for this! Two of you hold his legs! Dozy, there's a huge blutwurst in my desk drawer!'

'. . . *Let me valk in sunshine, Living not in vein* . . .' Otto crooned.

'Oh, my gods, his eyes are glowing red!' said William. 'What shall we do?'

'We could try cutting his head off again?' said Boddony.

'That was a very poor joke, Boddony,' Sacharissa snapped.

'Joke? I was smiling?'

Otto stood up, the cursing dwarfs hanging off his sparse frame.

'*Through thunderstorm and dreadful night, ve vill carry on zer fight . . .*'

'He's as strong as an ox!' said Goodmountain.

'Hang on, maybe it would help if we joined in!' said Sacharissa. She fumbled in her bag and produced a slim blue pamphlet. 'I picked this up this morning from the mission in Abattoirs Lane. It's their songbook! And,' she started to sniff again, 'it's so *sad*, it's called "Walking In Sunshine" and it's so—'

'You want us to have a *singsong*?' said Goodmountain, as the struggling Otto lifted him off the ground.

'Just to give him moral support!' Sacharissa dabbed at her eyes with a handkerchief. 'You can see he's trying to fight it! And he *did* lay down his life for us!'

'Yes, but then he picked it up again!'

William bent down and took up something from the wreckage of Otto's iconograph. The imp had escaped, but the picture that it had painted was just visible. Perhaps it'd show—

It wasn't a good one of the man who'd called himself Brother Pin; his face was just a white blob in the glare of the light that humans couldn't see. But the shadows behind him . . .

He looked closer.

'Oh, my gods . . .'

The shadows behind him were alive.

It was sleeting. Brother Pin and Sister Tulip slid and slithered through the freezing drops. Behind them, whistles were blowing in the murk.

'Come on!' Pin yelled.

'These —ing sacks are *heavy*!'

There were whistles blowing off to one side now, too. Mr Pin wasn't used to this. Watchmen shouldn't be enthusiastic, or organized. He'd been chased by watchmen before, when plans hadn't quite worked out. Their job was to give up at the second corner, out of breath. He felt quite angry about that. The watchmen here were doing it *wrong*.

He was aware of an open space to one side of him, full of damp swirling flakes. Below him there was a sluggish sucking noise, like a very bad digestion.

'This is a bridge! Chuck 'em in the river!' he commanded.

'I fort we wanted to find—'

'Doesn't matter! Get rid of *all* of 'em! Right now! End of problem!'

Sister Tulip grunted a reply and skidded to a halt at the parapet. The two whining, yapping sacks went straight on over.

'Did that sound like a —ing splash to you?' said Sister Tulip, peering through the sleet.

'Who cares? Now *run*!'

Mr Pin shivered as he sped on. He didn't know what

had been done to him back there, but he'd felt like he'd walked over his own grave.

He felt he had more than just watchmen after him. He speeded up.

In reluctant but marvellous harmony, because no one could sing like a group of dwarfs, even if the song was 'May I Suck Of Water Pure',* the dwarfs seemed to be calming Otto down.

Besides, the horrible black emergency blutwurst had finally been produced. For a vampire this was the equivalent of a cardboard cigarette to a terminal nicotine addict, but it was at least something he could get his teeth into. When William finally tore his gaze away from the horror of the shadows, Sacharissa was mopping Otto's brow.

'Oh, vunce again I am so ashamed, vhere can I put my head, it's so—'

William held up the picture. 'Otto, what's this?'

In the shadows were mouths, screaming. In the shadows were eyes, wide. They didn't move while you watched them, but if you looked at the picture a second time you got a feeling that they weren't quite in the same place.

Otto shuddered. 'Oh, I used all zer eels I had,' he said.

'And—?'

'Oh, they're *awful*,' breathed Sacharissa, looking away from the tortured shadows.

---

* In other circumstances it would have been as likely as cows singing 'Let Me Be Covered In Rapturous Gravy'.

'I feel so wretched,' said Otto. 'Obviously they vere too stronk—'

'Tell us, Otto!'

'Vell . . . the iconograph does not lie, you have heard zis?'

'Of course.'

'Yes? Vell . . . under stronk dark light, the picture *really* does not lie. Dark light reveals zer truth to the dark eyes of zer mind . . .' He paused and sighed. 'Ah, vunce again no ominous roll of thunder, vot a vaste. But at least you could look apprehensively at the shadows.'

All heads turned towards the shadows, in the corner of the room and under the roof. They were simply shadows, haunted by nothing more than dust and spiders.

'But there's just dust and—' Sacharissa began.

Otto held up a hand. 'Dear lady . . . I have just told you. Philosophically, the truth can be vot is *metaphorically* there . . .'

William stared at the picture again.

'I had hoped that I could use filters and so on to cut down zer, er, *unvanted* effects,' said Otto behind him. 'But alas—'

'This gets worse and worse,' said Sacharissa. 'It gives me the humorous vegetables.'

Goodmountain shook his head. 'This is unholy stuff,' he said. 'No more meddling with it, understand?'

'I didn't think dwarfs were religious,' said William.

'We're not,' said Goodmountain. 'But we know

unholy when we see it, and I'm looking at it right now, I'm *telling* you. I don't want any more of these, these . . . prints of darkness!'

William grimaced. *It shows the truth*, he thought. But how do we know the truth when we see it? The Ephebian philosophers think that a hare can never outrun a tortoise, and they can *prove* it. Is that the truth? I heard a wizard say that everything is made of little numbers, whizzing around so fast that they become *stuff*. Is that true? I think a lot of things that have been happening over the last few days are not what they seem, and I don't know why I think that, but I think it's not the truth . . .

'Yes, no more of this stuff, Otto,' he said.

'Damn right,' said Goodmountain.

'Let's just try to get back to normal and get a paper out, shall we?'

'You mean normal where mad priests start to collect dogs, or normal where vampires mess around with evil shadows?' said Gowdie.

'I mean like normal before that,' said William.

'Oh, I *see*. You mean like back in the old days,' said Gowdie.

After a while, though, silence settled on the press room, although there was an occasional sniff from the desk opposite.

William wrote a story about the fire. That was easy. Then he tried to write a coherent account of the recent events, but found he couldn't get beyond the first word. He'd written 'The'. It was a reliable word, the definite article. The trouble was, all the things he was definite about were bad.

He'd expected to ... what? Inform people? Yes. Annoy people? Well, some people, at least. What he hadn't expected was that it *wouldn't make any difference.* The paper came out, and it *didn't matter.*

People just seemed to *accept* things. What was the point of writing another story on the Vetinari business? Well, of course, it had a lot of dogs in it, and there was always a lot of human interest in a story about animals.

'What did you expect?' said Sacharissa, as if she was reading his thoughts. 'Did you think people would be marching in the streets? Vetinari isn't a very nice man, from what I hear. People say he probably deserves to be locked up.'

'Are you saying people aren't interested in the truth?'

'Listen, what's true to a lot of people is that they need the money for the rent by the end of the week. Look at Mr Ron and his friends. What's the truth mean to them? They live under a bridge!'

She held up a piece of lined paper, crammed edge to edge with the careful looped handwriting of someone for whom holding a pen was not a familiar activity.

'This is a report of the annual meeting of the Ankh-Morpork Caged Birds Society,' she said. 'They're just ordinary people who breed canaries and things as a hobby. Their chairman lives next door to me, which is why he gave me this. This stuff is important to him! My goodness, but it's dull. It's all about Best of Breed and some changes in the show rules about parrots which they argued about for two hours. But the people who were arguing were people who mostly spend their day mincing meat or sawing wood and basically leading little lives that are controlled by other people, do you see? They've got no say in who runs the city but they can damn well see to it that cockatoos aren't lumped in with parrots. It's not their fault. It's just how things are. Why are you sitting there with your mouth open like that?'

William closed his mouth. 'All right, I understand—'

'No, I don't think you do,' she snapped. 'I looked you up in *Twurp's Peerage*. Your family have never had to worry about the small stuff, have they? They've been some of the people who really run things. This ... paper is a kind of hobby for you, isn't it? Oh, you believe in it, I'm sure you do, but if it all goes wahoonie-shaped you'll still have money. I won't. So if the way it can be kept going is by filling it with what you sneer at as *olds*, then that's what I'll do.'

'I don't have money! I make my own living!'

'Yes, but you were able to choose! Anyway, aristo-crats don't like to see other toffs starving. They find them silly jobs to do for serious wages—'

She stopped, panting, and pushed some hair out of her eyes. Then she looked at him like someone who has lit the fuse and is now wondering if the barrel at the other end is bigger than they thought.

William opened his mouth, went to shape a word, and stopped. He did it again. Finally, a little hoarsely, he said: 'You're more or less right—'

'The next word's going to be "but", I just know it,' said Sacharissa.

William was aware that the printers were all watch-ing. 'Yes, it is—'

'Aha!'

'But it's a big but. Do you mind? It's important! *Someone* has to care about the ... the big truth. What Vetinari mostly does not do is *a lot of harm*. We've had rulers who were completely crazy and very, very nasty. And it wasn't that long ago, either. Vetinari might not be "a very nice man", but I had breakfast today with someone who'd be a lot worse if *he* ran the city, and there are lots more like him. And what's happening now is *wrong*. And as for your damn parrot fanciers, if they don't care about anything much beyond things that go squawk in cages then one day there'll be someone in charge of this place who'll make them choke on their own budgies. You want that to happen? If we don't make an effort all they'll get is silly ... *stories* about talking dogs and Elves Ate My Gerbil, so *don't* give me lectures on what's important and what's not, understand?'

They glared at one another.

'Don't you talk to me like that.'

'Don't *you* talk to *me* like that.'

'We're not getting enough advertising. The *Inquirer's* getting huge adverts from the big Guilds,' said Sacharissa. 'That's what'll keep us going, not stories about how much gold weighs.'

'What am I supposed to do about it?'

'Find a way of getting more ads!'

'That's not my job!' William shouted.

'It's part of saving your job! We're just getting penny-a-line advertisements from people wanting to sell surgical supports and backache cures!'

'So? The pennies add up!'

'So you want us to be known as The Paper You Can Put Your Truss In?'

'Er . . . excuse me, but are we producing an edition?' said Goodmountain. 'Not that we aren't enjoying all this, but the colour's going to take a lot of extra time.'

William and Sacharissa looked round. They were the focus of attention.

'Look, I know this means a lot to you,' said Sacharissa, lowering her voice, 'but all this . . . political stuff, this is the Watch's job, not ours. That's all I'm saying.'

'They're stuck. That's what Vimes was telling me.'

Sacharissa stared at his frozen expression. Then she leaned over and, to his shock, patted his hand.

'Perhaps you *are* having an effect, then.'

'Hah!'

'Well, if they're going to pardon Vetinari, maybe it's because they're worried about *you*.'

'Hah! Anyway, who are "they"?'

'Well . . . you know . . . *them*. The people who run things. *They* notice things. They probably read the paper.'

William gave her a wan smile. 'Tomorrow we'll find someone to get more ads,' he said. 'And we'll definitely need those extra staff. Er . . . I'm going to go for a little walk,' he added. 'And I'll get you that key.'

'Key?'

'You wanted a dress for the ball?'

'Oh. Yes. Thank you.'

'And I don't think those men will be back,' said William. 'I've got a feeling that there isn't a shed anywhere in town that's as well guarded as this one right at the moment.'

Because Vimes is waiting to see who tries to get at us next, he thought. But he decided not to say so.

'What exactly are you going to do?' said Sacharissa.

'First, I'm going to the nearest apothecary,' said William, 'and then I'm going to drop in at my lodgings for that key, and then . . . I'm going to see a man about a dog.'

The New Firm hurtled through the door of the empty mansion and bolted it behind them.

Mr Tulip ripped off the bride of innocence outfit and hurled it on to the floor.

'I *told* you —ing clever plans never work!' he said.

'A *vampire*,' said Mr Pin. 'This is a sick city, Mr Tulip.'

'What was that he —ing did to us?'

'He took some kind of picture,' said Mr Pin. He closed his eyes for a moment. His head was aching.

'Well, I was in disguise,' said Mr Tulip.

Mr Pin shrugged. Even with a metal bucket over his head, which would probably begin to corrode after a few minutes, there would be something recognizable about Mr Tulip.

'I don't think that will do any good,' he said.

'I —ing *hates* pictures,' snarled Mr Tulip. 'Remember that time in Mouldavia? All them posters they did? It's bad for a man's health, seeing his —ing phiz on every wall with "Dead or Alive" under it. It's like they can't —ing decide.'

Mr Tulip fished out a small bag of what he had been

assured was primo Smudge, but which would turn out to be sugar and powdered pigeon guano.

'Anyway, we *must*'ve got the —ing dog,' he said.

'We can't be sure,' said Mr Pin. He winced again. The headache was getting quite strong.

'Look, we done the —ing job,' said Mr Tulip. 'I don't recall no one telling us about —ing werewolves and vampires. That's *their* —ing problem! I say we scrag the geek, take the money and head for Pseudopolis or someplace!'

'You mean quit on a contract?'

'Yeah, when it's got small print you can't —ing see!'

'Someone'll recognize Charlie, though. Seems it's hard for the dead to stay dead around here.'

'I reckon I could help in that —ing respect,' said Mr Tulip.

Mr Pin chewed his lip. He knew better than Mr Tulip that men in their business needed a certain . . . reputation. Things didn't get written down. But *the word* got about. The New Firm sometimes dealt with very serious players, and they were people who took a lot of notice of the word . . .

But Tulip did have a point. This place was getting to Mr Pin. It jarred his sensibilities. Vampires and werewolves . . . springing that sort of thing on a body, that wasn't according to the rules. That was *taking liberties.* Yes . . .

. . . there was more than one way to keep a reputation.

'I think we should go and explain things to our lawyer friend,' he said slowly.

'Right!' said Mr Tulip. 'And then I'll rip his head off.'

'That doesn't kill zombies.'

'Good, 'cos then he'll be able to see where I'm gonna —ing *shove* it.'

'And then . . . we'll pay another visit to that newspaper. When it's dark.'

To get that picture, he thought. That was a good reason. It was a reason that you could tell the world. But there was another reason. That . . . burst of darkness had frightened Mr Pin to his shrivelled soul. A lot of memories had come pouring back, all at once.

Mr Pin had made a lot of enemies, but that hadn't worried him until now because all his enemies were dead. But the dark light had fired off bits of his mind and it had seemed to him that those enemies had not vanished from the universe but had merely gone a long way away, from which point they were watching him. And it was a long way away only from his point of view – from their point of view they could reach out and touch him.

What he wouldn't say, even to Mr Tulip, was this: they'd need all the money from this job because, in a flash of dark, he'd seen that it was time to retire.

Theology was not a field in which Mr Pin had much knowledge, despite accompanying Mr Tulip to a number of the more well-designed temples and chapels, on one occasion to scrag a High Priest who'd tried to double-cross Frank 'Nutboy' Nabbs, but the little he had absorbed was suggesting to him that this might be the very best time to take a bit of an interest. He could send them some money, maybe, or at least return some of the stuff he'd taken. Hell, maybe he could start not eating beef on Tuesdays or whatever it was you had to do. Maybe that would stop this feeling that the back of his head had just been unscrewed.

He knew that would have to be later, though. Right now, the code allowed them to do one of two things: they could follow Slant's instructions to the letter, which would mean they'd maintain a reputation for efficiency, or they could scrag Slant and maybe a few bystanders and leave, perhaps setting fire to a few things on the way out. That was also news that got around. People would understand how upset they were.

'But first we'll—' Mr Pin stopped, and in a strangled voice said: 'Is someone standing behind me?'

'No,' said Mr Tulip.

'I thought I heard . . . footsteps.'

'No one here but us.'

'Right. Right.' Mr Pin shuddered, straightened his jacket and then looked Mr Tulip up and down.

'Clean yourself up a bit, will you? Sheesh, you're leaking dust!'

'I can handle it,' said Mr Tulip. 'Keeps me sharp. Keeps me alert.'

Pin sighed. Mr Tulip had amazing faith in the contents of the next bag, whatever it was. And it was usually cat flea powder cut with dandruff.

'Force isn't going to work on Slant,' he said.

Mr Tulip cracked his knuckles. 'Works on everyone,' he said.

'No. A man like him will have a lot of muscle to call on,' said Pin. He patted his jacket. 'It's time Mr Slant said hello to my little friend.'

* * *

A plank thumped down on to the crusted surface of the river Ankh. Shifting his weight with care, and gripping the rope tightly in his teeth, Arnold Sideways swung himself on to it. It sank a little in the ooze, but stayed – for want of a better word – afloat.

A few feet away the depression that had been left by the first sack landing in the river was already filling up with – for want of a better word – water.

He reached the end of the plank, steadied himself and managed to lasso the remaining sack. It was moving.

'He's got it,' shouted the Duck Man, who was watching from under the bridge. 'Heave away, everybody!'

The sack came out of the muck with a sucking sound, and Arnold pulled himself aboard as it was dragged back to the bank.

'Oh, very well done, Arnold,' said the Duck Man, helping him off the sodden sack and back on to his trolley. 'I really doubted if the surface would support you at this stage of the tide!'

'Bit of luck for me, eh, when that cart ran over my legs all them years ago!' said Arnold Sideways. 'I'd have drowned, else!'

Coffin Henry slit the sacking with his knife and tipped the second lot of little terriers on to the ground, where they coughed and sneezed.

'One or two of the little buggers look done for,' he said. 'I'll give 'em mouth to mouth respiritoriation, shall I?'

'Certainly not, Henry,' said the Duck Man. 'Have you no idea of hygiene?'

'Jean who?'

'You can't kiss dogs!' said the Duck Man. 'They could catch something dreadful.'

The crew looked at the dogs that were clustering round their fire. How the dogs had landed in the river was something they didn't bother to wonder about. All sorts of things landed in the river. It was the kind of thing that happened all the time. The crew took a keen interest in floating things. But it was unusual to get this many all at once.

'Maybe it's been raining dogs?' said Altogether Andrews, who was being steered by the mind known as Curly. The crew liked Curly. He was easy to get along with. 'I heard the other day that's been happening lately.'

'You know what?' said Arnold Sideways. 'What we ort to do, right, is get some stuff, like . . . wood and stuff, and make a boat. We could get a lot more stuff if we had a boat.'

'Ah, yes,' said the Duck Man. 'I used to mess about in boats when I was a boy.'

'*We* could boat about in mess,' said Arnold. 'Same thing.'

'Not . . . exactly,' said the Duck Man. He looked at the circle of steaming, retching dogs.

'I wish Gaspode was here,' he said. 'He knows how to think about this sort of thing.'

'A jar,' said the apothecary carefully.

'Sealed with wax,' William repeated.

'And you want an ounce each of . . .'

'Oil of aniseed, oil of rampion and oil of scallatine,' said William.

'I can do the first two,' said the apothecary, looking at the little list he'd been given. 'But there is no such thing as a whole ounce of oil of scallatine in the city, you realize? It's fifteen dollars for enough to go on a pinhead. We've got about enough to fill a mustard spoon and we have to keep *that* in a soldered lead box under water.'

'I'll take a pinhead's worth, then.'

'You'll never get it off your hands, you know. It isn't really for the average—'

'In a bottle,' said William patiently. 'Sealed with wax.'

'You won't even smell the other oils! What do you want *them* for?'

'Insurance,' said William. 'Oh, and after you've sealed it, wash off the bottle with ether, and then wash the ether off.'

'Is this going to be used for some illegal purpose?' said the apothecary. He caught William's expression. 'Just interested,' he added quickly.

When he'd gone to make up the order William called in at a couple of other shops and bought a pair of thick gloves.

When he returned, the apothecary was just bringing the oils to the counter. He held a small glass flask, filled with liquid. Inside floated a much smaller phial.

'The outer liquid's water,' he said, pulling some plugs out of his nose. 'Take it carefully, if you don't mind. Drop it and we can kiss our sinuses goodbye.'

'What does it smell of?' said William.

'Well, if I said "cabbage",' said the apothecary, 'I wouldn't be saying the half of it.'

Next, William went to his lodgings. Mrs Arcanum was averse to boarders coming back to their rooms during the day, but at the moment William appeared to be outside her frame of reference and she merely gave him a nod as he went upstairs.

The keys were in the old trunk at the end of his bed. It was the one he'd taken to Hugglestones; he'd kept it ever since, so that he could kick it occasionally.

His chequebook was also in there. He took that, too.

His sword rattled as his hand brushed against it.

He'd enjoyed swordsmanship at Hugglestones. It was in the dry, you were allowed to wear protective clothing and no one attempted to stamp your face into the mud. He'd actually been the champion of the school. But this wasn't because he was much good. It was simply that most of the other boys were so bad. They approached the sport as they approached all others, in a great big keen screaming rush, using the sword as a sort of club. That meant that if William could avoid the first wild stroke, then he was going to win.

He left the sword in the trunk.

After some reflection he pulled out one of his old socks and pulled it over the apothecary's bottle. Hurting people with broken glass wasn't part of the plan, either.

Peppermint! Not a bad choice, but they hadn't known what else was available, had they . . . ?

Mrs Arcanum was a great believer in net curtains,

so that she could see out while outsiders couldn't see in. William lurked behind the ones in his room until he was certain that an indistinct shape among the rooftops opposite was a gargoyle.

This wasn't natural gargoyle territory, any more than Gleam Street.

The thing about gargoyles, he reflected as he stepped back and headed down the stairs, was that they didn't get bored. They were happy to stay and watch *anything* for days. But, while they moved faster than people thought, they didn't move faster than people.

He ran through the kitchen so quickly that he only heard Mrs Arcanum gasp, and then he was through the back door and over the wall into the alley beyond.

Someone was sweeping it. For a moment William wondered if it was a watchman in disguise, or even Sister Jennifer in disguise, but probably there was no one who'd disguise themselves as a gnoll. You'd have to strap a compost heap to your back, to begin with. Gnolls ate almost everything. What they didn't eat they collected obsessively. No one had ever studied them to find out why. Perhaps a carefully sorted collection of rotted cabbage stalks was a sign of big status in gnoll society.

''ar'tn'n, M'r W'rd,' croaked the creature, leaning on its shovel.

'Er . . . hello . . . er . . .'

'Sn'g'k.'

'Ah? Yes. Thank you. Goodbye.'

He hurried down another alley, crossed the street and found yet another alley. He wasn't sure how many gargoyles were watching him, but it took them some time to cross streets . . .

How was it that the gnoll had known his name? It wasn't as though they'd met at a party or something. Besides, the gnolls all worked for . . . Harry King . . .

Well, they did *say* that the King of the Golden River never forgot a debtor . . .

William ducked and dodged across several blocks, making as much use as he could of the alleys and walkthroughs and noisome courts. He was sure a normal person wouldn't be able to keep track of him. But then, he'd be amazed if a normal person was following him. Mister Vimes liked to refer to himself as a simple copper, just as Harry King thought of himself as a rough diamond. William suspected that the world was littered with the remains of those people who had taken them at their word.

He slowed down and climbed some outside stairs. And then he waited.

You're a fool, said the internal editor. Some people have tried to kill you. You're concealing information from the Watch. You're mixing with strange people. You're about to do something that's going to get so far up Mister Vimes's nose it will raise his hat. And why?

Because it makes my blood tingle, he thought. And because I'm not going to be used. By anyone.

There was a faint sound at the end of the alley, which might not have been heard by anyone who wasn't expecting it. It was the sound of something sniffing.

William looked down and saw, in the gloom, a four-legged shape break into a trot while keeping its muzzle close to the ground.

William measured the distance carefully. Declaring independence was one thing. Assaulting a member of the Watch was a very *different* thing.

He lobbed the fragile bottle so that it would land twenty feet ahead of the werewolf. Then he dropped from the stairs on to the top of a wall and jumped down on to a privy roof just as the glass broke with a 'pof!' inside the sock.

There was a yelp, and the sound of scrabbling claws.

William jumped from the roof on to another wall, inched along the top of it and climbed down into another alley. Then he ran.

It took five minutes, dodging into convenient cover and cutting through buildings, to arrive at the livery stables. In the general bustle no one took any notice of him. He was just another man coming to fetch his horse.

The stall that might or might not have contained Deep Bone was occupied by a horse now. It looked down its nose at him.

'Don't turn round, Mister Paper Man,' said a voice behind him.

William tried to remember what *had* been behind him. Oh, yes . . . the hay lift. And huge bags of straw. Plenty of room for someone to hide.

'All right,' he said.

'Hark, hark, the dogs do bark,' said Deep Bone. 'You must be *ment'l.*'

'But I'm on the right track,' said William. 'I think I've—'

311

''ere, you sure you weren't followed?'

'Corporal Nobbs was on my trail,' said William. 'But I shook him off.'

'Hah! Walkin' round the corner'd shake off Nobby Nobbs!'

'Oh, no, he kept right up. I *knew* Vimes would have me tracked,' said William proudly.

'By Nobbs?'

'Yes. Obviously . . . in his werewolf shape . . .' There. He'd said it. But today was a day for shadows and secrets.

'A werewolf shape,' said Deep Bone flatly.

'Yes. I'd be grateful if you didn't tell anyone else.'

'Corporal Nobbs,' said Deep Bone, still in the same dull monotone.

'Yes. Look, Vimes told me not to—'

'*Vimes* told you Nobby Nobbs was a werewolf?'

'Well . . . no, not *exactly*. I worked that out for myself, and Vimes told me not to tell anyone else . . .'

'About Corporal Nobbs bein' a werewolf . . .'

'Yes.'

'Corporal Nobbs is not a werewolf, mister. In any way, shape or form. Whether he's human is another matter, but he ain't a lycr— a lynco— a lycantro— a bloody werewolf, that's for sure!'

'Then whose nose did I just drop a scent bomb in front of?' said William triumphantly.

There was silence. And then there was the sound of a thin trickle of water.

'Mr Bone?' said William.

'What kind of a scent bomb?' said the voice. It sounded rather strained.

'I think oil of scallatine was probably the most active ingredient.'

'Right in front of a werewolf's nose?'

'More or less, yes.'

'Mister Vimes is going to go round the twist,' said the voice of Deep Bone. 'He's going to go totally Librarian-poo. He's going to invent new ways of being angry just so's he can try them out on you—'

'Then I'd better get hold of Lord Vetinari's dog as soon as possible,' said William. He produced his chequebook. 'I can give you a cheque for fifty dollars, and that's all I can afford.'

'What's one of them, then?'

'It's like a legal IOU.'

'Oh, *great*,' said Deep Bone. 'Not much good to me when you're locked up, though.'

'Right now, Mr Bone, there's a couple of very nasty men hunting down every terrier in the city, by the sound of it—'

'Terriers?' said Deep Bone. '*All* terriers?'

'Yes, and while I don't expect you to—'

'Like . . . pedigree terriers, or just people who might happen to look a bit terrier-like?'

'They didn't look like they were inspecting any paperwork. Anyway, what do you *mean*, "people who look like terriers"?'

Deep Bone went silent again.

William said, 'Fifty dollars, Mr Bone.'

At length the sacks of straw said, 'All right. Tonight. On the Misbegot Bridge. Just you. Er . . . I won't be there but there will be . . . a messenger.'

'Who shall I make the cheque to?' said William.

There was no answer. He waited a while and then eased himself into a position where he could peer around the sacks. There was a rustling from them. Probably rats, he thought, because certainly none of them could hold a man.

Deep Bone was a very tricky customer.

Some time after William had gone, looking surreptitiously into the shadows, one of the grooms turned up with a trolley and began to load up the sacks.

One of them said: 'Put me down, mister.'

The man dropped the sack and then opened it cautiously.

A small terrier-like dog struggled out, shaking itself free of clinging wisps.

Mr Hobson did not encourage independence of thought and an enquiring mind, and at 50 pence a day plus all the oats you could steal he didn't get them. The groom looked owlishly at the dog.

'Did you just say that?' he said.

''course not,' said the dog. 'Dogs can't talk. Are you stupid or somethin'? Someone's playin' a trick on you. Gottle o' geer, gottle o' geer, vig viano.'

'You mean, like, throwing their voice? I saw a man do that down at the music hall.'

'That's the ticket. Hold on to that thought.'

The groom looked around. 'Is that you playin' a trick, Tom?' he said.

'That's right, it's me, Tom,' said the dog. 'I got the trick out of a book. Throwin' my voice into this harmless little dog what cannot talk at all.'

'What? You never told me you were learnin' to read!'

'There were pictures,' said the dog hurriedly. 'Tongues an' teeth an' that. Dead easy to understand. Oh, now the little doggie's wanderin' off . . .'

The dog edged its way to the door.

'Sheesh,' it appeared to say. 'A couple of thumbs and they're lords of bloody creation . . .'

Then it ran for it.

'How will this work?' said Sacharissa, trying to look intelligent. It was much better to concentrate on something like this than think about strange men getting ready to invade again.

'Slowly,' mumbled Goodmountain, fiddling with the press. 'You realize that this means it'll take us much longer to print each paper?'

'You vanted colour, I gif you colour,' said Otto sulkily. 'You never said *qvick*.'

Sacharissa looked at the experimental iconograph. Most pictures were painted in colour these days. Only really cheap imps painted in black and white, even though Otto insisted that monochrome 'vas an art form in itself'. But *printing* colour . . .

Four imps were sitting on the edge of it, passing a very small cigarette from hand to hand and watching with interest the work on the press. Three of them wore goggles of coloured glass – red, blue and yellow.

'But not green . . .' she said. 'So . . . if something's green – have I got this right? – Guthrie there sees the . . . blue in the green and paints *that* on the plate in blue' – one of the imps gave her a wave – 'and Anton sees the yellow and paints *that*, and when you run it through the press—'

'. . . very, very slowly,' muttered Goodmountain. 'It'd be quicker to go round to everyone's house and *tell* 'em the news.'

Sacharissa looked at the test sheets that had been done of the recent fire. It was definitely a fire, with red, yellow and orange flames, and there was some, yes, blue sky, and the golems were a pretty good reddish-brown, but the flesh tones . . . well, 'flesh-coloured' was a bit of a tricky one in Ankh-Morpork, where if you picked your subject it could be any colour except maybe light blue, but the faces of many of the bystanders did suggest that a particularly virulent plague had passed through the city. Possibly the Multicoloured Death, she decided.

'Zis is only the beginning,' said Otto. 'Ve vill get better.'

'Better maybe, but we're as fast as we can go,' said Goodmountain. 'We can do maybe two hundred an hour. Maybe two hundred and fifty, but someone's going to be looking for their fingers before this day's out. Sorry, but we're doing the best we can. If we had a day to redesign and rebuild properly—'

'Print a few hundred and do the rest in black and white, then,' said Sacharissa, and sighed. 'At least it'll catch people's attention.'

'Vunce zey see it, the *Inqvirer* vill vork out how it vas done,' said Otto.

'Then at least we'll go down with our colours flying,' said Sacharissa. She shook her head as a little dust floated down from the ceiling.

'Hark at that,' said Boddony. 'Can you feel the floor shake? That's their big presses again.'

'They're undermining us everywhere,' said Sacharissa. 'And we've all worked so hard. It's so *unfair*.'

'I'm surprised the floor takes it,' said Goodmountain. 'It's not as though anything's on solid ground round here.'

'Undermining us, eh?' said Boddony.

One or two of the dwarfs looked up when he said this. Boddony said something in dwarfish. Goodmountain snapped something in reply. A couple of other dwarfs joined in.

'Excuse *me*,' said Sacharissa tartly.

'The lads were . . . wondering about going in and having a look,' said Goodmountain.

'I tried going in the other day,' said Sacharissa. 'But the troll on the door was *most* impolite.'

'Dwarfs . . . approach matters differently,' said Goodmountain.

Sacharissa saw a movement. Boddony had pulled his axe out from under the bench. It was a traditional dwarf axe. One side was a pickaxe, for the extraction of interesting minerals, and the other side was a war axe, because the people who own the land with the valuable minerals in it can be so unreasonable sometimes.

'You're not going to *attack* anyone, are you?' she said, shocked.

'Well, someone *did* say that if you want a good story you have to dig and dig,' said Boddony. 'We're just going to go for a walk.'

'In the cellar?' said Sacharissa, as they headed for the steps.

'Yeah, a walk in the dark,' said Boddony.

Goodmountain sighed. 'The rest of us will get on with the paper, shall we?' he said.

After a minute or two there was the sound of a few axe blows, below them, and then someone swore in dwarfish, very loudly.

'I'm going to see what they're doing,' said Sacharissa, unable to resist any more, and hurried away.

The bricks that once had filled the old doorway were already down when she got there. Since the stones of Ankh-Morpork were recycled over the generations no one had ever seen the point of making strong mortar, and especially not for blocking up an old doorway. Sand, dirt, water and phlegm would do the trick, they felt. They always had done up to now, after all.

The dwarfs were peering into the darkness beyond. Each one had stuck a candle on his helmet.

'I thought your man said they filled up the old street,' said Boddony.

'He's not my man,' said Sacharissa evenly. 'What's in there?'

One of the dwarfs had stepped through with a lantern.

'There's like . . . tunnels,' he said.

'The old pavements,' said Sacharissa. 'It's like this all round this area, I think. After the big floods they built up the sides of the road with timber and filled it in, but they left the pavements on either side because not all the properties had built up yet and people objected.'

'What?' said Boddony. 'You mean the roads were higher than the pavements?'

'Oh, yes,' said Sacharissa, following him into the gap.

'What happened if a horse pi— if a horse made water on the street?'

'I'm sure I don't know,' sniffed Sacharissa.

'How did people cross the street?'

'Ladders.'

'Oh, come on, miss!'

'No, they used ladders. And a few tunnels. It wasn't going to be for very long. And then it was simpler just to put heavy slabs over the old pavements. And so there's these – well, forgotten spaces.'

'There's rats up here,' said Dozy, who was wandering into the distance.

'Hot damn!' said Boddony. 'Anyone brought the cutlery? Only joking, miss. Hey, what do we have here . . . ?'

He hacked at some planks, which crumbled away under the blows.

'Someone didn't want to use a ladder,' he said, peering into another hole.

'It goes right *under* the street?' said Sacharissa.

'Looks like it. Must have been allergic to horses.'

'And . . . er . . . you can find your way?'

'I'm a dwarf. We are underground. *Dwarf. Underground.* What was your question again?'

'You're not proposing to hack through to the cellars of the *Inquirer*, are you?' said Sacharissa.

'Who, us?'

'You are, aren't you?'

'We wouldn't do anything like that.'

'Yes, but you are, aren't you?'

'That'd be tantamount to breaking in, wouldn't it?'

'Yes, and that's what you're planning to do, isn't it?'

Boddony grinned. 'Well . . . a little bit. Just to have a look round. You know.'

'Good.'

'What? You don't mind?'

'You're not going to kill anyone, are you?'

'Miss, we don't do that sort of thing!'

Sacharissa looked a little disappointed. She'd been a respectable young woman for some time. In certain people, that means there's a lot of dammed-up dis-reputability just waiting to burst out.

'Well . . . perhaps just make them a bit sorry, then?'

'Yes, we can probably do that.'

The dwarfs were already creeping along the tunnel at the other side of the buried street. By the light of their torches she saw old frontages, bricked-up doors, windows filled with rubble.

'This should be about the right place,' said Boddony, pointing to a faint rectangle filled with more low-grade brick.

'You're just going to break in?' said Sacharissa.

'We'll say we were lost,' said Boddony.

'Lost underground? Dwarfs?'

'All right, we'll say we're drunk. People'll believe *that*. Okay, lads . . .'

The rotten bricks fell away. Light streamed out. In the cellar beyond a man looked up from his desk, mouth open.

Sacharissa squinted through the dust. '*You?*' she said.

'Oh, it's you, miss,' said Cut-Me-Own-Throat Dibbler. 'Hello, boys. Am I glad to see you . . .'

The crew were just leaving when Gaspode arrived at the gallop. He took one look at the other dogs that were huddled around the fire, then dived under the trailing folds of Foul Ole Ron's dreadful coat and whined.

It took some time for the whole of the crew to understand what was going on. These were, after all, people who could argue and expectorate and creatively misunderstand their way through a three-hour argument after someone said 'Good morning'.

It was the Duck Man who finally got the message. 'These men are hunting terriers?' he said.

'Right! It was the bloody newspaper! You can't bloody trust people who write in newspapers!'

'They threw these doggies in the river?'

'Right!' said Gaspode. 'It's all gone fruit-shaped!'

'Well, we can protect you too.'

'Yeah, but *I've* got to be out and about! I'm a figure in this town! I can't lie low! I need a disguise! Look, we could be looking at fifty dollars here, right? But you need me to get it!'

The crew were impressed with this. In their cashless economy fifty dollars was a fortune.

'Blewitt,' said Foul Ole Ron.

'A dog's a dog,' said Arnold Sideways. 'On account of bein' called a dog.'

'Gaarck!' crowed Coffin Henry.

'That's true,' said the Duck Man. 'A false beard isn't going to work.'

'Well, your huge brains had better come up with *somethin'*, 'cos I'm staying put until you do,' said Gaspode. 'I've *seen* these men. They are not nice.'

There was a rumble from Altogether Andrews. His face flickered as the various personalities reshuffled themselves, and then settled into the waxy bulges of Lady Hermione.

'We *could* disguise him,' she said.

'What could you disguise a dog as?' said the Duck Man. 'A cat?'

'A dog is not *just* a dog,' said Lady Hermione. 'Ai think ai have an idea . . .'

The dwarfs were in a huddle when William got back. The epicentre of the huddle, its huddlee, turned out to be Mr Dibbler, who looked just like anyone would look if they've been harangued. William had never seen anyone to whom the word 'harangued' could be so justifiably applied. It meant someone who had been talked at by Sacharissa for twenty minutes.

'Is there a problem?' he said. 'Hello, Mr Dibbler . . .'

'Tell me, William,' said Sacharissa, while pacing slowly around Dibbler's chair. 'If stories were food, what kind of food would Goldfish Eats Cat be?'

'What?' William stared at Dibbler. Realization dawned. 'I think it would be a sort of long, thin kind of food,' he said.

'Filled with rubbish of suspicious origin?'

'Now, there's no need for anyone to take that

tone—' Dibbler began, and then subsided under Sacharissa's glare.

'Yes, but rubbish that's sort of attractive. You'd keep on eating it even though you wished you weren't,' said William. 'What's going on here?'

'Look, I didn't *want* to do it,' Dibbler protested.

'Do *what*?' said William.

'Mr Dibbler's been writing those stories for the *Inquirer*,' said Sacharissa.

'I mean, no one *believes* what they read in the paper, right?' said Dibbler.

William pulled up a chair and sat straddling it, resting his arms on the back.

'So, Mr Dibbler . . . when did you *start* pissing in the fountain of Truth?'

'William!' snapped Sacharissa.

'Look, times haven't been good, see?' said Dibbler. 'And I thought, this news business . . . well, people like to hear about stuff from a long way away, you know, like in the *Almanacke*—'

' "Plague of Giant Weasels in Hersheba"?' said William.

'That's the style. Well, I thought . . . it doesn't sort of *matter* if they're, you know, *really* true . . . I mean . . .' William's glassy grin was beginning to make Dibbler uncomfortable. 'I mean . . . they're *nearly* true, aren't they? Everyone knows that sort of thing happens . . .'

'You didn't come to *me*,' said William.

'Well, of *course* not. Everyone knows you're a bit . . . a bit unimaginative about that sort of thing.'

'You mean I like to know that things have *actually* happened?'

'That's it, yes. Mr Carney says people won't notice the difference *anyway*. He doesn't like you very much, Mr de Worde.'

'He's got *wandering hands*,' said Sacharissa. 'You can't trust a man like that.'

William pulled the latest copy of the *Inquirer* towards him and picked a story at random.

'"Man Stolen by Demons",' he said. 'This refers to Mr Ronnie "Trust Me" Begholder, known to owe Chrysoprase the troll more than two thousand dollars, last seen buying a very fast horse?'

'Well?'

'Where do the demons fit in?'

'Well, he *could*'ve been stolen by demons,' said Dibbler. 'It could happen to anybody.'

'What you mean, then, is that there is no evidence that he *wasn't* stolen by demons?'

'That way people can make up their own minds,' said Dibbler. 'That's what Mr Carney says. People should be allowed to choose, he said.'

'To choose what's true?'

'He doesn't clean his teeth properly, either,' said Sacharissa. 'I mean, I'm not one of those people who think cleanliness is next to godliness, but there are *limits*.'*

Dibbler shook his head sadly. 'I'm losin' my touch,' he said. 'Imagine – me, working for someone? I

---

* Classically, very few people have considered that cleanliness is next to godliness, apart from in a very sternly abridged dictionary. A rank loincloth and hair in an advanced state of matted entanglement have generally been the badges of office of prophets whose injunction to disdain earthly things starts with soap.

must've been mad. It's the cold weather getting to me, that's what it is. Even . . . *wages*,' he said the word with a shudder, 'looked attractive. D'you know,' he added, in a horrified voice, 'he was telling me what to do? Next time I'll have a quiet lie-down until the feeling goes away.'

'You are an immoral opportunist, Mr Dibbler,' said William.

'It's worked so far.'

'Can you sell some advertising for us?' said Sacharissa.

'I'm not going to work for anyone ag—'

'On commission,' snapped Sacharissa.

'What? You want to *employ* him?' said William.

'Why not? You can tell as many lies as you like if it's *advertising*. That's allowed,' said Sacharissa. 'Please? We need the money!'

'Commission, eh?' said Dibbler, rubbing his unshaven chin. 'Like . . . fifty per cent for you two and fifty per cent for me, too?'

'*We'll* discuss it, shall we?' said Goodmountain, patting him on the shoulder. Dibbler winced. When it came to hard bargaining, dwarfs were diamond-tipped.

'Have I got a choice?' he mumbled.

Goodmountain leaned forward. His beard was bristling. He wasn't currently holding a weapon but Dibbler could see, as it were, the great big axe that wasn't there.

'*Absolutely*,' he said.

'Oh,' said Dibbler. 'So . . . what would I be selling, exactly?'

'Space,' said Sacharissa.

Dibbler beamed again. 'Just space? *Nothing?* Oh, I can do *that.* I can sell nothing like *anything*!' He shook his head sadly. 'It's only when I try to sell *something* that everything goes wrong.'

'How did you come to be here, Mr Dibbler?' William asked.

He was not happy with the answer.

'That sort of thing could work both ways,' he said. 'You can't just dig into other people's property!' He glared at the dwarfs. 'Mr Boddony, I want that hole blocked up right now, understand?'

'We only—'

'Yes, yes, you did it for the best. And now I want it bricked up, properly. I want the hole to look as though it has never been there, thank you. I don't want anyone coming up the cellar ladder that didn't climb down it. Right now, please!'

'I think I'm on to a real story,' said William, as the disgruntled dwarfs filed away. 'I *think* I'm going to see Wuffles. I've got—'

As he pulled out his notebook something dropped on to the floor with a tinkle.

'Oh, yes . . . and I got the key to our town house,' he said. 'You wanted a dress . . .'

'It's a bit late,' said Sacharissa. 'I'd forgotten all about it, to tell the truth.'

'Why not go and have a look while everyone else is busy? You could take Rocky, too. You know . . . to be on the safe side. But the place is empty. My father stays at his club if he has to come to town. Go on. There's got to be more to life than correcting copy.'

Sacharissa looked uncertainly at the key in her hand.

'My sister has quite a *lot* of dresses,' said William. 'You want to go to the ball, don't you?'

'I *suppose* Mrs Hotbed could alter it for me if I take it to her in the morning,' said Sacharissa, expressing mildly peeved reluctance while her body language begged to be persuaded.

'That's right,' said William. 'And I'm sure you can find someone to do your hair properly.'

Sacharissa's eyes narrowed. 'It's true, you know, you *have* got an amazing way with words,' she said. 'What are *you* going to do?'

'I'm going,' said William, 'to see a dog about a man.'

Sergeant Angua peered up at Vimes through the steam from the bowl in front of her.

'Sorry about this, sir,' she said.

'His feet won't touch the ground,' said Vimes.

'You can't arrest him, sir,' said Captain Carrot, putting a fresh towel over Angua's head.

'Oh? Can't arrest him for assaulting an officer, eh?'

'Well, that's where it gets tricky, doesn't it, sir?' said Angua.

'You're an officer, Sergeant, whatever shape you happen to be currently in!'

'Yes, but . . . it's always been a bit convenient to let the werewolf thing stay a rumour, sir,' said Carrot. 'Don't you think so? Mr de Worde writes things down. Angua and I aren't particularly keen on that. Those who need to know, know.'

'Then I'll ban him from doing it!'

'How, sir?'

Vimes looked a little deflated. 'You can't tell me that as Commander of Police I can't stop some little ti—some idiot from writing down *anything* he likes?'

'Oh, no, sir. Of course you can. But I'm not sure you can stop him writing down that you stopped him writing things down,' said Carrot.

'I'm amazed. Amazed! She's your . . . your—'

'Friend,' said Angua, taking another deep sniff of the steam. 'But Carrot's right, Mister Vimes. I don't want this going any further. It was my fault for under-estimating him. I walked right into it. I'll be fine in an hour or two.'

'I saw what you were like when you came in,' said Vimes. 'You were a mess.'

'It was a shock. The nose just shuts down. It was like walking around a corner and running into Foul Ole Ron.'

'Ye gods! *That* bad?'

'Maybe not quite as bad as that. Let it lie, sir. Please.'

'He's a quick learner, our Mr de Worde,' said Vimes, sitting down at his desk. 'He's got a pen and a printing press and everyone acts like he's suddenly a major player. Well, he's going to have to learn a bit more. He doesn't want us watching? Well, we won't, any more. He can reap what he sows for a while. We've got more than enough other things to do, heavens know.'

'But he is technically—'

'See this sign on my desk, Captain? See it, Sergeant? It says "Commander Vimes". That means the buck starts here. It was a command you just got. Now, what else is new?'

Carrot nodded. 'Nothing good, sir. No one's found the dog. The Guilds are all battening down. Mr Scrope has been getting a lot of visitors. Oh, and High Priest Ridcully is telling everyone that he thinks Lord Vetinari went mad because the day before he'd been telling him about a plan to make lobsters fly through the air.'

'Lobsters flying through the air,' said Vimes flatly.

'And something about sending ships by semaphore, sir.'

'Oh, dear. And what is Mr Scrope saying?'

'Apparently he says he's looking forward to a new era in our history and will put Ankh-Morpork back on the path of responsible citizenship, sir.'

'Is that the same as the lobsters?'

'It's political, sir. Apparently he wants a return to the values and traditions that made the city great, sir.'

'Does he *know* what those values and traditions *were*?' said Vimes, aghast.

'I assume so, sir,' said Carrot, keeping a straight face.

'Oh my gods. I'd rather take a chance on the lobsters.'

It was sleeting again, out of a darkening sky. The Misbegot Bridge was more or less empty; William lurked in the shadows, his hat pulled down over his eyes.

Eventually a voice out of nowhere said, 'So . . . you got your bit of paper?'

'Deep Bone?' said William, startled out of the reverie.

'I'm sending a . . . a guide for you to follow,' said the

hidden informant. 'Name of ... name of ... Trixiebell. Just you follow him and everything will be okay. Ready?'

'Yes.'

Deep Bone is watching me, William thought. He must be really close.

Trixiebell trotted out of the shadows.

It was a poodle. More or less.

The staff at Le Poil du Chien, *the* doggie beauty salon, had done their very best, and a craftsman will give of his or her *all* if it means getting Foul Ole Ron out of the shop any faster. They'd cut, blown, permed, crimped, primped, coloured, woven, shampooed, and the manicurist had locked herself in the lavatory and refused to come out.

The result was ... pink. The pinkness was only one aspect of the thing, but it was so ... *pink* that it dominated everything else, even the topiary-effect tail with the fluffy knob on the end. The front of the dog looked as though it had been fired through a large pink ball and had only got halfway. Then there was also the matter of the large glittery collar. It glittered altogether too much; sometimes glass glitters more than diamonds because it has more to prove.

All in all, the effect was not of a poodle but of malformed poodleosity. That is to say, everything about it suggested 'poodle' except for the whole thing itself, which suggested walking away.

'Yip,' it said, and there was something wrong with this, too. William was aware that dogs like this yipped, but this one, he was sure, had *said* 'yip'.

'There's a good ...' he began, and finished '... dog?'

'Yip yipyip sheesh yip,' said the dog, and walked off.

William wondered about the 'sheesh', but decided the dog must have sneezed.

It trotted away through the slush and disappeared down an alley.

A moment later its muzzle appeared around the corner.

'Yip? Whine?'

'Oh, yes. Sorry,' said William.

Trixiebell led the way down greasy steps to the old path that ran along the riverside. It was littered with rubbish, and anything that stays thrown away in Ankh-Morpork is *real* rubbish. The sun seldom got down here, even on a fine day. The shadows contrived to be freezing *and* running with water at the same time.

Nevertheless, there was a fire among the dark timbers under the bridge. William realized, as his nostrils shut down, that he was visiting the Canting Crew.

The old towpath had been deserted to start with, but Foul Ole Ron and the rest of them were the reason that it stayed that way. They had nothing to steal. They had precious little even to keep. Occasionally the Beggars' Guild considered running them out of town, but without much enthusiasm. Even beggars need someone to look down on, and the crew were so far down that in a certain light they sometimes appeared to be on top. Besides, the Guild recognized crafts-manship when they saw it; no one could spit and ooze like Coffin Henry, no one could be as legless as Arnold Sideways and nothing in the *world* could smell like

Foul Ole Ron. He could have used oil of scallatine as a deodorant.

And, as that thought tripped through William's brain, he knew where Wuffles was.

Trixiebell's ridiculous pink tail disappeared into the mass of old packing cases and cardboard known variously to the crew as 'What?', 'Bugrit!', 'Ptooi!' and Home.

William's eyes were already watering. There wasn't much breeze down here. He made his way to the pool of firelight.

'Oh ... good evening, gentlemen,' he managed, nodding to the figures around the green-edged flames.

'Let's see the colour of your bit of paper,' commanded the voice of Deep Bone, from out of the shadows.

'It's, er, off-white,' said William, unfolding the cheque. It was taken by the Duck Man, who scanned it carefully and added noticeably to its off-whiteness.

'It seems to be in order. Fifty dollars, signed,' he said. 'I have explained the concept to my associates, Mr de Worde. It was not easy, I have to tell you.'

'Yeah, and if you don't put up we'll come to your house!' said Coffin Henry.

'Er ... and do what?' said William.

'Stand outside for ever and ever and ever!' said Arnold Sideways.

'Lookin' at people in a funny way,' said the Duck Man.

'Gobbin' on their boots!' said Coffin Henry.

William tried not to think about Mrs Arcanum. He said: 'Now can I see the dog?'

'Show him, Ron,' commanded the voice of Deep Bone.

Ron's heavy coat fell open, revealing Wuffles blinking in the firelight.

'*You* had him?' said William. 'That was all there was to it?'

'Bugrit!'

'Who's going to search Foul Ole Ron?' said Deep Bone.

'Good point,' said William. 'Very good point. Or smell him out.'

'Now, you got to remember he's old,' said Deep Bone. 'An' he wasn't exactly Mr Brain to start with. I mean, we're talkin' dogs here – not *talking dogs*,' said the voice hurriedly, 'but talking *about* dogs, I mean – so don't expect a philosophical treatise, is what I'm sayin'.'

Wuffles begged geriatrically when he saw William looking at him.

'How did he come to be with you?' said William as Wuffles sniffed his hand.

'He came running out of the palace straight under Ron's coat,' said Deep Bone.

'Which is, as you point out, the last place anyone would look,' said William.

'You'd better believe it.'

'And not even a werewolf would find him there.' William took out his notebook, turned to a fresh page, and wrote: 'Wuffles.' He said, 'How old is he?'

Wuffles barked.

'Sixteen,' said Deep Bone. 'Is that important?'

'It's a newspaper thing,' said William. He wrote:

'Wuffles (16), formerly of The Palace, Ankh-Morpork.'

I'm interviewing a dog, he thought. Man Interviews Dog. That's nearly *news*.

'So . . . er, Wuffles, what happened before you ran out of the palace?' he said.

Deep Bone, from his hiding place, whined and growled. Wuffles cocked an ear and then growled back.

'He woke up and experienced a moment of horrible philosophical uncertainty,' said Deep Bone.

'I thought you said—'

'I'm *translatin'*, right? And this was on account of there being two Gods in the room. That's two Lord Vetinaris, Wuffles being an old-fashioned kind of dog. But he knew one was wrong because he smelled wrong. And there were two other men. And then—'

William scribbled furiously.

Twenty seconds later Wuffles bit him hard on the ankle.

The clerk in Mr Slant's front office looked down from his high desk at the two visitors, sniffed and carried on with his laborious copperplate. He did not have a lot of time for the notion of customer service. The Law could not be hurried—

A moment later his head was rammed into the desktop and held down by some enormous weight.

Mr Pin's face appeared in his limited vision.

'I *said*,' said Mr Pin, 'that Mr Slant wants to see us . . .'

'Sngh,' said the clerk. Mr Pin nodded and the pressure was relieved slightly.

'Sorry? You were saying?' said Mr Pin, watching the man's hand creep along the edge of the desk.

'He's ... not ... seeing ... anyone ...' The words ended in a muffled yelp.

Mr Pin leaned down. 'Sorry about the fingers,' he said, 'but we can't have them naughty little things creeping to that little lever there, can we? No telling *what* might happen if you pulled that lever. Now ... which one's Mr Slant's office?'

'Second ... door ... on ... left ...' the man groaned.

'See? It's so much nicer when we're polite. And in a week, two at the outside, you'll be able to pick up a pen again.' Mr Pin nodded to Mr Tulip, who let the man go. He slithered to the floor.

'You want I should —ing scrag him?'

'Leave him,' said Mr Pin. 'I think I'm going to be nice to people today.'

He had to hand it to Mr Slant. When the New Firm stepped into his office the lawyer looked up and his expression barely flickered.

'Gentlemen?' he said.

'Don't press a —ing *thing*,' said Mr Tulip.

'There's something you should know,' said Mr Pin, pulling a box out of his jacket.

'And what is that?' said Mr Slant.

Mr Pin flicked a catch on the side of the box.

'Let's hear about yesterday,' he said.

The imp blinked.

'... nyip ... nyapnyip ... nyapdit ... nyip ...' it said.

'It's just working its way backwards,' said Mr Pin.

'What is this?' said the lawyer.

'... nyapnyip ... sipnyap ... nip ... *is valuable, Mr Pin. So I will not spin this out. What did you do with the dog?*' Mr Pin's finger touched another lever. '... wheedlewheedle whee ... *My ... clients have long memories and deep pockets. Other killers can be hired. Do you understand me?*'

There was a tiny 'Ouch' as the Off lever hit the imp on the head.

Mr Slant got up and walked across to an ancient cabinet.

'Would you like a drink, Mr Pin? I am afraid I have only embalming fluid ...'

'Not yet, Mr Slant.'

'... and I think I probably have a banana somewhere ...'

Mr Slant turned, smiling beatifically, at the sound of the smack of Mr Pin catching Mr Tulip's arm.

'I *told* you I'm gonna —ing *kill* him—'

'Too late, alas,' said the lawyer, sitting down again. 'Very well, Mr Pin. This is about money, is it?'

'All we're owed, plus another fifty thousand.'

'But you haven't found the dog.'

'Nor have the Watch. And *they*'ve got a werewolf. *Everyone*'s looking for the dog. The dog's gone. But that doesn't matter. This little box matters.'

'That is very little in the way of evidence ...'

'Really? You asking us about the dog? Talking about killers? I reckon that Vimes character will niggle away at something like that. He doesn't sound like the sort to let things go.' Mr Pin smiled humourlessly. 'You've got stuff on us but, well, between you and me,' he leaned closer, 'some of the things we've done might be considered, well, tantamount to crimes—'

'All them —ing murders, for a start,' said Mr Tulip, nodding.

'Which, since we *are* criminals, could be called typical behaviour. Whereas,' Pin went on, 'you're a respectable citizen. Doesn't look good, respectable citizens getting involved in this sort of thing. People talk.'

'To save . . . misunderstandings,' said Mr Slant, 'I will do you a draft of—'

'Jewels,' said Mr Pin.

'We *like* jewels,' said Mr Tulip.

'You have made copies of that . . . thing?' said Slant.

'I'm not saying anything,' said Mr Pin, who hadn't and didn't even know how. But he took the view that Mr Slant was in no position to be other than cautious, and it looked as though Mr Slant thought so too.

'I wonder if I can trust you?' said Mr Slant, as if to himself.

'Well, you see, it's like this,' said Mr Pin, as patiently as he could. His head was feeling worse. 'If news got around that we'd shopped a client, that wouldn't be good. People would say, you can't trust a person of that kind of ilk. They do not know how to behave. But if the people *we* deal with heard we'd scragged a client because the client had not played fair, then they would say to themselves, these are businessmen. They are businesslike. They do business . . .'

He stopped and looked at the shadows in the corner of the room.

'And?' said Mr Slant.

'And . . . and . . . the hell with this,' said Mr Pin, blinking and shaking his head. 'Give us the jewels, Slant, or Mr Tulip'll do the asking, understand? We're getting out of here, with your damn dwarfs and vampires and trolls and dead men walking. This city gives me the creeps! So give me the diamonds! Right now!'

'Very well,' said Mr Slant. 'And the imp?'

'It goes with us. We get caught, it gets caught. We die mysteriously, then . . . some people find out about things. When we are safely away . . . you're in no position to argue, Slant.' Mr Pin shuddered. 'I am not having a good day!'

Mr Slant pulled open a desk drawer and tossed three small velvet bags on to the leather top. Mr Pin mopped his brow with a handkerchief.

'Take a look at 'em, Mr Tulip.'

There was a pause while both men watched Mr Tulip pour the gems into one enormous palm. He scrutinized several through an eyeglass. He sniffed at them. He gingerly licked one or two.

Then he picked four out of the heap and tossed them back to the lawyer.

'You think I'm some kind of a —ing idiot?' he said.

'Don't even think of arguing,' said Mr Pin.

'Perhaps the jewellers made a mistake,' said Mr Slant.

'Yeah?' said Mr Pin. His hand darted into his jacket again, but this time came out holding a weapon.

Mr Slant looked into the muzzle of a spring-gonne. It was technically and legally a crossbow, in that human strength compressed the spring, but it had been reduced by patient technology to a point where it was more or less a pipe with a handle and a trigger. Anyone caught with one by the Assassins' Guild, it was rumoured, would find its ability to be hidden on the human body tested to extremes; any city watch that found one used against them would see to it that the offender's feet did not touch the ground but instead swung gently as the breeze pushed them around.

There must have been a switch in this desk, too. A door flew open and two men burst in, one armed with two long knives, one with a crossbow.

It was quite horrible, what Mr Tulip did to them.

It was, in its way, a kind of skill. When an armed man runs into a room in the knowledge that there is trouble he needs a fraction of a second to assess, to decide, to calculate, to *think*. Mr Tulip didn't need a fraction of a second. He didn't think. His hands moved by themselves.

It required, even for the calculating eyes of Mr Slant, a mental action replay. And even in the slow-mo of horror, it was hard to see Mr Tulip grab the nearest chair and swing it. At the end of the blur two men lay unconscious, one with an arm twisted in a disconcerting way, and a knife was shuddering in the ceiling.

Mr Pin hadn't turned round. He kept the gonne pointed at the zombie. But he produced from a pocket a small cigarette lighter in the shape of a dragon, and *then* Mr Slant ... Mr Slant, who crackled when he walked and smelled of dust ... Mr Slant saw, wrapped around the evil little bolt that just projected from the tube, a wad of cloth.

Without taking his eyes off the lawyer Mr Pin applied the flame. The cloth flared. And Mr Slant was very dry indeed.

'This is a bad thing I'm about to do,' Pin said, as if hypnotized. 'But I've done so many bad things, this one'll hardly count. It's like . . . *a* killing is a big thing, but *another* killing, that's kind of half the size. You know? So it's, like, when you've done twenty killings, they barely notice, on average. But . . . it's a nice day today, the birds is singing, there's stuff like . . . kittens and stuff, and the sun is shining off the snow, bringin' the promise of spring to come, with flowers, and fresh grass, and more kittens and hot summer days an' the gentle kiss of the rain and wonderful clean things *which you won't ever see if you don't give us what's in that drawer 'cos you'll burn like a torch you double-dealing twisty dried-up cheating son of a bitch!'*

Mr Slant scrabbled in the drawer and threw down another velvet bag. Glancing nervously at his partner, who'd never even *mentioned* kittens before except in the same sentence as 'water barrel', Mr Tulip took it and examined the contents.

'Rubies,' he said. '—ing good ones.'

'Now go away from here,' rasped Mr Slant. 'Right away. Never come back. I've never heard of you. I've never seen you.'

He stared at the spluttering flame.

Mr Slant had faced many bad things in the last few hundred years, but right now nothing seemed more menacing than Mr Pin. Or more erratically deranged, either. The man was swaying, and his gaze kept flickering into the shadowy corners of the room.

Mr Tulip shook his partner's shoulder. 'Let's —ing scrag him and go?' he suggested.

Pin blinked. 'Right,' he said, appearing to return to his own head. 'Right.' He glanced at the zombie. 'I think I shall let you live today,' he said, blowing out the flame. 'Tomorrow . . . who knows?'

It wasn't a bad threat, but somehow his heart wasn't in it.

Then the New Firm had gone.

Mr Slant sat down and stared at the closed door. It was clear to him, and a dead man has experience in these matters, that his two armed clerks, veterans of many a legal battle, were beyond help. Mr Tulip was an expert.

He took a sheet of writing paper from a drawer, wrote a few words in block letters, sealed it in an envelope and sent for another clerk.

'Have arrangements made,' he said, when the man stared at his fallen colleagues, 'and then take this to de Worde.'

'Which one, sir?'

For a moment Mr Slant had forgotten that point.

'*Lord* de Worde,' he said. 'Definitely *not* the other one.'

William de Worde turned a page in his notebook and continued to scribble. The crew were watching him as if he was a public entertainment.

'That's a grand gift you have there, sur,' said Arnold Sideways. 'It does the heart good to see the pencil waggling like that. I wish I had the knowing of it, but I've never been mechanical.'

'Would you care for a cup of tea?' said the Duck Man.

'You drink tea down here?'

'Of course. Why not? What kind of people do you think we are?' The Duck Man held up a blackened teapot and a rusty mug with an inviting smile.

It was probably a good moment to be polite, thought William. Besides, the water would have been boiled, wouldn't it?

'. . . no milk, though,' he said quickly. He could imagine what the milk would be like.

'Ah, I said you were a gentleman,' said the Duck Man, pouring a tarry brown liquid into the mug. 'Milk in tea is an abomination.' He picked up, with a dainty gesture, a plate and pair of tongs. 'Slice of lemon?' he added.

'Lemon? You have *lemon*?'

'Oh, even Mr Ron here would rather wash under his arms than have anything but lemon in his tea,' said the Duck Man, plopping a slice into William's mug.

'And four sugars,' said Arnold Sideways.

William took a deep draught of the tea. It was thick and stewed, but it was also sweet and hot. And slightly lemony. All in all, he considered, it could have been much worse.

'Yes, we're very fortunate when it comes to slices of lemon,' said the Duck Man, busily fussing over the tea things. 'Why, it is indeed a bad day when we can't find two or three slices floating down the river.'

William stared fixedly at the river wall.

Spit or swallow, he thought, the eternal conundrum.

'Are you all right, Mr de Worde?'

'Mmf.'

'Too much sugar?'

'Mmf.'

'Not too hot?'

William gratefully sprayed the tea in the direction of the river.

'Ah!' he said. 'Yes! Too hot! That's what it was! Too hot! Lovely tea but – too hot! I'll just put the rest down here by my foot to cool down, shall I?'

He snatched up his pencil and pad.

'So . . . er, Wuffles, *which* man was it that you bit on the leg?'

Wuffles barked.

'He bit all of them,' said the voice of Deep Bone. 'When you're biting, why stop?'

'Would you know them if you bit them again?'

'He says he would. He says the big man tasted of . . . you know . . .' Deep Bone paused, 'like a . . . wossname . . . big, big bowl with hot water and soap in it.'

'A bath?'

Wuffles growled.

'That'd . . . be the word,' said Deep Bone. 'An' the other one smelled of cheap hair oil. And the one who looked like G— like Lord Vetinari, he smelled of wine.'

'Wine?'

'Yes. Wuffles also says he'd like to apologize for biting you just now, but he got carried away with the recollection. We— that is to say, dogs have very *physical* memories, if you see what I mean.'

William nodded and rubbed his leg. The description of the invasion of the Oblong Office had been carried out in a succession of yelps, barks and growls, with Wuffles running around in circles and snapping at his own tail until he bumped into William's ankle.

'And Ron's been carrying him around in his coat ever since?'

'No one bothers Foul Ole Ron,' said Deep Bone.

'I believe you,' said William. He nodded at Wuffles.

'I want to get an iconograph of him,' he said. 'This is ... amazing stuff. But we must have a picture to prove I've really talked to Wuffles. Well ... via an interpreter, obviously. I wouldn't want people to think this is one of the *Inquirer*'s stupid "talking dog" stories ...'

There was some muttering amongst the crew. The request was not being favourably received.

'This is a select neighbourhood, you know,' said the Duck Man. 'We don't allow just anybody down here.'

'But there's a path running right under the bridge!' said William. 'Anyone could walk right past!'

'Werll, yerss,' said Coffin Henry. 'They *could*.' He coughed and spat with great expertise into the fire. 'Only they don't no more.'

'Bugrit,' explained Foul Ole Ron. 'Choking a tinker? Garn! I *told* 'em. Millennium hand *and* shrimp!'

'Then you'd better come back to the office with me,' said William. 'After all, you've been carrying him around while you've been selling the papers, haven't you?'

'Too dangerous now,' said Deep Bone.

'Would it be less dangerous for another fifty dollars?' said William.

'*Another* fifty dollars?' said Arnold Sideways. 'That'll make it *fifteen* dollars!'

'A hundred dollars,' said William wearily. 'You do realize, don't you, that this is in the public interest?'

The crew craned their necks.

'Don't see anyone watching,' said Coffin Henry.

William stepped forward, quite accidentally knocking over his tea.

'Come on, then,' he said.

Mr Tulip was beginning to worry now. This was unusual. In the area of worry, he had tended to be the cause rather than the recipient. But Mr Pin was not acting right, and since Mr Pin was the man who did the thinking this was a matter of some concern. Mr Tulip was good at thinking in split-seconds, and when it came to art appreciation he could easily think in centuries, but he was not happy over middle distances. He needed Mr Pin for that.

But Mr Pin was talking to himself, and kept staring at shadows.

'We'll be heading off now?' said Mr Tulip, in the hope of directing matters. 'We've got the —ing payment with a —ing big bonus, no —ing point in hanging around?'

He was also worried about the way Mr Pin had acted with the —ing lawyer. It wasn't like him to point a weapon at someone and then not use it. The New Firm didn't go round threatening people. They *were* the threat. All that —ing stuff about 'letting you live for today' . . . that was amateur stuff.

'I said, are we heading—'

'What do you think happens to people when they die, Tulip?'

Mr Tulip was taken aback. 'What kind of —ing question is *that*? You *know* what happens!'

'Do I?'

'Certainly. Remember when we had to leave that guy in that —ing barn and it was a week before we got to bury him properly? Remember how his—'

'I don't mean bodies!'

'Ah. Religion stuff, then?'

'Yes!'

'I never worry about that —ing stuff.'

'Never?'

'Never —ing give it a thought. I've got my potato.'

Then Mr Tulip found that he'd walked a few feet alone, because Mr Pin had stopped dead.

'Potato?'

'Oh, yeah. Keep it on a string round my neck.' Mr Tulip tapped his huge chest.

'And that's religious?'

'Well, yeah. If you've got your potato when you die, everything will be okay.'

'What religion is that?'

'Dunno. Never ran across it outside our village. I was only a kid. I mean, it's like gods, right? When you're a kid, they say "that's God, that is". Then you grow up and you find there's —ing *millions* of 'em. Same with religion.'

'And it's all okay if you have a potato when you die?'

'Yep. You're allowed to come back and have another life.'

'Even if . . .' Mr Pin swallowed, for he was in territory which had never before existed on his internal atlas, '. . . even if you've done things which people might think were bad?'

'Like chopping up people and —ing shovin' 'em off cliffs?'

'Yeah, that kind of thing . . .'

Mr Tulip sniffed, causing his nose to flash. 'We-ell, it's okay so long as you're really —ing sorry about it.'

Mr Pin was amazed, and a little suspicious. But he could feel things . . . catching up. There were faces in the darkness and voices on the cusp of hearing. He dared not turn his head now, in case he saw anything behind him.

You could buy a *sack* of potatoes for a dollar.

'It *works*?' he said.

'Sure. Back home people'd been doing it for hundreds of —ing years. They wouldn't be doing it if it didn't —ing work, would they?'

'Where *was* that?'

Mr Tulip tried to concentrate on this question, but there were many scabs in his memory.

'There was . . . forests,' he said. 'And . . . bright candles,' he muttered. 'An' . . . secrets,' he added, staring into nothing.

'And potatoes?'

Mr Tulip came back to the here and now.

'Yeah, them,' he said. 'Always lots of —ing potatoes. If you've got your potato, it will be all right.'

'But . . . I thought you had to pray in deserts and go to a temple every day, and sing songs, and give stuff to the poor . . . ?'

'Oh, you can do all that too, sure,' said Mr Tulip. 'Just so long as you've got your —ing potato.'

'And you come back alive?' said Mr Pin, still trying to find the small print.

'Sure. No point in coming back dead. Who'd notice the —ing difference?'

Mr Pin opened his mouth to reply, and Mr Tulip saw his expression change.

'Someone's got their hand on my shoulder!' he hissed.

'You feeling all right, Mr Pin?'

'You can't see anyone?'

'Nope.'

Clenching his fists, Mr Pin turned round. There were plenty of people in the street, but no one gave him a second glance.

He tried to reorganize the jigsaw that his mind was rapidly becoming.

'Okay. Okay,' he said. 'What we'll do . . . we'll go back to the house, okay, and . . . and we'll get the rest of the diamonds, and we'll scrag Charlie, and, and . . . we'll find a vegetable shop . . . any special *kind* of potato?'

'Nope.'

'Right . . . but first . . .' Mr Pin stopped, and his mind's ear heard footsteps stop behind him a moment later. The damn vampire had *done* something to him, he knew. The darkness had been like a tunnel, and there had been *things* . . .

Mr Pin believed in threats, and in violence, and at a time like this he believed in revenge. An inner voice that currently passed for sanity was making a clamour, but it was overruled by a deeper and more automatic response.

'That bloody vampire did this,' he said. 'And killing a vampire . . . *hey* . . . that's practically *good*, right?' He brightened. Salvation beckoned through Holy Works. 'Everyone knows they have evil occult powers. Could even count in a man's favour, eh?'

'Yeah. But . . . who cares?'

'I do.'

'Okay.' Even Mr Tulip didn't argue with that tone of voice. Mr Pin could be inventively unpleasant. Besides, part of the code was that you did not leave an insult unavenged. Everyone knew that.

It was just that nervousness was beginning to percolate even into the bath-salt-and-worming-powder-ravaged pathways of his own brain. He'd always admired the way Mr Pin wasn't frightened of difficult things, like long sentences.

'What'll we use?' he said. 'A stake?'

'No,' said Mr Pin. 'With this one I want to be *certain*.'

He lit a cigarette, with a hand that shook just a little, and then let the match flare up.

'Ah. Right,' said Mr Tulip.

'Let's just *do* it,' said Mr Pin.

Rocky's brow furrowed as he looked at the seals nailed around the doors of the de Worde town house.

'What's dem things?' he said.

'They're to say the Guilds will interest themselves in anyone who breaks in,' said Sacharissa, fumbling with the key. 'It's a sort of curse. Only it works.'

'Dat one's the Assassins?' said the troll, indicating a crude shield with the cloak-and-dagger and double-cross.

'Yes. It means there's an automatic contract out on anyone who breaks in.'

'Wouldn't want dem interested in *me*. Good job you got a key . . .'

The lock clicked. The door opened at a push.

Sacharissa had been in a number of Ankh-Morpork's great houses, when the owners had thrown parts of them open to the public in aid of some of the more respectable charities. She hadn't realized how a building could change when people no longer wanted to live in it. It felt threatening and out of scale. The doorways were too big, the ceilings too high. The musty, empty atmosphere descended on her like a headache.

Behind her Rocky lit a couple of lanterns. But even their light left her surrounded by shadows.

At least the main staircase wasn't hard to find, and William's hasty directions led her to a suite of rooms bigger than her house. The wardrobe, when she found it, was simply a room full of rails and hangers.

Things glittered in the gloom. The dresses also smelled strongly of mothballs.

'Dat's interestin',' said Rocky, behind her.

'Oh, it's just to keep the moths away,' said Sacharissa.

'I'm lookin' at all the footprints,' said the troll. 'Dey were in the hall, too.'

She tore her gaze away from the rows of dresses and looked down. The dust was certainly disturbed.

'Er . . . cleaning lady?' she said. '*Someone* must come in to keep an eye on things?'

'What she do, *kick* der dust to death?'

'I suppose there must be . . . caretakers and things?' said Sacharissa uncertainly. A blue dress was saying: wear me, I'm just your type. See me shimmer.

Rocky prodded a box of mothballs that had spilled out across a dressing table and rolled into the dust.

'Looks like dem moths are really keen on dese things,' he said.

'You don't think a dress like this would be a bit . . . forward, do you?' said Sacharissa, holding the dress against herself.

Rocky looked worried. He hadn't been hired for his dress sense, and certainly not for his grasp of colloquial Middle Class.

'You're quite a lot forward already,' he opined.

'I *meant* make me look like a fast woman!'

'Ah, right,' said Rocky, getting there. 'No. Def'nitly not.'

'Really?'

'Sure. No one could run much in a dress like dat.'

Sacharissa gave up. 'I suppose Mrs Hotbed could let it out a bit,' she said, reflectively. It was tempting to stay, because some of the racks were quite full, but she felt like a trespasser here and part of her was certain that a woman with hundreds of dresses was *more* likely to miss one than a woman with a dozen or so.

In any case, the empty darkness was getting on her nerves. It was full of other people's ghosts. 'Let's get back.'

When they were halfway across the hall someone started to sing. The words were incoherent and the tune was being modulated by alcohol, but it was singing of a sort and it was under their feet.

Rocky shrugged when Sacharissa glanced at him.

'Maybe all dem moths is having a ball?' he said.

'There *must* be a caretaker, mustn't there? Maybe we'd better just, you know, mention we've been here?' Sacharissa agonized. 'It hardly seems polite, just taking things and running . . .'

She headed for a green door tucked away beside the staircase and pushed it open. The singing went louder for a moment but stopped as soon as she said, 'Excuse me?' into the darkness.

After a few moments' silence a voice said: 'Hello! How are you? I'm fine!'

'It's only, er, me? William said it was all right?' She presented the statement like a question, in the voice of someone who was apologizing to a burglar for discovering him.

'Mr Mothball Nose? Whoops!' said the voice in the shadows at the bottom of the stairs.

'Er . . . are *you* all right?'

'Can't get . . . it's a . . . hahaha . . . it's all chains . . . hahaha . . .'

'Are you . . . ill?'

'No, I'm fine, not ill at all, jus' had a few too many . . .'

'Few too many what?' said Sacharissa, speaking from a sheltered upbringing.

'. . . wazza . . . things you put drink in . . . barrels?'

'You're *drunk*?'

'Tha's right! Tha's the word! Drunk as a . . . thing . . . smellything . . . ahahaha . . .'

There was a tinkle of glass.

The lantern's weak glow showed what looked like a wine cellar, but a man was slumped on a bench against one wall and a chain ran from his ankle to a ring set in the floor.

'Are you . . . a *prisoner*?' said Sacharissa.

'Ahaha . . .'

'How long have you been down here?' She crept down.

'Years . . .'

'Years?'

'Got lots of years . . .' The man picked up a bottle and peered at it. 'Now . . . Year of the Amending Camel . . . that was bloodigoodyear . . . and this one . . . Year of the Translated Rat . . . another bloodigoodyear . . . bloodigoodyears, the lot of them. Could do with a biscuit, though.'

Sacharissa's knowledge of vintages extended just as far as knowing that Chateau Maison was a very popular wine. But people didn't have to be chained up to drink wine, even the stuff from Ephebe that stuck the glass to the table.

She moved a little closer and the light fell on the man's face. It was locked in the grin of the seriously drunk, but it was very recognizable. She saw it every day, on coins.

'Er ... Rocky,' she said. 'Er ... can you come down here a minute?'

The door burst open and the troll came down the steps at speed. Unfortunately, it was because he was rolling.

Mr Tulip appeared at the top of the stairs, massaging his fist.

'It's Mr Sneezy!' said Charlie, raising a bottle. 'The gang's all here! Whoopee!'

Rocky got up, weaving slightly. Mr Tulip strolled down the steps, ripping out the doorpost as he passed. The troll raised his fists in the classic boxer's pose, but Mr Tulip didn't bother with niceties of that kind and hit him hard with the length of ancient wood. Rocky went over like a tree.

Only then did the huge man with the revolving eyes try to focus them on Sacharissa.

'Who the —ing hell are you?'

'Don't you dare swear at me!' she said. 'How dare you swear in the presence of a lady!'

This seemed to nonplus him. 'I don't —ing swear!'

'Here, I've seen you before, you're that— I *knew* you weren't a proper virgin!' said Sacharissa triumphantly.

There was the click of a crossbow. Some tiny sounds carry well and have considerable stopping power.

'There are some thoughts too dreadful to think,' said the skinny man looking at her from the top of the steps and down the length of a pistol bow. 'What are *you* doing here, lady?'

'And you were Brother Pin! You haven't got any right here! *I've* got a key!' Some areas of Sacharissa's mind that dealt with things like death and terror were signalling to be heard at this point, but, being part of Sacharissa, they were trying to do it in a ladylike way, and so she ignored them.

'A key?' said Brother Pin, advancing down the stairs. The bow stayed pointing at her. Even in his current state of mind, Mr Pin knew how to aim. 'Who'd give you a key?'

'Don't you come near me! Don't you *dare* come near me! If you come near me I'll – I'll write it down!'

'Yeah? Well, one thing I know is, words don't hurt,' said Mr Pin. 'I've heard lots of—'

He stopped and grimaced, and for a moment it looked as if he'd fall to his knees. He righted himself and focused on her again.

'*You* are coming with *us*,' he said. 'An' don't say you're going to scream, because we're all alone here and I've ... heard ... lots ... of ... screams ...'

Once again he seemed to run down, and again he recovered. Sacharissa stared in horror at the weaving crossbow. Those parts of her advocating silence as a survival aid had finally made themselves heard.

'What about these two?' said Mr Tulip. 'We're scragging 'em now?'

'Chain them up and leave them.'

'But we *always*—'

'Leave them!'

'You sure you feel all right?' said Mr Tulip.

'No! I don't! Just leave them, okay? We haven't got time!'

'We've got lots of—'

'I haven't!' Mr Pin strode up to Sacharissa. 'Who gave you that key?'

'I'm not going to—'

'Do you want Mr Tulip here to say goodbye to our drunken friends?' In his buzzing head, and with his shaky grasp of how things were supposed to work in a moral universe, Mr Pin reckoned that this was all right. After all, their shadows would follow Mr Tulip, not him . . .

'This house belongs to Lord de Worde and his son gave me the key!' said Sacharissa triumphantly. 'There! He was the one you met at the newspaper! *Now* you know what you've got yourself into, eh?'

Mr Pin stared at her.

Then he said, 'I'm going to find out. Don't run. *Really* don't scream. Walk normally and everything—' He paused. 'I was going to say it will be all right,' he said. 'But that would be silly, wouldn't it . . . ?'

It wasn't fast, going through the streets with the crew. To them the world was a permanent theatre, art gallery, music hall, restaurant and spittoon, and in any case no member of the crew would dream of going anywhere in a straight line.

The poodle Trixiebell accompanied them, keeping as close to the centre of the group as possible. Of Deep Bone there was no sign. William had offered to carry Wuffles, because in a way he felt he owned him. A hundred dollars' worth of him, at least. It was a hundred dollars he hadn't got but, well, *surely* tomorrow's edition would pay for that. And anyone after the dog now surely wouldn't try anything out here on the street, in broad daylight, especially since it was barely narrow daylight now. Clouds filled the sky like old eiderdowns, the fog that was descending was meeting the river mist coming up, and the light was draining out of everything.

He tried to think of the headline. He couldn't quite get a grip on it yet. There was too much to say, and he wasn't good at getting the huge complexities of the world into fewer than half a dozen words. Sacharissa was better at it, because she treated words as lumps of letters that could be hammered together any old how. Her best one had been on some tedious inter-Guild squabble and, in single column, read:

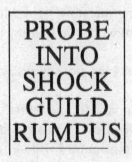

PROBE
INTO
SHOCK
GUILD
RUMPUS

William just wasn't used to the idea of evaluating words purely in terms of their length, whereas she'd picked up the habit in two days. He'd already had to stop her calling Lord Vetinari CITY BOSS. It was technically correct that if you spent some time with a thesaurus you *could* arrive at that description, and it did fit in a single column, but the sight of the words had made William feel extremely exposed.

It was self-absorption like this that allowed him to walk into the printing shed, with the crew tagging along, and not notice anything wrong until he saw the expression on the faces of the dwarfs.

'Ah, our writer man,' said Mr Pin, stepping forward. 'Shut the door, Mr Tulip.'

Mr Tulip slammed the door with one hand. The other was clamped over Sacharissa's mouth. She rolled her eyes at William.

'And you've brought me the little doggie,' said Mr Pin. Wuffles started to growl as he approached. William backed away.

'The Watch will be here soon,' said William. Wuffles still growled, on a rising note.

'Doesn't worry me now,' said Mr Pin. 'Not with what I know. Not with *who* I know. *Where's the damn vampire?*'

'I don't know! He's not always with us!' snapped William.

'Really? In that case let me retort!' said Mr Pin, his pistol bow inches from William's face. 'If it doesn't arrive within two minutes I will—'

Wuffles leapt out of William's arms. His bark was the frantic *whurwhur* of a small dog mad with fury. Pin reared back, one arm raised to protect his face. The bow fired. The arrow hit one of the lamps over the press. The lamp exploded.

A cloud of burning oil rained down. It splattered across type metal and old rocking horses and dwarfs.

Mr Tulip let go of Sacharissa to help his colleague, and in the slow dance of rushing events Sacharissa spun round and planted her knee hard and firmly in the place that made a parsnip a very funny thing indeed.

William grabbed her on the way past and rushed

her out into the freezing air. When he fought his way back in through the stampeding crew, who had the same instinctive reaction to fire as they did to soap and water, it was into a room full of burning debris. Dwarfs were fighting fires in the rubbish. Dwarfs were fighting fires in their beards. Several were advancing on Mr Tulip, who was on his hands and knees and throwing up. And Mr Pin was spinning around, flailing at an enraged Wuffles, who was managing to growl while sinking his teeth into Pin's arm all the way to the bone.

William cupped his hands. 'Get out right now!' he yelled. 'The tins!'

One or two dwarfs heard him, and looked around at the shelves of old paint tins just as the first one blew off its lid.

The tins were ancient, no more now than rust held together with chemical sludge. Several others were starting to burn.

Mr Pin danced across the floor, trying to shake the enraged dog from his arm.

'Get the damn thing off'f me!' he yelled.

'Forget the —ing dog, my —ing *suit's* on fire!' shouted Mr Tulip, flailing at his own sleeve.

A tin of what had once been enamel paint took off from the blazing mess, spinning with a *wzipwzip* noise, and exploded on the press.

William grabbed Goodmountain's shoulder. 'I said *come on*!'

'My press! It's on fire!'

'Better it than us! Come *on*!'

* * *

It was said of the dwarfs that they cared more about things like iron and gold than they did about people, because there was only a limited supply of iron and gold in the world whereas there seemed to be more and more people everywhere you looked. It was said mostly by people like Mr Windling.

But they *did* care fiercely about things. Without things, people were just bright animals.

The printers clustered around the doorway, axes at the ready. Choking brown smoke billowed out. Flames licked out among the roof eaves. Several sections of tin roof buckled and collapsed.

As they did so a smouldering ball rocketed out through the door and three dwarfs who took a swipe only just missed hitting one another.

It was Wuffles. Patches of fur were still smoking, but his eyes gleamed and he was still whining and growling.

He let William pick him up. He had a triumphant air about him, and turned to watch the burning doorway with his ears cocked.

'That must be it, then,' said Sacharissa.

'They might have got out of the back door,' said Goodmountain. 'Boddony, some of you go round and check, will you?'

'Plucky dog, this,' said William.

' "Brave" would be better,' said Sacharissa distantly. 'It's only five letters. It would look better in a single-column sidebar. No . . . "Plucky" *would* work, because then we'd get:

PLUCKY
DOG PUTS
BITE ON
VILLAINS

. . . although that first line is a bit shy.'

'I wish I could think in headlines,' said William, shivering.

It was cool and damp down here in the cellar.

Mr Pin dragged himself to a corner and slapped at the burns on his suit.

'We're —ing trapped,' moaned Tulip.

'Yeah? This is *stone*,' said Pin. 'Stone floor, stone walls, stone ceiling! Stone doesn't burn, okay? We just stay nice and calm down here and wait it out.'

Mr Tulip listened to the sound of the fire above them. Red and yellow light danced on the floor under the cellar hatchway.

'I don't —ing like it,' he said.

'We've seen worse.'

'I don't —ing *like* it!'

'Just keep cool. We're going to get out of this. I wasn't born to fry!'

The flames roared around the press. A few late paint tins pinwheeled through the heat, spraying burning droplets.

The fire was yellow-white at the heart, and now it

crackled around the metal formes that held the type.

Silver beads appeared around the leaden, inky slugs. Letters shifted, settled, ran together. For a moment the words themselves floated on the melting metal, innocent words like 'the' and 'truth' and 'shall make ye fere', and then they were lost. From the red-hot press, and the wooden boxes, and amongst the racks and racks of type, and even out of the piles of carefully stockpiled metal, thin streams began to flow. They met and merged and spread. Soon the floor was a moving, rippling mirror in which the orange and yellow flames danced upside down.

On Otto's workbench the salamanders detected the heat. They *liked* heat. Their ancestors had evolved in volcanoes. They woke up and began to purr.

Mr Tulip, walking up and down the cellar like a trapped animal, picked up one of the cages and glared at the creatures.

'What're these —ing things?' he said, and dropped it back on the bench. Then he noticed the dark jar next to it. 'And why's it —ing got "Handle viz Care!!!" on this one?'

The eels were already edgy. They could detect heat too, and they were creatures of deep caves and buried, icy streams.

There was a flash of dark as they protested.

Most of it went straight through the brain of Mr Tulip. But such as was left of that ragged organ had survived his every attempt at scrambling and in any case Mr Tulip didn't use it much, because it hurt such a lot.

But there was a brief remembrance of snow, and fir woods, and burning buildings, and the church. They'd sheltered there. He'd been small. He remembered big shining paintings, more colours than he'd ever seen before . . .

He blinked and dropped the jar.

It shattered on the floor. There was another burst of dark from the eels. They wriggled desperately out of the wreckage and slithered along the edge of the wall, squeezing into the cracks between the stones.

Mr Tulip turned at a sound behind him. His colleague had collapsed to his knees and was clutching at his head.

'You all right?'

'They're right behind me!' Pin whispered.

'Nah, just you and me down here, old friend.'

Mr Tulip patted Pin on the shoulder. The veins on his forehead stood out with the effort of thinking of something to do next. The memory had gone. Young Tulip had learned how to edit memories. What Mr Pin needed, he decided, was to remember the *good* times.

'Hey, remember when Gerhardt the Boot and his lads had us cornered in that —ing cellar in Quirm?' he said. 'Remember what we did to him afterwards?'

'Yes,' said Mr Pin, staring at the blank wall. 'I *remember.*'

'And that time with that old man who was in that house in Genua and we didn't —ing know? So we nailed up the door and—'

'Shut up! Shut up!'

'Just trying to look on the —ing bright side.'

'We shouldn't have killed all those people . . .' Mr Pin whispered, almost to himself.

'Why not?' said Mr Tulip, but Pin's nervousness had got through to him again. He pulled at the leather cord around his neck and felt the reassuring lump on the end. A potato can be a great help in times of trial.

A pattering behind him made him turn round, and he brightened up.

'Anyway, we're okay now,' he said. 'Looks like it's —ing raining.'

Silver droplets were pouring through the cellar hatch.

'That's not water!' screamed Pin, standing up.

The drops ran together, became a steady stream. It splashed oddly and mounded up under the hatch, but more liquid poured on top of it and spread out across the floor.

Pin and Tulip backed against the far wall.

'That's hot lead,' said Pin. 'They print their paper with it!'

'How —ing much is there going to be?'

'Down here? Can't end up more than a couple of inches, can it?'

At the other side of the cellar Otto's bench started to smoulder as the pool touched it.

'We need something to stand on,' said Pin. 'Just while it cools! It won't take long in this chill!'

'Yeah, but there's nothing here but us! We're —ing *trapped*!'

Mr Pin put his hand over his eyes for a moment and took a deep breath of air that was already getting very warm in the soft silver rain.

He opened his eyes again. Mr Tulip was watching him obediently. Mr Pin was the thinker.

'I've . . . got a plan,' he said.

'Yeah, good. Right.'

'My plans are pretty good, right?'

'Yeah, you come up with some —ing wonders, I've always said. Like when you said we should twist the—'

'And I'm always thinking about the good of the Firm, right?'

'Yeah, sure, right.'

'So . . . this plan . . . it's not, like, a *perfect* plan, but . . . oh, the hell with it. Give me your potato.'

'What?'

Suddenly Mr Pin's arm was stretched out, his cross-bow an inch from Mr Tulip's neck.

'No time to argue! Gimme the damn potato right now! This is no time for you to *think*!'

Uncertain, but trusting as ever in Mr Pin's survival abilities in a tight corner, Mr Tulip pulled the thong of the potato over his head and handed it to Mr Pin.

'Right,' said Mr Pin, one side of his face beginning to twitch. 'The way I see it—'

'You better hurry!' said Mr Tulip. 'It's only a coupla inches away!'

'—*the way I see it*, I'm a small man, Mr Tulip. You couldn't stand on me. I wouldn't do. You're a big man, Mr Tulip. I wouldn't want to see you suffer.'

And he pulled the trigger. It was a good shot.

'Sorry,' he whispered, as the lead splashed. 'Sorry. I'm sorry. Sorry. But I wasn't born to fry . . .'

* * *

Mr Tulip opened his eyes.

There was darkness around him, but with a suggestion of stars overhead behind an overcast sky. The air was still, but there was distant soughing, as of wind in dead trees.

He waited a while to see if anything would happen, and then said: 'Anyone —ing there?'

JUST ME, MR TULIP.

Some of the darkness opened its eyes, and two blue glows looked down at him.

'The —ing bastard stole my potato. Are you —ing Death?'

JUST DEATH WILL SUFFICE, I THINK. WHO WERE YOU EXPECTING?

'Eh? For what?'

TO CLAIM YOU AS ONE OF THEIRS.

'Dunno, really. I never —ing thought . . .'

YOU NEVER SPECULATED?

'All I know is, you got to have your potato, and then it will be all right.' Mr Tulip parroted the sentence without thinking, but it was coming back now in the total recall of the dead, from a vantage point of two feet off the ground and three years of age. Old men mumbling. Old women weeping. Shafts of light through holy windows. The sound of wind under the doors, and every ear straining to hear the soldiers. Us or theirs didn't matter, when a war had gone on this long . . .

Death gave the shade of Mr Tulip a long, cool stare.

AND THAT'S IT?

'Right.'

YOU DON'T THINK THERE WERE ANY BITS YOU MIGHT
HAVE MISSED?

. . . the sound of wind under the doors, the smell of
the oil lamps, the fresh acid smell of snow, blowing in
through the . . .

'And . . . if I'm sorry for everything . . .' he
mumbled. He was lost in a world of darkness, without
a potato to his name.

. . . candlesticks . . . they'd been made of gold,
hundreds of years ago . . . there were only ever
potatoes to eat, grubbed up from under the snow, but
the candlesticks were of gold . . . and some old
woman, she'd said: 'It'll all turn out right if you've got
a potato . . .'

WAS ANY GOD OF SOME SORT MENTIONED TO YOU AT
ANY POINT?

'No . . .'

DAMN. I WISH THEY DIDN'T LEAVE ME TO DEAL WITH
THIS SORT OF THING, Death sighed. YOU *BELIEVE*, BUT
YOU DON'T BELIEVE *IN* ANYTHING.

Mr Tulip stood with his head bowed. More
memories were trickling back now, like blood under a
closed door. And the knob was rattling, and the lock
had failed.

Death nodded at him.

AT LEAST YOU STILL HAVE YOUR POTATO, I SEE.

Mr Tulip's hand flew to his neck. There was something wizened and hard there, on the end of a string. It
had a ghostly shimmer to it.

'I thought he got it!' he said, his face alight with hope.

AH, WELL. YOU NEVER KNOW WHEN A POTATO MIGHT
TURN UP.

'So it's all going to be all right?'

WHAT DO *YOU* THINK?

Mr Tulip swallowed. Lies did not survive long out here. And more recent memories were squeezing under the door now, bloody and vengeful.

'I think it's gonna take more than a potato,' he said.

ARE YOU SORRY FOR EVERYTHING?

More unused bits of Mr Tulip's brain, which had shut down long ago or had never even opened up, came into play.

'How will I know?' he said.

Death waved a hand through the air. Along the arc described by the bony fingers appeared a line of hourglasses.

I UNDERSTAND YOU ARE A CONNOISSEUR, MR TULIP. IN A SMALL WAY, SO AM I. Death selected one of the glasses and held it up. Images appeared around it, bright but insubstantial as shadow.

'What are they?' said Tulip.

LIVES, MR TULIP. JUST LIVES. NOT ALL MASTERPIECES, OBVIOUSLY, OFTEN RATHER NAIF IN THEIR USE OF EMOTION AND ACTION, BUT NEVERTHELESS FULL OF INTEREST AND SURPRISE AND, EACH IN THEIR OWN WAY, A WORK OF SOME GENIUS. AND CERTAINLY VERY ... COLLECTABLE. Death picked up an hourglass as Mr Tulip tried to back away. YES. COLLECTABLE. BECAUSE, IF I HAD TO FIND A WAY TO DESCRIBE *THESE* LIVES, MR TULIP, THAT WORD WOULD BE 'SHORTER'.

Death selected another hourglass. AH. NUGGA VELSKI. YOU WILL NOT REMEMBER HIM, OF COURSE. HE WAS SIMPLY A MAN WHO WALKED INTO HIS RATHER SIMPLE

LITTLE HUT AT THE WRONG TIME, AND YOU ARE A BUSY MAN AND CANNOT BE EXPECTED TO REMEMBER *EVERYONE*. NOTE THE MIND, A BRILLIANT MIND THAT MIGHT IN OTHER CIRCUMSTANCES HAVE CHANGED THE WORLD, DOOMED TO BE BORN INTO A TIME AND PLACE WHERE LIFE WAS NOTHING BUT A DAILY, HOPELESS STRUGGLE. NEVERTHELESS, IN HIS TINY VILLAGE, RIGHT UP UNTIL THE DAY HE FOUND YOU STEALING HIS COAT, HE DID HIS BEST TO—

Mr Tulip raised a trembling hand. 'Is this the bit where my whole life passes in front of my eyes?' he said.

NO, THAT WAS THE BIT JUST NOW.

'Which bit?'

THE BIT, said Death, BETWEEN YOUR BEING BORN AND YOUR DYING. NO, THIS . . . MR TULIP, THIS IS YOUR WHOLE LIFE AS IT PASSED BEFORE *OTHER PEOPLE'S* EYES . . .

By the time the golems arrived it was all over. The fire had been fierce but short-lived. It had stopped because there wasn't anything left to burn. The crowd that always turns up to watch a fire then dispersed until the next one, reckoning that this one had not scored very highly, what with no one dying.

The walls were still standing. Half the tin roof had fallen in. Sleet had begun to fall, too, and now it hissed on the hot stone as William picked his way cautiously through the debris.

The press was visible in the light of the few fires still smouldering. William heard it sizzling under the sleet.

'Repairable?' he said to Goodmountain, who was following him.

'Not a chance. The frame, maybe. We'll salvage what we can.'

'Look, I'm so sorry—'

'Not your fault,' said the dwarf, kicking at a smoking can. 'And look on the bright side . . . we still owe Harry King a lot of money.'

'Don't remind me . . .'

'I don't need to. *He'll* remind you. Us, rather.'

William wrapped his jacket around his sleeve and pushed aside some of the roof.

'The desks are still here!'

'Fire can be funny like that,' said Goodmountain gloomily. 'And the roof probably kept the worst of it away.'

'I mean, they're half charred but they're still usable!'

'Oh, *well*, we're home and dry, then,' said the dwarf, now sliding towards 'glumly'. 'How soon do you want the next edition?'

'Look, even the spike . . . there's even bits of paper that are hardly charred!'

'Life is full of unexpected treasure,' said Goodmountain. 'I don't think you should come in here, miss!'

This was to Sacharissa, who was picking her way across the smouldering ruins.

'It's where I work,' she said. 'Can you repair the press?'

'No! It's . . . done for! It's scrap! We've got no press and no type and no metal! Can you both *hear* me?'

'Okay, so we've got to get another press,' said Sacharissa evenly.

'Even an old scrap one would cost a thousand

dollars!' said Goodmountain. 'Look, it's *over*. There is nothing *left*!'

'I've got some savings,' said Sacharissa, pushing the rubble off her desk. 'Perhaps we can get one of those little hand presses to be going on with.'

'I'm in debt,' said William, 'but I could probably go into debt another few hundred dollars.'

'Do you think we could go on working if we put a tarpaulin over the roof, or should we move to somewhere else?' said Sacharissa.

'I don't want to move. A few days' work should get this place in shape,' said William.

Goodmountain cupped his hands around his mouth. '*Hel-looo!* This is sanity calling! *We have no money.*'

'There's not much room to expand, though,' said Sacharissa.

'In what way?'

'Magazines,' said Sacharissa, as the sleet settled in her hair. Around her the other dwarfs spread out on a hopeless salvage operation. 'Yes, I know the paper's important, but there's a lot of dead time on the press and, well, I'm sure there'd be a market for something like, well, a magazine for ladies . . .'

'Dead time on the press?' said Goodmountain. 'The press is *dead*!'

'What about?' said William, completely ignoring him.

'Oh . . . fashion. Pictures of women wearing new clothes. Knitting. That sort of thing. And don't you go telling me it's too dull. People will buy it.'

'Clothes? Knitting?'

'People are interested in that sort of thing.'

'I don't like that idea much,' said William. 'You might as well say we should have a magazine just for men.'

'Why not? What would you put in it?'

'Oh, I don't know. Articles about drink. Pictures of women *not* wearing ... Anyway, we'd need more people to write for them.'

'Excuse me?' said Goodmountain.

'Lots of people can write well enough for that sort of thing,' said Sacharissa. 'If it was clever, *we* wouldn't be able to do it.'

'That's true.'

'And there's another magazine that would sell, too,' said Sacharissa. Behind her a piece of the press collapsed.

'Hello? Hello? I *know* my mouth is opening and shutting,' said Goodmountain. 'Is any sound getting out?'

'Cats,' said Sacharissa. 'Lots of people like cats. Pictures of cats. Stories about cats. I've been thinking about it. It could be called ... *Completely Cats.*'

'To go with *Completely Women*, and *Completely Men*? *Completely Knitting*? *Completely Cake*?'

'I had thought of calling it something like *The Ladies' Home Companion*,' said Sacharissa, 'but your title has got a certain ring, I must admit. Ring ... yes. Now, that's another thing. There's all the dwarfs in the city. We could produce a magazine for them. I mean ... what's the modern dwarf wearing this season?'

'Chain mail and leather,' said Goodmountain,

suddenly perplexed. 'What are you talking about? It's always chain mail and leather!'

Sacharissa ignored him. The two of them were in a world of their own, Goodmountain realized. It had nothing to do with the real one any more.

'Seems a bit of a waste, though,' said William. 'A waste of words, I mean.'

'Why? There's always more of them.' Sacharissa patted him gently on the cheek. 'You think you're writing words that'll last for ever? It's not like that. This newspaper stuff . . . that's words that last for a day. Maybe a week.'

'And then they get thrown away,' said William.

'Perhaps a few hang on. In people's heads.'

'That's not where the paper ends up,' said William. 'Quite the reverse.'

'What did you expect? These aren't books, they're . . . words that come and go. Cheer *up*.'

'There's a problem,' said William.

'Yes?'

'We haven't got enough money for a new press. Our shed has been burned down. We are out of business. It's all over. Do you understand?'

Sacharissa looked down. 'Yes,' she said meekly. 'I just hoped you didn't.'

'And we were so close. So *close*.' William pulled out his notebook. 'We could have run with this. I've got nearly the whole thing. All I can do with it now is give it to Vimes—'

'Where's the lead?'

William looked across the wreckage. Boddony was crouching by the smoking press, trying to see under it.

'There's not a *sign* of the lead!' he said.

'It's got to be *somewhere*,' said Goodmountain. 'In my experience twenty tons of lead does not just get up and walk away.'

'It must've melted,' said Boddony. 'There's a few blobs on the floor . . .'

'The cellar,' said Goodmountain. 'Give me a hand here, will you?' He grabbed a blackened beam.

'Here, I'll help,' said William, coming round the stricken desk. 'It's not as though I've got anything better to do . . .'

He got a grip on a tangle of charred wood and pulled—

Mr Pin arose from the pit like a demon king. Smoke poured off him and he was screaming one long, incoherent scream. He rose and rose and knocked Goodmountain aside with a round-arm sweep and then his hands clamped around William's neck and still his leap propelled him up.

William fell backwards. He landed on the desk and felt a stab of pain as some piece of debris went through the flesh of his arm. But there was no time to think about pain that had happened. It was imminent pain that occupied all his future. The face of the creature was inches away, eyes wide and staring *through* him at something horrible, but his hands were tight around William's neck.

William would never have dreamed of using a cliché as tired as 'vice-like grip' but, as consciousness became a red-walled tunnel, the editor inside him said, yes, that's what it would be like, the sheer mechanical pressures that—

The eyes crossed. The scream stopped. The man staggered sideways, half crouched.

As William raised his head he saw Sacharissa stepping backwards.

The editor chittered away in his head, watching him watching her. She'd kicked the man in the . . . Er, You Know. It had to be the influence of those humorous vegetables. It had to be.

And he had to get the Story.

William rose to his feet and waved frantically at the dwarfs, who were advancing with their axes at the ready.

'Wait! Wait! Look . . . you . . . er . . . Brother Pin . . .' He winced at the pain in his arm, looked down and saw, with horror, the evil length of the spike poking through the cloth of his jacket.

Mr Pin tried to focus on the boy grappling with his arm, but the shadows wouldn't let him. He wasn't certain, now, that he was still alive. Yes! That was it! He *must* be dead! All this smoke, people shouting, all the voices whispering in his ear, this was some kind of hell but, *aha*, he had a return ticket . . .

He managed to straighten up. He fished the potato of the late Mr Tulip out of his shirt. He held it aloft.

'G't m' 'tato,' he said proudly. ''m all right, okay?'

William stared at the smoke-stained, red-eyed face, with its horrible expression of triumph, and then at the shrunken vegetable on the end of its string. His grip on reality was at the moment almost as slippery as Mr Pin's, and people showing him a potato seemed to mean only one thing.

'Er ... it's not a very funny one, is it?' he said, wincing as he tugged at the spike.

Mr Pin's last train of thought jumped the rails. He let go of the potato and with a movement that owed nothing to thought and everything to instinct pulled a long dagger from inside his jacket. The figure in front of him was fading into just another shadow among many now, and he lunged madly.

William pulled the metal free, and his hand flew out in front of him—

And that, for the moment, was everything that Mr Pin ever knew.

The sleet hissed on a few remaining embers.

William stared into the puzzled face as the light in the eyes went out and the attacker sagged slowly to the ground, one hand fiercely hanging on to the potato.

'Oh,' said Sacharissa distantly. 'You *spiked* him ...'

Blood dripped down William's sleeve.

'I ... er ... I think I could do with a bandage,' he said. Ice shouldn't be hot, he knew, but shock was filling his veins with a burning chill. He was *sweating* ice.

Sacharissa ran forward, tearing at the sleeve of her blouse.

'I don't think it's *bad*,' said William, trying to back away. 'I just think it's one of those ... enthusiastic wounds.'

'Vot *has* been happening here?'

William looked at the blood on his hand and then at Otto, standing on top of a pile of rubble with an amazed look on his face and a couple of packages in his hands.

'I just go away for five minutes to buy some more acids and suddenly zer whole place . . . Oh dear . . . oh dear . . .'

Goodmountain pulled a tuning fork out of his pocket and twanged it on his helmet.

'*Quick*, lads!' He waved the fork in the air. '"*Oh will you come to the mission—*"'

Otto waved his hand gently as the dwarfs began to sing.

'No, I am vell on top of it, thank you all the same,' he said. 'Ve know vot all this is about, don't ve? It vas a mob, yes? Zere is alvays a mob, sooner or later. Zey got my friend Boris. He showed them zer black ribbon but zey just laughed and—'

'I think they were after all of us,' said William. 'I wish I'd had a chance to ask him a few questions, even so . . .'

'You mean like "Is this the first time you've strangled anyone?"' said Boddony. 'Or "How old are you, Mr Killer?"'

Something started to cough.

It seemed to be coming from the pocket of the man's jacket.

William looked around at the stunned dwarfs to see if anyone else had a clue about what he should do next. Then he reluctantly patted the greasy suit with extreme care and pulled out a slim, polished box.

He opened it. A small green imp peered out of its slot.

''m?' it said.

'What? A personal Dis-organizer?' said William. 'A *killer* with a personal Dis-organizer?'

'The Things To Do Today section is going to be interesting, then,' said Boddony.

The imp blinked at him. 'Do you want me to reply or not?' it said. 'Insert Name Here requested silence, despite my range of sounds to suit any mood or occasion.'

'Um . . . your previous owner is . . . previous,' said William, looking down at the cooling Mr Pin.

'You're a new owner?' said the imp.

'Well . . . possibly.'

'Congratulations!' said the imp. 'Warranty not applicable if said device is sold, hired, transferred, gifted or stolen unless in original packaging and extraneous materials which by then you will have thrown away and Part Two of the warranty card which you have lost has been filled in and sent to Thttv ggj, thhtfjhsssjk the Scors and quoting the reference number which you did not in fact make a note of. Do you want me to wipe the contents of my memory?' It produced a cotton-wool bud and prepared to insert it into one very large ear. 'Erase Memory Y/N?'

'Your . . . memory . . . ?'

'Yes. Erase Memory Y/N?'

'N!' said William. 'And now tell me what exactly it is you are remembering,' he added.

'You have to press the Recall button,' said the imp impatiently.

'And that will do what?'

'A small hammer hits me on the head and I look to see what button you pressed.'

'Why don't you just, well, recall?'

'Look, I don't make the rules. You've got to press the button. It's in the manual—'

William carefully pushed the box to one side. There

were several velvet bags in the dead man's pocket. He put these on the desk, too.

Some of the dwarfs had gone a little way down the iron ladder into the cellar. Boddony climbed back out again, looking thoughtful.

'There's a man down there,' he said. 'Lying in ... lead.'

'Dead?' said William, looking carefully at the bags.

'I hope so. I really hope so. You could say he made a bit of an impression. He's a bit on the . . . cooked side. And there's an arrow through his *head*.'

'William, you realize that you are robbing a corpse?' said Sacharissa.

'Good,' said William distantly. 'Best time.' He upended a bag and jewels spilled across the charred wood.

There was a strangled noise from Goodmountain. Next to gold, jewels were a dwarf's best friend.

William emptied the other bags.

'How much do you think this lot is worth?' he said, when the gems stopped rolling and twinkling.

Goodmountain had already whipped an eye glass from an inside pocket and was inspecting a few of the larger stones. 'What? Hey? Oh, tens of thousands. Could be a hundred thousand. Could be a lot more. This one here is worth fifteen hundred, I reckon, and it's not the best of 'em.'

'He must've stolen them!' said Sacharissa.

'No,' said William calmly. 'We'd have heard about a theft this big. We hear about things. A young man would certainly have told you. Check to see if he has a wallet, will you?'

'The very idea! And what—'

'Check for a damn wallet, will you?' said William. 'This is a *story*. I'm going to check his legs, and I'm not looking forward to *that*, either. But this is a *story*. We can have hysterics *later*. Do it. Please?'

There was a half-healed bite on the dead man's leg. William rolled up his own trouser leg for comparison while Sacharissa, her eyes averted, pulled a brown leather wallet out of the jacket.

'Any clue to who he is?' said William, carefully measuring toothmarks with his pencil. His mind felt strangely calm. He wondered if he was actually thinking at all. It all seemed like some dream, happening in another world.

'Er . . . there's something done on the leather in pokerwork,' said Sacharissa.

'What does it say?'

' "Not A Very Nice Person At All" ,' she read. 'I wonder what kind of person would put *that* on a wallet?'

'Someone who wasn't a very nice person,' said William. 'Anything else in there?'

'There's a piece of paper with an address,' said Sacharissa. 'Er . . . I didn't have time to tell you this, er, William. Um . . .'

'What does it *say*?'

'It's 50 Nonesuch Street. Er. Which is where those men caught me. They had a key and everything. Er . . . that's *your* family's house, isn't it?'

'What do you want me to *do* with these jewels?' said Goodmountain.

'I mean, you gave me a key and everything,' said

Sacharissa nervously. 'But there was this man in the cellar, *highly* inebriated, and he looked just like Lord Vetinari, and then these men turned up and knocked out Rocky and then—'

'I'm not suggesting anything,' said Goodmountain, 'but if these aren't stolen, then I know plenty of places that'd give us top dollar, even at this time of night—'

'—and of course they were *most* impolite but really there was nothing I could do—'

'—we could do with a bit of immediate cash, is the point I'm trying to make—'

It dawned on the girl and the dwarf that William was no longer listening. He seemed locked, blank-faced, in a little bubble of silence.

Slowly, he pulled the Dis-organizer towards him and pressed the button marked 'Recall'. There was a muffled 'Ouch'.

'. . . *nyip-nyap mapnyap nyee-wheedlewheedle-wheee* . . .'

'What's that noise?' said Sacharissa.

'It's how an imp remembers,' said William distantly. 'It . . . sort of plays its life backwards. I used to have an early version of this,' he added.

The noise stopped. The imp said, very apprehensively, 'What happened to it?'

'I took it back to the shop because it wasn't working properly,' said William.

'That's a relief,' said the imp. 'You'd be amazed at some of the terrible things people did to the Mk I. What went wrong with it?'

'It got flung through a third-floor window,' said William, 'for being unhelpful.'

This imp was a little brighter than most of the species. It saluted smartly.

'. . . *wheeeewheedlewheedle nyap-nyark* . . . *Testing, testing . . . seems okay*—'

'That's Brother Pin!' said Sacharissa.

'—*say something, Mr Tulip*,' and the voice became the damp growl of Sister Jennifer, '*What'll I say? It's not natural, talkin' to a —ing box. This box, Mr Tulip, may be a passport to better times. I thought we were getting the —ing money. Yes, and this'll help us keep it . . . nyipnyip . . .*'

'Go forward a bit,' William commanded.

'—*whee . . . nyip dog has got personality. Personality counts for a lot. And the legal precedents*—'

'That's Slant!' said Boddony. 'That lawyer!'

'*What* shall I *do* with the *jewels*?' said Goodmountain.

'. . . *nyipnyip* . . . *I can add another five thousand dollars in jewels to your fee . . . nyip . . . I want to know who's giving me these orders . . . nyip . . . not be stupid, either. My . . . clients have long memories and deep pockets . . .*' In its terror the imp was skipping.

William pressed the Pause button.

'Slant gave him the money,' he said. 'Slant was paying him. Did you hear him mention clients? You understand? This is one of the men who attacked Vetinari! And they had a *key* to our house?'

'But we can't just keep the money!' said Sacharissa.

William pressed the button again.

'. . . *nyip* . . . *they say a lie can run round the world before the truth has got its boots on . . .*'

'Obviously, we—' Sacharissa began.

He pressed the button.

'*Wheeewheedlewheedle lie can run round the world before the truth has got its boots on.*'

He pressed the button again.

'*Wheeewheedlewheedle can run round the world before the truth has got its boots on.*'

'*Wheeewheedlewheedle round the world before the truth has got its boots on.*'

'*Wheeewheedle the truth has got its boots on.*'

'Are you all right, William?' said Sacharissa, as he stood motionless.

'Delayed shock,' Goodmountain whispered. 'It can take people that way.'

'Mr Goodmountain,' said William sharply, still with his back to them. 'Did you say you could get me another press?'

'I said they cost a—'

'—handful of rubies, perhaps?'

Goodmountain opened his hand. '*Are* these ours, then?'

'*Yes!*'

'Well ... in the morning I could buy a dozen presses, but it's not like buying sweets—'

'I want to go to press in half an hour,' said William. 'Otto, I want pictures of Brother Pin's leg. I want quotes from everyone, even Foul Ole Ron. And a picture of Wuffles, Otto. And I want a printing press!'

'I told you, where could we get a printing press at this time of ni—'

The floor shook. The heaps of rubble shifted.

All eyes turned to the high lighted windows of the *Inquirer*.

Sacharissa, who had been watching William wide-eyed, breathed so heavily that Otto groaned and averted his face and started to hum frantically.

'There's your press!' she shouted. 'All you have to do is get it!'

'Yeah, but just stealing a—' the dwarf began.

'*Borrowing*,' said William. 'And half the jewels are yours.'

Goodmountain's nostrils flared. 'Let's just—' he began to yell, and then said, 'You did say half, did you?'

'Yes!'

'Let's just do it, lads!'

One of the *Inquirer*'s overseers knocked politely on Mr Carney's door.

'Yes, Causley? Has Dibbler turned up yet?' said the *Inquirer*'s proprietor.

'No, sir, but there's a young lady to see you. It's that Miss Cripslock,' said the overseer, wiping his hands on a rag.

Carney brightened up. 'Really?'

'Yes, sir. She's in a bit of a state. And that de Worde fellow is with her.'

Carney's smile faded a little. He'd watched the fire from his window with great glee, but he had been bright enough not to step out into the street. Those dwarfs were pretty vicious, from what he'd heard, and would be bound to blame him. In fact, he hadn't the faintest idea why the place had caught fire, but it was hardly unexpected, was it?

'So ... it's time for the humble pie, is it?' he said, half to himself.

'Is it, sir?'

'Send them up, will you?'

He sat back and looked at the paper spread out on his desk. Damn that Dibbler! The odd thing was, though, that those things he wrote were like the wretched sausages he sold – you knew them for what they were, but nevertheless you kept on going to the end, and coming back for more. Making them up wasn't as easy as it looked, either. Dibbler had the knack. He'd make up some story about some huge monster being seen in the lake in Hide Park and five readers would turn up swearing that they'd seen it, too. Ordinary, everyday people, such as you might buy a loaf off. How did he do it? Carney's desk was covered with his own failed attempts. You needed a special kind of imagi—

'Why, Sacharissa,' he said, standing up as she crept into the room. 'Do take the chair. I'm afraid I don't have one for your ... friend.' He nodded at William. 'May I say how sad I was to hear about the fire?'

'It's your office,' said William coldly. 'You can say anything you like.' Beyond the window he could see the torches of the Watch, arriving at the ruins of the old shed. He took a step back.

'Don't be like that, William,' said Sacharissa. 'It's because of that, you see, Ronnie, that we've come to you.'

'Really?' Carney smiled. 'You have been a bit of a silly girl, haven't you ...?'

'Yes, er ... well, all our money was ...' Sacharissa

sniffed. 'The fact is . . . well, we've just got nothing now. We . . . worked so hard, so *hard*, and now it's all gone . . .' She started to sob.

Ronnie Carney leaned over the desk and patted her hand.

'Is there anything I can do?' he said.

'Well, I did hope . . . I wondered if . . . I mean, d'you think you could see your way clear to . . . letting us use one of your presses tonight?'

Carney rocked back. 'You what? Are you mad?'

Sacharissa blew her nose. 'Yes, I thought you'd probably say that,' she said sadly.

Carney, slightly mollified, leaned forward and patted her hand again. 'I know we used to play together when we were children—' he began.

'I don't think we actually *played*,' said Sacharissa, fishing in her handbag. 'You used to chase me and I used to hit you over the head with a wooden cow. Ah, here it is . . .' She dropped the bag, stood up and aimed one of the late Mr Pin's pistol bows straight at the editor.

'Let us use your "ing" presses or I'll "ing" shoot your "ing" head "ing" off!' she screamed. 'I think that's how you're supposed to say it, isn't it?'

'You wouldn't dare pull that trigger!' said Carney, trying to crouch in his chair.

'It was a lovely cow, and one day I hit you so hard one of the legs broke off,' said Sacharissa dreamily.

Carney looked imploringly at William. 'Can't you talk some sense into her?' he said.

'We just need the loan of one of your presses for an hour or so, Mr Carney,' said William, while Sacharissa kept the barrel of the bow aimed at the man's nose with what he judged to be a very strange smile on her face. 'And then we'll be gone.'

'What are you going to do?' said Carney hoarsely.

'Well, firstly I'm going to tie you up,' said William.

'No! I'll call the overseers!'

'I think they're ... busy at the moment,' said Sacharissa.

Carney listened. It seemed unusually quiet downstairs.

He sagged.

The printing staff of the *Inquirer* were in a ring around Goodmountain.

'Right, lads,' said the dwarf, 'here's how it works. Every man who goes home early tonight 'cos of a headache gets a hundred dollars, all right? It's an old Klatchian custom.'

'And what happens if we don't go?' said the foreman, picking up a mallet.

'Vell,' said a voice by his ear, 'that's ven you *get* a ... headache.'

There was a flash of lightning and a roll of thunder. Otto punched the air triumphantly.

'Yes!' he shouted, as the printers ran madly towards the doors. 'Ven you really, really need it, zere it is! Let's try vunce more ... Castle!' The thunder rolled again. The vampire jumped up and down excitedly, vest tails flying. 'Vow! *Now* ve are cooking! Vunce more mit feelink! Vot a big ... *castle*...' The thunder was even louder this time.

Otto did a little jig, beside himself with joy, tears running down his grey face.

'Music viz Rocks In!' he yelled.

In the silence after the thunder roll William pulled a velvet bag from his pocket and tipped it out on to the desk blotter.

Carney stared goggle-eyed at the jewels.

'Two thousand dollars' worth,' said William. 'At least. Our admission to the Guild. I'll just leave them here, shall I? No need for a receipt. We trust you.'

Carney said nothing, because of the gag. He had been tied to his chair.

At this point Sacharissa pulled the trigger. Nothing happened.

'I must've forgotten to put the pointy arrow bit in,' she said, as Carney fainted away. 'What a silly girl I am. "Ing". I feel so much better for saying that, you know? "Ing". "Inginginging". I wonder what it means?'

Gunilla Goodmountain looked expectantly at William, who swayed as he tried to think.

'All right,' he said, closing his eyes and pinching the bridge of his nose. 'Triple-decker heading, as wide as you can. First line: "Conspiracy Revealed!" Got that? Next line: "Lord Vetinari is Innocent!"' He hesitated at that one, but let it go. People could argue about its general application later on. That wasn't the important thing at the moment.

'Yes?' said Goodmountain. 'And the next line?'

'I've written it down,' said William, passing him a

page torn from the notebook. 'Caps, please. Big caps. Big as you can. The sort the *Inquirer* used for elves and exploding people.'

'This?' said the dwarf, reaching for a case of huge black letters. 'Is *this* news?'

'It is now,' said William. He flicked back through the pages of his notebook.

'Are you going to write the story down first?' said the dwarf.

'No time. Ready? "A plot to illegally seize control of Ankh-Morpork was exposed last night after days of patient detective work by the Watch." Paragraph. "The *Times* understands that two assassins, both now dead, were hired from outside the city to blacken the character of Lord Vetinari and depose him as Patrician." Paragraph. "They used an innocent man with a remarkable resemblance to Lord Vetinari in order to trick their way into the palace. Once inside"—'

'Hold on, hold on,' said Goodmountain. 'The Watch didn't get to the bottom of this, did they? *You* did!'

'I just said they've been working for days,' said William. 'That's true. I don't have to say they weren't getting anywhere.' He saw the look in the dwarf's eye. 'Listen, very soon I'm going to have a lot more unpleasant enemies than anyone really needs. I'd like Vimes to be angry at me for making him look good rather than for making him look bad. Okay?'

'Even so—'

'Don't argue with me!'

Goodmountain didn't dare. There was a *look* in

William's face. The boy had frozen when he was listening to the box, and now he'd unfrozen into . . . someone else.

Someone a lot more touchy and a lot less patient. He looked as though he was running a fever.

'Now . . . where was I?'

'"Once inside". . .' said the dwarf.

'Okay . . . "Once inside" . . . no . . . Make it: "The *Times* understands that Lord Vetinari was" – Sacharissa, you said the man in the cellar looked just like Vetinari?'

'Yes. Haircut and *everything*.'

'Right. "The *Times* understands that Lord Vetinari was overwhelmed in the moment of shock on seeing himself entering his office"—'

'Do we understand that?' said Sacharissa.

'Yes. It makes sense. Who's going to argue? Where was I . . . "Their plan was foiled by Lord Vetinari's dog, Wuffles (16), who attacked both men." Paragraph. "The noise of this attracted the attention of Lord Vetinari's clerk, Rufus Drumknott" – damn, I forgot to ask him how old he was – "who was then knocked unconscious." Paragraph. "The attackers tried to put the interruption to good use in their" – what's the good word? Oh, yes – "their dastardly plan and stabbed Drumknott with one of Lord Vetinari's own daggers in an attempt to make it look as if he was insane or murderous." Paragraph. "Acting with vicious cunning"—'

'You're getting really *good* at this,' said Sacharissa.

'Don't interrupt him,' hissed Boddony. 'I want to find out what the dastards did next!'

'—"with vicious cunning they forced the bogus Lord Vetinari"—'

'Good word, good word,' said Goodmountain, setting furiously.

'Are you certain about "forced"?' said Sacharissa.

'They aren't— they weren't the kind of men who ask nicely,' said William brusquely. 'Er . . . "forced the bogus Lord Vetinari . . . to make a false confession to some servants who were attracted by the noise. Then all three, carrying the unconscious Lord Vetinari and harried by the dog, Wuffles (16), took the stairs to the stables." Paragraph. "There they had set up a scene to suggest that Lord Vetinari had been trying to rob the city, as already reported in"—'

' "*Exclusively* in",' Sacharissa said.

'Right, "*exclusively* in the *Times*." Paragraph. "However, the dog Wuffles escaped and began a city-wide search by Watch and criminals alike. He was found by a group of public-spirited citizens, who"—'

A piece of type dropped from Goodmountain's fingers. 'You mean Foul Ole Ron and that bunch?'

'—"public-spirited citizens",' William repeated, nodding furiously, ' "who kept him hidden, while"—'

Cold winter storms had the whole of the Sto Plains in which to build up speed. By the time they hit Ankh-Morpork they were fast and heavy and laden with malice.

This time it took the form of hail. Fist-sized balls of ice smashed into tiles. They blocked gutters and filled the streets with shrapnel.

They hammered on the roof of the warehouse

in Gleam Street. One or two windows smashed.

William paced up and down, shouting out his words above the force of the storm, occasionally flicking back and forth through the pages of his notebook. Otto came out and handed the dwarfs a couple of iconograph plates. The crew limped and sidled in, ready for the edition.

William stopped. The last letters clicked into place.

'Let's see what it looks like so far,' said William.

Goodmountain inked the type, put a piece of paper over the story and ran a hand-roller over it. Wordlessly, he handed it to Sacharissa.

'Are you *sure* of all this, William?' she said.

'Yes.'

'I mean, some bits – are you sure it's all true?'

'I'm sure it's all journalism,' said William.

'And what is that supposed to mean?'

'It means it's true enough for now.'

'But do you know the *names* of these people?'

William hesitated. Then he said:

'Mr Goodmountain, you can insert an extra paragraph anywhere in the story, can't you?'

'That's not a problem.'

'Right. Then set this: "The *Times* can reveal that the assassins were hired by a group of prominent citizens led by" . . . "The *Times* can reveal that" . . .' He took a deep breath. 'Start again: "The plotters, the *Times* can reveal, were headed by". . .' William shook his head. ' "Evidence points to" . . . uh . . . "Evidence, the *Times* can reveal" . . . "All the evidence, the *Times* can reveal . . . can reveal . . ."' His voice trailed off.

'This is going to be a long paragraph?' said Goodmountain.

William stared miserably at the damp proof.

'No,' he said wretchedly. 'I think that's it. Let it go at that. Put in a line saying that the *Times* will be helping the Watch with its inquiries.'

'Why? We're not guilty of anything, are we?' said Goodmountain.

'Just do it, please.' William screwed the proof into a ball, tossed it on to a bench and wandered off towards the press.

Sacharissa found him a few minutes later. A print room offers a mass of holes and corners, mostly used by those whose duties require the occasional bunk-off for a quiet smoke. William was sitting on a pile of paper, staring at nothing.

'Is there something you want to talk about?' she said.

'No.'

'Do you know who the conspirators are?'

'No.'

'Then would it be true to say that you *suspect* you know who the conspirators are?'

He gave her an angry look. 'Are you trying journalism on me?'

'I'm just supposed to try it on everyone else, then, am I? Not you, then?' she said, sitting down beside him.

William absent-mindedly pressed a button on the Dis-organizer.

'*Wheeewheedle the truth has got its boots on . . .*'

'You don't get on very well with your father, is tha—' Sacharissa began.

'What am I supposed to *do*?' said William. 'That's his favourite saying. He says it proves how gullible people are. Those men had the run of our house. He's in this up to his neck!'

'Yes, but perhaps he just did it as a favour to some other—'

'If my father is involved in anything, he'll be the leader,' said William flatly. 'If you don't know that you don't know the de Wordes. We don't join any team if we can't be captain.'

'But it'd be a bit silly, wouldn't it, to let them use your own house—'

'No, just very, very arrogant,' said William. 'We've always been privileged, you see. Privilege just means "private law". That's exactly what it means. He just doesn't believe the ordinary laws apply to him. He doesn't really believe they can touch him, and if they do he'll just shout until they go away. That's the de Worde tradition, and we're *good* at it. Shout at people, get your own way, ignore the rules. It's the de Worde way. Up until me, obviously.'

Sacharissa was careful not to let her expression change.

'And I didn't expect this,' William finished, turning the box over and over in his hands.

'You said you wanted to get at the truth, didn't you?'

'Yes, but not this! I . . . must have got something wrong. I must have. I *must* have. Even my father couldn't be this . . . this *stupid*. I've got to find out what's really been happening.'

'You're not going to see him, are you?' said Sacharissa.

'Yes. By now he'll know it's over.'

'Then you ought to take someone with you!'

'No!' snapped William. 'Look, you don't know what my father's friends are like. They are brought up to give orders, they know that they're on the right side because if they are on it then it *must* be the right side, by definition, and when they feel threatened they are bare-knuckle fighters, except that they never take their gloves off. They are thugs. Thugs and bullies, *bullies*, and the worst kind of bully, because they *aren't* cowards and if you stand up to them they only hit you harder. They grew up in a world where, if you were enough trouble, they could have you . . . disappeared. You think places like the Shades are bad? Then you don't know what goes on in Park Lane! And my father is one of the worst. But I'm family. We . . . care about family. So I'll be all right. You stay here and help them get the paper out, will you? Half a truth is better than nothing,' he added bitterly.

'Vot vas all zat about?' said Otto, coming up as William strode out of the room.

'Oh, he's . . . he's off to see his father,' said Sacharissa, still taken aback. 'Who is not a nice man, apparently. He was very . . . heated about him. Very upset.'

''scuse me,' said a voice. The girl turned, but there was no one behind her.

Now the invisible speaker sighed. 'No, down here,' it said. She looked down at the malformed pink poodle.

'Let's not mess around, eh?' it said. 'Yeah, yeah, dogs can't talk. Got it in one, well done. So maybe you've got some strange ment'l power. That's *that* sorted out, then. I couldn't help overhearin', 'cos I was listenin'. The lad's heading into trouble, right? I can *smell* trouble—'

'Are you some kind of verevolf?' said Otto.

'Yeah, right, I get very hairy every full moon,' said the dog dismissively. 'Imagine how much that interferes with my social life. Now, look—'

'But surely dogs can't talk—' Sacharissa began.

'Oh dear oh dear oh dear,' said Gaspode. 'Did I *say* I was talking?'

'Well, not in so many words—'

'Right. Wonderful thing, phenomenology. Now, I just seen a hundred dollars walk out the door and I want to see it walk back, right? Lord de Worde is as nasty a piece of work as you'll find in this town.'

'*You* know nobility?' said Sacharissa.

'A cat can look at a king, right? That's *legal*.'

'I suppose so—'

'So it works for dogs, too. Got to work for dogs if it works for ratbag moggies. I know everyone, I do. Lord de Worde used to get his butler to put down poisoned meat for the street dogs.'

'But he wouldn't *hurt* William, would he?'

'I'm not a betting man,' said Gaspode. 'But if he does, right, we still get the hundred dollars, yes?'

'Ve cannot stand by and let him do zis,' said Otto. 'I like Villiam. He was not brought up nice but he tries to be a nice person, vithout even cocoa and a singsong to help him. It is hard to go against your nature. Ve must . . . help him.'

Death placed the final hourglass back on to the air, where it faded away.

THERE, he said, WASN'T THAT *INTERESTING*? WHAT
NEXT, MR TULIP? ARE YOU READY TO GO?

The figure sat on the cold sand, staring at nothing.

MR TULIP? Death repeated. The wind flapped his
robe, so that it streamed out a long ribbon of
darkness.

'I . . . got to be really sorry . . . ?'

OH YES. IT IS SUCH A SIMPLE WORD. BUT HERE . . . IT
HAS MEANING. IT HAS . . . SUBSTANCE.

'Yeah. I know.' Mr Tulip looked up, his eyes red-
rimmed, his face puffy. 'I reckon . . . to be that sorry,
you got to take a —ing good run at it.'

YES.

'So . . . how long have I got?'

Death looked up at the strange stars.

ALL THE TIME IN THE WORLD.

'Yeah . . . well, maybe that'll —ing do it. Maybe
there won't be no more world to go back to by then.'

I BELIEVE IT DOES NOT WORK LIKE THAT. I UNDERSTAND
REINCARNATION CAN TAKE PLACE ANYWHEN. WHO SAYS
LIVES ARE SERIAL?

'You sayin' . . . I could be alive before I was born?'

YES.

'Maybe I can find me and kill myself,' said Mr Tulip,
staring at the sand.

NO, BECAUSE YOU WILL NEVER KNOW. AND YOU MAY BE
LEADING QUITE A DIFFERENT LIFE.

'Good . . .'

Death patted Mr Tulip on the shoulder, which
flinched under his touch.

I SHALL LEAVE YOU NOW—

'Th't's a good scythe you got there,' said Mr Tulip,

slowly and laboriously. 'That silverwork's craftsman-ship if ever I saw it.'

THANK YOU, said Death. AND NOW, I REALLY MUST BE GOING. BUT I WILL PASS THROUGH HERE SOMETIMES. MY DOOR, he added, IS *ALWAYS* OPEN.

He strode off. The hunched figure fell behind into the darkness, but a new one appeared, running madly across the not-exactly-sand.

It was waving a potato on a string. It stopped when it saw Death and then, to Death's amazement, turned to look behind it. This had never happened before. Most people, upon coming face to face with Death, ceased worrying about *anything* behind them.

'Is there anyone after me? Can you see anyone?'

ER . . . NO. WERE YOU EXPECTING ANYONE?

'Oh, right. No one, eh? Right!' said Mr Pin, squaring his shoulders. 'Yeah! Hah! Hey, look, I've got my potato!'

Death blinked and then took an hourglass out of his robe.

MR PIN? AH. THE OTHER ONE. I HAVE BEEN EXPECTING *YOU*.

'That's me! And I've got my potato, look, and I'm very sorry about everything!' Mr Pin was feeling quite calm now. The mountains of madness have many little plateaux of sanity.

Death stared into the madly smiling face. YOU ARE VERY SORRY?

'Oh, yes!'

ABOUT EVERYTHING?

'Yep!'

AT THIS TIME? IN THIS PLACE? YOU DECLARE YOU ARE SORRY?'

'That's right. You got it. You're bright. So if you'll just show me how to get back—'

YOU WOULD NOT LIKE TO RECONSIDER?

'No arguing, I want what's due,' said Mr Pin. 'I've got my potato. Look.'

AND I SEE. Death reached into his robe and pulled out what looked to Mr Pin, at first sight, like a miniature model of himself. But there was a rat skull looking out from under the tiny cowl.

Death grinned. SAY HELLO TO *MY* LITTLE FRIEND, he said.

The Death of Rats reached out and snatched the string.

'Hey—'

DO NOT PUT ALL YOUR TRUST IN ROOT VEGETABLES. WHAT THINGS SEEM MAY NOT BE WHAT THEY ARE, said Death. YET LET NO ONE SAY I DON'T HONOUR THE LAW. He snapped his fingers. RETURN, THEN, TO WHERE YOU SHOULD GO . . .

Blue light flickered for a moment around the astonished Pin, and then he vanished.

Death sighed and shook his head.

THE OTHER ONE . . . HAD SOMETHING IN HIM THAT COULD BE BETTER, he said. BUT THAT ONE . . . He sighed deeply. WHO KNOWS WHAT EVIL LURKS IN THE HEART OF MEN?

The Death of Rats looked up from the feast of potato.

SQUEAK, he said.

Death waved a hand dismissively. WELL, YES,

OBVIOUSLY *ME*, he said. I JUST WONDERED IF THERE WAS ANYONE ELSE.

William, ducking from doorway to doorway, realized that he was taking the long way round. Otto would have said that it was because he didn't want to arrive.

The storm had abated slightly, although stinging hail still bounced off his hat. The much bigger balls from the initial onslaught filled the gutters and covered the roads. Carts had skidded, pedestrians were hanging on to the walls.

Despite the fire in his head, he took out his notebook and wrote: *hlstns bggr than golf blls?* and made a mental note to check one against a golf ball, just in case. Part of him was beginning to understand that his readers might have a very relaxed attitude about the guilt of politicians but were red hot on things like the size of the weather.

He stopped on the Brass Bridge and sheltered in the lee of one of the giant hippos. Hail peppered the surface of the river with a thousand tiny sucking noises.

The rage was cooling now.

For most of William's life Lord de Worde had been a distant figure staring out of his study window, in a room lined with books that never got read, while William stood meekly in the middle of acres of good but threadbare carpet and listened to . . . well, viciousness mostly, now that he thought about it, the opinions of Mr Windling dressed up in more expensive words.

The worst part, the *worst* part, was that Lord de

Worde was never wrong. It was not a position he understood in relation to his personal geography. People who took an opposing view were insane, or dangerous, or possibly even not really people. You couldn't have an argument with Lord de Worde. Not a proper argument. An argument, from *arguer*, meant to debate and discuss and persuade by reason. What you could have with William's father was a flaming row.

Icy water dripped off one of the statues and ran down William's neck.

Lord de Worde used words with a tone and a volume that made them as good as fists, but he'd never used actual violence.

He had people for that.

Another drop of thawed hail coursed down William's spine.

Surely even his father couldn't be *this* stupid?

He wondered if he should turn over *everything* to the Watch right now. But whatever they said about Vimes, in the end the man had a handful of men and a lot of influential enemies who had families going back a thousand years and the same amount of honour that you'd find in a dog fight.

No. He was a de Worde. The Watch was for other people, who couldn't sort out their problems their own way. And what was the worst that could happen?

So many things, he thought as he set out again, that it would be hard to decide which one *was* the worst.

A galaxy of candles burned in the middle of the floor. In the corroded mirrors around the room they looked like the lights of a shoal of deep-sea fishes.

William walked past overturned chairs. There was one upright, though, behind the candles.

He stopped.

'Ah . . . William,' said the chair. Then Lord de Worde slowly unfolded his lanky form from the embracing leather and stood up in the light.

'Father,' said William.

'I thought you'd come here. Your mother always liked the place, too. Of course, it was . . . different in those days.'

William said nothing. It had been.

'I think this nonsense has got to stop now, don't you?' said Lord de Worde.

'I think it *is* stopping, Father.'

'But I don't think you mean what I mean,' said Lord de Worde.

'I don't know what you think you mean,' said William. 'I just want to hear the truth from you.'

Lord de Worde sighed. 'The truth? I had the best interests of the city at heart, you know. You'll understand, one day. Vetinari is ruining the place.'

'Yes . . . well . . . that's where it all becomes difficult, doesn't it?' said William, amazed that his voice hadn't even begun to shake yet. 'I mean, *everyone* says that sort of thing, don't they? "I did it for the best", "the end justifies the means" – the same words, every time.'

'Don't you agree, then, that it's time for a ruler who listens to the people?'

'Maybe. Which people did you have in mind?'

Lord de Worde's mild expression changed. William was surprised it had survived this long.

'You are going to put this in your *rag* of a news-paper, aren't you?'

William said nothing.

'You can't prove anything. You know that.'

William stepped into the light and Lord de Worde saw the notebook.

'I can prove enough. That's all that matters, really. The rest will become a matter of . . . inquiry. Do you know they call Vimes "Vetinari's terrier"? Terriers dig and dig and don't let go.'

Lord de Worde put his hand on the hilt of his sword.

And William heard himself think: *Thank you. Thank you. Up until now, I couldn't believe it . . .*

'You have no honour, do you?' said his father, still in the voice of infuriating calm. 'Well, publish and be damned to you. *And* to the Watch. We gave no order to—'

'I expect you didn't,' said William. 'I expect you said "make it so" and left the details to people like Pin and Tulip. Bloody hands at arm's length.'

'As your father I *order* you to cease this . . . this . . .'

'You used to order me to tell the truth,' said William.

Lord de Worde drew himself up. 'Oh, William, *William!* Don't be so naive.'

William shut his notebook. The words came easier now. He'd leapt from the building and found that he could fly.

'And which one is this?' he said. 'The truth that is so precious it must be surrounded by a bodyguard of lies? The truth that is stranger than fiction? Or the truth that is still putting on its boots when a lie is running round the world?' He stepped forward. 'That's your little phrase, isn't it? It doesn't matter any more. I think Mr Pin was going to try blackmail and, you know, so am I, naive as I am. You're going to leave the city, right now. That shouldn't be too hard for you. And you had better hope that nothing happens to me, or anyone I work with, or anyone I know.'

'Really?'

'Right now!' screamed William, so loud that Lord de Worde rocked backwards. 'Have you gone deaf as well as insane? Right now and don't come back, because if you do I'll publish *every* damn word you've just said!' William pulled the Dis-organizer out of his pocket. 'Every damn word! D'you hear me? And not even Mr Slant will be able to grease your way out of that! You even had the arrogance, the stupid *arrogance*, to use our house! How dare you! Get out of the city! And either draw that sword or take . . . your . . . hand . . . off . . . it!'

He stopped, red-faced and panting.

'The truth has got its boots on,' he said. 'It's going to start kicking.' His eyes narrowed. '*I told you to take your hand off that sword!*'

'So silly, so silly. And I believed you were my son . . .'

'Ah, yes. I nearly forgot that,' said William, now rocketing on rage. 'You know one of the customs of the dwarfs? No, of course you don't, because they're not really people, are they? But I know one or two of them, you see, and so . . .' He pulled a velvet bag out of his pocket and threw it down in front of his father.

'And this is . . . ?' said Lord de Worde.

'There's more than twenty thousand dollars in there, as close as a couple of experts could estimate,' said William. 'I didn't have a lot of time to work it out and I didn't want you to think I was being unfair, so I've erred on the generous side. That must cover everything I've cost you over the years. School fees, clothes, everything. I have to confess you didn't make such a good job of it, given that I'm the end result. I'm buying myself off you, you see.'

'Oh, I see. The dramatic gesture. Do you really think that family is a matter of *money*?' said Lord de Worde.

'We-ell, *yes*, according to history. Money, land and titles,' said William. 'It's amazing how often we failed to marry *anyone* who didn't have at least two out of three.'

'Cheap jibe. You know what I mean.'

'I don't know if I do,' said William. 'But I do know I got that money a few hours ago off a man who tried to kill me.'

'Tried to kill you?' For the first time there was a note of uncertainty.

'Why, yes. You're surprised?' said William. 'If you throw something into the air, don't you have to worry about where it bounces?'

'Indeed you do,' said Lord de Worde. He sighed, made a little hand signal, and William saw shadows detach themselves from deeper shadows. And he remembered that you couldn't run the de Worde estates without a lot of hired help, in every department of life. Hard men in little round hats, who knew how to evict and distrain and set mantraps . . .

'You have been overdoing it, I can see,' said his father, as they advanced. 'I think you need ... yes, a long sea voyage. The Isles of Fog, perhaps, or possibly Fourecks. Or Bhangbhangduc. There's fortunes to be made there, I understand, by young men prepared to get their hands dirty. Certainly there's nothing for you here ... nothing good.'

William made out four figures now. He'd seen them around on the estates. They tended to have one-word names, like Jenks or Clamper, and no visible pasts at all.

One of them said, 'Now, if you'll just see a bit o' sense, Mr William, we can all do this nice and quiet ...'

'Small sums of money will be sent to you periodically,' said Lord de Worde. 'You will be able to live in a style which—'

A few wisps of dust spiralled down from the shadowy ceiling, twirling like sycamore leaves.

They landed next to the velvet bag.

Overhead, a shrouded chandelier jingled gently.

William looked up. 'Oh, no,' he said. 'Please ... don't kill anyone!'

'What?' said Lord de Worde.

Otto Chriek dropped to the floor, hands raised like talons.

'Good evening!' he said to a shocked bailiff. He looked at his hands. 'Oh, vot am I thinking of!' He bunched his fists and danced from foot to foot. 'Put zem up in the traditional Ankh-Morpork pugilism!'

'Put them up?' said the man, raising a cudgel. 'Blow that!'

A jab from Otto lifted him off his feet. He landed on his back, spinning, and slid away across the polished floor. Otto spun round so fast that he blurred, and there was a smack as another man went down.

'Vot's this? Vot's this? I'm using your civilized fisticuffs, and you don't vant to fight?' he said, springing back and forth like an amateur boxer. 'Ah, you, sir, you show fight—' The fists blurred into invisibility and pummelled a man like a punchbag. Otto straightened up as the man fell, and absent-mindedly punched sideways to catch the charging fourth man on the chin. The man actually spun in the air.

This happened in a few seconds. And then William got enough of a grip to shout a warning. He was too late.

Otto looked down at the length of sword blade sticking too far into his chest.

'Oh, vill you look at zis,' he said. 'You know, in zis job I just cannot make a shirt last two days?'

He turned to Lord de Worde, who was backing away, and cracked his knuckles.

'Keep it away from me!' shouted his lordship.

William shook his head.

'Oh, yes?' said Otto, still advancing. 'You think I am an *it*? Vell, let me act like an *it*.'

He grabbed Lord de Worde's jacket and held him up in the air, with one hand, at arm's length.

'Ve have people like you back home,' he said. 'Zey are the vuns that tell the mob vot to do. I come here to Ankh-Morpork, zey tell me things are different, but really it is alvays the same. Alvays zere are damn people like you! And now, vot shall I do viz you?'

He wrenched at his own jacket and tossed the black ribbon aside.

'I never liked zer damn cocoa anyvay,' he said.

'Otto!'

The vampire turned. 'Yes, Villiam? Vot is it you vish?'

'That's going too far.' Lord de Worde had gone pale. William had never seen him so obviously frightened before.

'Oh? You say? You think I *bite* him? Shall I bite you, Mister Lordship? Vell, maybe not, because Villiam here thinks I am a good person.' He pulled Lord de Worde close, so their faces were a few inches apart. 'Now, maybe I have to ask myself, *how* good am I? Or maybe I just have to ask myself . . . am I better zan you?' He hesitated for a second or two and then in a sudden movement jerked the man towards him.

With great delicacy, he planted a kiss on Lord de Worde's forehead. Then he put the trembling man back down on the floor and patted him on the head.

'Actually, maybe zer cocoa is not *too* bad and zer young lady who plays zer harmonium, sometimes she *vinks* at me,' he said, stepping aside.

Lord de Worde opened his eyes, and looked at William.

'How dare you—'

'Shut up,' said William. 'Now, I'm going to tell you what's going to happen. I'm not going to name names. That's my decision. I don't want my mother to have been married to a traitor, you see. Then there's Rupert. And my sisters. And me, too. I'm protecting the name. That's probably very wrong of me, and I'm going to do it anyway. I'm going to disobey you one more time, in fact. I won't tell the truth. Not the whole truth. Besides, I am sure that those who want to know these things will find out soon enough. And I daresay they'll sort it out quietly. You know . . . just like you do.'

'Traitor?' whispered Lord de Worde.

'That is what people would say.'

Lord de Worde nodded, like a man caught in an unpleasant dream.

'I could not possibly take the money,' he said. 'I wish you joy of it, *my son*. Because . . . you are most *certainly* a de Worde. Good day to you.' He turned and walked away. After a few seconds the distant door creaked open and shut quietly.

William staggered to a pillar. He *was* shaking. He replayed the meeting in his head. His brain hadn't touched the ground the whole time.

'Are you okay, Villiam?' said Otto.

'I feel sick, but . . . yeah, I'm all right. Of all the bone-headed, stubborn, self-centred, arrogant—'

'But you make up for it in other vays,' said Otto.

'I *meant* my father.'

'Oh.'

'He's just so certain he's in the right all the time—'

'Sorry, this is still your father ve're talking about?'

'Are you saying I'm *like* him?'

'Oh, no. Qvite different. Absolutely qvite different. No similarities votsoever.'

'You didn't need to go that far!' He stopped. 'Did I say "thank you"?'

'No, you did not.'

'Oh, dear.'

'No, you *noticed* that you didn't, so zat is okay,' said Otto. 'Every day, in every vay, ve get better and better. By the vay, vould you mind pulling this sword out of me? Vot kind of idiot just sticks it in a vampire? All it does is mess up zer linen.'

'Let me help—' William gingerly withdrew the blade.

'Can I put zis shirt on my expenses?'

'Yes, I think so.'

'Good. And now it is all over and time for revards and medals,' said the vampire cheerfully, adjusting his jacket. 'So vhere are your troubles now?'

'Just starting,' said William. 'I think I'm going to be seeing the inside of the Watch House in less than an hour.'

In fact it was forty-three minutes later that William de Worde was Helping the Watch, as they say, with Their Inquiries.

On the other side of the table Commander Vimes was carefully rereading the *Times*. He was, William knew, taking longer than necessary in order to make him nervous.

'I can help you with any long words you don't recognize,' he volunteered.

'It's very good,' said Vimes, ignoring this. 'But I need to know more. I need to know the *names*. I think you know the *names*. Where did they meet? Things like that. I need to know them.'

'Some things are a mystery to me,' said William.

'You've got more than enough evidence to release Lord Vetinari.'

'I want to know more.'

'Not from me.'

'Come *on*, Mr de Worde. We're on the same side here!'

'No. We're just on two different sides that happen to be side by side.'

'Mr de Worde, earlier today you assaulted one of my officers. Do you know how much trouble you are in already?'

'I expected better of you than that, Mister Vimes,' said William. 'Are you saying I assaulted an officer in uniform? An officer who identified themself to me?'

'Be careful, Mr de Worde.'

'I was being followed by a werewolf, Commander. I took steps to . . . inconvenience it so that I could get away. Would you like to debate this publicly?'

I'm being an arrogant, lying, supercilious bastard, thought William. And I'm *good* at it.

'Then you give me no choice but to arrest you for concealing—'

'I demand a lawyer,' said William.

'Really? And who did you have in mind at this time of night?'

'Mr Slant.'

'*Slant*? You think he'll come out for *you*?'

'No. I *know* he'll come out. Believe me.'

'Oh, he *will*, will he?'

'Trust me.'

'Come now,' said Vimes, smiling. 'Do we need this? It's the duty of every citizen to help the Watch, isn't it?'

'I don't know. I know the *Watch* think it is. I've never seen it written down,' said William. 'There again, I never knew it was the right of the Watch to spy on innocent people.'

He saw the smile freeze.

'It was for your own good,' Vimes growled.

'I didn't know it was your job to decide what was good for me.'

This time Vimes won a small prize. 'I'm not going to be led, either,' he said. 'But I have reason to believe that you are withholding information about a major crime, and that *is* an offence. That's against the law.'

'Mr Slant will come up with something. There's some precedent, I'll bet. He'll go back hundreds of years. The Patricians have always set great store by precedent. Mr Slant will dig and dig. For *years* if necessary. That's how he got where he is today, by digging.'

Vimes leaned forward. 'Between you and me, and without your notebook,' he muttered, 'Mr Slant is a devious dead bastard who can bend such law as we have into a puzzle ring.'

'Yep,' said William. 'And he's my lawyer. I guarantee it.'

'Why would Mr Slant speak up on *your* behalf?' said Vimes, staring at William.

William matched him eyeball for eyeball. It's true, he thought. I'm my father's son. All I have to do is *use* it.

'Because he's a very fair man?' he said. 'Now, are you going to send a runner to fetch him? Because if you're not you've got to let me go.'

Without taking his gaze off William, Vimes reached down and unhooked the speaking tube from the side of his desk. He whistled into it and then put it to his ear. There was a sound like a mouse pleading for mercy at the other end of a drainpipe.

'Yata whipsie poitl swup?'

Vimes put the tube to his mouth. 'Sergeant, send someone up to take Mr de Worde down to the cells, will you?'

'Swyddle yumyumpwipwipwip?'

Vimes sighed and replaced the pipe. He got up and opened the door.

'Fred, send someone to take Mr de Worde down to the cells, will you?' he yelled. 'I'm calling it protective custody for now,' he added, turning to William.

'Protecting me from whom?'

'Well, I personally have an overwhelming urge to give you a ding alongside the ear,' said Vimes. 'And I suspect there are others out there without my self-control.'

It was in fact quite peaceful in the cells. The bunk was comfortable. The walls were covered with graffiti, and William passed the time correcting the spelling.

The door was unlocked again. A stony-faced constable escorted William back up to Vimes's office.

Mr Slant was there. He gave William an impassive nod. Commander Vimes was sitting in front of a small yet significant pile of paper and had the look of a beaten man.

'I believe Mr de Worde can go free,' said Mr Slant.

Vimes shrugged. 'I'm only amazed you aren't asking me to give him a gold medal and an illuminated

413

scroll of thanks. But I'm setting bail at one thou—'

'Ah?' said Mr Slant, raising a grey finger.

Vimes glowered. 'One hun—'

'Ah?'

Vimes grunted and reached into his pocket. He tossed William a dollar. 'Here,' he said, with extensive sarcasm. 'And if you aren't in front of the Patrician at ten o'clock tomorrow you've got to give it back. Satisfied?' he said to Slant.

'Which Patrician?' said William.

'Thank you for that smart answer,' said Vimes. 'Just you be there.'

Mr Slant was silent as he walked out into the night air with his new client, but after a while he said: 'I have presented a writ of *exeo carco cum nihil pretii* on the basis of *olfacere violarum* and *sini plenis piscis*. Tomorrow I shall move that you are *ab hamo*, and in the event of this not working I—'

'Smelling of violets?' said William, who had been translating in his head, 'and pockets full of fish?'

'Based on a case some six hundred years ago when the defendant successfully pleaded that, although he had indeed pushed the victim into a lake, the man came out with his pockets full of fish, to his net benefit,' said Mr Slant crisply. 'In any case, I shall argue that if withholding information from the Watch is a crime, every person in the city is guilty.'

'Mr Slant, I do not wish to have to say how and where I got my information,' said William. 'If I have to, I shall have to reveal *all* of it.'

The light from the distant lamp over the Watch

House door, behind its blue glass, illuminated the lawyer's face. He looked ill.

'You really believe those two men had . . . accomplices?' he said.

'I'm sure of it,' said William. 'I'd say it's a matter of . . . record.'

At that point he almost felt sorry for the lawyer. But only almost.

'That might not be in the public interest,' said Mr Slant slowly. 'This ought to be a time for . . . reconciliation.'

'Absolutely. So I'm sure you will see to it that I don't have to pour all those words into Commander Vimes's ear.'

'Strangely enough, there was a precedent in 1497 when a cat successfully—'

'Good. And you will have one of your special quiet words with the Engravers' Guild. You are *good* at quiet words.'

'Well, of course I will do my best. The bill, however—'

'—won't exist,' said William.

Only then did Mr Slant's parchment features really crease up in pain.

'*Pro bono publico?*' he croaked.

'Oh, yes. You will certainly be working for the public good,' said William. 'And what is good for the public, of course, is good for you. Isn't that nice?'

'*On the other hand,*' said Mr Slant, 'perhaps it would be in the interests of everyone to put this sorry affair behind us, and I will be, uh, happy to donate my services.'

'Thank you. Mr Scrope is now Lo— is now the Patrician?'

'Yes.'

'By the vote of the Guilds?'

'Yes. Of course.'

'The unanimous vote?'

'I don't have to tell—'

William raised a finger. 'Ah?' he said.

Mr Slant squirmed. 'The Beggars and the Seamstresses voted to adjourn,' he said. 'So did the Launderers and the Guild of Exotic Dancers.'

'So . . . that would be Queen Molly, Mrs Palm, Mrs Manger and Miss Dixie Voom,' said William. 'What an interesting life Lord Vetinari must have led.'

'No comment.'

'And would you say Mr Scrope is looking forward to getting to grips with the manifold problems of running the city?'

Mr Slant considered this one. 'I think that may be the case,' he conceded.

'Not least of which is the fact that Lord Vetinari is, in fact, completely innocent? And that therefore there is a very large question mark over the appointment? Would you advise that he takes up his duties with several spare pairs of underpants? You don't have to answer that last one.'

'It is not my job to instruct the assembly of Guilds to reverse a legitimate decision, even if it turns out to have been based on . . . erroneous information. Nor is it my responsibility to advise Mr Scrope on his choice of undergarments.'

'See you tomorrow, Mr Slant,' said William.

* * *

William barely had time to undress and lie down before it was time to get up again. He washed as best he could, changed his shirt and went cautiously down to breakfast. He was in fact the first at the table.

There was the usual stolid silence as the other guests gathered. Most of Mrs Arcanum's boarders didn't bother to talk unless they had something to say. But when Mr Mackleduff sat down he pulled out a copy of the *Times* from his pocket.

'Couldn't get the paper,' said Mr Mackleduff, shaking it open. 'So I got the other one.'

William coughed. 'Anything much in it?' he said. He could see his headline from where he sat, in huge bold caps:

DOG BITES MAN!

He'd *made* it news.

'Oh ... Lord Vetinari got away with it,' said Mr Mackleduff.

'Well, of course he would,' said Mr Prone. 'Very clever man, whatever they say.'

'And his dog's all right,' said Mr Mackleduff. William wanted to shake the man for reading so slowly.

'That's nice,' said Mrs Arcanum, pouring out the tea.

'Is that *it*?' said William.

'Oh, there's a lot of political stuff,' said Mr Mackleduff. 'It's all a bit far-fetched.'

'Any good vegetables today?' said Mr Cartwright.

Mr Mackleduff carefully inspected the other pages. 'No,' he said.

'My firm are thinking of approaching that man to see if he'd let us sell his seeds for him,' Mr Cartwright went on. 'It's just the sort of thing people like.' He caught Mrs Arcanum's eye. 'Only those vegetables suitable for a family environment, of course,' he added quickly.

'Aye, it does you good to laugh,' said Mr Mackleduff solemnly.

It crossed William's mind to wonder if Mr Wintler could grow an obscene pea. But of course he could.

'I would have thought it's quite important,' he said, 'if Lord Vetinari isn't guilty.'

'Oh, yes, I daresay, to them as has to deal with these things,' said Mr Mackleduff. 'I don't quite see where we come into it, though.'

'But surely—' William began.

Mrs Arcanum patted her hair. 'I've always thought Lord Vetinari was a most handsome man,' she said, and then looked flustered when they all stared at her. 'I meant, I'm just a little surprised there isn't a Lady Vetinari. As it were. Ahem.'

'Oh well, you know what they say,' said Mr Windling.

A pair of arms shot out across the table, grabbed the surprised man by the lapels and pulled him up so that his face was a few inches from William's.

'*I* don't know what they say, Mr Windling!' he shouted. 'But *you* know what they say, Mr Windling! Why don't you tell us what they say,

418

Mr Windling! Why don't you tell us who told *you*, Mr Windling?'

'Mr de Worde! Really!' said Mrs Arcanum. Mr Prone pulled the toast out of the way.

'I'm very sorry about this, Mrs Arcanum,' said William, still holding the struggling man, 'but I want to know what everyone knows and I want to know how they know it. Mr Windling?'

'They *say* he's got some sort of a lady friend who's very important in Uberwald,' said Mr Windling. 'And I'll thank you to let go of me!'

'And that's *it*? What's so sinister about that? It's a friendly country!'

'Yes, but, yes, but they say—'

William let go. Windling rocked back into his chair, but William stayed standing, breathing heavily.

'Well, *I* wrote the article in the *Times*!' he snapped. 'And what's in there is what *I* say! Me! Because I found things out, and checked things, and people who say "ing" a lot tried to kill me! I'm not the man that's the brother of some man you met in the pub! I'm not some stupid rumour put about to make trouble! So just remember that, before you try any of that "everyone knows" stuff! And in an hour or so I've got to go up to the palace and see Commander Vimes and whoever is the Patrician and a lot of other people, to get this whole thing sorted out! And it's not going to be very nice, but I'm going to have to do it, because I wanted you to know things that are *important*! Sorry about the teapot, Mrs Arcanum, I'm sure it can be mended.'

In the ensuing silence Mr Prone picked up the paper and said: '*You* write this?'

'Yes!'

'I ... er ... I thought they had special people ...'

All heads turned back to William.

'There isn't a they. There's just me and a young lady. We write it all!'

'But ... who tells you what to put in?'

The heads turned back to William.

'We just ... decide.'

'Er ... is it true about big silver discs kidnapping people?'

'No!'

To William's surprise Mr Cartwright actually raised his hand.

'Yes, Mr Cartwright?'

'I've got quite an important question, Mr de Worde, what with you knowing all this stuff ...'

'Yes?'

'Have you got the address of the funny vegetable man?'

William and Otto arrived at the palace at five minutes to ten. There was a small crowd around the gates.

Commander Vimes was standing in the courtyard, talking to Slant and some of the Guild leaders. He smiled in a humourless way when he saw William.

'You're rather late, Mr de Worde,' he said.

'I'm early!'

'I meant that things have been happening.'

Mr Slant cleared his throat. 'Mr Scrope has sent a note,' he said. 'It appears that he is ill.'

William pulled out his notebook.

The civic leaders focused on it. He hesitated. And then uncertainty evaporated. *I'm a de Worde*, he thought, *don't you dare look down your noses at me! You've got to move with the* Times. Oh well . . . here goes . . .

'Was it signed by his mother?' he said.

'I don't follow your meaning,' said the lawyer, but several of the Guild leaders turned their heads away.

'What's happening now, then?' said William. 'We don't have a ruler?'

'*Happily*,' said Mr Slant, who looked like a man in a private hell, 'Lord Vetinari is feeling very much better and expects to resume his duties tomorrow.'

'Excuse me, is he allowed to write that down?' said Lord Downey, head of the Assassins' Guild, as William made a note.

'Allowed by who?' said Vimes.

'Whom,' said William, under his breath.

'Well, he can't just write down *anything*, can he?' said Lord Downey. 'Supposing he writes down something we don't *want* him to write down?'

Vimes looked William firmly in the eye.

'There's no law against it,' he said.

'Lord Vetinari is not going to go on trial, then, Lord Downey?' said William, holding Vimes's gaze for a second.

Downey, baffled, turned to Slant.

'Can he ask me that?' he said. 'Just come out with a question, just like that?'

'Yes, my lord.'

'Do I have to answer it?'

'It is a reasonable question in the circumstances, my lord, but you don't *have* to.'

'Do you have a message for the people of Ankh-Morpork?' said William sweetly.

'Do we, Mr Slant?' said Lord Downey.

Mr Slant sighed. 'It may be advisable, my lord, yes.'

'Oh, well, then – no, there won't be a trial. Obviously.'

'And he's not going to be pardoned?' said William.

Lord Downey turned to Mr Slant, who gave a little sigh.

'Again, my lord, it is—'

'All right, all right . . . No, he's not going to be pardoned because it is quite clear that he is quite guiltless,' said Downey testily.

'Would you say that this has become clear because of the excellent work done by Commander Vimes and his dedicated band of officers, aided in a small way by the *Times*?' said William.

Lord Downey looked blank. '*Would* I say that?' he said.

'I think you possibly would, yes, my lord,' said Slant, sinking further in gloom.

'Oh. Then I would,' said Downey. 'Yes.' He craned his neck to see what William was writing down. Out of the corner of his eye William saw Vimes's expression; it was a strange mixture of amusement and anger.

'And would you say, as spokesman for the Guild Council, that you are commending Commander Vimes?' said William.

'Now see here—' Vimes began.

'I suppose we would, yes.'

'I expect there's a Watch Medal or a commendation in the offing?'

'Now *look*—' Vimes said.

'Yes, very probably. Very probably,' said Lord Downey, now thoroughly buffeted by the winds of change.

William painstakingly wrote this down, too, and closed his notebook. This caused a general air of relief among the others.

'Thank you very much, my lord, and ladies and gentlemen,' he said cheerfully. 'Oh, Mister Vimes . . . do you and I have anything to discuss?'

'Not right at this moment,' growled Vimes.

'Oh, that's good. Well, I must go and get this written up, so thank you once—'

'You will of course show this . . . article to us before you put it in the paper,' said Lord Downey, rallying a little.

William wore his haughtiness like an overcoat. 'Um, no, I don't think I will, my lord. It's my paper, you see.'

'Can he—'

'*Yes*, my lord, he can,' said Mr Slant. 'I'm afraid he can. The right to free speech is a fine old Ankh-Morpork tradition.'

'Good heavens, is it?'

'Yes, my lord.'

'How did that one survive?'

'I couldn't say, my lord,' said Slant. 'But Mr de Worde,' he added, staring at William, 'is, I believe, a young man who would not go out of his way to upset the smooth running of the city.'

William smiled at him politely, nodded to the rest of the company and walked back across the courtyard and out into the street. He waited until he was some distance away before he burst out laughing.

A week went past. It was notable because of the things that *didn't* happen. There was no protest from Mr Carney or the Engravers' Guild. William wondered if he had been carefully moved into the 'to be left alone' file. After all, people might be thinking, Vetinari probably owed the *Times* a favour, and no one would want to be that favour, would they? There was no visit from the Watch, either. There *had* been rather more street cleaners around than usual, but after William sent a hundred dollars to Harry King, plus a bouquet for Mrs King, Gleam Street was no longer gleaming.

They'd moved to another shed while the old one was being rebuilt. Mr Cheese had been easy to deal with. He just wanted money. You know where you stand with simple people like that, even if it *is* with your hand in your wallet.

A new press had been rolled in, and once again money had made the effort almost frictionless. It had already been substantially redesigned by the dwarfs.

This shed was smaller than the old one, but Sacharissa had contrived to partition off a tiny editorial space. She'd put a potted plant and a coat rack in it, and talked excitedly of the space they'd have when the new building was finished, but William reckoned that however big it was it would never be neat. Newspaper people thought the floor was a big flat filing cabinet.

He had a new desk, too. In fact it was better than a new desk; it was a genuine antique one, made of genuine walnut, inlaid with leather, and with two inkwells, lots of drawers and genuine woodworm. At a desk like that a man could *write*.

They hadn't brought the spike.

William was pondering over a letter from the Ankh-Morpork League of Decency when the sense that someone was standing nearby made him look up.

Sacharissa had ushered in a small group of strangers, although after a second or two he recognized one of them as the late Mr Bendy, who was merely strange.

'You remember you said we ought to get more writers?' she said. 'You know Mr Bendy, and this is Mrs Tilly' – a small white-haired woman bobbed a curtsey to William – 'who likes cats and really nasty murders, and Mr O'Biscuit' – a rangy young man – 'who's all the way from Fourecks and looking for a job before he goes home.'

'Really? What did you do in Fourecks, Mr O'Biscuit?'

'I was at Bugarup University, mate.'

'You're a wizard?'

'No, mate. They threw me out, 'cos of what I wrote in the student magazine.'

'What was that?'

'Everything, really.'

'Oh. And . . . Mrs Tilly, I think you wrote a lovely well-spelled and grammatical letter to us suggesting that everyone under the age of eighteen should be flogged once a week to stop them being so noisy?'

'Once a day, Mr de Worde,' said Mrs Tilly. 'That'll teach 'em to go around being young!'

William hesitated. But the press needed feeding, and he and Sacharissa needed time off. Rocky was supplying some sports news, and while it was unreadable to William he put it in on the basis that anyone keen on sport probably couldn't read. There had to be more staff. It was worth a try.

'Very well, then,' he said. 'We'll give you all a trial, starting right— Oh.'

He stood up. Everyone turned round to see why.

'Please don't bother,' said Lord Vetinari from the doorway. 'This is meant to be an informal visit. Taking on new staff, I see?'

The Patrician walked across the floor, followed by Drumknott.

'Er, yes,' said William. 'Are you all right, sir?'

'Oh, yes. Busy, of course. Such a lot of reading to catch up on. But I thought I should take a moment to come and see this "free press" Commander Vimes has told me about at considerable length.' He tapped one of the iron pillars of the press with his cane. 'However, it appears to be firmly bolted down.'

'Er, no, sir. I mean "free" in the sense of what is printed, sir,' said William.

'But surely you charge money?'

'Yes, but—'

'Oh, I *see*. You meant *you* should be free to print what you like?'

There was no escape. 'Well . . . broadly, yes, sir.'

'Because that's in the, what was the other interesting term? Ah, yes . . . the public interest?' Lord

Vetinari picked up a piece of type and inspected it carefully.

'I think so, sir.'

'These stories about man-eating goldfish and people's husbands disappearing in big silver dishes?'

'No, sir. That's what the public is interested in. We do the other stuff, sir.'

'Amusingly shaped vegetables?'

'Well, a *bit* of that, sir. Sacharissa calls them human interest stories.'

'About vegetables and animals?'

'Yes, sir. But at least they're real vegetables and animals.'

'So . . . we have what the people are interested in, and human interest stories, which is what humans are interested in, and the public interest, which no one is interested in.'

'Except the public, sir,' said William, trying to keep up.

'Which isn't the same as people and humans?'

'I think it's more complicated than that, sir.'

'Obviously. Do you mean that the public is a different thing from the people you just see walking about the place? The public thinks big, sensible, measured thoughts while *people* run around doing silly things?'

'I think so. I may have to work on that idea too, I admit.'

'Hmm. Interesting. *I* have certainly noticed that groups of clever and intelligent people are capable of really stupid ideas,' said Lord Vetinari. He gave William a look which said 'I can read your mind, even the small print', and then gazed around the press room again. 'Well, I can see you have an eventful future ahead of you, and I wouldn't wish to make it any more difficult than it is clearly going to be. I notice you have work going on . . . ?'

'We're putting up a semaphore post,' said Sacharissa proudly. 'We'll be able to get a clacks straight from the big trunk tower. And we're opening offices in Sto Lat and Pseudopolis!'

Lord Vetinari raised his eyebrows. 'My word,' he said. 'Many new deformed vegetables will become available. I shall look forward with interest to seeing them.'

William decided not to rise to this one.

'It amazes me how the news you have so neatly fits the space available,' Lord Vetinari went on, staring down at the page Boddony was working on. 'No little gaps anywhere. And every day something happens that is important enough to be at the top of the first page, too. How strange— Oh, "receive" takes an e after the c . . .'

Boddony looked up. Lord Vetinari's cane swung around with a hiss and hovered in the middle of a densely packed column. The dwarf looked closer and nodded, and took out a small tool.

It's upside down to him, and back to front, thought William. And the word's in the middle of the text. And he spotted it.

'Things that are back to front are often easier to comprehend if they are upside down as well,' said Lord Vetinari, tapping his chin with the silver knob of his cane in an absent-minded way. 'In life as in politics.'

'What have you done with Charlie?' said William.

Lord Vetinari looked at him in nothing but innocent surprise. 'Why, nothing. Should I have done something?'

'Have you locked him up,' said Sacharissa suspiciously, 'in a deep cell, and made him wear a mask all the time and have all his meals brought by a deaf and dumb jailer?'

'Er ... no, I don't *think* so,' said Lord Vetinari, giving her a smile. 'Although it would make a very good story, I've no doubt. No, I understand he's enrolled in the Guild of Actors, though of course I realize that there are those who would consider a deep dungeon a preferred alternative. I foresee a happy career for him, nevertheless. Children's parties, and so on.'

'What . . . as being you?'

'Indeed. Very risible.'

'And perhaps when you have some boring duty to perform, or have to sit for an oil painting, you'll have a little job for him?' said William.

'Hmm?' said Vetinari. William had thought that Vimes had a blank look, but he'd been wreathed in smiles compared to his lordship when Lord Vetinari wanted to look blank. 'Do you have any more questions, Mr de Worde?'

'I will have a lot,' said William, pulling himself together. 'The *Times* will be taking a very close interest in civic affairs.'

'How commendable,' said the Patrician. 'If you contact Drumknott here I'm sure I will find time to grant you an interview.'

The Right Word in the Right Place, William thought. Unpleasant though the knowledge was, his ancestors had always been amongst the first to get to grips in any conflict. In every siege, every ambush, every stricken dash against fortified emplacements, some de Worde had galloped towards death or glory and sometimes both. No enemy was too strong, no wound was too deep, no sword was too heavy for a de Worde. No grave was too deep, either. As his instincts wrestled with his tongue, he could feel his ancestors behind him, pushing him into the fray. Vetinari was too obviously playing with him. *Oh well, at least let's die for something decent . . . Onward to death or glory or both!*

'I am sure, my lord, that whenever you wish for an interview, the *Times* will be quite prepared to grant you one,' he said. 'If space allows.'

He hadn't realized how much background noise there was until it stopped. Drumknott had closed his eyes. Sacharissa was staring straight ahead. The dwarfs stood like statues.

Finally, Lord Vetinari broke the silence.

'The *Times*? You mean you, and this young lady here?' he said, raising his eyebrows. 'Oh, I *see*. It's like the Public. Well, if I can be of any help to the *Times*—'

'We won't be bribed, either,' said William. He knew he was galloping in among the sharpened stakes here, but he'd be damned before he'd be patronized.

'Bribed?' said Vetinari. 'My dear sir, seeing what you're capable of for nothing, I'd hesitate to press even a penny in your hand. No, I have nothing to offer you except thanks, which of course are notorious for their evaporative tendencies. Ah, a little idea occurs. I shall be having a small dinner on Saturday. Some of the Guild leaders, a few ambassadors ... all rather dull, but perhaps you and your very bold young lady ... I do beg your pardon, I meant of course the *Times* ... would like to attend?'

'I don't—' William began, and stopped suddenly. A shoe scraping down your shin can do that.

'The *Times* would be delighted,' said Sacharissa, beaming.

'Capital. In that case—'

'There *is* a favour I need to ask, to tell the truth,' said William.

Vetinari smiled. 'Of course. If I can do *anything* for the *Ti*—'

'Will you be going to Harry King's daughter's wedding on Saturday?'

To his secret delight, the look that Vetinari gave him seemed to be blank because the man hadn't got anything to fill it with. But Drumknott leaned towards him and there were a few whispered words.

'Ah?' said the Patrician. 'Harry King. Ah, yes. A positive incarnation of the spirit that has made our city what it is today. Haven't I always said that, Drumknott?'

'Yes indeed, sir.'

'I shall certainly attend. I expect a lot of other civic leaders will be there?'

The question was left delicately spinning in the air.

'As many as possible,' said William.

'Fine carriages, tiaras, stately robes?' said Lord Vetinari, to the knob of his cane.

'Lots.'

'Yes, I'm sure they will be there,' said Lord Vetinari, and William knew that Harry King would walk his daughter past more top nobs than he could count, and while the world of Mr King did not have a lot of space for letters he could count very carefully indeed. Mrs King was going to have joyful hysterics out of sheer passive snobbery.

'In return, however,' said the Patrician, 'I must ask you not to upset Commander Vimes.' He gave a little cough. 'More than necessary.'

'I'm sure we can pull together, sir.'

Lord Vetinari raised his eyebrows. 'Oh, I do hope not, I really do hope not. Pulling together is the aim of despotism and tyranny. Free men pull in all kinds of directions.' He smiled. 'It's the only way to make progress. That and, of course, moving with the times. Good day to you.'

He nodded to them and walked out of the building.

'Why is everyone still here?' William demanded, when the spell had broken.

'Er ... we still don't know what we should be doing,' said Mrs Tilly hopelessly.

'Go and find out things that people want to put in the paper,' said Sacharissa.

'And things that people don't want put in the paper,' William added.

'And interesting things,' said Sacharissa.

'Like that rain of dogs there was a few months ago?' said O'Biscuit.

'There was *no* rain of dogs two months ago!' William snapped.

'But—'

'One puppy is *not* a rain. It fell out of a window. Look, we are *not* interested in pet precipitation, spontaneous combustion, or people being carried off by weird things from out of the sky—'

'Unless it happens,' said Sacharissa.

'Well, *obviously* we are if it *does* happen,' said William. 'But when it doesn't, we're not. Okay? News is unusual things happening—'

'And usual things happening,' said Sacharissa, screwing up a report from the Ankh-Morpork Funny Vegetable Society.

'And usual things, yes,' said William. 'But news is mainly what someone somewhere doesn't want you to put in the paper—'

'Except that sometimes it isn't,' said Sacharissa again.

'News is—' said William, and stopped. They watched him politely as he stood with his mouth open and one finger raised.

'News,' he said, '*all depends*. But you'll know it when you see it. Clear? Right. Now go and find some.'

'That was a bit abrupt,' said Sacharissa after they'd filed out.

'Well, I was thinking,' said William. 'I mean, it's been a . . . a funny old time all round, what with one thing and another—'

'—people trying to kill us, your being imprisoned, a plague of dogs, the place catching on fire, your being cheeky to Lord Vetinari—' said Sacharissa.

'Yes, well . . . so would it really matter if you and I, you know . . . you and I . . . took the afternoon off?

I mean,' he added desperately, 'it doesn't *say* anywhere that we have to publish every day, does it?'

'Except at the top of the newspaper,' said Sacharissa.

'Yes, but you can't believe *everything* you read in the newspapers.'

'Well . . . all right. I'll just finish this report—'

'Messages for you, Mr William,' said one of the dwarfs, dropping a pile of paper on his desk. William grunted and glanced through them. There were a few test clackses from Lancre and Sto Lat, and already he could see that pretty soon he'd have to go out into the country to train some real, yes, *reporters* of news, because he could see there was only a limited future in these earnest missives from village grocers and publicans who'd be paid a penny a line. There were a couple of carrier pigeon messages, too, from those people who couldn't get a grip on the new technology.

'Ye gods,' he said, under his breath. 'The Mayor of Quirm has been struck by a meteorite . . . *again*.'

'Can that happen?' said Sacharissa.

'Apparently. This is from Mr Pune at the council offices there. Sensible chap, not much imagination. He says that *this* time it was waiting for the mayor in an alley.'

'Really? The woman we get our linen from has got a son who is the lecturer in Vindictive Astronomy at the University.'

'Would he give us a quote?'

'He smiles at me when he sees me in the shop,' said Sacharissa firmly. 'So he will.'

'O-kay. If you can—'

'Afternoon, folks!'

Mr Wintler was standing at the counter. He was holding a cardboard box.

'Oh, dear . . .' murmured William.

'Just you take a look at *this* one,' said Mr Wintler, a man who would not take a hint if it was wrapped around a lead pipe.

'I think we've had enough funny ve—' William began.

And stopped.

It was a big potato that the rubicund man was lifting from his box. It was knobbly, too. William had seen knobbly potatoes before. They could look like faces, if that was the way you wanted to amuse yourself. But with this one you didn't have to imagine a face. It had a face. It was made up of dents and knobs and potato eyes, but it looked very much like a face that had been staring madly into his and trying to kill him very recently. He remembered it quite well, because he still occasionally woke up around 3 a.m. with it in front of him.

'It's . . . not . . . exactly . . . *funny*,' said Sacharissa, glancing sideways at William.

'Amazing, isn't it?' said Mr Wintler. 'I wouldn't have brought it round, but you've always been very interested in them.'

'A day without a bifurcated parsnip,' said Sacharissa sweetly, 'is a day without sunshine, Mr Wintler. William?'

'Huh?' said William, tearing his eyes away from the potato head. 'Is it me, or does it look . . . surprised?'

'It does rather,' said Sacharissa.

'Did you just dig this up?' said William.

'Oh, no. It's been in one of my sacks for months,' said Wintler.

. . . which upset an occult train of thought that had started to trundle through William's head. But . . . the universe was a funny place. Cause and effect, effect and cause . . . He'd rip off his right arm rather than write that down, though.

'What are you going to do with it?' he said. 'Boil it?'

'Bless you, no. The variety's far too floury. No, this one's going to be chips.'

'Chips, eh?' said William. And it seemed, strangely, exactly the right thing to do.

'Yes. Yes, that's a good idea. Let it fry, Mr Wintler. *Let it fry.*'

The clock moved on.

One of the reporters came in to say that the Alchemists' Guild had exploded, and did this count as news? Otto was summoned from his crypt and sent out to get a picture. William finished his piece about yesterday's events and passed it over to the dwarfs. Someone came in and said there was a big crowd in Sator Square because the Bursar (71) was sitting on a roof seven floors up, looking puzzled. Sacharissa, wielding her pencil with care, crossed out every adjective in a report of the Ankh-Morpork Floral Arranging Society, reducing its length by half.

William went out to find out about the Bursar (71), then wrote a few short paragraphs. Wizards doing odd things wasn't news. Wizards doing odd things was *wizards*.

He threw the piece into the Out tray, and looked at the press.

It was black, and big, and complex. Without eyes, without a face, without life . . . It looked back at him.

He thought: you don't need old sacrificial stones. Lord Vetinari was wrong about that. He touched his forehead. The bruise had long ago faded.

You put your mark on me. Well, I'm wise to you.

'Let's go,' he said.

Sacharissa looked up, still preoccupied. 'What?'

'Let's go. Out. Now. For a walk, or tea, or shopping,' said William. 'Let's not be here. Don't argue, please. Coat on. Now. Before it realizes. Before it finds a way to stop us.'

'What *are* you talking about?'

He pulled her coat off the peg and grabbed her arm. 'No *time* to explain!'

She allowed herself to be dragged out into the street, where William took a deep breath and relaxed.

'Now would you mind telling me what that was all about?' said Sacharissa. 'I've got a pile of work in there, you know.'

'I know. Come on. We're probably not far enough away. There's a new noodle place opened in Elm Street. Everyone says it's pretty good. How about it?'

'But there's all that work to do!'

'So? It'll still be there tomorrow, won't it?'

She hesitated. 'Well, an hour or two won't hurt, probably,' she admitted.

'Good. Let's go.'

They'd reached the junction of Treacle Mine Road and Elm Street when it caught up with them.

There were cries further along the street. William swivelled his head, saw the four-horse brewer's dray thundering out of control. He saw the people diving and scuttling out of the way. He saw the soup-plate hooves throw up mud and ice. He saw the brasses on the harness, the gleam, the steam . . .

His head swivelled the other way. He saw the old woman with two sticks crossing the street, quite oblivious of the onrushing death. He saw the shawl, the white hair . . .

A blur went past him. The man twisted in the air, landed on his shoulder in the centre of the street, rolled upright, grabbed the woman, and leapt—

The wayward wagon went by in a rush of steam and slush. The team tried to corner at the crossroads. The dray behind them did not. A mêlée of hooves and horses and wheels and sleet and screams whirled onwards and took the windows out of several shops before the cart rammed up against a stone pillar and stopped dead.

In obedience to the laws of physics and the narrative of such things, its load did not. The barrels burst their bonds, crashed down on to the street and rolled onwards. A few smashed, filling the gutter with suds. The others, thumping and banging into one another, became the focus of attention of every upright citizen who could recognize a hundred gallons of beer which suddenly didn't belong to any-one any more and was heading for freedom.

William and Sacharissa looked at one another.

'Okay – I'll get the story, you go and find Otto!'

They said that at the same time, and then stared defiantly at each other.

'All right, all right,' said William. 'Find some kid,

bribe him to get Otto, I'll talk to that Plucky Watchman who grabbed the old lady in A Mercy Dash, you cover the Big Smash, okay?'

'I'll find the kid,' said Sacharissa, pulling out her own notebook, 'but *you* cover the accident and the Beer Barrel Bonanza and I'll talk to the White-Haired Granny. Human interest, right?'

'All right!' William conceded. 'That was Captain Carrot who did the rescue. Make sure Otto gets a picture, and get his age!'

'Of course!'

William headed towards the crowd around the smashed wagon. Many people were in distant pursuit of the barrels, and the odd scream suggested that thirsty people seldom realize how hard it is to stop a hundred gallons of beer in a big oak cask when it's on a roll.

He dutifully noted down the name on the side of the dray. A couple of men were helping the horses up, but they did not appear to have much to do with beer delivery. They appeared to be men who simply wanted to help lost horses, and take them home and make them better. If this had to mean dyeing areas of their coats and swearing blind they'd owned them for the past two years, then so be it.

He approached a bystander not obviously engaged in any felonious activity.

'Exc—' he began. But the citizen's eyes had already detected the notebook.

'I saw it all,' he said.

'Did you?'

'It was a ter-ri-ble scene,' said the man, at dictation

speed. 'But the watch-man made a death-defying plunge to res-cue the old lady and he de-serves a med-al.'

'Really?' said William, scribbling fast. 'And you are—'

'Sa-muel Arblaster (43), stone-mason, of 11b The Scours,' said the man.

'I saw it too,' said a woman next to him, urgently. 'Mrs Florrie Perry, blonde mother of three, from Dolly Sisters. It was a scene of car-nage.'

William risked a glance at his pencil. It *was* a kind of magic wand.

'Where's the iconographer?' said Mrs Perry, looking around hopefully.

'Er . . . not here yet,' said William.

'Oh.' She looked disappointed. 'Shame about the poor woman with the snake, wasn't it? I expect he's off taking pictures of her.'

'Er . . . I hope not,' said William.

It was a long afternoon. One barrel had rolled into a barber shop and exploded. Some of the brewer's men turned up, and there was a fight with several of the barrels' new owners, who claimed rights of salvage. One enterprising man tapped a barrel by the roadside and set up a temporary pub. Otto arrived. He took pictures of barrel rescuers. He took a picture of the fight. He took pictures of the Watch arriving to arrest everyone still standing. He took pictures of the white-haired old lady and the proud Captain Carrot and, in his excitement, of his thumb.

It was a good story all round. And William was

halfway through writing his part of it back at the *Times* when he remembered.

He'd watched it happening. And he'd *reached for his notebook*. That was a worrying thought, he told Sacharissa.

'So?' she said, from her side of the desk. 'How many ls in "gallant"?'

'Two,' said William. 'I mean, I didn't try to *do* anything. I thought: this is a Story, and I have to tell it.'

'Yep,' said Sacharissa, still bowed over her writing. 'We've been press-ganged.'

'But it's not—'

'Look at it like this,' said Sacharissa, starting a fresh page. 'Some people are heroes. And some people jot down notes.'

'Yes, but that's not very—'

Sacharissa glanced up and flashed him a smile. 'Sometimes they're the same person,' she said.

This time it was William who looked down, modestly.

'You think that's really true?' he said.

She shrugged. 'Really true? Who knows? This is a newspaper, isn't it? It just has to be true until tomorrow.'

William felt the temperature rise. Her smile had really been attractive. 'Are you . . . sure?'

'Oh, yes. True until tomorrow is good enough for me.'

And behind her the big black vampire of a printing press waited to be fed, and to be brought alive in the dark of the night for the light of the morning. It chopped the complexities of the world into little stories, and it was always hungry.

And it needed a double-column story for page two, William remembered.

And, a few inches under his hand, a woodworm chewed its way contentedly through the ancient timber. Reincarnation enjoys a joke as much as the next philosophical hypothesis. As it chewed, the woodworm thought: 'This is —ing good wood!'

Because nothing has to be true for ever. Just for long enough, to tell you the truth.

THE END

SOUL MUSIC
Terry Pratchett

'Classic English humour, with all the slapstick,
twists and dry observations you could hope for'
The Times

*'Be careful what you wish for. You never know who
might be listening.'*

THERE'S no getting away from it. From whichever
angle, Death is a horrible, inescapable business. But
someone's got to do it. So if Death decides to take a
well-earned moment to uncover the meaning of life and
discover himself in the process, then there is going to be
a void of specific dimensions that needs to be occupied,
particularly so when there is trouble brewing in
Discworld. There aren't too many who are qualified to
fill Death's footsteps and it certainly doesn't help the
imminent cataclysm that the one person poised
between the mortal and the immortal is only sixteen
years old…

'Very clever madcap satire which has universal
appeal. If you haven't tried him, this is a fun one
to start with'
Today

'Pratchett lures classical themes and popular
mythologies into the dark corners of his
imagination, gets them drunk and makes them
do things you wouldn't dream of doing with
an Oxford don'
Daily Mail

9780552153195

INTERESTING TIMES
Terry Pratchett

'Funny, delightfully inventive and refuses to lie
down in its genre'
Observer

'A foot in the neck is nine points of the law.'

THERE are many who say that the art of diplomacy is
an intricate and complex dance between two
informed partners, determined by an elaborate set of
elegant and unwritten rules. There are others who
maintain that it's merely a matter of who carries the
biggest stick. Like when a large, heavily fortified and
armoured empire makes a faintly menacing request of a
much smaller, infinitely more cowardly neighbour. It
would be churlish, if not extremely dangerous, not to
comply – particularly if all they want is a wizard, and
they don't specify whether competence is an issue...

'Imagine a collision between Jonathan Swift at his
most scatological and J.R.R. Tolkien on speed...
This is the joyous outcome'
Daily Telegraph

'Like Dickens, much of Pratchett's appeal lies in his
humanism, both in a sentimental regard for his
characters' good fortune, and in that his writing is
generous-spirited and inclusive'
Guardian

9780552153218

MASKERADE
Terry Pratchett

'As funny as Wodehouse and as witty as Waugh'
Independent

'*I thought: opera, how hard can it be? Songs. Pretty girls dancing. Nice scenery. Lots of people handing over cash. Got to be better than the cut-throat world of yoghurt, I thought. Now everywhere I go there's…*'

DEATH, to be precise. And plenty of it. In unpleasant variations. This isn't real life. This isn't even cheesemongering. It's opera. Where the music matters and where an opera house is being terrorised by a man in evening dress with a white mask, lurking in the shadows, occasionally killing people, and most worryingly, sending little notes, writing maniacal laughter with five exclamation marks. Opera can do that to a man. In such circumstances, life has obviously reached that desperate point where the wrong thing to do **has** to be the right thing to do…

'Cracking dialogue, compelling illogic and unchained whimsy…Pratchett has a subject and a style that is very much his own'
Sunday Times

'Entertaining and gloriously funny'
Chicago Tribune

9780552153232

FEET OF CLAY
Terry Pratchett

'The work of a prolific humorist at his best'
Observer

'Sorry?' said Carrot. 'If it's just a thing, how can it commit murder? A sword is a thing' – he drew out his own sword; it made an almost silken sound – 'and of course you can't blame a sword if someone thrust it at you, sir.'

FOR members of the City Watch, life consists of troubling times, linked together by periods of torpid inactivity. Now is one such troubling time. People are being murdered, but there's no trace of anything alive having been at the crime scene. Is there ever a circumstance in which you can blame the weapon not the murderer? Such philosophical questions are not the usual domain of the city's police, but they're going to have to start learning fast...

'Like most true originals, Pratchett defies categorization... Deliciously and amiably dotty... Driven by Swiftian logic and equally intellectually inventive'
The Times

'Fantastical, inventive and finally serious... It's enjoyable as crime fiction, but the real attraction is the laughter waiting to be uncovered on every page'
Observer

'An explosion of imaginative lunacy'
Daily Express

9780552153256

JINGO
Terry Pratchett

'Generous, amusing and the ideal boarding point for
those who have never visited Discworld'
Sunday Telegraph

*'Neighbours…hah. People'd live for ages side by side,
nodding at one another amicably on their way to work,
and then some trivial thing would happen and someone
would be having a garden fork removed from their ear.'*

THROUGHOUT history, there's always been a perfectly
good reason to start a war. Never more so if it is over
a 'strategic' piece of old rock in the middle of nowhere.
It is after all every citizen's right to bear arms to defend
what they consider to be their own. Even if it isn't. And
in such pressing circumstances, you really shouldn't let
small details like the absence of an army or indeed the
money to finance one get in the way of a righteous fight
with all the attendant benefits of out-and-out
nationalism…

'Pratchett's writing is a constant delight. No one mixes
the fantastical and the mundane to better comic effect
or offers sharper insights into the absurdities of
human endeavour'
Daily Mail

'One of those very rare writers who appeals to
everyone…He satisfies the need for fast-moving,
breathtaking plots with entirely satisfying endings, and
the equally primitive desire for an alternative world, full
of thrills but benign, into which one can step for pleasure
and enlivenment'
Daily Express

'Vintage Pratchett…Perennially funny…A sharp satire
on the futility of war'
Metro

9780552154161

Visit

www.**terrypratchett**.co.uk

to discover everything you need to know
about Terry Pratchett and his writing, plus all
manner of other things you may find interesting, such as
videos, competitions, character profiles and games.

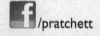 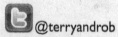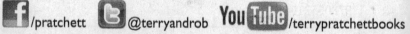